"A generation which ignores history has no past and no future."
Robert Heinlein, American author (1907-1988)

GRIMSBY BEACH, BELL PARK. AUTUMN 1989

My garden rake rattled as I pulled it through the lawn. I was rolling up the bumper crop of walnuts that fell into our front yard. It was a perennial task, and the cleanup required the repetitive motion of rake and scoop, rake and scoop as I pulled the pungent fruit into my shovel and dumped it into the wheelbarrow. To take the labour out of the job I told myself it was a meditation. As if on cue, a kid across the park added a ring to the autumn air as he struck the bell with rock. It wasn't the long resonance of a Tibetan prayer wheel but in the foggy autumn air the muffled gong added to the contemplative atmosphere.

The bell was forged in 1876 in Troy, N.Y. and it sat on a concrete pad, lifted off its rocker many years ago with its clapper removed. Still, the attempts to render it silent were not entirely successful. The ring was muffled, but everyone within a hundred yards heard it. Years ago, when it was perched up on its stand, it must have peeled out for many miles. It would call residents of the Methodist Campground to church services, signal the arrival of steam driven ferries from Toronto and Hamilton and in more desperate times, called together bucket brigades that worked to keep cottages from burning to the ground.

A part of me bristled every time I heard the bell struck with a rock because that is what five-year-old's do to make it ring. I could easily reconcile that small children couldn't have an appreciation for historical artifacts but their parents should know better. Maybe it's too much to ask for the young to honour the history of the last century. Life is obvious and simple for them. They don't have the perspective that time and experience give. They are blind to the layers of human activity that when explored and untangled reveal a history that is rich and interesting. Just how interesting our local history was, was a lesson I was just about to learn.

I had filled the fifth wheelbarrow with walnuts when a car pulled up into the lot across from my home. It was a black sedan, a BMW or Audi, I wasn't certain, but it was a swankier car than anyone in our community might own.

A man got out and asked if he might take a picture of our house. It is an older cottage that my wife and I had renovated and decorated, adding gingerbread and painting the trim orange and gold to accentuate the deep green of the board and batten walls. The roof is pitched at forty-five degrees and at the peak is a fish weathervane that is forever swimming into the wind. It generally faces the back of our house as that is where you will find the lake and the prevailing breeze. The cottage is well over a century old and is nestled under the walnut tree that is another century and half older. Its branches splay up and over the house protecting it from the sun and wind but at this time of year, pepper its roof with falling nuts. It was a cottage that became a home.

"Sure," I said, "just let me get out of your way."

As I wheeled the barrow and my rake out of view of his camera lens the passenger door of the sedan opened, and an elderly man pulled himself out and onto his feet. Wherever they came from, this old guy was stiff from the ride but once up on his trembling legs, he took half a dozen uneasy steps towards me, stopped to put his hands on his hips and said,

"I used to live here."

As he said this his back straightened and he lifted his head and let his eyes gaze up to the top of the walnut tree. There was a brightness to them. A flash in the blue of his iris that was young and alive in contrast to his loose and translucent skin and there was an unusual scar on his right temple that etched its way from his earlobe to his eyebrow.

"You must be Jacob or Robert Birk?" I guessed.

"I'm Robert," he said as he held out his hand. "Jacob was my brother. We had the time of our lives here."

I shook his hand, surprised by his strength and his height. Despite his advanced years, he was taller than me and I found myself looking up at a face that in its youth must have been chiselled and handsome.

"That tree has always been a giant. It's nice to see that it is still here. Jacob and I used to swing on a rope from that branch."

The old man's face beamed. It was obvious that the moment he was reliving brought joy to every part of him. Meanwhile, the other guy was still taking pictures, trying to include the older man in the photos.

"You'll have to excuse my son here. John's a bit of a shutterbug. How did you know my name was Birk?"

"If you've got time to come inside, I'll show you," I said and motioned for both men to follow. "I'm sure you will notice some changes," I said as I led them inside.

Having moved the front door and changed what was the laundry room into a bathroom and the dining room into a living room and the living room and kitchen into a larger kitchen, I knew that Robert would not recognize very much of what used to be his family's summer cottage. He silently looked around trying to make sense of it all, searching for some piece of architecture that would still have a presence in his memory. But his face faltered with blankness and confusion. It wasn't until he turned back towards the door we had entered that he said anything.

"Well, well...." his voice trailed off and he began wringing his hands together as he walked over the stone fireplace on the west wall.

"Did you build this?" I asked, looking from him to the fireplace and back again.

We were looking at the stonework that was one of the main inspirations for buying the house. Beach stones, the size of large potatoes were mortared into place from the floor to the ceiling with a wooden mantle half way up. The whole thing had been painted a dark brown and there were sculptures and tiny figurines embedded throughout. A plaster cast of seven heads, tiny elephants, a skull with a top hat brought intrigue to whoever laid eyes on it. The more you looked at it, the more you saw. When we bought the house, an electric heater sat in the hearth, but we had since replaced it with a natural gas stove.

"My father, Jacob and I. Yes, we built it in the summer of '21. We picked up the rocks and carried them up from the beach. Jacob and I added the toys.

My Dad was proud of this. He didn't work with his hands much. He'd be happy to see that it's still here. I'm happy to see it's still here."

Robert was reaching out to touch the past. His fingertips traced the smooth stones, the plaster heads and the toy elephants to verify that his memories were real. It was at this moment that I presented to him a piece of wood I had salvaged from a renovation on the second floor. It was from a tongue and groove plank of pine that lined a closet. I was using the old boards to build a new wall when I noticed that written faintly in pencil were the names Robert and Jacob Birk with the date, 1910, etched clearly beside it. I cut out the section of board and have kept it with our other interesting odds and ends.

"This is Jacob's writing," he said, rubbing the edges of the wood with his thumbs. "I never had penmanship like that. 1910. I was nine years old when he wrote this. Where did you find this?" Robert asked. His face was full of wonder and excitement, and this had the effect of infecting his son and I. John busied himself catching every angle of the fireplace. He took close-up shots of his father holding the signed plank up beside his face.

"Upstairs. Come upstairs and I'll show you."

I found myself taking the stairs two at a time. In the tearing out and renovation work I'd come across square nails, old bottles, irons, pantry inventories, measurements written on the original timbers and knob and tube wiring. I often used the discoveries as touchstones. Artifacts that would inspire my imagination. I would daydream about who hammered this nail, who wrote on this board, or who drank from this bottle? The bodies and souls who inhabited my house left behind traces of who they were, but they were only traces and silent ones at that. Here, on this very day, while I was raking leaves in my front yard, a living breathing artifact made its way into my house, and I intended on learning as much as I could from Robert Birk.

"Jacob and I used to sit up here at night and listen to the adults when they thought we were in bed. There was a vent right here on the floor that went down to the kitchen, and we could hear their voices clear as blue sky. And this

is our bathtub, although I can't say as I was in it very much. When we got dirty, Mom would tell us to go jump in the lake. We were always in the lake."

"Do you have a copy of this?" I asked him, pointing to a newspaper article from 1944. My wife had come across it at a flea market. It described our house in that year and how the Birk family had renovated their summer cottage into a home. It even had a picture of the stone fireplace. We had it laminated and hung it on the bathroom wall.

"I do not. Well look at that. I would fancy a copy of that if it is possible. My Dad would have seen this but I have no recollection of it. I am a little bit of a collector, and this would be a nice addition. Could I copy it?"

"Of course," I said, and the tour continued.

"And in this room, there stayed one of the most beautiful women you would ever see. I have a photo of her at home. She was my second cousin and she stayed in this room with her son in the last years of the war. She hobnobbed at parties with the likes of Winston Churchill before her family shipped her here for safety. She ended up marrying a Count from somewhere and moving to South America."

It felt odd to have a stranger guide me through my own house. He led his son and I through some of its history and the tour ended out onto the second-floor balcony. From this vantage point we could see out to the lake below and a glimpse of the beach.

"See those rows of concrete blocks. That was where George Barber's boathouse was and just beyond that, see that concrete pad? That's where the tuck shop was and that's where I got my nickname."

"Your nickname, Dad?" asked John.

"Yes, son. I had a nickname. I had it for most of my life. Got it when I was six years old and I carried it around every day we were in Grimsby Beach. I even had someone use it when I was last here, sometime in the sixties when I met up with Mr. Vannetter's son, Glen. He used it right away when he saw me, like I'd never left."

"Well, what was it, Dad? What was your nickname?"

"Toke."

"Toke?" asked John.

"When I was six I didn't speak so well and when I was down by the tuck shop on a hot day I had the cheek to ask for a 'coke' but I guess it came out more as 'Toke'. The crowd around there that day thought it was funny and that's how I got the name. Never bothered me much. Most people had a nickname back then."

While Robert Birk was explaining this to his son, I stepped back into the house. Fearing that he was losing a member of his audience, he turned from the shoreline and said over his shoulder,

"Have you heard about the murder that happened here?"

That caught my attention and halted my retreat. I had never heard of a murder or anything salacious at all associated to a place I'd always considered peaceful and bucolic. It also caught the attention and ire of his son, John, who instantly stopped playing the part of photojournalist and began to slander his father.

"You'll have to forgive my father," he said to me, "He has a fondness for hyperbole and bending the truth."

"There is no bending in it," came his father's heated retort. "What I say is true. Check the archives if you must. It was in the paper." and turning towards me he added, "And you'll have to forgive my son. He is a 'detail' man, an affliction no doubt due to his training as an Engineer. Only believes what's directly in front of his nose and has great difficulty in accepting that there is always more than meets the eye and more than the ear can hear. Mind you it took me most of my life to learn that so maybe there is hope for him yet. Anyway, it happened at 3:00 am on August 3rd, 1914, outside the veranda of the Park House Hotel and by it, I mean the murder."

The specificity of these details was meant to authenticate the mention of murder and once they came out of his mouth Robert Birk straightened his spine and glared at his son. I became aware that I was witnessing just another small skirmish in a long-drawn-out war between this father and son, and I didn't want it to ruin the moment. I sought to calm the waters so that the flow of historic information continued. I had no delusions of solving disputes that were decades old, but I did think some Earl Grey might salvage a pleasant and educational morning.

"I'd really like to hear about that. Do you two have time to sit and have some tea?" I offered.

With that, a smile returned to Robert Birk's face. He was not showing any signs of being elderly, his energy and enthusiasm for revealing this juicy tidbit of the past was robust. He was obviously pleased to have an audience and I, for one, was most happy to oblige him. His son, on the other hand, looked like he had somewhere he'd rather be but to his credit, he sat and drank coffee while his father talked. Between sips of Earl Grey, this is the story Robert Birk told us.

THE PARK HOUSE HOTEL, GRIMSBY BEACH 4:00 AM

AUGUST 3RD, 1914

"C'mon Toke, grab his wrists and let's go." Though soft and muffled, his words were still very much a command.

"I don't want to touch it."

My words came out a little more girlish than I would have liked but this was the first dead body I'd ever seen, let alone touched. And I was still bleary-eyed with sleep. I had been awoken from a blissful calm. My dream of fishing with Fiona Falconbridge in her dad's boat was shattered when my older brother Jacob shook me awake. He worked for the Park House Hotel doing all manner of things and this morning the job called for dragging a body out of view of its entrance. I helped Jacob work in the storerooms from time to time which is how I found myself on one end of a corpse and Jacob cursing at me under his breath, at the other.

"It's not an 'It' Toke. It's a man or was a man. Now grab him before anyone sees."

Jacob had a way of making his intentions sound imperative even while he was whispering, so I took a deep breath, tried to avert my gaze at the deceased and obliged my brother's orders.

I was surprised at how heavy the corpse was. I'm not as big as my brother, but I'm pretty strong, and still, we couldn't lift him off the ground. He was a big man. We managed to lift his limbs high enough that his arse dragged as we pulled him sideways toward the storeroom door of the hotel. Thankfully the entrance to the door was at ground level and only ten yards away. I don't think we could have managed to haul him up any stairs. The second thing that surprised me, something that didn't register with me until I let his arms flop down on the cellar floor was that he was still warm. I had never associated death with warmth but like I said, I hadn't had any experience with dead people. I learned later that the body was still warm because this guy was freshly dead.

Jacob put a sheaf of canvas over the body, put a broom in my hand and pushed me out of the storeroom. "We ain't done yet." He told me to sweep out the gulley we made in the dirt dragging the carcass around the side of the hotel. I wasn't about to argue so I swung the broom back and forth in the dirt to cover our tracks while Jacob went back into the storeroom alone. I was sweeping my way to the front of the hotel when four men came out of the entrance and walked to the edge of the veranda. They were overlooking the crime scene. I recognized the hotel manager, Mr. Vannetter, Officer Belcher, one of the Park's two policemen, Doctor Campbell and Mr. H.H. Wylie, the Owner of Grimsby Park. Only Officer Belcher was in uniform. The rest of the men were in various stages of dress, a strange combination of trousers and night dresses. Mr. Vannetter even had on a sleeping cap. The men were whispering amongst themselves but through the soft whoosh of my broom I heard Mr. Wylie say, "Belcher, the boys have put it in the storeroom. Do whatever investigation you must do and then arrange for the body to be moved before daybreak. We do not want Mr. Vannetter's guests to catch sight of this. Boyle is upstairs with the accused and we'd very much like you to take him out the back way as soon as possible."

"Yes sir," replied the policeman and he came down the stairs toward me, veered right and headed towards the storeroom.

Turning back to Doc Campbell, Mr. Wylie asked, "You, say he was alive when you got to him Doctor? Did he say anything?"

"He tried but he was silenced by his wound. He had a deep cut laterally across his throat. Odd that there was little blood where he fell. I found one bullet wound in his back, but I suspect there might be more. I distinctly heard two shots. It was the gunfire that brought me here. You say the suspect is up in his room?"

Wylie nodded towards Mr. Vannetter who spoke.

"I heard the same shots, followed by scuffling across the 2nd floor balcony and then down the stairs. When I came out of my office, I saw Mr. Sparling stagger out the door, down the stairs and collapse there," pointing to the ground. "When I saw the Doctor coming, I set off to find Boyle, but he was already on his way. I directed the Constable to Room 16 where Mr. Sparling, the victim, was staying and together we found the accused sitting in the adjoining room on his bed holding a cloth to his throat for he had been cut as well."

I was just about finished the job when I reached a dark wet splotch about the size of my fist on the ground. I hesitated my sweeping not wanting to soil the broom when Jacob came up beside me.

"Blood" was all he said as he took the broom out of my hand and kicked dust and dirt into the gelatinous blob.

"Doc Smith said he was still alive when he got here," I whispered. "He said he had a gash on his throat and a bullet in his back."

I couldn't quite believe what I was telling my brother even though I helped drag the body from the scene only moments before. But I had averted my gaze and the darkness didn't allow me to take in much. I took careful pains not to look. All I saw were the victim's shirt cuffs, slightly frayed and striped with thin blue thread. It was an old shirt but at one time, it had been a fancy one and that's all I saw. I couldn't tell you if he was sandy haired or a blood nut or raven-haired cause I didn't want to look. I had no intention of becoming intimately acquainted with a cadaver. I only knew he was male because he was wearing britches. As I was reliving it all, I was getting wheezy and weak, and I must have wobbled a little. The blood in my head must have settled down into my feet and I'm sure my face was pale and luminous even in the early morning darkness.

"You gonna be okay Toke? You look like you're gonna faint," Jacob grabbed me by the elbow and led me back around to the storeroom door. Staring me directly in the eye he gave me his last instruction that morning. "You go back to the cottage. I've got more to do here and don't breathe a word to Mom or anyone else for that matter."

I nodded and slowly turned up the path towards the Temple. In my weakened state the shadows of trees and cottages became surreal and ominous. This was a path I'd walked a thousand times before, but this was like sleepwalking in a strange and awkward dream. I recognized the cottages on either side of the laneway, even knew who slumbered inside, all unaware of the tragedy that occurred just a short distance away. The whimsical and unique pattern of their gingerbread trim appeared strange and menacing. The neat and vertical lines of board and batten became slanted and skewed and I could feel the towering pine trees and sugar maples looming over me. It was though they were judging all humanity for bringing murder to their peaceful community and although I was just a bystander, I felt complicit, just for being human.

A few more plodding steps and I was before the mass of the Auditorium. As if the morning wasn't odd enough, I could hear a preacher from deep inside the structure working out his sermon for that morning. I could see the flutter of his lamp as I passed the open curtains and even though he muffled his voice so as not to rouse the adjacent cottagers, I could tell that he was working his way up to the fire and brimstone part. The pitch of his voice was rising as his fists thumped on the lectern. Made me wonder if God was telling him that I had just aided the removal and concealment of a dead body not 50 yards away. I quickened my pace. As his voice faded behind me, I turned onto Temple Lane just as the sun was bleeding red on the horizon. "Red sky at morning..." I whispered.

The walkway to Victoria Terrace was a wind tunnel. The narrow gap between the cottages worked like a funnel to squeeze the breeze into a gust. But the air off the lake was fresh and the sound of the waves crashing on the beach brought me back to consciousness. I stopped, took a deep breath and let the rhythm of the surf reset my pulse. It seemed like I was waking from a bad dream. The events of the morning were at odds with the tranquility of this place, a place I'd spent every summer, a place so peaceful and calm I normally had to work pretty hard to find adventure. A place where a dead body was foreign and incongruent. So, in the short time it took to get from the hotel to our cottage, I had nearly convinced myself that the incident had never happened.

Not wanting to arouse my mother, I crept up the steps to our porch, avoided the creaky board at the threshold and slowly swung the screen and the outside door open. I knew enough to push the doors in against their hinges to keep them from squealing, just like I knew that the floorboards along the wall saw little traffic and were still fastened securely to the joists, so they didn't pop up when you took your weight off of them. I expertly stole my way to my bunk in the pantry, rolled my weight onto its springs gently and pulled the blanket over me. I was wide eyed and not anywhere close to sleep, wondering just how I could get myself back to that dream with Fiona in the boat. I clasped the edges of my blanket, but these were bordered by blue and white stripes, just like the dead man's shirt cuffs and my thoughts returned to the patch of earth in front of the Park House Hotel. I lay there looking at my hands.

"These fingertips," I told myself, "have touched a dead person."

TWELVE MILE CREEK, LOCK 6, APRIL 1ST 1914

Five months earlier Percy Sparling was looking at his fingertips. They were more blue than pink. He could barely feel them, so he rubbed the digits together and stuffed them under his armpits. The chisel had felt like ice in his left hand and while the right had gripped the wooden handle of a mallet, it didn't feel any warmer. The sun had crested the horizon not an hour before. His breath hung in a cloud around him every time he exhaled.

He was blowing into his cupped hands when the Foreman approached, a man in tow. He knew very well the waddling gait of his boss, the result of some accident some years in the past. Percy didn't know the details. He didn't even know his boss's name; he was always introduced as 'Foreman'. It was a little early for his daily visit.

"Sparling, this is Jesse Ward. You are going to show Ward here how to cut a straight edge. You've got another drill and chisel for him?"

While Percy conjured an answer for his boss, he tried to assess this new recruit, but the sun was in his eyes. All he could see was Ward's silhouette. He was short and thin and did not have the broad shoulders of a mason.

"I have the tools. Where are the Nelles brothers?"

"They got pulled into the Fourth. There's a big push to get the Big Ditch done. The big wigs in Toronto don't seem to understand that we need to keep this canal going while they dig the new one, which means you and Ward here are going to have to work twice as fast before they make you trade in your chisel for a shovel. This gate has to keep working for another two years at least, so make it good." The Foreman paused, nodded in Sparling's direction, turned and began hobbling away, his low muttering fading.

"I think he'd rather be working on the Fourth," were the first words the newcomer said.

"I think he'd rather not be all gimped up bossing the lot of us around on this petty little project," returned Sparling. "All the big boys are working on the new canal and it's making him feel old. Take this drill and follow this line. Drill down as far as the mandrel will take you and brush the dust off as you go. When you're done, I follow with the chisel and split it."

"What happened here, to this gate?"

Ward was looking at the battered door and top three courses of stone blocks that served as a hinge. The stone blocks had been smashed and the hinge had been jerry-rigged to make it work. Sparling nodded up to the train bridge that spanned the canal just above them.

"Derailment. Bridge wasn't closed proper. The locomotive stayed up on the bridge, but the coal car came down and hit this gate. They patched it up, but the bridge needs more attention. And they want it done before the shipping season gets into full swing."

With that, the conversation ended, and Sparling went back to smacking his chisel with his mallet. Picking up the drill, Ward looked along the line scored across the face of the stone. This was dolomite, a relatively hard variety of limestone and the line showed up white against the grey surface. He carefully placed the point of the drill in a crevice and began to crank the drill around until a bead of sweat rose on his forehead, the grinding bit reverberating up from his hand to his arm and into his chest. The drill was sharp and his progress fast and he found the work satisfying and oddly soothing, if unfamiliar.

The cold of the morning produced a mist that hung over the canal. The sun wouldn't settle on them for another hour, so they had to keep warm with their labour. There was the gurgle of the water nearby and countless birds fulfilling their springtime rituals of finding food, building nests and performing courtship displays but the men on this worksite were ignorant of it all. They could only hear the peel of their hammers and the grinding of the drills on the limestone. They only saw the steady progress of their force on the stone.

"She's done". Percy's monotonous beat with the hammer was only interrupted with Ward's declaration. Wordlessly, Sparling came over to inspect the line of holes Ward's drill had made across the rock. He placed the edge of his chisel along the line and motioned for Ward to move behind him. Sparling raised the hammer high above his head and brought it down squarely and swiftly onto the chisel and the boulder split in two flat pieces with a reasonably straight edge on both. Percy turned to look up at Ward standing behind him. "You've done this before." It wasn't a question, but a statement said evenly without emotion.

"Well, no, but my biography is wide and diverse. I've been a cowboy, a lumberjack, a miner, a grocer, a tailor, a stevedore,"

"But not a mason," interrupted Sparling.

"I haven't had the pleasure, no I've never been a mason. But one time...."

Sparling interrupted again. "Let's get back to work."

And that was all Sparling said to Ward for the next two hours. The entire morning, Sparling scribed lines for Ward to drill, and then came in to cleave the stone with his tools. The pace of their work increased. They became two pistons driving each other, their actions humming with efficiency. In time, the men had removed their coats and didn't take time to warm their hands. Foreman came to inspect their progress later that morning, even though he didn't say anything, it pleased him to see that the two were making a good team.

Once the sun had made its way overhead, all the men on site shuffled downstream to the lunch meal. A couple of them nodded cautious greetings to Ward. He nodded back and noted the morose atmosphere of the place. Two dozen tents were scattered between the canal and the forest. There hadn't been much effort to organize the layout of the camp. A larger canvas tent built over a timber platform stood at the edge of the wood while the rest were smaller pup tents facing every which way. No doubt whomever set up the tents did so to take advantage of any level ground that could be found. There had been no attempt to level the site and logs and boulders sat amongst the canvas shelters. The encampment looked haphazard and temporary, as though the surrounding Nature could grow over it and make it disappear in a matter of hours.

Halfway between the water and the wood was the largest tent. It had a black stove pipe poking up and sooty smoke was drifting up above. Beneath it a line of men shuffled inside each holding their mess kit. This was the kitchen tent and one of its walls was tied back to let in the workmen and the light.

Jesse noted a joyless tension amongst those standing in line. It hung in the air like a funereal pall. The Cook stood behind a table ladling out something that looked like a watery stew and tried his best to engage the men in conversation. "How's the work progressing today, gents?" He asked cheerfully. "You'll be making the chips fly once you've had some grub."

One man grumbled out some words while the others shuffled forward in silence. As each man came before the cook, he held out his bowl to receive the colourless liquid and a truncheon of bread. Not one soul seemed grateful as they moved away to find a log or stump to sit on. When the cook ladled the stew into Ward's bowl, Jesse could see why. A gristly piece of beef floated in a murky broth. It did not look appetizing.

"Ahhh, a new recruit. Welcome to the mess tent. I am Cook."

"I am Jesse Ward. It is a pleasure to meet you. You have a warm place to work, not that I begrudge you the pleasure, I'm sure it's unpleasantly hot in the summer" he said, returning the cook's smile. He wanted to acknowledge the man's efforts to bring some energy and joy into this group of men, even though the food that he made obviously did not.

"Welcome Jesse Ward. It is a pleasure to meet your acquaintance!" he said with a flourish. The men in line shuffled impatiently.

"Would Cook be your given or your surname?"

"Neither. It's just what they call me."

"Could you two make your acquaintances after dinner?" protested someone behind.

"Sorry, sorry, I'm a bit long winded," Ward said as he moved out of the line. "Runs in my family. Words are in my veins." and he nodded his thanks to Cook who silently mouthed 'Harold' back.

"Well, thank you Harold. It is a pleasure to meet you." Ward meandered around the guy lines of the tent, a rock, and a stump on his way to a circle of logs surrounding a fire pit. He noticed that Sparling made an effort to sit alone by the stream and with no invitation to eat together, Ward took it upon himself to sit with the others.

"Hey there, you are welcome to join us." The words came from a large man sitting on the logs with other large men.

Jesse as he took a place within the group. "Much obliged."

"Worked on the canal before?"

"No, but I worked with masons on Booth's Railway as a kid," he said, nodding in a northerly direction.

"Weren't you up there Lucius?" asked the large man to another in the circle.

"Stuck it out there for three days before the black flies carried me away. That was a nasty job. My eyes puffed up so that I couldn't see. Those little black buggers had it in for me," said Lucius.

"They had it in for everyone, Lucius. Your blood is just sweeter than the average nave, at least that's what the ladies say," said another.

"Well, I wish the ladies swarmed me like those blasted bugs. I wouldn't mind being bitten by some lovely lass right now and me giving her some nibbles back. Say, who is good to go into Merritton tomorrow night?"

The mention of Merritton, the closest village to the worksite, brought lightness and laughter as the conversation degraded into various personal conquests and innuendo that brightens the eyes and lightens the tongue of most working men. But the large man still held Ward's attention.

"We see the Foreman teamed you with Sparling?" His tone told Jesse that he and Percy Sparling didn't get along. It was a simple statement that held an unspoken message. Ward decided to answer in the most positive way he could.

"That man sure can handle a chisel. He speaks to the stone and makes it do his bidding. He is very good at what he does."

"That is so. But he's gone through every driller Foreman has set him with. He's a might fussy and cantankerous. Prefers to work alone and...." motioning to the man seated at the edge of the camp, "likes to eat alone. I only mention it because he will likely try and take the piss out of you like he has everyone else."

"I think I can handle him. I once had trouble with a lumberjack by the name of Jacque Larue, biggest, meanest axeman in the camp. Told me to take my English ass back to the city and leave the real work to the Habitant. But he came around when he saw that I could handle the horses, I'm a bit of a horse whisperer you know, and worked the gantry. And he liked my stories once we sat down to supper. He'd lie on his bunk and ask me to tell some stories over and over again. He was partial to stories about trains. Anyway, all to say, if I can handle Jacque Larue, I think I can handle him," as he pointed his chin in Sparling's direction.

"Well maybe you can. Just mind his temper. He has a short fuse, and it seems to be getting shorter. Once this gate is done, they're going to float us downstream to work on the new canal which will mean trading in our hammers for shovels and none of us wants to be replaced by a cement mixer, least of all Percy Sparling."

"Well thanks for the heads up. Is the food always like this? When I was driving cattle on the Prairie, the chuckwagon always had this smell ....".

THE IRONWORKERS

When Ward made his way to the worksite the following day his boot broke through a skim of puddle ice. There was a mist wafting up from the creek and he could hear a cardinal chirping high in the trees, a flash of scarlet in the first light of morning. The sun was just skimming the tops of the trees on the escarpment, and he couldn't wait for it to creep down into the river valley where they worked so he could feel its warmth on his back. It was frigid and the sound of steel hammers on steel chisels only made it seem colder.

Sparling was already hunched over a stone, skillfully cleaving and squaring the rock into a block that would dovetail into the older blocks already lining the canal. This canal had twelve locks each one hundred and ten feet long and fifty feet wide. Each block was the size of a steamer trunk, and it took five hundred of them to complete a lock. Repairs like this one were usually routine but the gate on lock six was failing and it was important to make the repairs in a timely manner.

Over the last forty years countless skiffs and schooners had made their way up and down the escarpment separating Lake Ontario from Lake Erie. Trade up and down the canal had grown exponentially over the last decade and any delays would upset the economy of the entire Great Lakes region on both sides of the border. Blocks had to be cut, old and decrepit ones removed, and the new ones put into place as quickly as possible so that the supply of ore and grain could float out of the heart of North America, down the St. Lawrence and to ports beyond.

"Ward! Get down here with your drill and do some work!" Sparling spat.

Jesse brushed off the angry words, shook his head and replied in a singsong voice. "You are a taskmaster, Percy Sparling. You do love to work, and you are surely good at cutting stone. You know I've been called a 'dandy" in my day, but I tell you, I can hold my own with anyone. I am not shy with respect to adversity. 'Do what is right, not what is easy' is what me Dad always said, and a wiser man never spoke."

"And did he yammer on as much as you?"

"Oh yes, Mr. Ignatius Ward liked to tell a story. He was known to start talkin' when he sat up in bed and waggle his tongue til' his eyes closed at night; words flowed out of his mouth like water in the stream, a river in fact, and it became a torrent once he got to the pub, only stopping to take a breath and a swig of stout. One time....."

"Foreman wants the header blocks and gate hinges done this week." Sparling said, handing him the drill.

"Of course, of course. There's no working if you're talkin'. I'll shut me trap now and assist you. There is no task beneath me. I am at your service..."

Sparling's glare interrupted him and motioned the drill towards him again.

"I see, I see, my lips are sealed. I am in the present, the here and now. I will shut up now." and Ward exaggerated the motion of pressing his lips together and took the drill.

"That would be Christian of you," Sparling said as he got down to work and in seconds his red hair flecked with chips of limestone. Ward kneeled at the block beside him and began the monotonous turning of the drill. The grinding was hypnotic which helped to soothe the chronic pain in his shoulder. He tried switching the hand he used to turn the auger but found this made his accuracy suffer. Sparling noticed every time Ward was using his left hand and admonished him for it, so to maintain good working relations, Ward's shoulder ached.

It was approaching noon when the iron workers showed up. Sparling and Ward had just begun rounding off the gate blocks that sat adjacent to the rail line. They kept to their work, but each man listened intently to the voices and sounds coming from the tracks above. Over the sound of the gurgling stream, they could hear their leader shout out commands and the singsong responses of the other workers, the men who would hoist and fit and rivet new beams where cracked and damaged ones stood.

This bridge was something Ward had never seen before. It was designed to swing 90 degrees so that it wouldn't catch on the masts and rigging of the ships moving up and down the canal.

"Craziest bridge construction I've ever seen," said Ward, breaking the silence. "Did you work on the footing?"

"That was well before my time".

"But three footings?"

"You've seen a swing bridge before?" sneered Sparling. He glanced up at Jesse long enough to glower at him.

"No, but....."

"Then let's get back to drillin'."

While the locomotive sat hissing on the west side of the bridge the stonemasons could hear commands to set up a gantry. They heard the men call together as they lifted the steel girders off the flatbed cars and the jarring clang of chains being pulled over the edge of I-beams. Through the sound of the drill and the chisel, Sparling and Ward were picturing the ironworkers who would join their camp while the bridge was being repaired but whatever mental picture they conjured, it wasn't anything like the real image they saw when the newcomers entered the camp at lunch time.

"They're staying here with us?" one mason asked

"And eatin' with us?" a second asked in disgust.

"Well, I'm not eating here," said another and he left with his plate to sit further downstream.

Their facial expressions proved the ironworkers knew they weren't welcome. It was an expression that has been etched on their faces for much of their lives. Nearly all of them lined up at the grub table and paid no attention to the crews already sitting down. One of them glared at any mason who dared look back. He was monstrous in size and wore a menacing scowl and his long black hair tied behind his head. The silence in the camp was broken only by the caw of a crow flying by and the scraping of spoons on enamel plates. Not a single word was spoken by either side. It took only seconds for the lines to be drawn, the walls to be erected and the territories to be mapped out. All the ironworkers took their plates upstream and sat at the footings of the bridge. Conversation amongst the masons resumed when they were out of earshot from the new arrivals.

"Best hide your valuables," advised someone.

"Best sleep with your hammer," advised another.

Ward finished up his lunch and made his way upstream beyond the bridge to find Sparling already hammering away on a new block. As he crossed the tracks, he could see that the locomotive had steamed its way back to wherever it came from and that the Ironworkers were busy setting up their camp on the opposite shore of the stream. He picked his way down to Sparling. "Well, that was some welcome."

"They are Mohawk. Good workers. Can last all day and have no fear," informed Sparling.

It was the first time Ward had heard Sparling say anything complementary about anyone. "You've worked with them before?"

"I have," responded Sparling in a tone that meant that he wanted the conversation to be over.

But Jesse had been working with him now for over a week and he longed to use his voice. It was as though there was a log jam of words and phrases inside him. He let one escape hoping it would loosen the rest that were waiting to burst free. "Where?"

"Erie," was all Ward got out of him. By Erie, Jesse knew that Sparling had worked on the Erie canal, the three-hundred-and-sixty-mile waterway connecting Buffalo to New York City and the inspiration for the first Welland Canal. While it had been completed many years before, there was constant maintenance, expansions and bridge footings for skilled masons to work. And although it was just a single word answer, "Erie" was another piece of the puzzle, another scrap of evidence that Jesse Ward was working beside the right man.

"Do you think there'll be trouble with them?"

"I think Conners, and the rest of his crew will be beat to a pulp if they don't mind their business." Sparling was glaring at Jesse Ward again with that unmistakable and silent message that said, "And you should mind your own business too!"

And so, Ward reined in his words and posed no more questions. They worked through the afternoon in silence, went their separate ways at the grub table and like every worker in the camp that day, collapsed into their own tents as the darkness fell upon their camp.

NIGHTWATCH

Ward was sleeping soundly well into the night when something flashed across his face and caused him to stir. The flap of his tent fluttered in a light breeze and the moonlight came across his eyes. He turned his face away from the opening, groaned as he lay on his sore shoulder and tried to get back to sleep. He was nearly back into his slumbers when he heard a twig snap downstream from his tent. Jesse was alert instantly and recalling his co-worker's warning to sleep with your hammer, sat up and slowly pushed aside the flap for a better look.

In this camp, every man had his own small pup tent. They were company property, but government issued. Apparently, these were the same tents used by cadets and servicemen currently training in the Canadian light infantry. Temporary work crews like this one had to "rough it" compared to the barrack style accommodations offered to the large teams working on the Fourth Canal further downstream. The Government had supplied these tents to the Canal Project because of its economic and subsequent military importance. Apparently, the Government of Canada valued these workers as much as the young men that were currently training to be its soldiers.

Ward's tent was one of twenty clustered together downstream from the bridge and on the east side of the canal. He wasn't on the outside edge of the encampment, but he did have a clear view of the water from his entrance. One quick glance told him that the noise did not come from a Mohawk warrior sneaking into the mason's camp. Against the moonlight, he easily recognized the profile of Sparling wading across the water flow and holding his boots aloft in his outstretched hand. Sparling didn't appear to be concerned about getting his clothes wet. In the middle of the canal, in the deepest pool, the black water was swirling around his waist. From the shelter of his tent, Ward sat watching while he reached out for his boots. He was going to follow even though the moon was bright and full.

Ward knelt at the opening of his tent with his own boots in hand waiting for Sparling to make his way up the opposite bank. Questions percolating in his mind. Just what was on the opposite side of the canal that would be of interest? Why didn't he use the bridge to make the crossing? What was so secretive that he snuck out in the middle of the night to cross at its most difficult point?

When Sparling disappeared, Ward silently made his way to the edge of the river and followed. He nearly fell, was wet up to his chest by the time he made it across and had dipped his boots underwater twice to regain his balance. He rested on the same rock Percy had sat on and slipped on his boots. His heart was pounding as he climbed the berm and wove his way along Sparling's trail. The woods were thick, casting a dark shadow and he felt invisible until the path opened into a clearing. Jesse stepped off the trail, crouched down amongst the brush and steadied his breath.

Moonlight bounced off the metal roofs of two small sheds. There was no sign of Percy. In the shelter of the leaves, Jesse scanned his surroundings. There was not a breath of wind. A nighthawk hovered over the clearing and dove at its prey while Jesse sat motionless. He was alert and focused and readied himself for what might be a long vigil. He didn't have to wait long. Sparling came out of the larger of the two sheds carrying a bag. His movements were slow and deliberate, almost mechanical. Percy then turned, closed the door, slid a padlock through a hasp, locked it, and disappeared behind the shed. Jesse was certain that Sparling didn't know he was being watched and it was agonizing to just sit and wait.

Less than a minute later, Sparling walked back across the clearing with empty hands. He passed just ten feet from where Ward was holding his breath and hiding in the brush. Sparling must have hidden the bag and its contents somewhere behind the shed. Jesse listened for Sparling's fading footsteps and waited another moment before he dared move. Cautiously, he came out of the trees and crept across the clearing. He reached up and pulled on the padlock, but it was securely locked. The lock had either been picked or Sparling had a key.

He rounded the corner of the structure to see what Sparling had done with the bag. The trees and shrubs were thick there and the moonlight could not penetrate the darkness. Ward waited for his eyes to adjust but he could not see the bag or any place to hide one. Walking around the shed twice searching unsuccessfully he decided he would try to find an opportunity to come back in the light of day. Right now, he needed to get back to camp and slip into his tent without anyone, particularly Sparling, knowing.

Deciding that following Sparling across the river and back into the camp was risky, Ward made his way upstream with the idea of crossing over the railway bridge and then approaching the camp from the other side. If he was seen, it wouldn't look like he'd been trailing Sparling.

He turned towards the bridge and found that the path on this side of the canal was well used. In the bright moonlight it was easy to follow and within a minute he was scrambling up the gravel to the railway tracks. He had just stepped over the first rail when a voice calmly said, "Oh nihsatiѐhrha?"

Ward tripped on the next railway tie and nearly fell on his face. "Huh?"

A thin man stepped out of the shadows of the bridge and in the same calm voice said, "What are you doing?"

As the light fell upon his face, Ward realized that this was a boy and not a man. He did not possess the wide shoulders of the other ironworkers and his hair, while black as a raven, was cropped short. Ward looked about assessing if there were more ironworkers and realized that this boy was standing alone as a guard for their camp. Maybe the Mohawk were sleeping with their hammers too?

"Just out for a walk. Beautiful moonlight tonight."

"Eayehnekì:ra oghne:kanos?" laughed the boy. Obviously, Jesse was the butt of his joke, but it just made him smile as he watched the boy double up with laughter. It had been a long while since he had heard that kind of joy and it instantly lightened his mood.

"What?"

"I ask if you walk on water? You are on the wrong side of the river," the boy explained still chuckling. Jesse wasn't sure that he completely understood the joke. He decided to ask some questions of his own.

"You are Mohawk?"

The boy nodded and his chest puffing out proudly.

"You are an ironworker?"

The boy nodded again.

"My friend says that Mohawks are good workers, strong and brave."

"It is true," the boy smiled.

"Then you are welcome here." offered Ward.

"Are we?" The boy's smile faded as he cocked his head and looked Jesse over with an inquiring eye.

"Well, I'm welcoming you. What is your name?"

"Yaweko. In my language it means 'sweet'." The boy's smile returned.

"Well, it's nice to meet you Yaweko. My name is Jesse Ward. Maybe we can talk another time but now I must get back to camp."

"Sentà:wha."

"Huh?"

"To sleep. You go to sleep."

"Yes, whatever you said. Goodnight Yaweko" and Jesse picked his way carefully across the bridge taking care not to step between the ties.

"O:nen ki wehi" came the soft voice behind him.

Ward made his way silently back. Upon entering the camp, he scanned Sparling's tent for movement. It was dark and quiet. He lowered himself beneath his own canvas and pulled off his boots and wet clothes. He lay back and pulled his blanket over himself. Ward lay awake, eyes staring up at the ridge of his tent wondering about Percy Sparling's late-night walk, the shed in the clearing and the Mohawk boy with the infectious laugh.

The repair of the bridge began the next day. It wasn't two hours before a thirty-foot beam had been replaced. As Sparling and Ward laboriously chipped away at the stone below, they could hear the musical voices of the ironworkers above. There was laughter and much cajoling. Even though the language was incomprehensible to them, they could tell that this crew did their work with joy. The jokes and taunts distracted Jesse on more than one occasion; he'd looked up to see the Mohawk workers efficiently move about and fit the steel girders together. One lithe and muscular man climbed up the vertical I-beam post using his feet on the outside to push against his hands gripping the inside.

In this manner he scaled the vertical post to the top, got one foot on the top of the I-beam and then stood up on its end. He was up on the end of a vertical post, a full sixty feet above the riverbed. Sparling seemed to be impervious to the sounds. His focus was on his chisel.

"You did say that they had no fear."

Sparling stopped his work to look up at the sight. In a rare departure from his taciturn mood, Sparling explained to Ward what was going on. Ward watched the man's face, saw respect in his expression as much as in his words. "That kid there is the heater. He fires up the forge and gets the rivets red hot. See now he's got the rivets in his tongs. He drops them in that bucket which is pulled up by the guy with the blue shirt. He's the stick-in. He sticks the rivet in the hole once the bucker-up removes that temporary bolt and then he braces the rivet with his dolly bar while the riveter peens over the stem of the rivet. It takes teamwork 'cause that rivet only stays hot enough for a moment."

Throughout this dissertation, Jesse recognized the kid, the heater, as he glanced down in their direction.

"Hey Yaweko!" Jesse shouted up to him.

"Hey Jesse Ward!" shouted back, and for a moment the Mohawk crew stopped what they were doing and marveled at this exchange. Sparling looked too; all the observers were left to wonder how and when these two had the opportunity to share names.

"Get drillin'," commanded Sparling. Work resumed up on the bridge and below in the river.

All day Jesse looked for the chance to cross the river and investigate the mysterious shed on the other side of the creek, but no opportunity presented itself. When night fell the clouds made a low ceiling that eclipsed the moon. He knew he would not be visible in the darkness, but he also knew it would be difficult to see the slippery rocks should he cross the river, the uneven ties should he go over the bridge or Sparling should he be lurking in the dense brush that ringed the huts. So, he did nothing. He lay awake under his blanket listening for movement, straining to sense if Sparling was up and about. He listened to the gurgling stream and the hoot of an owl but heard no footsteps within the camp. Eventually he fell asleep vowing that he would try tomorrow.

THE SKIRMISH

The trouble began the next day. It came in like some great bird soaring down on the silent wings to catch its prey. A Great Horned owl that surprised everyone, except maybe the two adversaries challenging each other on the bridge. A large cart carrying a four-ton stone was being pulled up the berm of the railway tracks. The stone was needed on the opposite bank and had to cross the bridge. However, the Ironworker's railcar bearing the numbered beams and trusses sat in the center of the span blocking the way. The conflict could have been solved with some polite words and decorum, but neither manners or patience were in great supply among the masons.

"Get that shit out of our way!" shouted Carson. He was the individual who'd thoughtfully warned all in the camp to guard our possessions when the Mohawks had arrived. Whatever had shaped Carson's image of the First Nations Peoples left a sharp and jagged edge. It was clear that he had no love for the ironworkers and that he was willing to fight to prove it. In solidarity, the other masons stood shoulder to shoulder behind Carson, threatening expressions on their faces. The Mohawk crew all stopped working. Their laughter and smiles faded. All stood their ground except for one. The tallest and widest of them stepped forward onto the tracks and positioned himself between the mason's cart and the ironworker's railcar. All the masons except Carson took a step back and immediately looked less menacing. By this time Ward and Sparling had left their tools down by the river and were scrambling their way across the bridge to the perimeter of the confrontation. They had heard Carson's angry words and like everyone within earshot, came to investigate.

Staring directly into Emmet's eyes, this giant of a man uttered one word in Mohawk.

"Okà:ta"

"What's that you say Chief?" Carson sneered as he slowly drew a knife from his belt.

Yaweko, took a step forward and with a slight smile, translated. "He called you an anus."

The insult caused Carson to crouch down and hold out his knife as if ready to pounce. He began to take deep breaths and sway from side to side, shifting his weight from one foot to the other.

The large Mohawk did not move. He stood his ground, unarmed and seemingly unalarmed. Only his lips moved to repeat the insult again. "Okà:ta".

The cadence of Carson's swaying quickened. His eyes narrowed and he turned the blade back and forth in his hand, sunlight reflecting off the steel. His challenger just stared him in the eye. Every steelworker stood still. They were expressionless, like they had seen this scenario play out before, and they knew how it was going to end. Every mason, other than Carson, could also foresee the outcome and wisely took a step back, their solidarity crushed. Other than the crunching gravel under Carson's shuffling feet there was silence until...

"Gentlemen!" The shout came from the far side of the bridge. Foreman was quickly making his way along the tracks and as he did, Carson straightened up and slid his knife behind his back and into his belt. "Let's get this railway car across the bridge so we can get on with our day. Everyone put your shoulder to it! Carson, I need to talk to you."

And with that, Mohawks and masons put their combined force to the car and easily rolled it out of the way while the Foreman gave Emmet Carson a talking to. Ward found himself beside Yaweko as they pushed at the load of steel girders.

"The Big guy is right. Emmet Carson is an Okà:ta".

This made the boy laugh and translate the message for his crew to hear. Many laughed as well but the giant man just looked at Ward and nodded his head.

"Doesn't that guy know how to smile?" Ward asked.

"I have never seen it. Tsitsókwen is very still. He is a deep river."

With the railcar out of the way, the gate stone was moved over the bridge and the crews went back to their work. Foreman had sent Carson to work elsewhere and the tension in the air blew away as quickly as it had arrived. Ward and Sparling were about to make their way back down the embankment when the Foreman called. "Sparling and Ward. Come here." They turned and walked towards their boss. "Sparling, you've worked with Mohawk before. Ward, you seem to have struck up a friendship with that boy. I want you both to make this right. I want you to smooth this over with them."

"I thought our job was to finish this gate by the end of the month," said Sparling flatly. His expression was challenging and joyless. Ward on the other hand, relished the idea of a more social assignment. Working along Sparling was like working alone. Moreover, he wanted to learn more about Yaweko and his workmates.

"You'll do both," commanded the Foreman, looking only at Sparling, assessing his willingness to comply. "Now, get back to work."

When the masons retired to their tents that night, the moon was full. As was his habit, Sparling was the first to seek privacy and solitude. Ward crawled into his tent shortly thereafter but didn't untie or take off his boots. Peering through the tent flap he watched the other men retire one by one until the last left the fire. He lay waiting until there was a chorus of snores erupting around him. Then he knelt at the flap of the tent for several moments keeping a watchful eye for movement at Sparling's tent. Gusts of wind were weaving their way through the trees causing the leaves to flutter and rattle and it was under this sound that Ward left his tent and made his way up the path to the bridge. He'd prepared his alibi. If discovered, he was practicing good public relations. He thought he could avoid suspicion saying that he'd sought out the company of Yaweka.

As it turned out, Yaweka was not standing guard on the bridge. The previous day's confrontation lifted the tension between the two groups of men and the Mohawk's posted no guard. He was able to cross the bridge and turn down the path on the opposite side of the river unchallenged. From the train tracks the Mohawk camp looked as still as his own. They used the same government issued tents and had built a fire pit in the center of them. The only distinguishing feature were the bundles and packs hung in the trees; in the darkness they looked like giant fruit in the branches. Jesse assumed it was food and other valuables suspended out of reach of animals. With an urgency in his step, Jesse wove his way down the berm and onto the earthen path. It tunneled its way through some sumac, opened to a meadow of tall grass and then ducked back into sumac again before ending in the clearing with the two sheds. He sat on his haunches and waited before venturing out into the clearing; he had to consider that Sparling might take advantage of the brightness of the night and return.

A solitary cloud passed over the moon, casting a dark shadow on the scene before him. The air up high was traveling at great speeds, chasing the cloud away; the moonlight lit the scene once more. Branches creaked and moaned around him, and he could faintly hear an owl's call far in the distance. Ward held his breath and strained to listen towards the stream and his camp. He ignored the thumping heart in his chest and tuned his senses. For him, stealth had been an acquired skill. He had been sequestered for this job for other attributes. Namely, his congenial and affable character, his ability to win friends and gain the confidence of others. After some moments he was able to calm himself and when another darkening cloud passed, he quickly crossed the open space to the first shed. He was safely hidden in the shadow of its eaves when the moonlight returned.

A sign read 'Property of Welland Canal Company'. The shed was a dilapidated shell of grey and checked barn board. The door had been painted but it was chipped and peeling, and it didn't quite close properly. Ward recognized that it was locked with the same hasp and lock that was on the other structure. He tried to peer in through a crack between the door and the door frame but being windowless, there was total blackness within. Conscious of his time and exposure, Jesse crossed the clearing to the second shed.

With his shadow directly beneath him, he slid through the dewy grass and read on its sign. 'DANGER, EXPLOSIVES'. Though he could see the lock clicked firmly in place, he reached up and gave it a gentle pull. Its resistance was firm and made him wonder how Sparling came into the possession of its key. This shed was quite unlike the first. It was stoutly built and obviously of new construction. It too, was windowless but its lumber was solid and sound, the roof capped with metal sheets. There was no opening to peer into this structure, so he edged his way to the back of the building. Another cloud passed overhead extinguishing the moonlight. A quick glance at the sky told Jesse that more were on the way and that the brightness of the moon wasn't going to last.

Picking up a stick, he used it and the fleeting light to sweep the grass and shrubs. The open area was small, and it took him only seconds to search it. Another cloud passed, making him blind once more. In the darkness he made one last sweep of the grass, gave up and tossed the stick into the brush. It landed with a '*thunk*'. He turned again, picked up the stick and tapped on the earth beside. The same hollow sound rose from the ground. He knelt down, brushed dry grass away as the moonlight returned once more. He found wooden planks fastened together in a square. He lifted a corner of the cover and in the dim light could make out a hole two feet by two feet that was lined with a metal box. Three canvas bags lay there. He reached down and felt firm cylinders lying in bundles beneath the fabric. He didn't need to open the sacs to know that they were filled with sticks of dynamite.

Carefully replacing the wooden boards, Ward covered them with grass, removed his stick and quietly made his way up the path and to the bridge. He crept back into camp, slid into his tent and closed his eyes. In his mind he retraced his steps and his discovery. He filtered through all the information and decided on the most salient details for the report he would write and post tomorrow.

MAIL

Mail was a weekly occurrence in the mason's camp. On Tuesday evenings the postman and his horse would clop their way into the clearing in front of the mess tent where he would reach into his saddle bags to retrieve a small stack of envelopes and a package. He always handed them over to Foreman who, in turn, would hand them out to the men.

Jonathan Book was the only one who got regular packages. Each week the postman handed over the same battered tin box filled with baked goods packed by his wife. Nearly all the masons and the Postman watched as Jonathan would pry off the bent lid of the box. He would share the contents and a moment later, hand it back to the Postman who was still sitting on his horse. Ward thought this quite generous until he was informed that Jonathan Book had been threatened, black mailed really, into sharing his wife's baking with every soul in the camp. This was to ensure that Mrs. Book did not find out that Mr. Book had an ongoing relationship with a widow named Milly who worked at the hotel in a nearby town. "Milly Merritton" was a favorite topic of conversation in the camp, one that all the men wanted to keep alive so that cakes and biscuits kept coming their way. All the rest of the mail was usually addressed to the Foreman and contained directives from the Welland Canal Company managers, but today was different.

"Sparling. Ward. You got mail," said Foreman with some surprise.

The other men watched with envy and curiosity. While the envelopes could not have contained the sweet morsels of Book's tin box, private information was just as delicious to a group of workmen isolated in a labour camp, miles from their family and friends. To the group's disappointment both men had no interest in sharing their news. Each stuffed their envelopes in their pockets intent on reading them in privacy. To the surprise of everyone, Ward held out an envelope to the man on the horse.

"Can you deliver this for me?"

"Of course." The postman eyed the address while everyone gathered in the clearing stood aghast. This was the first mason in the camp to have ever posted outgoing mail, other than an empty baking tin. Some stared at Ward in awe while others looked at him with disdain and suspicion. Reading and writing were not requisite skills for stone cutters and although some read religiously, usually the Bible, very seldom had one ever picked up a pen or pencil to record their thoughts to share with others. Scribing was reserved for conveying a work plan and usually involved a stick sketch in the dirt or the edge of a chisel on limestone. Ward promised himself to find a more discreet way to post his mail.

"Okay, back to work!" came Foreman's command.

Ward and Sparling took the path up the river to the stone waiting for them, each feeling the burn of the envelope in their pocket. Both had been expecting correspondence, both hiding their desire to rip the envelope and devour the contents. It was only when they reached the worksite and sat by the bank of the river with a large block of stone between them, that they finally did.

Ward was reading his pages a second time when he heard the scratch of a match being lit and seconds later detected the unmistakable and acrid scent of sulphur and smoke. Folding his letter and stuffing it deep into his breast pocket he stood to see Sparling, his back to him, burning his letter. Sparling was turning the single page to be sure that the flames consumed every word, and he dropped the ashes into the swirling eddy at his feet. Ward sat back down behind the rock and watched the flakes spin and float past him and become swallowed in the current. Seconds later, there was the pounding of a hammer on a chisel.

Later that same morning, Jesse heard his name called from above. He looked up to the bridge to see the silhouette of Yaweko waving to him. The young man stood beneath the new beams and girders. The bridge had been repaired and his crew were moving down the line to rebuild and maintain other iron structures that kept the rail service moving across the region. As Ward raised his hand to wave back, he felt regret that he hadn't gotten to know him or any of the Mohawk better. He never did smooth things over as the Foreman wanted him to, like he wanted to. Ward sensed that there was much to learn from Yaweko and his people and that this rare chance had passed him by. He shouted up, "Yaweko!" and vowed to himself not to squander the opportunity if it ever presented itself again.

FOUND BY THE LORD

Emmet Carson noticed it before anyone. Mind you, he was always one to scrutinize others before putting his own character under a lens. He is one of those men who looks for the negative in everyone so that he could rationalize his own boorishness and self-interests. He painted a backdrop where his own sins blended and were lost with everyone else's. It was during dinner on mail day. Sparling was sitting alone on the same rock by the river where he always was, scraping the beans off his plate with a spoon. He then mopped up the residue with a slice of bread and stuffed it in his mouth. It was shortly thereafter that Carson spoke.

"Did you see that?"

"See what?" said several of the men, all together.

"Sparling just crossed himself." Emmet said this in an accusatory tone as though Percy Sparling had just committed a sin, or an insult against the Order of Masons. Crossing oneself was not a common sight in the camp but there were, from time to time, traces of religious piety. Charles and Alistair McConnell, two brothers from Hamilton, crossed themselves when they remembered. A shy youngster known only as Browning had the habit of crossing himself before laying his bookmark between the pages of his Bible. Jonathan Book, weekly recipient and distributor of his wife's baked goods, supposedly, went to church in Merritton every Sunday morning. What Emmet noticed and gloated over now was that this was the first time he'd seen Percy Sparling make the signum crucis or show any leaning towards spirituality at all.

It was a curious observation but most of the men just shrugged their shoulders and went back to chasing the remaining beans around their plates. There wasn't any mention of it again until the act was repeated the next morning at breakfast and then again at lunch.

"Jesus, I think he's found Jesus," scoffed Carson.

"There is no time like the present," Browning said without looking up from his Bible, "and there is still time for you," he continued. Everyone knew the comment was directed to Emmet but Browning's eyes never left the page of Luke 33:1.

This left Carson in the unusual position of being speechless. Browning rarely said a peep and to imply that Emmet Carson might consider the future of his soul temporarily silenced him.

It was the next day that Ward noticed a cross around Sparling's neck. It was small, silver in colour, probably pewter, and more like what you'd see around the neckline of a woman. It was held in place with a delicate chain that glinted in the sunlight. Like his habit of crossing himself, the crucifix around Percy's neck was a new thing.

"Where'd you get the cross?"

"It was my mom's."

"My mother was a big one for church, too," Ward said. "My Dad wasn't. He always said that work was the best way to feed your soul and that it helped to fill your belly at the same time. He'd stay at home and do chores while Mom took us to church. I think my dad enjoyed the solitude. Did it come in the mail?" Jessie asked.

"Did what come in the mail?"

"Your cross. You only started wearing it after mail day. I assumed it came in the envelope."

"Yeah, that's when I got it."

"Well, it's nice. You're lucky. Apparently, nobody has ever thought of you as religious."

"Most people don't think enough," and with that Percy picked up his chisel and started beating it into a rock.

NEW ARRIVALS

"Carson! Sparling! I want to see you both in my office!" Foreman's growl was more fearsome than usual. He was blustering around the flap of his tent which doubled as a home and office.

Emmet Carson balanced his breakfast plate on the log on which he sat and groaned as he stood. Percy Sparling took a large mouthful of oatmeal and placed his plate on the boulder beside him. Both men silently walked across the camp and disappeared into the Foreman's tent while the Foreman, still glowering at everyone, held the flap aside. He followed the men into the tent and a string of cursing and swearing came out shortly thereafter. Each man in camp, whether finished their breakfast or not, craned their necks and stretched their hearing towards the cacophony. Foreman's blustering was not uncommon, but it didn't usually start this early in the day.

Charles and Alistair McConnell's names were heard as the Foreman punctuated his discourse with shouts. "Damn" and "Big Ditch" and "Recruits" were also audible, and each mason did his best to reason out the conversation. A Whiskey Jack had swooped down to help itself to Sparling's oatmeal. No one made a motion to shush it away. The men were still as mannequins, statues focused on the private conversation, knowing that the results of the meeting would almost certainly impact their lives. It could be longer days, less pay, or worse, being transferred to work on the fourth Canal.

Their stillness broke when Carson poked his head out of the tent. Each man raced to finish the last spoonful of breakfast and get to washing out their kit. As Sparling emerged from the tent his face was emotionless. His only expression was to point at Ward and then tilt his head back toward the Foreman's tent. "He wants to talk to you," he said and then he went to chase away the bird from his breakfast.

Ward entered a humid and foul-smelling dwelling. It was four times the size of anyone else's tent and had a plank floor. There was a stove with a black chimney that protruded up above the yellowing canvas. There was a folding desk at the entrance and beyond it a small bureau, and a cot. It smelled of cheap tobacco and sweat and Ward wished he'd taken a gulp of air before he let the flap fall behind him. He instinctively held his breath.

"Ward, you are going to oversee the repair on lock five. The hinge blocks on each gate need to be replaced and there are capstones along the lock that are cracked. You will supervise Sparling's crew. Foreman was red in the face and puffing. He hadn't counted on giving this speech more than once.

"Sir, shouldn't Percy Sparling take charge? He has much more experience than I."

"Yes," bellowed the Foreman. "Percy Sparling should be taking charge!" He was shouting this louder now with his face close to the tent opening so that all outside could hear. "He does have more experience than you but he has an engagement this weekend. Do you have an engagement this weekend Ward?" Foreman was drawing out and accentuating each word.

"No, sir, I do not."

"Excellent then! It's wonderful to have men who are dedicated to their craft!" he shouted at the tent walls. "Not like a McConnell who will run off to slog cement just so he doesn't have to bed down in a tent. The moment the work gets hot or heavy or tough, they're off for the comfort of four walls and a cot. What skatterblake gives up his chisel for a shovel?" The Foreman was really wound up now and Ward and Emmet Conners just stood in the cramped tent, twisting their hats in their hands and letting him bluster on.

"Yes, you can drop your tools and mix cement for the rest of your life but what kind of a mason would you be then? It's your choice. No one's keeping you here. Go to your engagements! Go to the Big Ditch! See if I care!" and with that, the Foreman sank into his chair, out of breath and pointed the men out of his tent.

The camp was deserted by the time Carson and Ward escaped the Foreman's office. No one asked Sparling what was under Foreman's skin. The men had the gist of the story and knew that Carson would fill in the blanks throughout the day. To avoid causing any more strife to their boss and to escape his wrath, they had all gone back to work.

Ward found Sparling spalling away on a boulder. At this point it was more of a block than a boulder. He was finishing off the working edge with a toothed chisel making the surface flat and smooth. This face was the show edge. The face everyone would see when the water was let out downstream and the boat in the lock would sink down to expose the gleaming limestone and the skill of the mason. Sparling knew his work would be scrutinized every time a guild member would take the canal from Erie to Ontario. It is for this reason that of all the guilds, masons carried the strongest sense of legacy. They knew that their work could last for centuries, that the eyes of their great-great-great-grandchildren could possibly look at the work they had done and bestow praise or condemnation. Consequently, Sparling like every other mason took great care and pride in their work.

"What engagement takes you away this weekend Mr. Sparling?" Ward tried to sound a little miffed that Sparling was slipping out of the camp for three days. He wanted Percy to get a sense that he resented being left here to drill and cut stone. That he had envy for his associate for taking a holiday. He had to feign being disgruntled because he already knew that Percy Sparling was packing up his tools and heading off to the Park at Grimsby Beach for the weekend. That information had come to Ward in the same post.

"I'm off to hear a speaker." replied Sparling between blows of his hammer.

"And where is this speaker?" Ward pronounced each syllable with a dilute measure of disdain. He knew that he was going to get less information from this discourse than he already possessed. He already knew that Sparling was booked into room sixteen at the Park House Hotel. He already knew that Sparling was going there to meet Father Joseph McGarrity and he knew that he needed to be more vigilant.

"I'm attending the Auditorium at Grimsby Beach this weekend. There is a preacher I need to hear."

"I've heard of that place," said Ward, adding a heaviness to his voice.

A heaviness on which Sparling could float on. A heaviness that would make Sparling believe that he was free of watchful eyes and free of suspicion.

"Well, say a prayer for me" said Jesse which to Sparling's relief, ended the conversation.

It was during lunch when they heard the train sputter and hiss to a stop near the bridge. Foreman threw back the flap of his tent and emerged into the circle of men. He looked like he'd recovered from his morning's tirade and launched into a string of demands to the Cook. "Add some water to your soup and break out your bowls Cook! We have company."

With that he strode off in the direction of the bridge. There was a moment of silence and stiffness amongst the men in the camp and they looked around at each other as if they didn't know what to do. And then like a congregation sucking in a lung full of air before launching into a hymn, the men feverishly mopped up the remains on their plates and followed Foreman's footsteps up the path. They were curious and wanted to gawk at who had come to help them lift and move blocks of stone.

They could all feel the great heat of the locomotive as they climbed up to the tracks. The men moved down the train past one passenger coach and a box car to the caboose at the back. There were men securing a ramp to the door of the boxcar on the far side. As they came around the end of the train a short and rotund man exited the door of the caboose and leaned over the railing.

"Hey there Bailey!" shouted the Foreman.

"Hey there Foreman!" came the reply. The conductor's attention was divided. He was talking to the Foreman but waving a flag at the young engineer who was looking back from the locomotive.

"Dumb as a post!" he said in disgust and he spit a voluminous wad of saliva down onto the tracks. "Send any more engineers to prepare for war and we'll have babies driving our trains!"

"There are shortages everywhere, Bailey. I lost two men just yesterday. Makes you wonder how they think we can get anything done. What did you bring us?"

"A dozen. As far as I can tell, most of them speak English. Half look like clerks but there are a couple of big farm boys."

"Any masons?" asked the Foreman with a curious anticipation in his voice.

"Nothing so exotic."

The masons that had left their lunch so quickly were disappointed. So mundane was the life of a stonecutter that no one wanted to miss out on the new arrivals but there was no show. Except for the shuffling feet and a depression that seem to cling to them, these new workers could be mistaken for anyone on any street in any Canadian town. Ward addressed each and every one of them on their walk to the mess tent. The rest of the masons dispersed to their work.

It wasn't until he'd made his way across the bridge and descended down to the river that Jesse realized his negligence. He had dashed off with the rest of the men to meet the train and was fully expecting to see Sparling with his hammer and chisel but there was no rhythmic pounding of a hammer. As their worksite came into view, he realized that Sparling was absent as well. He scoured his memory of lunch. Sparling was there perched on his rock by the stream but was he in the group that went to inspect the new arrivals? Jesse couldn't find the image in his memory. He stood by the river and the rock and his tools and replayed the sequence of events. His thoughts were interrupted by Percy Sparling scrambling down the bank behind him.

"Where have you been?" Ward fully expected Sparling to growl and respond with, "Mind your own business," but that isn't what he said.

"Cook's lunch isn't agreeing with me. I was sitting on the latrine. How are the new men?"

It was odd behaviour for Percy Sparling. Asking questions wasn't in his nature and all of Jesse's senses told him that he was lying.

"All of them are from Niagara. Three from Queenstown, two from Fort Erie, one from Welland and the other one no one knows."

"All I want to know is, can they lift stone?"

"I hope so." Jesse's voice trailed off as the two men picked up their tools. But his mind wasn't on the abilities of the new recruits. Jesse's thoughts were tumbling with the realization that he had let Sparling out of his sight the day before he was leaving to meet Father Joseph McGarrity.

GRIMSBY BEACH

Had a train been available, Sparling would have paid the fare. The weather looked threatening and it was well over a full morning's walk to Grimsby Beach but there was no train scheduled until the end of the day. Percy wanted to make the most out of his three days so he set off on foot before first light. He knew the way to Merritton in the dark. The cart path was level and smooth and less than two miles long but just as dawn was making it visible, great whorls of dark vapour spun above him dimming the morning light. He'd just walked into town when the first drops of rain splattered on his face, rendering pockmarks in the road, puffs of dust reeling upwards. A few skips and a long stride brought him under cover of the veranda of the Merritton Tavern just as the sky opened and let the rain down.

"You timed that well!" came a voice from the gloom.

Sparling turned to see the broad brim of a hat and a bearded face looking up at him. His dark clothes and the weak light made him almost invisible in the shadows.

"You think so?" It wasn't a friendly response but it did not deter the stranger.

"Looks like you're going somewhere?" He could see the bundle slung over Sparling's shoulder.

"Grimsby Beach." answered Percy.

"Well, haven't you been dealt the cards today? Too bad there's not a game going at present," and he pointed his thumb behind him into the Tavern. "You could have cleaned up!" blurted out the stranger.

"Excuse me?" Percy was confused.

The pang of the rain on the metal roof and slapping the growing puddles made hearing a challenge.

"I said," shouted the old man, "you're in luck. That's just where I'm to take that load after this blessed deluge is done with." He pointed to a wagon getting soaked in the rain across the street. "You can catch a ride with me." He kept his gaze on Sparling." Is it business or pleasure that takes you to Grimsby Beach?"

Sparling took a second look at the wagon. It was drawn by two glistening horses who were doing their best to shake off the water flowing down their coats. The cargo was covered by an oiled tarp presumably keeping everything beneath it dry. Sparling turned to nod at the old man. "Revival," stated Percy.

"Then as soon as this blows over, we'll be on our way. I'll appreciate the company." A moment of silence ensued. "Revival, eh? I thought those days were over but I guess the preachers still have a pulpit there."

As quick as the sky closed in and soaked the town of Merritton it was equally quick to open up into sunshine. A rainbow arched across the storm's trailing edge and the old man stood up on creaky knees and ambled off towards his wagon, leaving a crooked set of boot prints in the street as he wove between the puddles. "Best help me give this tarp a shake," he said as he walked. Sparling followed his meandering trail, heaved his bundle up onto the buckboard seat and grabbed a corner of the tarp. Together they shook off the water droplets and the old man checked the cargo beneath.

"Can't let this load get damp," the old man said. "Wilson Morningstar would have my hide if this flour spoiled on the way. He just got the contract from the Park House Hotel and he wouldn't take it well if he lost it."

"That's where I'm staying. At the Park House Hotel." stated Percy.

"Then you truly must have a horseshoe up your ass. Door to door service, I tell you." The old man had retrieved two brushes from under the seat and tossed one to Percy. "If you'd be so kind as to give that gelding a good curry." After they combed the water out of the horse's coats, the old man adjusted the wet tack and they were soon on their way.

It wasn't a quick pace but the wagon was faster and easier than walking. Mud clung to the rims and spokes of the wheels and Sparling was feeling lucky to be keeping his boots dry and clean. The Old Man talked non-stop. He'd ask Sparling a question but begin another conversation before Sparling had a chance to answer. This suited him just fine. Less anyone knew about him the better. He was content to let the man carry the conversation. It was a small price to pay for a free ride.

The road remained in the shadow of the escarpment and this made them grateful for the occasional bite out of the tree canopy where sunlight beamed down to warm them. They meandered at the base of the talus slope ducking up ravines where Inns and Mills and lime kilns plied their trade. The old man knew every one of the proprietors and waved to each as they trundled by. Sparling got to hear every lurid and juicy tidbit of gossip about each and every one of them.

"I take it by the lilt in your voice that you've got O'Brien's in your bloodline?"

Percy sat up straight and said, "My Mom was Irish."

"Have you heard of the Battle of Slabtown?" offered the old man.

"I have not." Sparling leaned back, sensing another lengthy dissertation coming on.

"Well, since you work in the locale you should know that the Town known now as Merritton was at one point in its history known as Centreville and on its periphery was Slabtown, a smattering of shacks walled with the leftover bark slabs from Phelp's Lumber Mill. Canalers like yourself, made due in the shacks. Most were Catholic and they had a reputation as a cantankerous lot. Didn't get along with anyone. Fought the Protestants, of course, fought the non-Protestants and when no one else was handy, fought amongst themselves. When they weren't hammering out stone blocks for construction, they were hammering on some poor soul who happened across their path."

"Mind you, they say that life in Slabtown in those days was dire, so you can't blame them much. Work was hard and the pay was poor and most of their bosses were members of the Orangemen. Anyway, sixty plus years ago a mob of them gathered just before the "Glorious 12th" to protest King Billy's Victory on the Boyne. Makes me scratch my head how a battle fought in 1690 can still stir the blood of men a century and a half later."

"Anyway, at the same time, a group of Orangemen were gathered at Duffin's Inn in Centerville to celebrate the glory and privilege of being Protestant and that's when things got out of hand. While the Canalers were parading down Thorold Road making a menace of themselves, the brethren of

Orange Lodge 77 fortified themselves in the Inn and adjacent barn by cutting loopholes in the walls. As the Irish passed the Inn, the Protestants stuck their rifles through the loopholes and opened fire. They killed two and wounded a half a dozen more."

"Loyalist Bastards." Sparling hadn't meant to say anything but it slipped out.

"Oh, it doesn't end there," the old man continued. "All nineteen members of the Lodge were indicted for the murder but the Courts buried it. No doubt the Grand Jury were members of the Lodge as well. In fact, the Orangemen who fired from inside the Inn at the unarmed protesters were honoured and celebrated with medals for their valour."

Sparling sat rocking on the buckboard shaking his head, clenching his fists, trying to quell the rising anger inside of him. He'd heard stories like this before but never this one. A story that took place only steps from where he currently worked and, in his mind, little had changed. "Are you with the Canalers then?"

"I am with no one. I wish those that made the perilous journey to cross the ocean left their disputes at home. It does no one any favours to celebrate or protest battles from centuries ago. Still, I see who holds the reins here and it's not the likes of you or me. If you aren't an Orangemen, you are going to miss out on being connected. I just try to stay in the middle of the bridge and keep from falling into the churning waters below. My Dad always said, 'Don't go breaking your shin on a stool that's not in your way,' and I'll tell you, those are words to live by."

There were a few moments of silence after the story ended. Where the road met a rise Sparling could look North down the gentle plain to Lake Ontario glinting in the sunlight. Most of the plain had been cleared and planted as orchard; peach, plum and pear trees in neat rows from the escarpment to the lake. This was a place where nature had been tamed and organized but never completely out of sight. Overhead turkey vultures circled in great numbers. Percy lost count after fifty and he wondered why any bird would bother to soar so high and far from a nest or food. All the while, the old man found his voice again and just kept talking. Percy interrupted only once.

It was approaching noon and Percy could hear a low drone wafting on the breeze. It was not a common sound but he recognized the whine and sputter of a plane engine. He heard them before he saw them, for the sun was high and in his eyes. As they travelled north towards the lake he could make out the hum of several and far away. In the robin's egg blue he could see a glint reflect off a fuselage or a wing high in the sky. As with the vultures, Sparling began to count them but stopped when they kept slipping out of his sight. "What are they doing? I've never seen so many planes in one place."

"That's the Beamsville crew from the aerodrome on Sann Road. They're practicing their bombing skills. They drop dummy bombs on the Beach there. I gave a ride to one of those pilots last week. He made an impromptu landing in a potato patch. He was in fine shape but his plane was a sight. I tell you,.."

Sparling's attention drifted from the old man's story as he watched a plane circle and take its turn swooping down toward the edge of the lake. They were not unlike the vultures.

"The pilot who crashed expected to be in Europe before the year is out. 'War is imminent', he told me. That kid had a grin from ear to ear like he couldn't wait for it. Maybe it's a picnic in a plane but I'll tell you there's no glory on the ground when it comes to war."

"You've been a soldier then?"

"I served in the First Boer War. I was just a kid, a stupid starry-eyed kid. I lost my best friend there. It wasn't the adventure we thought it was going to be."

These were the last words the old man uttered for some time. There was only a muffled clop of hooves and creaking of the wagon as they gently rocked together over the rutted road. They were two separate entities, each lost in different worlds. Percy was visualizing the old man's story of Slabtown and how a group of unarmed Irish Catholics were murdered in the street. Meanwhile, the old man was in a trench hearing the whizz and ricochet of bullets echo off the rock walls of a Transvaal canyon. In his mind, Sparling could see clouds of smoke form outside the walls of William Duffin's Grog House while the old man heard the surprised shout of his childhood friend when a Boer Commando found his mark. Percy was imagining the Irish taunts becoming cries of anguish as the protestors felt the Orangemen's shot tear into their flesh and at the same moment, the old man felt the life of his best friend drain out of the hand that he held.

Regret and sadness fell upon the driver and he found himself staring at the reins in his hand wondering how this painful memory could still be so fresh. How was it that his mind had transported him and his wagon from a glorious spring day in Niagara to that fateful day in the hot and dusty South African outback? How could these hands be in both places at once? And sitting right next to him on the rocking buckboard of the wagon, occasionally knocking shoulders and a knee was Percy Sparling, who within him had a rage that was building like a storm cloud on a humid summer's day. In Sparling's mind's eye, he was standing in a St. Catharines courtroom hearing the judge declare there was "no bill" in the case against the nineteen Orangemen who murdered two Catholic Canalers and wounded six more.

It was as though the wagon that day held four men. One was affable and old and making his familiar delivery of flour from the Morningstar Mill to the Park House Hotel while the other was a young mason who, on leave from this repair work on the canal, was answering a mysterious summons to Grimsby Beach. The third man also held the reins but with much younger and innocent hands. He was the one pinned in a trench smelling the dust, hearing the ping of bullets and Afrikaans being shouted amongst the snipers above. The fourth man was the distillation of injustice carried out by every descendant of King Billy on the poor and peaceful Catholics of Ireland. He was angry and vengeful and dangerous. He carried inside of him every story describing the tyranny of the Loyalists both back home and here in North America. The stories were slivers buried deep within, sharp and painful and driven further into his soul by his verdant imagination.

It was late morning when the old man pulled the reins to the left and veered west. The change of light across their faces brought both men back to the present. There were five tall ships huddled together in a small bay, their masts visible from the distance. Two of them possessed dark smoke stacks and would let out a belch of black smoke at regular intervals. The wind carried these small clouds eastward, a fuzzy Morse code dotting the sky. "Dot-dot-dot, dash-dash-dash, dot-dot-dot. SOS." Sparling deciphered in his mind. The old man pointed to them and began the conversation again. He described how the ships were dropping empty barrels to the depot there and would be back in the fall to lower them into their hulls heavy with the fruit that would be transported across the lake and then to ports unknown.

Shortly thereafter, a stand of trees came into view. They were many times taller than the orchards in the foreground and appeared as a solid tangled mass against the neat rows. The road ran parallel to the rail line and in the distance, they could see a small building perched on the edge of the tracks.

"That's the Park stop. You should see that platform when the train pulls in. Busier than Union Station in Toronto, I tell you, and down here is the park gate."

The Old man guided the horses to turn right down Park Road. Sparling had to sit back on the buckboard and crane his neck to take in the height of the trees. The wispy green of white pine poked up through a dense canopy of giant oaks and sugar maples and their branches stretched high in every direction. Nestled under these shadowy giants were cottages. Each was of a modest size, but modest was no way to describe them. Their eaves were laced with gingerbread and their porches were supported with turned posts. Gardens flanked every porch and although it was too early in the season, Percy could see that great effort was made to encourage decorative plants and flowers. The paint on each looked glossy and new. Whoever built and maintained these dwellings did it with care and pride. The activity Percy observed as they rolled into the community reinforced this. Women and girls were bustling about sweeping and beating out carpets. Men and boys were delivering water and stacking firewood.

A short distance along, the old man turned the wagon west again and Sparling got small glimpses of an enormous structure looming through the trees. A dark funnel shaped mass sat inverted in the woods. High up flashes of sunlight bounced off of windows in a copula that sat nestled in the tree canopy.

A flag on top was higher than the tallest tree. The old man was watching the road but knew what had a hold on Sparling's attention.

"That's the auditorium or temple, depending on who's doing the performing. That's likely where you'll hear your preacher. It's a hundred feet high and they say it holds three thousand but take your umbrella if it rains; Leaks like a sieve."

Percy couldn't stop himself from smiling. This setting was quite unlike anything he'd seen before. It was a child's playroom. Doll houses scattered in a forest. It was one of the magical places described in the fairy tales his mother used to tell him. There was a holiday atmosphere about. Everyone was busy with their chores but they went about them with a joyful anticipation, like a crowd lining the street for a parade.

One hundred yards inside the park gate the old man pulled back on the reins and the wagon stopped before a large white building sitting on a stone foundation. There were two doors built into the stone walls and on the threshold of one sat a teenage boy petting his dog.

"Hey there Toke," called the old man.

"Hi Mr. Swanson."

"Would your brother Jacob be about? I could use his help unloading this wagon."

"Sure thing Mr. Swanson. I'll go fetch him."

Percy Sparling pulled his bundle from the wagon and slung it over his shoulder. "Well, I am most grateful for the ride Mr. Swanson." It was the first time Sparling had used the old man's name. "Would you like some help unloading the wagon?"

"Nah. Jacob will be along. You just get settled and enjoy yourself this weekend." Swanson said this as he held out his hand. Sparling shook it. Swanson held his hand and looking down said, "Now there's a mason's hand for you. Calluses like knots on a tree and a notch between the thumb and forefinger just aching for a hammer."

"Thanks again Mr. Swanson. I appreciate the ride."

"Don't mention it," said the old man, now starting to pull back on the tarp. "I enjoyed the company."

As he made his way around the hotel, Sparling once again felt the great mass of the temple. He marvelled at its size and structure. It was peculiar and strange, almost "other worldly". As a mason, he was curious about how it was supported. What had they used for a foundation? How did they support a circular roof? The answers to his questions were blocked by a ring of cottages that faced into the enormous circular building. He had seen bigger structures before but this one had its own gravity. He could feel it pulling at him as it competed for sunlight with the towering hardwoods.

The space in front of the hotel could hold six wagons but it appeared to be more of a hub for footpaths that radiated out in every direction. Presently, there was but one horse drawn cart tethered to a straight poplar and several pedestrians moving purposefully off in each direction. There was a general store on the left, another row of fancy porches beyond that and a large open space to the right, a park of some kind. Percy looked forward to exploring.

He turned on his heel to enter the hotel. It was impressive. There were half a dozen stairs on the veranda that stretched the full length of the building. A large awning read Park House and glossy white gingerbread ordained the railings on all three stories. It looked like a wedding cake. Percy climbed the steps and made his way to the front desk.

"Welcome to the Park House." said a middle-aged man a little short of breath.

He'd been busy moving boxes into an office when he saw Percy enter and approach the counter. Clearly, he was the manager, but had to fill in when menial duties called. Being 'short-handed' was a condition that existed here as well.

"Thank you."

The opportunity to stay in an establishment of this stature had never availed itself to Percy. He felt welcomed but out of place. He knew rooming houses. He didn't know the social graces of staying in a hotel. That he would have to supply a name so that the man before him could check the register and give him his room key didn't occur to him. After all, Percy Sparling didn't make the reservation.

"We hope you will enjoy your stay here Mr......" prompted the manager, leaning forward and letting the sentence dangle.

"Oh, ah, Sparling, Percy Sparling."

"Good that you booked in advance. Both hotels are full this weekend."

"There are two hotels?"

"Yes indeed. The Lakeview is across the park and up the road. It is a fine establishment as well. Some of our visitors prefer the view of the lake. It is quieter and more peaceful there. However, it's further from the Temple and the telegraph office and the beach. I manage both and can assure that you will have a pleasant stay whichever you choose." He drew an imaginary line down the page of his book with his forefinger, stopped near the bottom and tapped that finger twice. "Here we are. Mr. Sparling. Room sixteen. It is on the second floor. Will you need help with your bag?"

Noting the manager's glance at his bundle, Percy felt self-conscious for the first time that day. All of a sudden, his clothes weren't good enough and he needed to take a bath. "No, that will be fine. I can carry it," and he took the key from the manager and mounted the stairs.

Room sixteen was at the back of the hotel so Percy took a right turn after the first flight of stairs. This led him along a balcony railing. He stopped again to look at the front veranda of the hotel, this time from up above. Through the quaking leaves of the poplar's standing guard, he saw another wagon pass, two women climb the steps to a neighbouring mercantile store and the boy Toke with his dog coming up the street with his taller and older brother. He passed rooms fourteen and fifteen as he walked, his heals knocking on the glossy floor boards.

The hinges squealed as he entered his room. It had a narrow bed, a narrow chest of drawers, a chair and a small wash stand. It was simple and neat and when compared to his tent at the worksite, elegant. He threw his bundle onto the chair and poured a generous amount of water into the basin where he washed his face and neck. He was weary despite it being early afternoon. The bed looked inviting. How long had it been since he'd slept in one? He took off the delicate crucifix from around his neck, placed it on the washstand, lay on the bed and quickly fell asleep.

THE TURBINIA

It was evening when he awoke. The room had one small east facing window. In the dim light he wondered how long he'd slept. Percy could hear a bell clanging and wondered if that is what woke him. The bundle on the chair held his best shirt and another pair of trousers. He thought to avoid his earlier embarrassment so he unrolled the bundle and smoothed out the wrinkles in his good clothes.

The shirt had been a gift from his aunt in New York. He lived with her and his uncle for three years when he first came over to make a start in the New World and God bless, how that woman mothered him. His aunt fed and clothed him, which is how he came to possess the fine shirt he held in his hands. It was Egyptian cotton with a fine blue thread running through it. The cuffs were a little frayed as it had been first owned by his grandfather and then passed down to his uncle. Having been handed down twice over, this shirt was in reasonably good condition. Irish Immigrants had spare occasions to dress in their finery and other than the small cross that had belonged to his mother, it was the only family heirloom he possessed.

He dressed, pulled a comb through his hair and by dabbing the corner of his handkerchief in the water from the washbasin, made a weak attempt at rubbing mud off of his boots. Before reaching for the doorknob, he took a good look at himself in the mirror. His hair and beard had grown long during his time at the canal. Even with the fancy shirt, he looked older and wilder than he ever had. No wonder the hotel manager looked him up and down. Percy vowed to buy himself a haircut and shave first thing tomorrow.

His boots thumped on the deck boards of the second floor as he made his way to the staircase. He paused again to watch the commotion at the entrance of the hotel. Over the railing he could see wagons unloading passengers and their luggage onto the front steps of the veranda. He could hear the nasally voice of the manager giving orders and directions to the boy Jacob. From this perch, Sparling could see that the area in front of the hotel led out to five pathways, the largest of which was lined with a long succession of cottages that faced the empty expanse that Percy guessed was a park. He descended the stairs and crossed the lobby, going unnoticed as the staff were busy with the new arrivals. His nap was rejuvenating and he felt buoyant as he dodged a young man carrying baggage up the stairs. He wove his way around the wagons and strode towards a tall chestnut tree that guarded the entrance to a street and the park that sat beside it.

The view before him made him draw in a deep breath. Beams of sunlight pierced through the foliage of countless trees. It flitted here and there as the soft breeze swept through the treetops. In the park two children chased each other around a heart shaped pond while another sat poking the water with a stick. Two well dressed women stood beside a sign gawking at what was posted there while three young toughs sat on a raised platform that housed a large bell. Around the perimeter facing in on the park were the cottages all looking the same and yet different, a unity of structure and design but differing in colour and ornamentation. They were like the faces of brothers and sisters and their cousins all gathered in a family reunion.

All of the dwellings obeyed the same plan. Each roof sat at a forty-five-degree pitch shielding two floors beneath. Each floor was graced with a balcony that was festooned with turned posts and intricate gingerbread. Most dwellings occupied the entire plot of land on which they stood. Indeed, the cottages were so close to one another that neighbours could easily reach out and touch each other from their balconies. The paint used to preserve the board and batten walls varied from cottage to cottage. It was obvious to anyone who looked that while the same builder may have designed and created each structure, the owners made an effort to differ them in appearance, individual and unique.

Presently, each balcony showed life. There were people reading, relaxing, sweeping. On one porch a young man with an enormous moustache under a broad Panama hat was playing a guitar. The chords were awkward and poorly timed. Percy didn't recognize the tune but the music gently floated out onto the park and into the trees. The two women at the sign post turned to look at him. He smiled, nodded to them and made his way past, skirting the edge of the park and down a lane that led towards the lake. As he approached the end of it, he found himself standing at the crest of a bluff that ran along the shoreline. This fell down a long set of stairs leading to the water. The leaves trembled more violently here and in the cool breeze he detected the odour of oil and soot. As he put his weight on the top stair, he nearly lost his balance as the blast of a piercing horn traveled through his body.

Curious about the sound he quickened his descent and arrived on a wide path that opened up to a long sandy beach. A dozen or so people were scattered along the shore, their gaze focused out onto the water. He walked past a small hut and until he could feel the uneven and shifting surface of sand beneath his feet. The acrid smell of coal smoke was more intense here and he surmised that a steamer was in the process of docking. A few more steps brought into view of another small hut and a fence guarding the entrance to the pier. He could see two men standing expectantly there while two others walked out to join them. Beyond them, the glistening hull of a large passenger ship slowly approached, belching puffs of soot.

Percy was impressed by the length of the pier. It was built to accommodate large craft. Eight footings supported each span and together they jutted out seventy or eighty yards out into the lake.

"She's a beauty, isn't she?"

Percy hadn't noticed the unusually tall man come up beside him.

"Named after the first turbine steamer," the man continued. Percy hadn't responded to either of his comments but the man kept speaking anyway. "Can't say we're going to see her much longer. Suspect she'll be puffing her way to England soon. I'll be sorry to see her go."

He looked down for a response but Percy only nodded his agreement and watched the crew drop ropes down to the men on the pier. Disappointed that his attempts at conversation failed, the tall man left and Percy found a log on which to sit and watch the docking alone. It was cool here. The wind was stiff, the water choppy. Further out he could see whitecaps, like sheep grazing on the surface. The log on which he sat was damp and in the shade a chill went through him even as he hugged himself, wishing he'd brought his coat. Still, he couldn't tear himself away from the action on the pier. Long days cutting stone had dulled him. The monotony of his work was a pale reflection to what was going on before him. The contrast of his daily life as a mason and this place was stark and he felt an intoxication that no whisky had ever been able to achieve.

A gang plank rattled into place as the ship's twin stacks continued to pour out smoke. Passengers carrying carpet bags and suitcases descended and the dockhands helped to steady them as they stepped onto the pier. Percy could hear excited and happy greetings over the surf mixed with the cry of gulls and terns overhead. As they approached the beach the new arrivals were corralled by a fence on either side of the pier. It was some moments before they were allowed through a gate at the entrance. Whether they were accounting the arrivals or charging an entrance fee to enter the Park, Percy did not know. The chatter of the crowd grew. Presumably many of them had been here before and knew what delights awaited them. Despite the cold Percy continued to watch as the guests cleared the gate and began lugging their bags up the long staircase. Some of the better dressed ladies coerced some boys to haul their loads for them. They spoke excitedly as they ascended the embankment hugging themselves in their shawls. It took nearly thirty minutes for the crowd to disperse and then the Turbinia reversed her way clear of the pier and headed back west towards Hamilton.

With the faint smell of the ship's exhaust in his nostrils, Sparling made his way to the pier, slid through the unlocked gate, walked down the planks until he was surrounded by waves lapping around him on both sides. He was alone where scores of passengers had been only moments before. The breeze whistled faintly in his ears and the rush of the water grew with every step away from shore. The Turbinia was already a speck in the distance and her plume of smoke a small smudge on the fading sunset. When he reached the end of the pier he turned around and took in the view. Lights were becoming visible through the darkening foliage. Lanterns were being lit in the cottages on Victoria Terrace and to the west he could see the Lakeview hotel. Cottagers and hotel guests were unpacking their bags and settling in.

Above, the jagged horizon of a dense forest was interrupted by a flutter. It was the flag atop the auditorium and far beyond that was the greying and fuzzy line that was the Niagara Escarpment, the source of the stone with which he did his work. He drew in a deep breath. This place felt familiar to him. It didn't look like Skerries and it lacked the tangy scent of the sea but it did conjure memories of a happier time.

Despite these warm thoughts, the prolonged exposure to the onshore wind made him shiver. Under the falling darkness, he quickly retreated to shore, up the embankment and back to the hotel. Once in his room, he ate the half a loaf of bread Cook had given him and then crawled into bed. But sleep did not come easily. While his body was enjoying the soft mattress and bed sheets, his mind considered the reason he was summoned here, the mission and the instructions he was given. For many minutes these thoughts twisted and swirled in his stream of consciousness until they were caught by a current and he drifted off to sleep.

Percy awoke in the narrow bed before first light. He didn't know where he was until his eyes focused on the silhouette of the window frame. He swung his legs off the bed, relieved himself into the chamber pot and knew that he couldn't wait for the hotel staff to heat up water for his bath. He pulled on his work clothes, grabbed the bar of soap beside the washbasin and carried his boots out of the room. He walked in his stocking feet all along the balcony and down the stairs to the lobby. He tried to slip out the front door in silence but there was the faint glow of a lamp on the front desk and Mr. Vannetter's bald pate facing him as he crossed the floor.

"Ahhh, Mr. Sparling. You are off somewhere early. Clearly, you're more an early-bird than an owl." Vannetter whispered, raising his head. He had been looking over the register.

"Thought I'd take a swim."

"We could draw you a bath Mr. Sparling. It wouldn't be for some time but it will be nice and hot," offered the manager.

"Thank you, no. I will need a haircut and shave though."

"I can have Perkins here at nine. Shall I schedule you in?"

With that exchange, Percy had the first barber appointment he had had in three months. As he laced his boots on the front steps of the hotel, he was looking forward to getting himself cleaned up. In the soft morning air, he was already feeling like a new man and a haircut and shave would complete the picture. The early sky was washing out the eastern stars and what was left of the moon provided him with enough light to follow the path past the cottages and trees to the lake.

In contrast to the rolling waves of yesterday, the lake was flat as glass. Rushing waves and the clatter of beach stones rolling over each other gave way to an intermittent and soft hiss where the water met the gravelly shore. He felt the cold dampness of the stones as he removed his boots. His weight pushed aside the pebbles as he stepped to the shore. With water up to his ankles he stood marveling at the range of colours in the sky. The western horizon was nearly black behind the moon and as he arched his head upward the sky became shades and then tints of purple dotted with fading stars. Overhead he saw deep blue, and as he turned his head eastward, progressively lighter shades turned to green turned to a buttery yellow and finally the brilliant edge of white, like a giant eye peeking into a new day. Percy took a deep breath. He was happy that he was here in this place, in this moment, and simultaneously, it saddened him to know that he hadn't felt this way in a very, very long time. He took another deep breath, another two steps forward and with all of his clothes on, he plunged into the lake.

The coolness made him relaxed and alert. The upward push of the water on his body relaxed his muscles. He held a long steady breath and kept his face in the water even after he surfaced. When he couldn't hold it in any longer, Percy lifted his head and inhaled, letting his feet slowly sink to the bottom until he stood with only his shoulders above the surface. He watched the sunrise growing on the horizon. Ducks were bobbing some distance away and terns and gulls circled and swooped. He was the only human on the beach.

Reaching for his breast pocket, Percy removed the bar of soap and began to scrub his hair and clothes and his body. When he was sure that he had soaped every inch of himself, he tucked the bar back into his pocket and dove. Percy Sparling was a good swimmer. His mother had made sure of that.

When he was a child, he lived with his mother, Sarah Sparling and his grandfather in Skerries, just north of Dublin. They spent long hours on the beach there and many more hours in the water. His mother was the only child of a fisherman and he took pride at how his daughter could find her way around his boat, in and out of the water. And she made sure that she passed her talents on to her only child. Sarah Sparling taught him how to check his breathing, in and out quickly, 'bellow's breath' she'd called it. He would charge his blood with oxygen, take a half breath and dive and in this way be free to dive down further and stay underwater longer.

He kicked and paddled a good distance up the beach and rose clean, free of dirt and stone dust and soapy film. He plodded his way out of the water, sloshing back to the log where he had left his footwear. The pebbles on the beach were small and round and massaged his feet as he walked. The sun was nearly round, almost fully visible now and the pale blue sky had pushed all of the black and purple away. Its warmth was pleasant on his back and he could see that two young boys had arrived and were down near the pier. Percy sat down on the log, gazed out at the water and allowed himself to think once again on his childhood.

He could feel a chuckle percolating up inside of him. Like an air bubble zig zagging its way to the surface Percy could feel a memory rise within him until it burst forth and had him laughing to himself. Only the boys by the pier noticed. They stopped throwing stones in the water for a brief moment, shrugged their shoulders at one another and resumed their competition. The humour taking hold of Percy was his own and his only, for he was the only one alive to recall it. But many years ago, the anecdote was told and retold many times. It described how Sarah and her son snuck up under her father's skiff while he was mending his nets.

"Me Da' never suspected a thing as he was moored out some distance in the bay. Me and me boy swam beneath the surface, raised our hands to the gunwale and gave her a shake and me Dad jumped out of the skiff with shock. He was some mad until he saw Percy laughin' and sputterin' so hard he nearly drowned. Dad reached over and picked up Percy with one arm and started laughin' along with us, once he knew Percy was alright."

Sarah loved telling that story and Percy loved listening to her voice rise and fall with her laughter. Skerries was a magical place for the young lad. It was there that he felt warm and safe and loved. It was a sensation that he'd found nowhere else in the world and yet he was feeling it on this very morning, on this very beach. His laughter was an echo from history.

His clothes were still very damp but his feet were nearly dry. Percy put on his boots. He thought that he might try to slip back into his hotel room and change into his dry clothes before anyone could see him. He only met the water delivery wagon on his way back to the hotel. The driver of this wagon tipped his hat and gave no indication that he was shocked by Sparling's soggy appearance. Percy guessed that this delivery man had seen many people who had fallen in the lake by mistake or like him, had been taken over by the impulse to jump in fully clothed. The hotel lobby was quiet. Even manager Vannetter was nowhere to be seen and other than a few drops of water on the floor, Sparling made it up the staircase unnoticed. He walked along the second-floor balcony and could hear someone struggling around the corner. He rounded the edge of the building to see a woman in black dress dragging a carpet bag up to the door of room fifteen, the room right next to his.

"Can I help you with that?"

"Well, yes, that would be wonderful," said the woman, slightly out of breath. She stepped back and let Percy pick up the bag.

"How did you get this up the stairs? It's heavy."

The woman had turned to put her key in the door and worked it into the lock. Speaking to the door she said, "Oh it was a struggle."

She swung the door open and directed Percy into her room but remained at the threshold, out in plain view. "Just put it on the floor beside the bed, thank you."

Percy did as he was told, turned and tried to exit the room but the woman was too close to the threshold to let him pass.

"Mary Miller," she said, an attempt at an introduction. "Mrs. Mary Miller. Thank you so much Mr....?" letting her voice fade off. She was holding out her hand and apparently was not going to let him by without a proper greeting.

"Percy Sparling ma'am," he said grasping her hand and looking into her eyes for the first time.

She was incredibly beautiful. Her eyes were as dark as her dress and shone with intelligence. Her nose and lips were smooth and delicate and the corners of her mouth turned up into a smirk that made her look as though she was forever in a good mood.

"Oh please, Mr. Sparling. Don't call me 'Ma'am'. I have been wearing this dress so long that I think I've aged a decade and I can't bear to hear anyone consider that I am a,...a,....a ma'am."

"My apologies. And I am sorry about your husband." Percy cast his eyes over her black dress, a mourning dress adorned with lace that clung to her.

"My husband died for the glory of his King. There's no need to feel sorry when I don't feel sorry. He was an Imperialistic snob."

Mary turned her face as she said this. Percy was shocked and curious. Not many wives, or widows would talk so openly about their disdain for the deceased, let alone a deceased husband.

"Well, I'm sorry just the same," and he nodded and moved past her towards his room next door.

"Well, it was a pleasure to meet you Mr. Sparling. And thank you so much for carrying my bag."

She was facing him again and flashing her sparkling eyes. For the second time in an hour, he thought of his mother. Sarah Sparling and Mary Miller had little resemblance to one another. It was his mother's cameo that Mary resembled. He used to study it while he rested in her lap. The graceful curves cut in ivory pasted on a soft blue stone. The angle of the jaw, and the fine features of the carving were alive and present in the face of the woman standing before him.

"And it was a pleasure meeting you Mrs. Miller."

Percy emphasized the 'Mrs.', playfully reprimanding her for being disrespectful to her late husband. At the same time, Percy was intrigued. She'd called him an 'Imperialist'. These days, this was a treasonous thing to say anywhere in the British Commonwealth where men would soon be enlisting to defend it. Percy made his way awkwardly out of her room and along the balcony to his door.

"Perhaps we will meet again Mr. Sparling?" she said.

"Perhaps," he said as he unlocked his room and slipped inside. He closed the door to his room, changed his clothes and prepared to go downstairs for his haircut and shave.

CLAN NA GAEL

Perkins was stropping his razor when Percy entered the small room off of the hotel lobby.

"Mr. Percy Sparling?" he asked.

"That's me," Sparling replied, taking the chair.

"That will be 25 cents up front."

"Up front? What if I don't like the job you do?"

"You will have to suffer through it I suppose, besides, everyone knows there are only three days between a good and a bad cut." Perkins hesitated as if waiting for agreement. When he didn't get it, he continued. "If you don't like what I do, and you will, then wait three days and I'll straighten it out for you."

"But I won't be here in three days."

"Then you'll just have to be satisfied with what you get." and with that the barber laid a hot towel over Percy's face. If Sparling had a response, he would not have been able to be heard through the terrycloth soaking and warming his beard, so he remained silent.

The barber worked quickly. He had an oversized pair of scissors that he used to lop off large sums of hair. Percy watched as long strands dropped to the floor. In the mirror he was beginning to see his eyebrows again and his head was getting noticeably lighter with every moment. Perkins provided a one-sided conversation throughout. Sparling would have come to learn the name of every relation on the barber's family tree if he only had more hair.

"How's that sir?" asked Perkins as he adjusted his hand mirror so Percy could see the back of his head.

Percy's answer was muffled by the towel which was beginning to cool on his face.

"Pardon me sir," Perkins said, whipping off the towel. "Sometimes I forget."

"It's very fine. The shave...?" Percy started to say.

"The shave is coming right up!" Perkins turned to a table to retrieve his soap brush and dish. As the Barber rattled the brush in quick rotations, foam formed on the edges of the dish. "Is this your first visit to Grimsby Beach?"

"It is."

"I am sure that you will enjoy it. Not quite the pilgrimage it used to be. It's more relaxed in many ways but not nearly so relaxing, if you get my drift?" stated Perkins as he brushed a generous wad of foam onto Percy's beard.

"I don't know that I do."

"What I mean to say is that since Mr. Wylie took over Grimsby Beach, the Temple is more like an auditorium. Less hymns and more songs. Less praying and more playing. They put on plays and musicals now. He even brought in the midway and these woods have been hopping since."

"I came to hear Reverend McGarrity speak."

"There are still a few preachers, priests and ministers here to give talks. It's just more diversified now. Now you can have your soul saved in the morning and have your palm read in the afternoon." As Perkins was saying this, he unfolded a straight razor and began stropping it on a length of leather attached to the wall.

Percy's eyes went wide. He could never quell the nerves he felt when someone, other than him, took a razor to his throat. He took a deep breath and focused on the colourful bottles of hair tonic that lined the Barber's counter.

"And you can find ice cream and pies and egg sandwiches at McCoy's."

Perkins was pressing his thumb on Sparling's neck to bring the skin taught as he angled the blade. The edge glided down his cheek, over his jaw bone and followed his jugular down to his collarbone. The sharpness of the blade and Perkin's skill delivered only a mild pressure as it separated Percy's beard from his face. Perkins made six more passes, stood back and wiped the razor on the towel he had tucked in his belt.

"Take a breath sir."

"Sorry." Percy was embarrassed for letting his fear show, his face flushed from his distress and from the lack of oxygen.

"No need to be sorry sir. It's perfectly natural to have difficulty trusting anyone who holds a razor to your throat," he added, continuing his handiwork. "While you're here, you must do yourself a favour and see the snake charmer.

Now there's a brave man. He wraps a snake that must be over twenty feet long around his body. What a show………"

Perkin's voice trailed off until Sparling could only hear the thrum of his own pulse in his ears. He had done his best to stay calm, to breathe deeply and give himself over to the man with a steel razor.

Trust hadn't always been so elusive to Percy Sparling. As a young boy, he felt secure in his mother's arms or on the lap of his grandfather. Their home, his grandfather's home, was small and cozy. Many hours were spent in the weak light of the fire, around the hearth, as his grandfather told a yarn between puffs on his pipe. He would fall asleep there until his mother would lift him to the thick straw mattress and tuck him in. To this day the herbal fragrance of grass made him want to curl up and snooze.

As a young man in Skerrie he cultivated many friends. He was well liked and all of the villagers knew that they could count on the Sparling boy to lend a hand when there was work to do. Everyone knew him and looked out for him. But even the warp and weave of a community couldn't have protected Percy from his father.

Colonel Edgar Ballister was the son of Lord Ballister, the Earl of the Municipality of Skerries. His military position was a commission, paid for by his father and he'd been away on conquests for most of Percy's life. It was a shock to everyone, including Percy, when the Colonel showed up that day.

Just how Ballister ever got close enough to Sarah Sparling to father a son was a mystery that baffled all the residents of Skerrie. Sarah was helping out her father by delivering his catch to the wealthier kitchens in the district and Lord Ballister's Estate was the largest purchaser of goods in the region. What his cook didn't buy went into the Dublin market and Grandfather Sparling saw more profit if it sold locally. It was on one such delivery that Edgar cornered young Sarah and forced her into a stable. Sarah never revealed the sequence of events that followed to anyone, especially her father, for she knew he would lose the Ballister business and that would hurt and anger everyone. It was some months later when her father found out and got angry anyway. He took his pregnant daughter up to the Estate and demanded to see Lord Ballister.

While she waited in the hall, her father and his Lordship conferred on the best course of action. This turned out to be a small allowance to help raise the child and a promise that Edgar Ballister would restrain himself from seeing Sarah and the child once it was born. To seal the deal, the Lord bought Edgar his commission and had him sent to South East Asia. It was when the Lord of the Manor died, that the Colonel returned home to his inheritance, an inheritance that he believed should include Sarah Sparling and his illegitimate child.

Percy was fifteen years old at the time and he was on his way back from haying in Lester Finian's field when he saw the door to his grandfather's home ajar. From the distance he could see what looked like a lump of laundry bunched up by the door and the untidiness of it all made the hair on the back of his young neck stick up. He began to run and over the sound of his feet on the road he heard his mother's angry voice. When he was twenty strides from the front door he recognized the pile of laundry as his grandfather, lying motionless with his face down on the ground. He could hear his mother shouting from the pen behind the house but still he bent to check on his grandfather. He had a large purple contusion on his left temple. Once again, he heard his mother's cries and this set him in motion again. He rounded the corner of the house just in time to see a blond-haired man in a British Red Coat press the tip of his sword against his mother's throat. When Percy caught his mother's eye her last word to her son was, "Run!"

He wished that he had followed his mother's command but the shock of seeing her afraid and trapped, paralyzed him and when the Colonel dragged the edge of his sword across her throat his world changed forever. When she crumpled against the shed door and her knees gave way his instinct was to rush to her aid. If only he could catch her before she fell, maybe she might still be alright. But he was watching the light escape from her eyes, her pupils disappearing up and under her eyelids while her body folded and bent and deflated and it was then he knew that he couldn't get there in time. He knew that his mother would fall to the ground and not get up. The knowledge that he would never hear her laughter or her voice call or sing to him ever again settled on him like a weight he'd never known. He was aware how heavy his legs felt. How his feet felt stuck to the ground. Young Percy just stood there until the soldier, his father as he was slowly coming to realize, turned to face him.

Percy has never forgotten how his father's red serge matched perfectly the colour of his mother's blood staining the blade. Symbolic or not, he has thought since that the coats the English wore were stained with the blood of the Irish and the Scots and the Welch and any other race that they colonized. He came to believe that the colour was worn as a warning of how ruthless and cruel the Imperialists could be. These invaders would purposely slit your throat and stain their clothes in your blood to remind any survivors who controlled and owned them.

But in the moment of his mother's death Percy just saw the coat, the blade, the madman's long blond hair straying out in every direction and the deranged flash of his wild and familiar eyes. Eyes he had seen in the reflection of his mother's mirror. Eyes that were his own. Saliva and spittle escaped from the corner of the soldier's mouth. He was saying something to Percy but he could hear nothing. It was when the officer raised his sword that he felt the weight leave his legs. He turned and flew around the corner of the house, past the heap that had been his grandfather, over the stile and across the pasture. He did not turn to see if he was being pursued. He just ran.

From then on, Skerrie became a place to flee and although his grandfather and mother were no longer alive, he was not alone. The citizens of the small hamlet helped him escape. When he found himself back at Finian's Farm the speechless terror on his face told the story. Everyone had heard that a deranged Edgar Ballister had returned to the estate on the hill and they didn't need many clues to piece together why the Sparling boy who was typically calm and easy going was having trouble breathing and talking.

Angus Finian directed his youngest son to set up a space for Percy in the barn hayloft where he could remain hidden until they had a plan to move the boy to a safe and secure place. No one, including the brave and stoic Angus, believed that Colonel Ballister's crimes and misdemeanors would ever see the inside of any courtroom. Even though it made the blood in his veins boil, he knew that the scales of justice were not balanced in their favour. Still, under the cloak of darkness they did what they could do. They housed and they fed Edgar Ballister's illegitimate son for three days before whisking him off to his mother's brother in Belfast.

THE TEMPLE

Percy did as the barber suggested and took a deep breath. His pulse slowed and he could see in the mirror that the colour was coming back into his face. Perkins, having completed the job, folded up the razor and stood back to inspect his work.

"You are a new man Mr. Sparling. Now go out and enjoy what Grimsby Beach has to offer."

"Thank you. I will do my best." He did feel like a new man and the prospect of exploring the park on this sunny Saturday morning was a thrill. The shop he was in exited to the hotel lobby and when he emerged, he came into view of the reception desk and Mr. Vennetter.

"Mr. Sparling," said the manager in a generous and respectful tone, "A very good morning to you. I see Mr. Perkins worked his usual magic." The expression on Vannetter's face showed surprise and awe. "I don't think I would recognize you as the man who entered our foyer yesterday. Breakfast is served in the dining room until ten."

"Thankyou Mr. Vennetter. I am going to walk about the park this morning to get my bearings."

"Then I suggest starting with the midway before it gets too busy. It can get crowded on Saturdays. Turn left as you exit and go up Grand Avenue."

And then Percy did something he almost never did: he nodded, thanked the manager for the suggestion and followed his advice. The bath and haircut and the reaction to the fresh appearance gave him an air of respectability and he felt compelled to act the part. He left out the front door, descended the staircase, turned left and went up Grand Avenue. There he found the fish pond, where anyone with five cents could angle out a cupie doll, a butter dish or fancy milk jug from a waterless pond. There was the snake charmer who kept a large python in a shallow pit. Unfortunately, the python and the charmer were asleep - the python in his pit, the charmer in his hammock - so when Percy went by there wasn't much of a show. Across the lane the Electric Lady, a large corpulent woman in a striped dress, was reaching out her wand to deliver mild electric shocks. While Percy looked on, one young girl volunteered to be shocked over and over again until her hair stood out at odd angles and she couldn't quite pronounce "again". As she uttered, "Awain, awain, awain!" Repeatedly the sorcerous held her wand high and told the young girl that she had to move on. Percy did try his luck at the shooting gallery. He had little success and quit when he began to suspect that the barrel of the rifle wasn't true. Percy bit back his growing frustration, smiled at the carney and chastised himself out loud for being such a bad shot. As each pellet curved away from its target, Percy was reminded that not everything is as it appears. That truth is often illusive and hidden under the layers of everyday life. His presence here was a prime example of that.

A pang of hunger brought him to McCoy's where he had an egg sandwich. He was halfway into his breakfast when a buggy rattled by holding two unlikely looking passengers. The vehicle was a market cart that belonged to the hotel. It had only two wheels which made it more maneuverable in the narrow streets but rendered a less comfortable ride for the driver and passengers as it had a tendency to bob up and down as the horse stepped forward. Percy had seen it several times unloading luggage at the Park House after the Turbinia had arrived.

The driver was Jacob, Toke's older brother, who took to his work with a joyful energy that was in direct contrast to the temper of his present passengers. Sitting beside him was a stern and foul faced man dressed in a black silk suit. His frown accentuated the curve of his long white moustache and both of his hands were holding down a fedora to his head which was bouncing up and down with every step the gelding pulled on the rig. Sitting in the back of the buggy with the luggage was a large woman in an elegant dress. Her legs were dangling over the edge as she braced herself among the valises and carpet bags and they were swaying in the same cadence as her ear rings. She was holding on for her life and her face held an odd mix of terror and thrill. Clearly, Jacob's passengers were more accustomed to travelling by car but Grimsby Beach had no such luxury. Percy surmised that Jacob's passengers had arrived by train and had chosen not to walk to their hotel.

He passed them again on his way up the steps to the hotel. Jacob and the man with the moustache were trying to coax the woman out of the back of the wagon. Jacob had put down a stool on which she could step and although Jacob and the guest took a hold of each of her hands she was reluctant to step where she couldn't see. Her girth blocked her view of the stool and her feet. Despite words of encouragement from Jacob and words of derision from her travelling companion, the woman stayed perched on the edge of the wagon. The accents of the new guests, German he thought, made the scene more comical for Percy. "Oh Hans, don't let me vall!" Percy couldn't keep himself from chuckling into the lobby.

By twelve-fifty pm, Sparling was making his way back out of the Park House Hotel and towards the Temple. It was a short distance along a narrow path. The path emerged into another narrow circular street that looped around the structure and he followed this to an entrance covered with heavy canvas curtains. Percy brushed the canvas aside to reveal soaring timber rafters leading up to the cupola. Sunlight pierced it's windows and was beaming down to the pews below. The volume of space in this dome took one's breath away. It soared one hundred feet above the floor and at its base had a diameter of one hundred and twenty feet. There were no interior pillars or supports of any kind and it was said that the Auditorium could hold three thousand people. Today, however, the audience was small and the few in attendance scattered themselves amongst the pews on every side of the lectern. Percy found a place in a second row just as the speaker was taking the stage. Being a religious gathering, there was no applause.

Father McGarrity of Syracuse had come to speak about the Glory of the Afterlife. A poster advertised this throughout the community but it didn't do a good job of attracting a congregation. The priest had missed the puritanical and temperance fervour in this community by twenty years. In those days he would have been just one of twenty preachers and ministers, a team of holy men who would speak to a packed house all day long. But the feeble attendance seemed to have no impact on McGarrity. He would have been greatly disappointed for the turnout except for the single congregant seated on the aisle in the second-row center. Amongst the crowd of fourteen, there was Percy Sparling, faithfully where he was instructed to be.

"Ladies and Gentlemen, we are gathered here today to consider the Afterlife and how each and every one of us can ensure that we will win our place in Heaven at the feet of our Lord for all eternity. We are gathered here today to know that this is our destiny and that we must follow His word in order to fulfill His wishes. We are gathered here today," and here Father McGarrity paused and looked directly at Percy, "to carry out what is in our hearts to completion so that we might find the Glory that awaits us."

Percy fingered the crucifix that was strung around his neck. McGarrity's voice resonated through him and the words lifted him. It was as though the light from the copula above was pulling him up and off of the pew and away from the sawdust floor. As the sermon went on Percy closed his eyes and visualized himself transported up and out the top of the auditorium and into the clouds above. He had stopped listening to the words and was floating on the tone and rhythm of the Priest's voice. The sensation lasted for some time when he heard the preacher's tone change. As the pitch and energy of the delivery fell, Percy could feel his feet again on the floor and an alertness he hadn't experienced before. His eyes fluttered open and fell on a black dress one pew over. It hadn't been there at the start of the service and although the light was dim, he recognized the way her curly locks fell onto her shoulders. She was wearing a hat with a veil but he still knew who she was. Her silhouette was unmistakable and for the first time since the lecture began, Percy's attention was divided.

"May God be with you and take each and every one of us under His will and reveal to us all that heaven has to offer. He alone gives all that is offered in the glory of the afterlife" concluded Father McGarrity. "And now for those who would like to receive the flesh and blood of our Lord and Saviour, I will now conduct mass."

Percy didn't know where to look. He turned his head back and forth from the lectern to Mary Miller seated just a few yards over. Mary's attention was on her hands, still suspended with palms together and her lips mouthing a silent prayer. Percy watched as Father McGarrity swung a small chain over his bible, softly muttering words in Latin. A quick glance over showed Mary pulling some rosary beads through her fingers. McGarrity then unfolded a white handkerchief and swung the chain over it as well. Mary leaned forward and pressed her forehead to her hands. Her lips moving in earnest. McGarrity closed his bible, ceased chanting in Latin and descended the stairs.

"Come forward." he commanded and the congregation formed a line at the foot of the stage just beneath the lectern. Percy was the last to stand and join the line. He watched Mary, trancelike, file herself between an elderly woman and a rotund man. It appeared that she was still praying. To his disappointment, she took no notice of him and by the time he joined the line Mary and the others were ascending the aisles out of the auditorium. He wanted to follow her.

Percy had to wait a long time to receive the wafer on his tongue and the sip of wine from Father McGarrity's pewter chalice. The spinster in front of him was filibustering. She was trying to engage McGarrity in a conversation about the history of Catholicism in the Niagara Peninsula.

"We are so lucky to have you, Father. There are not many of us here. It is so good of you to come to our Park. You don't know how wonderful it is to have a proper mass. Just the other day, I was telling George, George is my brother, that it has been ages since I've done a confession,...."

But that's as far as the spinster got because the good Father, sensing that this was the beginning of a long monologue, interrupted her.

"And so good of you to be here this morning. God bless you." and with that, the priest ended the conversation, stepped to his right and motioned for Percy to come forward for his communion. The spinster, realizing her audience with the priest was over, walked away in disappointment.

"Good of you to be here my son," said McGarrity as he placed the wafer on Percy's tongue. Lowering his voice he added, "I trust you have found your accommodations comfortable?"

"I...." Percy had to bite, chew and swallow the pasty cracker before he could answer, "Yes they are. Thankyou Father McGarrity."

"You have Clan na Gael to thank." He brushed the crumbs from his hands and motioned for Percy to sit down once again amongst the pews. McGarrity sat beside him, leaned in close to Percy and though they were virtually alone in the auditorium, continued in a hushed tone. "Sparling, you must ready yourself. Things are about to change more rapidly than expected. I am told that the Kaiser's forces are moving into Belgium soon and that will bring England to declare war." He was looking directly into Percy's eyes assessing his comprehension. At Sparling's nodding, McGarrity went on. "When that happens, the militia here will step up their security of supply lines. Do you know what that means?

"It means my task will be more difficult."

"It means that we need the design plans. It will not be enough for one man to cripple one lock in the canal. We need a coordinated effort."

"But I can do more."

"You cannot do what a team of twenty can do, if we have the plans."

Sparling's eyes were wide as he considered the devastating effect of sabotaging all eleven locks on the canal at once. It would severely limit the flow of grain and supplies from Western Canada as land routes would have to take up the slack.

"You have twenty men to do this?" Percy was visualizing the steps needed to coordinate a mission of placing charges along strategic spots on all of the locks at the same time. Not only would you need twenty men, you would need twenty skilled men to carry and place the charges where they would do the most damage.

McGarrity smoothed the ceremonial tunic with his hands. "I have the uniform to gather the men that are needed."

The enormity of the mission fell on Sparling. He had been just one man working alone. It was safer and easier to control. McGarrity's suggestion required that he put his trust in others, others that he didn't know.

"Will these men be trained?"

"You will do the training."

"And how am I to work on the locks and train these men?"

"You will get the plans, make off like you are going to enlist in the Dominion of Canada's militia and then the training will begin. It is the only way to have an impact. Percy Sparling you are being called to wound our common enemy. You will be attacking them like our brothers attack them every day in Belfast and Dublin and Cork. And you will not be alone. There are those in Washington who can help us and at this very moment Clan na Gael is in Germany to secure Kaiser Wilhelm's support on our homefront. And do not forget, you will be compensated handsomely for your service. Our allies have been quite generous. Moreover, you will be following the footsteps of our Fenian Forefathers and you will be avenging your mother." McGarrity's preaching voice and the mention of the Fenians and his mother struck him.

Percy knew about the Fenian attacks on The Dominion of Canada. Attacks that were meant to strike at the outposts of the British Commonwealth to distract the English Imperialists from their hold over Ireland. For some it was political. There were two generations of Irish immigrants in the U S who had not forgotten the Great Famine and the expulsion of Irish farmers off of the English-controlled land. Half a century had gone by and the wounds were still fresh. For others, like Percy, it was a way to exact personal revenge. He had Colonel Edgar Ballister, his very own father, to blame for the destruction of his mother and grandfather and now he wanted every officer who wore the red serge to pay for it.

He was, however, unaware of Ireland's clandestine attempts to ally with Germany. The Irish Republicans saw the coming war as an attempt to stab England in the back while she was facing the Kaiser on the Continent and to know that they had emissaries in Washington buoyed his hopes of success.

"I will get the plans. I know where they are," Percy said with resolve.

McGarrity stood, placed his hand on Sparling's shoulder and said,

"I know you will, my son. I will be in touch with you when we are ready to move."

Sparling didn't know how long he sat inside the auditorium after the preacher left. He was considering all that needed to be done. There was no question that he would attempt it. He had many reasons to. His thoughts were only interrupted when a crew arrived to set up for the evening's performance.

"You're a little early," stated a stagehand carrying some lumber.

Percy just nodded his head and as an afterthought asked, "What's the play about?"

"Uncle Tom's Cabin." The response was so matter-of-fact that it suggested that Percy should know the story already. "This is our last show and the third sell out in a row."

"I guess I can't get a ticket?" fished Percy.

"No Sir, you can't. That's why it's called a"sell-out." The stagehand dropped his lumber and climbed the stairs for more.

Percy made his way out of the auditorium and back along the path to the hotel. He climbed up the stairs and along the balcony to his room. His key had just clicked inside the lock when Mary Miller popped out of the room next door. She appeared flustered. She swiftly pushed her key in her door and was struggling to lock it.

"Hello there." offered Percy.

Without turning her attention from the door, she responded, "Oh hello Mr. Sparling," while continuing to jiggle the key. She was having difficulty.

"May I be of some assistance?"

"Well, yes, if you wouldn't mind. I don't wish to be late. I am meeting Judge Falcanbridge's daughter at the train," she said as she straightened up and smiled. Her eyes were friendly and the upturned corners of her mouth made dimples and curves that caused Percy's head to swim. She was beautiful. He took the key from her hand and turned his wrist and felt the bolt slide easily into the door frame. Percy was surprised at his success on the first try.

"Well, there you go," he said, handing her back the key.

"Thank you so much."

She straightened her hat, turned and began walking, leaving him standing in front of the locked door. His heart fell at the swiftness of the exchange and her quick departure. He wanted it to last much longer and he hung his head in disappointment. But she only took four steps before she swung around.

"Mr. Sparling, would it be too much to ask, that is, if you have nothing else to occupy yourself with, that you help me with some luggage? You see, Fiona Falconbridge is a lovely girl but she is fickle when it comes to her clothing. She always brings more dresses than there are days in the week and I would have to hire a porter if you don't join me."

Percy raised his head and felt a surge in his chest. His cheeks pulled his lips into a smile. Something about her words, "join me" made his heart leap.

"By all means Mrs. Miller. I am at your service," and he gave her a truncated bow.

"We will have to rush if we are to meet the train. Can you join me now?"

"Of course."

So together their heels clattered down the stairs across the lobby and down the veranda. The station was half a mile away and in the distance, they could hear the far off whistle of an approaching train. Mary Miller picked up her pace and Percy had to jog a few steps to catch up.

"Can't the young lady wait at the station for your arrival?" he asked.

"I am in the employ of the Falconbridge's and they value promptness. Fiona is a lovely girl but I don't want any mention of my tardiness to make its way to the Judge. I take pride in my work record Mr. Sparling."

"As do I, Mrs. Miller."

They had just rounded the park gates and were beginning to breathe heavier with the added exertion. Both of them had settled into a lively pace and their ability to carry on a conversation showed that both were in the prime of their lives. It was an odd sight. Two adults lightly running in the holiday playground when no emergency called them to do so, was unusual.

"And what is it that you do, Mr. Sparling?" she asked between breaths.

"I am a mason." Percy was proud of his occupation but still he measured her reaction. He watched to see if she was impressed or repulsed by his trade.

"An honorable profession. How does it bring you to Grimsby Beach?"

"I came to hear Father McGarrity."

"He is a great speaker. I enjoyed his service today."

"I saw you there." Percy's words hung in the air. He was admitting that he noticed her. He was wondering if she noticed him. She made no comment, so they ran in silence for a moment.

"There it is." she said pointing East. Not far in the distance a pale plume of soot could be seen near the horizon. Peach and pear trees blocked their view of the tracks and train but they could see the platform and the small station up ahead on the road. The whistle sounded again and they both stopped running realizing that they had time before the train met them at the station.

"There aren't many Catholics here, are there?" asked Percy.

"Grimsby Beach was a Methodist Campground and many of the people in this area were United Empire Loyalists. This is very much English soil Mr. Sparling."

"So how do you find yourself here Mrs. Miller?"

Mary Miller was silent for a moment gathering her thoughts. Percy wondered if he had been too forward but to his relief, she began to describe her life.

"I was born an O'Rourke. My grandparents left home after the second famine and settled in Maine. My grandfather fished in the summer and cut wood in the winter and my father did the same. My mother kept the house, picked up some sewing jobs and raised kids. She was born in her village and she died in her village. She never saw another village other than that one and when I grew up, I vowed not to be stuck as she was. So, when Tommy stepped off a boat one day and offered to take me West, I left my family behind. At the time, his politics didn't matter to me. I just wanted out. Tommy's family had settled in the Eastern Townships of Lower Canada so that is where we went or should I say, where he left me.

"He left you?"

"We hadn't been there for two months before he went off to survey for the railway and he never came back. He left me with his Empire Loyalists parents who looked down on me the whole time I was there. When I learned of Tommy's death, I packed up and moved to Montreal. That's where I came under the employ of Judge Falconbridge.

Mary and Percy had arrived at the station. Three short blasts of a whistle that signaled the train was near. The platform was crowded.

"When did he die, I mean, your husband, if you don't mind me asking?" stammered Percy.

He knew the custom of wearing black to mourn a spouse usually lasted a year but for some it stretched out longer. He was wondering how deeply she was wounded by the tragedy and how soon she might be available to wear a more lively coloured dress. He wondered about his own curiosity. How could he live for years without a thought about settling down with a woman and have the notion present itself so mysteriously now? It was another surprise.

"There was an explosion. He wanted so much to be a part of the new Dominion of Canada and it blew him to pieces."

There was anger and resentment in her voice and Percy was looking for a way to regain the light and easy conversation they were having earlier. He was relieved as the train pulled in and a cloud of steam enveloped them. When the vapour cleared a pretty blond girl was waving at them from the window above. She was very excited to see Mary.

"There she is." said Mary and she moved with the crowd towards the conductor who had just dropped a stool to make up for the gap between the ground and the steps leading down from the car.

"We will wait until everyone gets off the train. We will have to go aboard to help her with her luggage," instructed Mary.

There was a happy noise on the platform. People were embracing and kissing one another. One woman had tears of joy streaming down her face as she bear-hugged a younger woman, presumably her long lost daughter. The porters were pushing carts down the track to unload the boxcars while the locomotive kept a slow and steady rhythm while expelling steam and smoke.

Once the crowd had cleared, Mary grabbed the railings and easily hauled herself up onto the passenger car. When Percy followed, he found Fiona and Mary in a close embrace. The young girl came up to Mary's shoulders. Her eyes were closed and her smile showed relief and security in her governess's arms.

There was a closeness here that went beyond a professional relationship. They acted more like sisters than employer and employee. Fiona opened her eyes.

"Who is this?" Fiona's voice was high and excited.

"This is Mr. Sparling. He is going to help us with your bags."

"Nice to meet you Mr. Sparling." She still had her arms tightly around Mary. "It's nice of you to help me."

"It is my pleasure," and Percy nodded and then moved to take down the only bags left in the overhead shelf.

"It is such a relief to be here, Mary. Mother is driving everyone crazy with her renovations. All of the help are flustered and on edge and Daddy just spends all his time at work. They told me to tell you that they will both be coming down on the train tomorrow."

"Well, I am glad to see you Fiona. This is Mr. Sparling's first time at Grimsby Beach."

"O Mr. Sparling, you are going to love it!" There is the Merry Go Round and ice cream and the beach and ice cream and auditorium and ..."

"Ice cream." filled in Mary. They all laughed. Fiona's youthful exuberance was infectious and for Percy, it made the load of her bags weightless as he carried them down the long dusty road. The time he had spent with women, young or old, was limited and he was marveling at how enjoyable he was finding it now. While he contemplated the mysteries of living a family life, Fiona chattered about the goings on in her family home in Toronto. From what Percy could glean from the conversation, her father was a high level judge and wealthy enough to keep servants and a wife who spent her time arranging and rearranging the contents and decor of their home. They were passing under the Park gates when Mary directed Percy down a new path.

"We have to go down Center Street."

Percy nodded and changed direction. They walked past a row of cottages, much like the others but each very much an individual. He stopped in front of one whose scroll sawn cornices and lathed turned posts were especially intricate.

"Mr. Sparling, the gingerbread patterns were originally cut as borders for tents when this was a campground. Because the tents looked so much the same, the women added some individual flair so that everyone could find their way into their own tent. When they were replaced by cottages, the decorations stayed on," explained Mary.

"Don't you love it Mr. Sparling?" asked Fiona.

"It is lovely," admitted Percy.

The last cottage was facing the lake. The breeze was refreshing here and the sound of the waves flowed into their ears. Percy watched the women climb the stairs and enter a screen door. A sign beside the door read, "The Courtroom", no doubt a reference to Mr. Falconbridge's occupation. He stopped at the edge of the porch and swung the bags onto the porch. He stood there awkwardly until Mary came out, apologized for not inviting him in. She explained that she needed to supervise Fiona until Mrs. Clements arrived.

"But I am free after dinner and I do have two tickets to the play tonight if you would like to join me?" offered Mary.

"I most certainly would," said Percy. "I was told the show was sold out and I'd surely like to see it. Shall I come by here?"

"At seven o'clock?"

"At seven o'clock." confirmed Percy. "I will see you then." He left the cottage headed back to the hotel and his room. He wanted to wash his shirt and hang it out to dry while the sun was still warm. It was a marvelous day. Light was fluttering its way through the canopy above and played on the ground and on the cottages below. It had been a long time since he'd felt so happy and he saw joy everywhere he looked. Children were running around the heart shaped pond in the park. One was trying to pull a kite into flight but the air was still and it wobbled behind him only inches from the ground. A group of boys were sitting on a raised platform that housed an enormous bell. One of them was rapping his knuckles on the iron and even from across the park, Percy could hear it resonate. This was an idyllic place, beautiful and relaxed and that is how he felt until he arrived at the Park House Hotel. He had just climbed the front steps, walked over the veranda and entered the building when he heard his name being called by Mr. Vannetter. Percy moved to the front desk where the manager leaned forward and discreetly said,

"Mr. Sparling, a Reverend McGarrity, is wanting you to join him and his guests in the dining room for dinner this evening. He has booked a table for six pm. Can I send him a message that you will attend?"

"I, uh, I, yes. Yes, I will."

Percy thought that he'd see McGarrity only once as outlined in his instructions. There must have been a change of plans and he wondered who the other guests might be. He hurried up to the second floor so that he could clean himself and his shirt. He now had a second reason to look presentable tonight.

DINNER AT THE PARK HOUSE

Through the doorway leading into the dining room Percy could see the serious looking man with a large handlebar mustache and the stout woman he'd seen struggling to get out of the market cart the day before seated with Reverend McGarrity at a table by the window. When Percy entered the dining room McGarrity saw Percy straight away and waved him over.

"So glad you could join us Mr. Sparling. May I introduce to you Mr. Tauscher and his wife Madame Johanna Gadski." McGarrity said their names with a flourish as though Percy should know who they were.

"It is nice to meet you," he said.

"It is our pleasure to dine with you Mr. Sparling," gushed Madame Gadski. She held out a pudgy hand. Percy shook it and wondered immediately if he was supposed to have kissed it instead. Mr. Tauscher stood, albeit reluctantly. Where his wife was welcoming and quick to smile, he paused, folded his napkin, carefully placed it beside his dinner plate before he straightened his legs. He made a show of making Percy wait. Tauscher forced a narrow smile, held out his hand and said insincerely, "A pleasure," as though it was no pleasure at all. Percy felt simultaneously welcomed by the woman and unwelcomed by the man. Though Percy towered in size and height over McGarrity's guest, he felt intimidated by his stature, his severe mustache and cold greeting.

Madame Gadski made a theatrical gesture towards the empty chair inviting Percy to sit down. She was a large woman, dressed in fine clothes and she enunciated every syllable she spoke. Her dramatic manner was a pleasant distraction from the frigid and quiet man that was her husband.

For his part, Father McGarrity appeared anxious. He was looking back and forth between Sparling and Tauscher. It was a startling contrast from the confident self-assured Preacher that spoke in the auditorium just hours before. McGarrity picked up a menu just as a waiter arrived.

"Shall we order?" he said cheerfully.

"Yes, let's. Oh, look Hans they have a soup of the day. You know how you love to try the soup of the day," prompted Madame Gadski. She was looking at her husband who sat staring at Father McGarrity. After some seconds of silence, he nodded.

"And I am going to have the roast pork with dumplings." she said excitedly.

"That's a fine choice. I'll have the same. What about you Mr. Sparling? This meal will be charged to your room so there is no need to go hungry."

"Thank you, Father McGarrity. I will also have the pork roast."

"I wanted you two to meet," the Priest began after the waiter had left.

He was holding his palms together, fingers splayed with matching tips beating in rapid succession against each other, almost prayer-like. He was nervous.

"As I was telling you both, Mr. Sparling here is a master stonemason working on the canal. He has a thorough working knowledge of its design and construction." In a hushed tone, McGarrity added, "and has experience with volatile charges".

It was clear that Mr. Tauscher had something to say by the way he was glaring at McGarrity. His eyebrows were raised and his face was becoming flushed. Percy could tell the man was dying to speak but something was holding him back. It was Madame Gadski who responded.

"What Hans would like to assure, Father, is that Mr. Sparling here can supervise his men to coordinate the job. It is one thing to have the knowledge. It is another to be able to complete the task."

"You have my word. We are assembling the best force possible. Mr. Sparling here has my every confidence."

As she spoke, Madame Gadski was staring directly into her husband's eyes. She was voicing his concerns. He was speaking through her. "Father McGarrity, you may not appreciate the peril we place ourselves in. While our adoptive country is not engaged with our homeland, they may soon be. Hans and I have become quite 'at-home' on this continent and we would like to keep it that way. So you see, we must be careful about who we associate and do business with. We trust actions. We do not trust words."

"And that is how it should be," agreed McGarrity. Sparling noticed a change in the timbre of his voice. His confidence had returned and he assumed the tone he used in the pulpit earlier that morning. "Trusting us is your decision. It is ours to prove that you were right to do so. Madame Gadski, when you start to wonder whether you can trust someone or not, you already know that you don't." McGarrity paused here for effect, looking from the Madame to her husband and back again. "All I have to offer you and Mr. Tauscher is faith. I have brought Mr. Sparling here so that you can see who you are dealing with. He has already acquired enough charge to cripple our target and he will soon be in possession of the plans for the entire system. We are prepared to expand on our original goal which will magnify the impact of our actions. Is it not better to inflict a blow that will take years for them to recover or a smaller one that will only inconvenience them for a few weeks?" He paused again looking from side to side but settled his gaze on Mr. Tauscher. "We need you. We need your assistance. You must trust and believe in us or this mission will be impossible."

Hans Tauscher took a deep breath. while everyone else at the table sat breathlessly. He paused and then again, nodded silently.

McGarrity grinned as did Madame Gadski. Tauscher continued to scowl and Percy sat there mostly confused. Fortunately, at that very moment, the food arrived.

"Now let's eat. Mr. Sparling, you may not know that you are dining in the presence of a diva." He glanced at Madam Gadski, who was feigning humbleness and trying her best to blush. "If you had spent any time in New York City or the major cities of Europe you would know that Johanna here is a household name." He turned towards Madame Gadski. "You were magnificent as Brumhilde and Isolde. I have only been to New York twice and both times I had the pleasure of watching you perform."

"Thank you, Father. You are so kind. And you, Mr. Sparling, are you a fan of the Opera?"

"I have never had the pleasure Madame," said Percy.

"Hmmpf" sounded Tauscher as he shot a scowl at Percy.

“Is there a problem we need to talk about because I’m getting tired of being stared down?” Percy was returning the glare of Tauscher now and his volume and tone had attracted the attention of those seated at adjacent tables.

“Now gentlemen.” The Priest had put his hands out as if to keep the two men from physically attacking one another. “Everything is fine. Mr. and Mrs. Tauscher have just had a long trip from Buffalo. We all just need a good meal and to rest for a few days here in this lovely spot and everything will be fine.”

Percy didn’t like the conciliatory tone in McGarrity’s voice. Here was a man that had preached a sermon that reaffirmed his faith in the Lord, a man that reminded him of his commitment to his Nationalist passions and a man that had convinced him that his salvation involved actions that might just get him hanged for treason. And now he was bending over backwards to this pompous foreigner. Percy’s respect for McGarrity plummeted.

“We will return to Buffalo tomorrow.”

These were the first words Hans Tauscher said out loud. HIs tone was crisp and commanding and the accent decidedly German. There was silence around the table and both Madame Gadski and Father McGarrity made subtle glances to their left and right, nervous about the conflict at their table. It was Madame Gadski who broke the silence.

“I do have a recital this week and it is always good to be well rested. Hans is correct. We do need to return tomorrow.”

“That is a shame. I have another service tomorrow I would have liked for you to attend.” McGarrity was speaking to the Madame only, preferring not to look at the other two men.

“We have been away for some time now, haven’t we Hans? We are one more week in Buffalo and then back home to Washington.”

“I thought your home was in New York City?” questioned the Priest.

“We have houses in both cities. Hans’s work is mostly in Washington and mine in New York. Thank goodness the trains are so efficient these days. Oh, the life of an Opera Singer!”

“The life of an Opera Star!” gushed McGarrity.

"Well, I need to be on my way," huffed Sparling as he placed both of his palms on either side of his untouched plate and pushed himself up to a standing position. The meal looked and smelled delicious but he'd lost his appetite. He glanced to his left to see Tauscher staring at his wife. He looked to his right to see Madame Gadski holding out her hand. He took it and shook it again. In the awkward silence McGarrity stood, walked around the table, took Percy by the elbow and led him out into the lobby.

"No mention of this meeting needs repeating, understand." Percy nodded but glared into the face of McGarrity. His stare conveyed his annoyance at the Priest and his dinner guests but he said nothing. "I will be in contact through the post. Enjoy your stay," and McGarrity quickly turned and re-entered the restaurant.

THE PLAY

The clock behind the hotel reception read six-fifty. Fortunately, he was dressed for the evening and didn't have to go back up to his room. He bounded down the stairs and walked briskly past the auditorium and down Temple Lane to Center Street. Mary Miller, still in her black dress, was sitting patiently with Fiona on the porch.

"Good evening, ladies."

"Good evening, Mr. Sparling," Fiona and Mary said together.

"Good evening Mr. Sparling?" came another voice from a woman carrying a tray out of the screen door. "And just who is this Mr. Sparling?" she asked, tilting her head back so that she could look at him through her spectacles.

"This is Mr. Sparling!" said Fiona. "I told you about him, Mrs. Clements. He's a mason."

"A mason you say?" She was still gawking at him up and down with her glasses balanced on the edge of her nose. She had a tray of tea in her hands and the screen door held open with her foot. "My Henry was a mason. Did you know Henry Clements, son?"

"No, I'm afraid not."

"Mr. Sparling is from Ithaca, Clara. He is not from Niagara," informed Mary.

"You must be up to work on the canal then. That's good work that is. That will keep you busy for a long while. My Henry would be gone for months when he had projects like that. It's not an easy life being in that line of work."

This made Percy smile and chuckle which left the three women on the porch looking at him in wonder.

"I just heard an opera singer say the same thing about her line of work." Percy explained. "I guess it doesn't matter who you are, there are always something to complain about."

"Well, we better go. The performance begins at half past seven and it will be crowded," suggested Mary.

"Enjoy yourselves. Whoever plays Evie is wonderful. I saw it last night."

"Thank you for staying with Fiona Mrs. Clements." said Mary in parting.

"Don't give it a second thought. Fiona and I are going to enjoy our tea and catch up." said Mrs. Clements as she put down the tray.

"Goodbye Mr. Sparling!" said Fiona. "Enjoy the show!"

Percy turned and waved.

"I think you have a fan," said Mary, tilting her head behind her. Her locks were curly chestnut. Percy liked the way they framed her face and cascaded down around her shoulders. Her skin, although not pale, looked alabaster against her black dress. Percy just smiled. Her company eclipsed every else in his life. He forgot about the rough work of cutting stone, the danger of handling explosives, the meeting with Father McGarrity and the dinner he had just left. In her presence, even the ache for revenge that consistently stewed inside of him cooled to a simmer and drifted out of his mind.

"I've looked forward to this all day. I've never been to a play."

"Well then, you are in for a treat. Do you know the story?" asked Mary.

"I can't say as I do."

"Well, it's good to know the background. Most plays are not like the book. The book was written years ago by Harriet Beecher Stowe. Some believe it was the inspiration for the American Civil War, that the story angered slave owners in the South and energized the anti-slave movement in the North. Her story outlines the inhumanity of the slave trade. There is no telling what we might see tonight. Most of the "Tom" plays depict the characters as simple folk who love to dance and sing and be slaves. I saw the movie and the slaves were dancing at a slave auction. The plays and film seem to have twisted Harriet's message. She must be turning in her grave."

"Well, I'm going to enjoy it anyway." said Percy smiling down on her.

"That's the spirit." smiled Mary back.

They joined the throng of theater goers and made their way down to their seats. Some of the audience brought their own cushions to place on the pews and as they sat down Percy was struck by the transformation. The lectern was gone and in its place was a scene of a cabin on the edge of a farm field. There was even a tree on stage.

"You sat right there this morning," said Percy pointing to a spot two pews over. When Mary didn't reply, he went on, "Do you attend every Mass?"

"I try." she said shyly. Her hands began to fidget with one another, like she was turning her rosary beads again.

The play began. There was song and dance throughout the story. All of the actors were white. Those who played black characters had black grease smoothed over their faces. The story revolved around Eliza who was running from her owner so that her daughter Evie would not have to be a slave. It was a tragic story. One that Percy could relate to.

"Did you enjoy it?" asked Mary as they walked up and out of the Auditorium.

"Very much, although it is a sad story."

"Sad indeed. Do you think Elizabeth Stowe would be turning in her grave?"

"I wouldn't know about that. My thoughts aren't very complicated. It did make me think of my family and your family and all the families that came over to escape English rule and how they had fallen into a kind of slavery here. Did you know that during the American Civil War, the Union Army had to leave the front to quell an Irish riot in New York City. It was our people who revolted because our boys kept getting conscripted and no one else was. They stuffed the conscription drum with Irish names and to buy your way out cost four hundred dollars and of course, no one had four hundred dollars. In effect, they put a price on our heads when black slaves were selling for twice the amount. We were worth less than slaves!"

The words flowed out of him in one breath. He had a library of the wrongs done to his people and this was just one anecdote within the volumes he carried inside.

"Well, Mr. Sparling, I think you just had a thought." and she smiled at him and he immediately felt the fury that had built up during his rant dissolve.

She slid her arm through his and they continued to walk in a direction that Percy hadn't been before. The pressure of her forearm on his was a thrill and he felt like he could walk like this all night long. The Park was a quieter place in the late evening. There were other couples walking about and a few groups of boys milling in places. Shadowy figures and the odd glowing pipe could be seen on the porches they passed. Some spoke soft greetings as they walked by. Fireflies were zigzagging their way through the trees and between the cottages. Here, well away from the Auditorium, everything was quiet and peaceful.

"I want you to see Spooney bridge," said Mary. "The views of the lake are lovely there this time of night."

Victoria Terrace climbed gently up a hill and they passed the Park's other hotel. The Lakeview House was slightly bigger than the Park House and owned by the same company. There were a few quiet voices coming from the veranda but most of the windows were dark. It appeared as though the lake had lulled the guests to sleep with the sound of the waves on the beach. A short way beyond, the path crossed an arched bridge. The fireflies were numerous here and their lights danced in the darkness of the ravine below. Mary was right. The view was beautiful.

"Mrs. Miller...?" started Percy.

"Mr. Sparling, my husband has been dead for most of a year. Please call me Mary."

"Well, alright, Mary, I have a job to do that will take me away from here for a long time. I was wondering if you have strong ties here?"

"Oh,"' Mary said as she turned to look down into the ravine. "Are you asking me to come with you?"

"I, I don't really know what I'm asking. I'm sorry. I really like you and I like being here with you and I don't really know what I am saying."

Sparling was embarrassed. His heart wasn't used to feeling like this and it was affecting his thoughts and what he said. A day ago there was nothing that he was uncertain of but now he was uncertain of everything.

"Percy, I've enjoyed meeting you and this evening has been wonderful but it is a little early to be making plans don't you think?" She reached out and put her hand on his arm. "What will we do tomorrow?"

He put his hand on hers and held it on his arm. This offer made him feel like his embarrassment had been worthwhile and she used his first name although he didn't recall telling her what it was.

"I do need to get back to the work site tomorrow, but we could rent a boat in the morning."

"That sounds delightful," and the two of them walked arm and arm back along the terrace. When Percy turned to go back in the direction of the hotel, Mary resisted.

"I'm staying at the Falconbridge's tonight. I will stay with Fiona."

"Well then, I will meet you there tomorrow morning. Is eight o'clock too early?"

"Eight o'clock would be just fine Mr. Sparling".

They kept on the path along the lakeshore. The air was soft and warm and the moonlight made a sparkling triangle of light on the water. Percy began to forgive himself for being so clumsy earlier. He was with a beautiful woman on a beautiful night. His past had turned him to stone and the present evening had softened who he was. His heart was remembering what it was to love. He helped Mary up the steps but stayed on the path before the porch.

"Goodnight" she said.

"Goodnight." he said.

A BOAT RIDE

At seven am the next morning, Percy was down on the beach looking for the boy who rented canoes. Twenty paces from the pier there was a hut that stood before two long boathouses. This is where he'd seen the boy and the sign "Canoe Rentals" before. The hut was locked up tight and the boy and the sign were nowhere to be seen. He knocked on the door just the same and was surprised to hear a rustling inside.

"Just a moment." came a muffled voice.

There was a metallic screech as a bolt slid open and the top hinge of a Dutch door swung open. A balding and middle-aged man squinted his eyes and shaded his face with his hand. Percy had awoken him. He could see the make-shift mattress of life preservers against the wall. The poor fellow was staggering in the bright morning light.

"Sorry to wake you."

"That's alright, I needed to get up anyway," said the man in a gravelly voice.

"Looks like an uncomfortable bed," stated Percy

"It was more comfortable than being in the house with my Mrs, I tell you. She was on a tear last night."

"Oh, well, I would like to rent a canoe this morning."

"Twelve or Sixteen feet?"

"Oh, well, I don't know."

"How many are you?"

"Just two."

"Then a twelve-footer will do. Just the morning you say?"

"Yes, just the morning."

"That will be twenty-five cents."

Percy took the money from his pocket and put it on the ledge of the door.

"I'll get it ready for you. It will be on the beach beside the pier."

Percy bounded up the steps and briskly walked along the terrace towards the Falconbridge cottage. He had not yet arranged a way back to Merritton. If all else failed, he could walk but that would take six hours. He would have to leave Grimsby by noon. He wanted the morning to be perfect and he wanted to spend every moment he could with Mary. He walked faster. He had just turned up the lane that ran along "The Courtroom" cottage and was stopped short by a man's voice. The voice was deep and confident and emanated from the back porch. Percy stood and listened.

"An opera singer? Are you sure Mary?" said the voice.

"Yes, sir. That is what he said." It was Mary's voice but it was softer, more subservient.

"You must confirm this," the voice commanded.

"I will sir."

"As quickly as possible." reaffirming the command. The conversation had ended with the slap of a screen door.

Percy tried to piece together his thoughts. Questions rose up into his brain like lightning. Was she talking about his dinner companions from last night? Why would Mary be talking about his dinner partners to her employer? What was it that she had to confirm? The list of questions left him wondering just what he knew about Mary Miller. He paused and turned. He took a few steps in the direction from which he came and then stopped again. His heart and mind were at odds with one another. He turned again and slowly paced to the front of the cottage. His mind needed to know more. His heart thought it knew everything it needed to know. As he rounded the cottage Mary came into view. She was still in black but her hair and face shone. Her smile was disarming and Percy tried to steel himself against it.

"Good morning Mr. Sparling." Mary's voice was bright and confident and musical once again.

"It's a fine day for a paddle." said Percy.

"Yes indeed, it is." She paused. "But do you mind, I have to get some of my things from the Park House before we go?"

"Well alright. The canoe is waiting for us. Will it take long?"

The skirmish going on within Percy persisted. His mind wanted to know her business at the hotel. His heart wanted to be bobbing up and down on the lake with her.

"No." she said.

"Then, let's be off." They walked in silence for some distance.

"Why do you have a room at the hotel when you can stay with Fiona and her family?"

"Judge Falconbridge lends out his cottage when he is not here. When I came down to prepare for Fiona, it was occupied, so I stayed in the hotel."

It was a reasonable explanation and his questions began to evaporate in the glorious sunshine and in her smile. An offshore breeze kept the humid air from building and the temperature stayed temperate. Sunday morning was a busy time in the Park. There were three different Sunday services in the Auditorium and the residents were walking every which way in their best clothes. Mary and Percy rounded the bend and came to the Park House. As they climbed the stairs, Mary asked,

"Can you take my key and open up the door? You know how finicky the lock can be. I just need to check in at the front desk," and she waved Percy up the stairs while she headed for the counter.

Reluctantly, Percy climbed to the second floor alone and walked around to Mary's door. He took out the key and placed it in the lock but it wouldn't turn. He jiggled it every which way but it wouldn't budge. Just as he withdrew the key for the third time, Mary rounded the corner holding another key aloft.

"Sorry, Mr. Sparling. I gave you the wrong one." She handed the replacement to him and he inserted it into the latch. It turned easily. She wedged herself between him and the door, stepped inside and as she closed it said,

"I will just be a moment."

And that is how Percy was left, standing alone outside of her room, wondering what she had to 'confirm' here at the hotel and what she had to come back to get. Suspicion was welling up inside him once again but, true to her word, she was just a moment. She beamed a smile at him and then wove her arm through his.

"Now, let us find your canoe Mr. Sparling."

The rest of the morning was less complicated. They spent an hour splashing about in the lake. They paddled out around the pier and headed into the sun. From the water Percy and Mary could see the layers of life that made up the holiday community. The mild chop of water gave way to sand and then to the boathouses. The boathouses sat at the foot of the embankment well away from the water. On the bluff grew trees and shrubs and through these a line of cottages was visible. The crest of the auditorium was just poking up above the trees. A union jack was fluttering on a pole sticking out of the cupola. The British flag, small as it was in the grand scene before him, was a small reminder of his mission and a sinking feeling crept into his heart. The sing-song inflection in Mary's voice pulled him back to the surface.

"See there. That is where Mr. Wylie is building a dance hall." she said.

She was pointing to a shoreline property just east of the Park. Percy couldn't tell if Mary thought this was a good idea or a bad one.

"I thought Grimsby Beach was supposed to be a religious retreat?"

"Well, it used to be but times change Mr. Sparling. People used to come here only for the holiday weekends and then go back to their farms and shops and mills for the rest of the year. Now, some people stay the entire summer and the boats and trains stop here every day."

"I can see why. It's beautiful." He was talking about Grimsby Beach but his eyes never left her profile.

"Indeed." she agreed, still gazing at the shore.

The wind had picked up and the canoe was pushed towards the shore.

"I guess we should go in," said Percy, and he dipped the paddle deep and pulled a long stroke. The bow made a shushing sound as it met the sand and Mary stepped out of the canoe with an impressive athletic agility. She had gathered up the folds of her dress and held the paddle in one hand and stepped out of the moving canoe in one fluid motion. Percy followed awkwardly, walking up the canoe until he could step out on dry land. The owner of the canoe was coming down to shore to meet them.

"Just leave it there. I'll have the boy come and take care of it."

This left them standing wondering where to go next.

"Shall we get some breakfast. I'm sorry to say that I missed eating something this morning." said Percy.

"I have an apple. Will that tide you over?"

"Sure, let's sit here and enjoy the water. I have to be leaving soon." Percy watched her face as he said this. He was hoping to detect disappointment in her expression but he couldn't tell if she felt one way or the other. They found a large log that must have drifted onto the beach some time ago. It was a popular place to sit throughout the day but no one was sitting on it now.

"And just where exactly do you have to be going?" Percy thought he could hear a note of disappointment in her question and his spirit was lifted.

"Presently we are near Merritton. We will be there for some time. The land starts to rise there so there're many locks clustered together."

"I see. And will you be coming back to Grimsby Beach Mr. Sparling?" Her question sounded like an invitation. He looked directly at her and she at him. He was feeling weightless and weak again and he said,

"I certainly hope so." They held their gaze like this until Mary opened the bag she carried and looked down into it. She reached in and pulled out an apple.

"Hungry?" she said while she continued to feel around in the bag.

"It's a start." said Percy, knowing that he would have to consume more than an apple if he were to walk back to the canal.

"Here, have another," and she withdrew a second one. He put it in his pocket. At that moment a dog barked down by the pier and Percy could see a family arriving at the water's edge for a swim. When he looked back to Mary, she was slicing the apple in half with a knife. She handed him his half, wiped the shiny blade on her sleeve and folded the blade back into the handle. Percy had seen knives like this. He'd even owned one once but this one was of a quality that he hadn't seen before. The blade was straight and sleek. From the way it slid through the fruit he could see that it was sharp and the sheen off the blade told him that she kept it well oiled. She handled it with a well-practiced grace.

"That's some knife," Percy said. "Do you always carry around a knife like that?"

"I eat a lot of apples," Mary giggled. "This was my father's knife. I keep it to remember him." and she slid it back into her bag.

They looked over the water. Percy was thinking about what his father left for him and once again he could feel an anger rising in him. His father left him no material possession, just the desire for revenge. His hands closed into fists. Mary reached out and with her fingertips touched the inside of his wrist. It was a soft and gentle intimate act and he opened his palm. She slid hers into his and all thoughts of his father vanished.

"I hope we can meet again." she said.

"As do I. I can come next month, during the Civic holiday."

Mary reached in her bag and removed a neatly folded paper.

"This is where I can be reached. If your plans change, you can write to me." She stood up and smiled. "I have to go back to be with Fiona. It has been a pleasure Mr. Sparling." and she held out her hand. He reached up and took it and Mary pulled him up to his feet.

"Thank you, Mrs. Miller, for a wonderful weekend." She looked at him with a disappointed look.

"Thank you, Mary, for a wonderful weekend." he tried again. She smiled this time, turned on her heel and left him there standing in the sand.

THE WAY BACK

The trip back to Merritton was glorious. The morning sun rose up into a cloudless sky and cast crisp dark shadows beneath anything standing. There was no humidity and Percy marched away from Grimsby Park at a great pace. His strides were long and his steps buoyant. Shortly after noon, he consumed the apple Mary had given him and his lunch included three small pears from a tree by the road. He found them sweet and flavourful.

He tipped his hat and smiled at drivers as they drove their wagons in the opposite direction and even though he was tempted to ask them for a ride back to Grimsby Park, he knew he was going in the right direction. He had a glimpse of what the future might hold for him and for the first time in a long time, he liked what he saw. It was as though he'd been travelling in a long dark tunnel for many years and now, he could see a light in the distance and that distance wasn't so far away. He just had a few things to do. He just had a short way to go. He was just reaching the tree line at the talus base of the escarpment when a voice called out.

"Hey there! Mr. Sparling! Climb aboard. I am going your way."

Percy turned to see a Rockaway carriage pull up beside him. The driver was shaded by a short roof and even though Percy couldn't see his face, he knew the voice at once.

"Fancy meeting you here," snarled Sparling. He was standing beside the carriage while Father McGarrity sat hunched over on the seat.

"Mr. Sparling, do get up here and ride with me."

Percy hesitated but knew that his destiny was tied to this man. Father McGarrity had lost his hold on Percy's spiritual salvation, but he did guard the door to his future. Percy swallowed his pride and he climbed up on the carriage.

"Mr. Sparling, I don't like Hans Tauscher any more than you do but it is necessary to work with him. He has resources that we need. He is a contact that we need. Did you know that there have been revolts in Dublin this week? Our countrymen are spilling their blood for Home Rule, as we speak, just as they've always done. We cannot let this opportunity pass when England is occupied with Europe. We must seize this opportunity."

Percy sat in silence. McGarrity continued.

"Clan na Gael has sent a delegation to Berlin. We think the Kaiser will supply us with the arms we need to finally stand on our own in our own land. Here in North America, Hans Tauscher is an important man. He is an Officer in the German military and he has diplomatic immunity in Washington and he is in the business of selling firearms. We must work with him. He is our only hope here in America to strangle England's supply chain."

Sparling was still silent; his distrust and anger was crumbling. He nodded his understanding and McGarrity flicked the leather again which sent them down the road.

"And he is the one who has supplied you with the keys."

At the mention of the keys, Percy felt their weight in his pocket. There were two of them. The larger one opened the padlock on the dynamite shed. The contents of which belonged to the Welland Canal Company. The smaller one locked up the Foreman's desk.

"And in an indirect way, paid for your room and meals at the hotel. They also suggested that I increase your compensation. They have been most generous."

This statement made Percy straighten from his slouched position. He didn't know who was pulling the strings before. It was a shock to know that it was the snotty wee German. That Tauscher was able to achieve this while living in Washington D.C. indicated his influence and political reach. Again, Percy nodded and a brooding silence sat with them both nearly all the way to Merritton. They were just clearing the east side of St Catharines when the carriage stopped and Percy asked the question that was nagging at him.

"You are not a preacher, are you?"

"Not in the strictest sense of the word," responded McGarrity, "but that isn't important. What is important is that you follow my instructions. I will have a team assembled within the month. You need to be ready. There is much at stake."

"I have been ready since I was a boy," and these were the last words Percy ever said out loud to McGarrity. When they reached Merritton, Percy got down from the buggy and walked away without looking back.

"Keep a watch for the post," the Preacher called after him.

Without turning Percy gave a backwards wave signalling that he had heard and understood. He was on the path to the canal and the daylight was nearly extinguished. A nighthawk hovered over the brush and shadows were stretching out before him, blending into darkness. He loved this time of day when work was done and the world relaxed. It brought him back to the pleasures of the morning. The sun, the surf, Mary's lilting voice and her face. He marveled at how deeply this woman had touched him in just two days. Images of her kept floating into his thoughts, her quiet reflection at McGarrity's sermon, her disdain for her Loyalist husband, her infectious laugh, intelligent eyes and her grace as she moved with athletic ease. And yet there were contrasts too. Her confidence and decisiveness against the subservient role she played with her employer, her prayer beads versus her polished knife. She was a mystery he wanted to explore. He could hardly wait for the month to go by.

It was dark when he came upon the camp. The embers of Cook's fire were still glowing and a faint trail of smoke rose up from the ashes. Everyone had turned in for the night and in the dim light it appeared as if little had changed. There were three new tents pitched on the outer edges of the camp. The new workers had found a place to lay their heads. His tent, although sagging somewhat, stood in its place. He shortened the ties to regain its shape and descended into it. He laid his head down, he slept soundly.

BACK AT CAMP

"Is Sparling back yet?" It was Foreman's voice.

"Haven't seen him," came a couple of replies.

"I'm here!" Percy shouted from beneath his blanket.

"Good! Ward is going to need your help today with that crew on number five."

This was his warm welcome back. It was as though he hadn't left. Nothing had changed here. There were broken stones that needed to be removed and new stones that needed to be shaped and fitted and lowered into place. Nothing here had changed. But he had. Percy had a new and improved outlook and with that he developed new habits. He was just as diligent once he began swinging a hammer but he stayed up later at night and slept in later in the morning. He became the last to rise each morning and he used the time to relive his days in Grimsby Beach with Mary. He was looking forward to the month to go by.

"Yes, sir!" He answered, still horizontal. When did he start to be Ward's help? He put on his boots and shuffled to the mess tent.

"Good trip Percy?" asked the Cook.

"Good trip Cook."

"Any women there?" asked the Cook.

"Lots of women there."

"Sounds like heaven." said Cook, looking wistful.

After a bowl of oatmeal and fried pork, Percy walked up to lock five. Ward and his crew had set up a gantry and were in the process of lowering a cap stone on the gate blocks. Percy stood from a good vantage point and watched. Under Ward's direction, the crew with the aid of a horse slowly lowered the cap stone into place. It was a delicate operation as the work took place on the edge of the lock and there was a thirty-foot drop to its bottom but it went smoothly and looked true when the stone came to rest. Percy was impressed that his protégé could do more than drill holes in rocks.

"Looks like that gate is done. Will we be taking our shovels down to the Big Ditch now?" he shouted to Ward.

"We're going up to six and after that nine. There is still enough work here to keep a hammer in our hands," replied Ward.

As Percy approached, he held out his hand. He did so awkwardly. Percy wasn't well practiced in the gesture and the surprise in Jesse Ward's face didn't help. They had worked alongside each other now for three months and this was the first physical contact between them. Percy wasn't used to putting himself in the vulnerable position of being rejected but the offer of shaking his co-worker's hand seemed like the right thing to do. Jesse smiled and grasped Percy's hand in a firm grip.

"Good trip?" asked Ward.

"Good trip," replied Sparling.

The crew noticed the changes in Percy Sparling. He slept a little later, took longer breaks and ate closer to the rest of the men. At first, he moved to a rock by the stream that was just on the periphery of the group. He kept his head cocked towards the circle of men to better hear the banter that bounced back and forth with every meal. But it was when he added his opinion to the discourse that he truly became a part of them. He rolled up a log end and over the span of three meals he moved closer and closer until he became part of the circle. It happened so gradually that it was almost forgotten that he ever sat alone. The change was referenced only once when O'Malley suggested to his brother that he needed a weekend in Grimsby Beach to cure a sour mood he was in.

To Jesse Ward, the transformation was especially interesting. Alone in his tent he took the time to write down some of these observations. He neatly folded them and locked in a box he kept at the foot of his bed. On Tuesdays he would put them in an envelope and give them to the Postman and this practice went on for three consecutive weeks until the fateful day of July 27th.

On that day, as usual, Jonathan Book received and shared his box of pound cake and shortbread and Jesse Ward received a letter wrapped in a brown envelope. When Percy heard his name called, he stood slowly as if surprised. When he got up and reached for the letter held out in the Postman's hand, he did so reluctantly. He did not extend his arm up and out enough to hold what was offered.

"Well, take it man!" said the Postman reaching to hand it off to Percy Sparling. "Do you want me to fall out of my saddle?"

Percy snatched it quickly then and without a word walked quickly to his tent, picked up his jacket and left for the worksite.

"Never seen anyone so spooked about getting mail, I'll be seeing you next week," said the Postman as he snapped the reins and rode off down the trail.

It was a peculiar exchange and reminded all in attendance how odd and distant Percy Sparling had been prior to his holiday in Grimsby Beach. The men collectively looked at each other, shrugged and went back to lunch. Jesse, however, was quick to follow Sparling to the worksite. He made a point of approaching quietly and wasn't a dozen yards from where Percy was sitting when he smelled the phosphorus smoke on the breeze. Sparling was burning his letters again.

Jesse kept his letter in his pocket. He would read it later. He felt the need to observe his work partner. There was a shift in Sparling's posture and demeanor that needed watching. He had picked up his hammer and chisel and started tapping on the block before him. It was without his characteristic energy. He seemed distracted.

"You alright?" asked Ward.

Percy looked up and glared. His eyes were dark. Gone was the light and levity present there in recent days. The old Percy Sparling had returned and he didn't say a word for the rest of the day. He ate dinner on his lonely rock by the stream and he slipped into his tent early without speaking to anyone. Jesse Ward did the same.

Ward became vigilant. He studied Sparling's movements and behaviours throughout the morning and afternoon of that day and suspected that his attention might be needed into the night as well. He turned in early. In the privacy of his tent, Jesse retrieved the unopened envelope from his breast pocket and read the contents. In a fine and flourishing cursive there were just two words on the page.

"*Anytime now.*"

Sometime through the night the wind came up. Jesse heard it first as a rustle in the canopy but in a short time large limbs were bending under the force of strong downdrafts. He reached up to tighten the tie on the tent flap that was vibrating above his head, only to learn that it was another piece of canvas that was making the noise. He poked his fingers through the flap and pulled the opening so he could eye Sparling's tent. Its entrance was untied and undulating and Jesse knew that Percy was not likely to be inside.

He slipped on his boots, got on his hands and knees and peered through the canvas door. He scanned the camp from side to side and strained to hear movement beyond the swaying branches and quaking leaves. Other than the wind in the trees and on the tents, nothing was moving. He kept low and stepped softly as he exited his tent and threaded his way out of the camp. When he came to the worksite trail, he picked up his pace, climbed up to the bridge and crossed the river.

Jesse proceeded warily. He suspected that Sparling was visiting the sheds again. Not wanting to meet him on the trail, he proceeded with caution. His eyes were in constant motion, sweeping the shadows for movement. As he neared the clearing, he could make out the roof line of each structure against the starlit sky and he slowed his approach. Percy was nowhere in sight but the door to one shed was ajar. He crouched down and waited. Seconds later, Sparling emerged from behind. He was carrying a large box. His steady and calculated movements suggested that the load was precious or volatile and Jesse knew that Sparling was retrieving the explosives from the buried box and putting them back into the shed, reversing the steps he witnessed weeks before.

When Sparling disappeared once more behind the shed, Ward turned back to camp. He quickly went up the trail, crossed the bridge and back down to the camp. He tiptoed through the tents and slipped into his own. He kept the ties loose so that he could sit and watch for Percy's return. He didn't have to wait long. Only a moment later, Percy returned, silent as a shadow and disappeared into his tent.

THE ROBBERY

"What do you mean you're enlisting? We're not at war, Sparling!"

The words were angry and they spewed forth from the Foreman's tent. It was breakfast time and Percy Sparling decided to break the news to the Foreman while everyone was spooning oatmeal into their mouths. Most of the men stopped chewing and sat with their mouths gaping open and their spoons in mid-air while they watched the Forman's tent burst open. The Foreman was the first out, waving his arms in the air as he continued his tirade.

"For Christ sakes, you are needed here. Not marching up and down and around like a tin soldier. We have work to do here. Important work and who is going to do it if the likes of you trade in your chisel for a gun. Blasted!" sputtered the Foreman and he stomped and huffed his way up the path and out of the camp.

Percy came out of the Foreman's tent expressionless. He didn't look at the men who were all looking at him. While the men sat still, he silently walked to his tent, picked up his tools and went to the jobsite.

"So, when are you leaving us?" Jesse had arrived at the site to find Percy was turning a block over with an iron bar.

"Friday will be my last day."

"Well, we'll be sorry to see you go. Foreman is in a fit."

"He'll get over it."

There was a pause before Jesse probed further.

"So did she break your heart?"

"Did who break my heart?"

"I don't know. The girl that you met when you went off to Grimsby Beach."

"Who says there's a girl?"

"Okay, a woman then. No man goes from being ill-tempered to joyful to back to being ill-tempered on his own. Only a woman can yank a man's heart around like that. She must be a beauty."

"Mind your business, Ward." And that was the end of the conversation.

The following day, the breakfast was interrupted once again but this time every man in the camp feared that the Foreman would die of heart failure right in front of them. He was apoplectic.

"Who was in my desk?" he shouted, looking accusingly at each man. When no one responded he took another deep breath and bellowed,

"Get to your tents and turn out your belongings!"

The men just sat, bowls in one hand, spoons in the other, and looked at one another.

"Get to your tents and turn out your belongings!" Foreman repeated and the men immediately put down their utensils and obeyed. Each went back to his own tent and began dragging the contents through tent flaps out onto the ground.

"Ward! Follow me," and Jesse who was only a few steps from his own tent turned and followed the Foreman. "You will make sure each tent is empty."

Both Foreman and Ward waited while Allan Brown pulled out his cot, his foot locker and a carpet bag.

"Open the bag Brown," demanded the Foreman. Brown crouched down and lifted the hasp from the bag and opened it. He turned the mouth of the bag towards Foreman for inspection and pulled out a shirt, a spare pair of socks and a framed picture that could only have been his mother.

"Now the footlocker. Ward, go into the tent and make sure it is empty."

Jesse looked sympathetically at Allan like he was seeking his approval. When Brown nodded to him, Jesse bent over and crawled in on his hands and knees into the tent.

Meanwhile, Allan Brown fumbled with the lock and lifted the lid on the box.

"All clear in here," reported Ward from inside the tent.

Foreman scanned the footlocker and looked up towards McNally who was standing outside the adjacent tent, his personal belongings scattered on the ground. And so the process was repeated for each member of the work crew.The procedure only changed when they got to Ward's tent and the Foreman directed Allan Brown to do the search. It took nearly half an hour before the Foreman had searched all of the tents and the effort was fruitless. All it accomplished was the embarrassment and anger that follows an invasion of privacy.

"It might help to know what was taken," offered McNally.

The Foreman responded with a grunt and proceeded to stomp his way back into his tent. Most of the men had reorganized and returned their belongings and were now milling around looking alarmed and disgruntled. Jesse Ward looked for forgiveness in the face of each man for invading their personal space. Most gave him a nod to let him know he was forgiven. Percy Sparling didn't meet his gaze at any time. Percy was nonplussed about the whole affair, as though turning out your personal effects for the inspection of Foreman was a normal part of the day.

"Does anyone know what was taken?" asked McNally to the group. There was no response. Just a lot of head shaking as the men gathered their tools and shuffled off to their work.

Ward watched Sparling carefully throughout the day. His attacks on the stone had subsided but he became silent and remote again. He had his head down into his work. There was an unfamiliar purposefulness in his character.

The Foreman's temper had not abated by lunchtime. It was not his custom to sit with the men at any mealtime but on this occasion he took a seat within the circle and scrutinized each face as it chewed the bread and stew. The men self-consciously ate their meal quickly and silently and hurried back to work. And at dinner it was the same. The Foreman took up his post around the circle and stared from man to man as though he could intimidate them to confess to the robbery. Some men turn away unable to withstand the examination. Finally, McNally exploded.

"What is it that you have lost Foreman? I cannot stand for this! I will not stand for this! We are made to feel indicted and sentenced guilty and none of us know what we are charged with. What is this about? State your grievance!"

The silence was thick as each man in the camp turned to look at the Foreman. All eyes were on him and their attention opened a crack in the Foreman's demeanor. To their astonishment, all recognized a sliver of fear in the older man's eyes before he focused them on the ground as he held his head in his hands.

"The lock on my desk was picked and documents were taken. Important documents that I was entrusted with. Do not ask the nature of these papers. Just know, if they are not recovered, you will have a new foreman. That is my grievance," he said as he raised his head and looked again into the faces of the men around him.

His plea, dramatic as it was, was no more effective as the search he conducted earlier in the day. His predicament created a pall over the men and one by one they retired early to their tents.

Jesse Ward was especially vigilant that night. He kept the ties on his tent flaps loosened. He kept his boots close by and he inspected his revolver. The Colt Single Action pistol had been bequeathed to him by his father and as he drank a cold cup of coffee in his tent he cleaned and oiled it. He knew what he needed to do.

For the first hour, the caffeine made him alert but hours passed and there was nothing to observe. When the drug left in his veins Jesse fell into a slumber that lasted until Foreman's voice woke him.

"Ward! Ward! I can't have you sleeping in when I'm down a man." The Foreman's voice did not have its characteristic harshness. Yesterday's robbery had diminished his zeal. The consequences of his negligence were weighing him.

"I'm up, I'm up," came Ward's response but as the fog in his head began to lift he digested the meaning of "I'm down a man."

"Foreman? Has Percy Sparling left camp?" Jesse asked.

"Before daybreak. He is in some hurry to get a pair of new boots and do some marching. I tried to convince him that he would do the Commonwealth more good cutting stone here but it was like talking to a wall."

"Did he say where he was going?" asked Jesse.

"The armory in St. Catharines. He headed off down the Merritton path."

"Foreman, you are going to be down two men today."

Jesse pulled on his boots and stood before his boss. He watched waves of emotions pass over the Foreman's face. Anger, wonder, surprise, distrust and gratitude flashed in the brief seconds it took the older man to process Jesse's intentions.

"Sparling? You think Sparling....?"

Jesse nodded as he buttoned up his shirt.

"I think I can get the plans back for you."

The Foreman squinted back. Months before, a request from Management had placed Jesse Ward in his camp and specified that he was to work with Percy Sparling. He thought it unusual at the time and mildly resented being told how to run his crew. But Sparling was a difficult one to pair anyone with and in the end, they turned out to be a good team. The direction from above had been fortuitous for the Foreman, but now he understood. Ward put up with Sparling's temper. Ward not only received mail, he sent mail. Ward knew what had been taken and who possessed it and now he was promising to retrieve sensitive documents.

"You know where the documents are?" The expression on his face was a strange mix of wonder, distrust and gratitude.

"No, I don't but I believe that I can get them back for you. You'll have to do without me Foreman. I have to find him."

The older man squinted at Ward as he tried to make sense of it all.

"Falconbridge?" whispered Foreman.

Jesse acknowledged the question with raised eyebrows. He said nothing but stared back with a look of determination that said that he must go. As he passed the kitchen tent Jesse downed a cup of lukewarm coffee and grabbed a thick slab of bread. Foreman followed him silently. Before he ran up the trail, Jesse turned to face his boss. The older man was still looking puzzled and worried.

Jesse nodded as he mouthed the name "Falconbridge" and he held his index finger vertically to his lips.

The Foreman returned the nod signaling that he understood the need for secrecy. Jesse turned up the trail and began running. It would be the last time he saw the Foreman again.

THE CHASE

The first day of August was hot. The humidity was climbing as the sun moved higher and Percy Sparling could see the billowing clouds of cumulus building in the west. There would be thunderstorms later in the day and he was happy to be nearing his destination. He had rented a horse from the stables in Merritton and had made good time along the Escarpment road. He was long past the armories in St. Catharines, and continued west through the villages of Jordan, Vineland and Beamsville.

Presently, he was riding north towards the lake. It had been some time since he had straddled a horse and he was becoming uncomfortable. Percy would have preferred walking but time was of the essence and he desired distance between himself and the work camp on the canal.

He scanned the sky and listened for biplanes practicing over the beach. He saw and heard none. He looked for a plume of smoke and soot at the station far down the tracks but he didn't find that either. He even tried to sniff the breeze for a hint of coal soot from a ferry delivering passengers to the pier. He would have preferred to enter Grimsby Beach with a crowd. He would have preferred to arrive unnoticed but he knew that he would be seen and recognized soon enough. His plan was to complete this business quickly, reconnect with Mary and be off at first light tomorrow. He resolved to arrive slowly and calmly. He thought it more inconspicuous to move through the park gates looking relaxed no matter how fast his heart was pumping.

The prospect of change was overwhelming. His life as a mason could very well be over. At the very least his life here in Niagara was over. After tomorrow, he would move on. After tomorrow he would be able to afford to set himself up on a farm and build his own house of stone. He could have a home like his grandfather's in Skerrie and live out his days in peace. He could put the oppression of Imperialism behind him. His was an open road with a big blue sky where anything was possible. Percy even thought and hoped love was a possibility.

He dismounted and walked his horse under the park gate. The streets were quiet and he saw very few cottagers on his way to the Park House Hotel. His approach brought him to the rear of the hotel and there, sitting by the storeroom doors, was the same boy petting the same dog as his first visit to Grimsby Beach. Because of my unusual name, Percy remembered it right away. I guess he never expected me to be a threat to his security because he asked me right away for my help.

"Hey there Toke. Remember me. I rode in a month ago with Mr. Swanson."

"Sure, I remember you," I said.

"Well, Toke, could you do me a favour? I rented this horse in Merritton and it needs to be delivered to Smith's Livery in Grimsby. Could you lead her there for me?" Sparling flipped a nickel which landed in the dust at my feet.

"Sure, I can. I know where it is," I said as I pocketed the coin. Sparling handed the reins to me, slung his bag over his shoulder and walked towards the entrance to the hotel and that was the last time I saw him alive. He went his own way. I went mine. While I led the horse to the stables on the west side of Grimsby Beach, he disappeared around the corner of the hotel. It was a brief but significant exchange.

Mr. Vannetter was sitting before the hotel register in his usual spot. At the sight of Percy, his eyes lit up and he said,

"Ah Mr. Sparling, welcome back to the Park House."

"Thank you," stammered Percy. He wasn't used to being welcomed back anywhere and he felt a pang of unease at hearing his name spoken out loud but reminded himself that this room was bought and paid for. He was expected.

The manager turned to a peg board and fetched a key.

"Here you are. Room sixteen. The same room you were in before. Second floor, go to your right."

"Thank you," said Percy a second time. He turned towards the stairs and didn't get two strides away from the desk when Mr. Vannetter spoke again.

"Oh, and Mr. Sparling, Father McGarrity left this for you."

Percy turned to see the manager holding out an envelope.

"Thank you," said Percy a third time and grasped the envelope. He turned once again, mounted the stairs, turned right and edged his way around the balcony. He couldn't stop looking down on the street and the park beyond as he walked. He was surprised and happy to be here again.

Once inside his room, Percy tossed his bag on the empty chair and flopped down on the bed. He turned the envelope around in his hands before forcing his index finger under the flap and tearing it open. A short note fell out onto his chest. He lifted it to read,

Exchange delayed. Will meet Sunday Service.

His heart sank. He wanted this business over with and to be as far from Niagara as possible. The delay made him nervous. Still, to his knowledge, no one connected with the Welland Canal Company knew that he was here and the added time would give him the opportunity to pursue what had been most elusive in his adult life.

Percy opened his pack and withdrew a sheaf of papers. He slid them into the top drawer of the bureau and went back to his pack. He pulled out his good shirt, smoothed it as best he could and traded it for the work smock he was wearing. A quick splash of water from the wash basin and a comb pull made his hair presentable. It had grown unruly since his visit a month ago but it would have to do. Percy stepped over the threshold and made his way through the lobby and out the entrance. He longed to stroll through Bell Park, past the pond and down to the pier but he decided there was no time to waste. Instead, he took the narrow path to Auditorium Circle, skirted the large round building and made his way towards the lake. He followed Temple Lane to Centre St. and down another laneway to 'The Courtroom' cottage.

Percy was hoping to see Mary Miller on the Judge's porch. There were two women there but neither had her dark locks.

"Hello Mr. Sparling!" It was young Fiona. "It is so nice to see you again!"

The other woman was Mrs. Clements. She stood, face like she just sucked a lemon, stepped behind Fiona and put her hands protectively on her shoulders.

"Well hello Fiona and good evening Mrs. Clements. I was wondering if I might call upon Mary?"

"Mrs. Miller is not available presently." This was said in a stern manner as she stepped forward and in front of Fiona.

"But she will be back soon," offered Fiona, peering around the older woman's shoulder.

"Shush child. Mr. Sparling, I will tell Mrs. Miller that you paid a visit." Her expression and tone uninviting, Percy decided to take his leave and hopefully find Mary on his own.

"Thank you, Mrs. Clements and good day Fiona. It was a pleasure seeing you both again." He gave the ladies a curt bow and did a good job of hiding his disappointment.

Percy followed Victoria Terrace towards the pier. He had time to kill and decided that he might find Mary by chance as he walked about. Dark clouds were forming to the west and were approaching the southern shore. White caps had formed on the lake and the streamers that were strung from the bluff down to the pier were flapping uncontrollably in the wind. The beach goers were hastily packing up their belongings and retreating back to their cottages and the canoe renters were moving their craft to higher ground. Percy picked up his pace as he moved west past the Lakeview Hotel and onto Spoony Bridge. He stopped at the bridge. He could think of no reason why Mary would go beyond this point so he turned around.

Large raindrops were beginning to pelt at him and the low rumble of thunder told of the coming storm. On his second pass of the Lakeview, he could see staff on all three floors fastening shutters. Anyone not already indoors was running for cover and Percy followed suit. He was halfway across Bell Park when the skies opened up. Sheets of water streaked down soaking everything in his path. Each stride he took across Fair Ave. landed in a puddle and with a leap and a bound he was safely under the awning of the Montreal Telegraph Company when a violent crack of lightning sounded overhead. Percy was standing there dripping, with a small crowd of others stranded in the storm. They all cowered beneath the heaving canvas and shivered as the temperature plummeted.

"That came up fast," said the man next to him. Percy shyly nodded and measured the distance to the Park House Hotel. The road was a minefield of puddles and yet he chose to run the gauntlet. He was already as wet as he could be. Right now, he wanted some dry clothes and a hot meal. He would resume his search for Mary Miller tomorrow.

The rain was cold on his face as he raced across the road. The wind whipped the branches above his head and he instinctively ducked though they were far above. By the time he made it under the hotel awning he was soaked from head to toe, his footsteps visible across the lobby floor as he climbed the stairs to the second story. Water was still dripping into his eyes when he placed his key in the lock. It was then he heard his name. He turned to see a face emerge a short distance along the balcony. It was just a silhouette but Percy knew instantly that it belonged to Mrs. Mary Miller.

"Mr. Sparling," she called out softly. She kept herself hidden in a crevice in the wall, exposing only her head. "Come here."

Leaving the key in the door, Percy stepped quietly to her. Her voice hinted at the need for discretion and so he moved carefully along the floor to the narrow niche in which she stood.

"Mrs. Miller?"

"I thought you were going to call me Mary from now on?"

"Mary, I mean. What are you doing here?"

"I thought you were looking for me."

"I was. I mean I am. I'm sorry. I'm all wet."

It wasn't the way Percy wanted this reunion to go. He was soaking, his best shirt clinging to him and his hair matted and pasted to his skull while she stood beautiful as ever, her dark locks curling around her. He didn't think to ask her how she managed to get herself to the hotel without a drop of rain soiling her black dress.

"I mean, here. What are you doing here?" he asked again looking around the cubby hole where she was concealed. On closer inspection he could see that Mary was standing on a small landing that led to a narrow flight of stairs leading to the lower floor.

"Service stairs." She explained and she smiled. "I'm happy to see you."

He stepped toward her. They were face to face and close enough Percy could breathe her perfume. "And I, too. Mary, we must talk. I will be leaving Niagara soon."

She reached up and silenced his lips with her fingers. "I will return tonight. Be in your room at eleven." Her dark eyes were pleading with his. He nodded that he understood and then she was gone. She turned and silently descended the stairs.

Back at his door Percy turned the key in the lock. As he entered the small room, he was full of hope. The chill in the evening air had evaporated and was replaced by a warm glow emanating from this heart. He peeled off his shirt, hung it to dry and used a towel to dry his body. A boyhood memory flashed. He was toweling sea water from his skin while his mother's laughter surrounded him. He recalled the coolness of his flesh and yet not feeling one bit cold. They had just spent twenty minutes in the Irish Sea and with the frigid water peeled away from him, he felt alive and invigorated and this is how he felt now. He was excited by the prospect of beginning a new life, one that might include Mrs. Mary Miller.

Jesse Ward was not having an easy time catching up with Sparling. He knew the way but he had to walk as all other modes of transportation were closed to him. He arrived in Merritton to find that Percy had rented the only horse available and the boy at the livery stable told him that Mr. Swanson had left with his Grimsby flour delivery hours before. He checked the hotel.

Merritton Milley happened to be working the desk that morning. It was his first time meeting her and he was surprised at how attractive she was. Jesse found a new respect for his fellow mason Jonathan Book, surprised that he could have a wife who diligently baked for him and a mistress who would turn most men's heads. It was no wonder Book walked the trail between the camp and Merritton so readily.

"This time of day, the wagons are all out Mr. Ward. Everyone who has a place to get to is already gone. The trains have left their stations and the ships have sailed. I'm afraid that you will have to rely on your legs and it's a fair jaunt."

Milley had a sing song lilt in her voice that was as pretty as her face. He thanked her for the information and started down the road.

He had just passed the village of Jordan and was heading down in the ravine of Twenty Mile Creek when the skies opened up. He was grateful for the cool air but the rain made the clay track into a heavy glue that stuck to his boots. Each step was heavier than the last. He was out of breath as he reached the west crest of the ravine where he bent to pick up a stick and scrape away the mud. It was slow going and he vowed to stop in Vineland to see if there was a cleaner way to travel.

But he was met with the same result in Vineland and then a third time in Beamsville. There was no easy way to get to Grimsby Beach. By that time, he was quite exhausted and damp from the rain. It was a miserable journey and he didn't know if he possessed the energy required to engage with Percy Sparling if the situation arose. He was losing the enthusiasm for his task and relished the promise that there was a clean and dry room for him waiting at the Park House Hotel.

Meanwhile, Percy felt like a new man. He had on dry clothes. His hair was combed. He made his way down to the dining room. The staff were clearing the hall from lunch and setting linens and dinnerware out for the evening crowd and so they were unable to serve him. It was going to be several hours before he was to meet Mary again, so he decided to revisit the Grand Avenue Midway. He would happily eat another of McCoy's egg sandwiches and perhaps he might find the Snake Charmer and his snake awake this time. He crossed the lobby, went down the stairs and turned left onto Grand Avenue.

There were still puddles on the streets but the air was clean and fresh from the passing rain. The cottagers were out in full force and the midway was a muddy mess but it was busy. He had overheard that both hotels were fully booked and that an extra ferry had dropped off an additional load of passengers. There were people everywhere. Children ran from booth to booth encouraging their parents and guardians to keep up. Colourful banners hung down over the street while the calliope music floated from the Merry-Go-Round. McCoy's had a line-up so Percy staved off his hunger and moved onto The Fortune Teller's tent.

Madame Zodski was reading palms for 5 cents and there was no line, so Percy brushed the tassels aside and entered her tent. It smelled of incense and was dimly lit with a hurricane lantern. Shadows played all around the canvas walls while Madame Zodski moved her hands slowly around a glass ball quietly chanting incantations in some foreign language. Her eyes were closed and when she didn't stop to acknowledge his presence, Percy sat down in a chair opposite the Madame and patiently waited.

"I have seen you here before, young man. You were searching then and you continue to search today. Whatever you search for, your search will end soon. Your journey will soon be over."

Madame Zodski opened her eyes and glared at him. Her stare was alarming. Her eyes were bulging out of her head as she scanned him. She found him curious. It was as though Percy was a strange kind of bug that she had never seen before. Percy found her unnerving.

"You have something others wish to possess. Guard it carefully for their intentions are not yours." The Medium's voice trailed off and her eyelids flickered and then closed and flickered again. Percy could see her swallow, open her mouth like she was about to speak and then swallow a second time.

"That is all I see."

This time her voice had a different timbre. She was out of her trance. The spooky inflection in her voice had dissipated and Percy could see that his time was up. She was staring directly at him and pointing into the ornate glass jar between them. It held several coins and Percy realized that she was asking him to pay.

"Can I ask questions?"

"You will have to ask tomorrow. Madame Zodski is finished for today."

"That is all I get for a nickel?"

"Madame Zodski must rest. It takes great energy to see beyond, to see what others cannot. Come back tomorrow and I will tell you more," and she pointed to the glass jar again.

Percy reached into his pocket for the coin, deposited it into the glass jar and stood. All the while the Madame's eyes never left Percy. She stared at him like she was still reading his fortune.

He turned and left her tent feeling like he had been swindled once again. He vowed to himself that the next nickel he spent would fill the void of his stomach.

The light outside the tent was brighter but fading. He decided to head towards McCoy's. He walked past the shooting gallery but got sidetracked by a crowd gathered five deep around the Snake Charmer. Percy forgot his hunger and shuffled his way into the crowd and peered over the heads in front of him.

"One hundred pounds of pure muscle. One hundred pounds of crushing flesh that will squeeze you to death. Ever so slowly, this python will tighten his grip around you every time you exhale until you will no longer be able to expand your lungs. He will slowly starve you of oxygen until you are his unwilling victim. Should this python choose to consume you he will open his gaping jaws and eat you head first so that your limbs fold down and you can be more easily swallowed." His voice rose and fell. The deep baritone had a hypnotic effect on the crowd. "In the jungles of Borneo and Sumatra these serpents will wait with great patience, camouflaged in the branches overhead and drop onto unsuspecting passersby knocking them down to the ground where they are helpless against its strength, power and speed."

The crowd groaned and gasped at the Snake Charmer's description. Percy could see the constrictive power of the snake under its glistening skin but speed? The animal's movements were nearly imperceptible and Percy couldn't imagine not being able to avoid being captured by simply walking away. So that is what he did. He walked on.

The fish pond and the Merry-Go-Round were beside McCoy's. He fell into the cue and sweet smell of frying onions and egg erased any repulsion he felt watching the giant snake wrapping itself around the Snake Charmer's torso. It was while he was waiting in this menagerie of sights and sounds that he had time to reflect. The midway was a collage of everything mysterious to him; the fake, the phoney, the future, the past but what stood out most as he waited for his sandwich were the children and parents and boyfriends and girlfriends moving about from tent to tent. He saw families and the memory of his mother and grandfather happy in their stone cottage appeared before him. He longed for those days and wondered how he was going to get back to the time where he felt the warmth of family love. Maybe soon his journey would be over. He was thinking of Mary when they called for him to pick up his sandwich.

The food satisfied his hunger. The barber's recommendation had been true and he considered that he might return here for a third time before he left. The daylight was disappearing and the lights along the midway began to glow. By his watch, he had three hours before Mary Miller would meet him at his room. He left the Midway and strolled away from the bustling crowd. He followed a dimly lit path that wove between some cottages. He could hear soft voices on the balconies he passed. Mother's whispering "sweet dreams" to their children, men quietly laughing and enjoying their last pipe of the day and crickets chirping. It was so peaceful here. He was wishing that he didn't have to leave but his new life would have to start somewhere else, somewhere like here, like Skerries. Before he knew it, the sound of his footsteps gave way to the waves rushing through the gravel beach. He could feel the warm moist air coming off the lake. He descended the bluff to the shoreline and was struck with the first beams of moonlight reflecting off the waves rolling on the water. How many times had he sat with his mother by the ocean staring at the same moon? It was so long ago.

And then he sat down in the sand and wondered where his anger went. It was as though this place had cleansed him of the need to avenge his mother. The revenge he vowed to take on his father was all of a sudden pointless and his current political mission foolhardy. The wind and the water were washing away the glory of Fenian raids and the tree branches swaying above were brushing away the importance of Irish Independence. Percy just wanted to be in the present. To enjoy the pleasure of each new day as it unfolded and not to mired in the conflicts of history. He had found a new reason to be and it didn't involve waging war on the British Commonwealth.

Still, he was up to his neck. He knew the Foreman would now suspect him of stealing the plans and perhaps begin to suspect that he was involved in the swing bridge derailment. When they found he didn't enlist at the St. Catharine's Armories they would put two and two together and follow him here to Grimsby Beach. But he would be gone by then. He would hand off the plans for the Welland Canal to McGarrity tomorrow and that would be the end of it. He was relieved that his assignment changed. That he was to steal and deliver the plans and let the sabotage be carried out by others. He would collect what was owed to him and leave Niagara to find his new life. He had heard of a similar community in New York called Chautauqua and there was Martha's Vineyard in Massachusetts and there was Skerries.

Percy stood and brushed the sand from his trousers. He still had time before his rendezvous with Mary and he decided he needed to look his most presentable. What he said to her in the next few hours could make a difference in his life and he wanted to be prepared. He walked back to the hotel, climbed the stairs to his room, washed, combed his hair, lay back on the bed, closed his eyes and dreamed of his future.

Two stories below, a tired and road weary Jesse Ward arrived at the rear door of the Hotel. He had been waiting and shivering in an orchard for nearly an hour in his rain-soaked clothes. Despite his miserable condition, he did not want Sparling to know that he was on his trail so he waited until darkness before he entered the park gates. This is when I first met Jesse Ward.

He was moving cautiously towards the back staircase of the Park House Hotel. He was just about to ascend the first flight when I startled him. I was sitting motionless beneath the stairs with my dog as I often did. We'd often sit and listen to Mr. Vannetter and Cook talk about the guests as they smoked above but tonight no one was on the landing. It was my pet who gave me away. He was a pretty sucky dog and began to whine as Ward approached.

"Hey there boy." Ward said as he knelt down to calm my dog. I don't think he had seen me as he registered surprise when we came face to face.

"And hello to you. What's your name, young man?"

"My name is Robert but most people call me Toke. What's your name?"

"I'm Jesse," he said. "Say, I've been walking all day. Are these the stairs to the second floor? I've got a room saved for me and I'm dying to lie down on a bed."

"Ya. You go up, past the kitchen and up again," I said. At the time I didn't think it odd that he didn't go through the front door and register like any other guest but he seemed friendly and honest and I guess I just wasn't thinking. My dog and I continued to sit there as we listened to him climb up to the landing and then up the service stairs to the second floor. A moment later we heard a soft knock on a door, the squeaking of hinges and the same door closing. Someone was waiting for Mr. Jesse Ward and had just let him into their room. You see and hear a lot of strange things when you hang around the back of a hotel.

It was getting late, so my dog and I left our hiding spot and went home. I never suspected that I would be back only a few hours later.

END OF A ROMANCE

The soft rap on the door did not arouse him. Mary had to repeat her tapping three times before Percy was off the bed and on his feet. When he opened the door Mary was looking to her left. Her profile was unmistakable. It took his breath away. He started to say, "Mary,...." but she put her palm on his chest and forcibly pushed him back into his room. She turned quickly, closed the door and turned again and smiled. Percy was elated that she came and even though it was all he thought about all day, he was still surprised that she was here.

"Mary..." he started again but she put her fingers to his lips and silenced him.

She moved close and whispered in his ear, "Let's go to the beach."

He stared at her in disbelief and she just nodded and turned to go. Percy didn't move until she was out of the door and down the hall. He followed, shut the door and was two steps behind her when he stopped, turned around and walked back to his room. He took out his key and locked it.

At first, Percy was confused as she led him away from the hotel entrance. He understood when he saw her disappear into the small niche of the service stairs. She turned, pressed her index finger to her own lips to instruct him to follow silently. They crept down the stairs and onto a landing that went into the hotel kitchens and past these was another short flight of stairs bringing them to the street behind the hotel storerooms. She waited for him at the bottom and he was thrilled when she took his hand and led him away from the hotel.

Mary selected the darkest of lanes. Here the cottages were close together and all was dim and quiet. They moved quickly and quietly, not daring to attract attention. There were few people out at this hour and by the time they made it to the shore they saw only one lone man smoking on the pier. They headed further down the beach and nestled down into the sand with a large driftwood log to lean against. Throughout the journey they said nothing to each other although their hands held fast. Mary spoke first.

"I'm sorry Mr. Sparling. A widow such as myself must maintain her reputation. I do hope you aren't scandalized by this late evening meeting." She was giggling as she said this and her laughter was infectious.

"I am no stranger to impropriety Mrs. Miller. It really is no shock at,......" and he would have finished his sentence but her lips were on his. Her kiss sent an electric shock through his body and he could swear that he was levitating above the sand. She withdrew to study his face.

"Did that shock you Mr. Sparling?"

"In a very nice way, Mrs. Miller," and he moved towards her to return her kiss.

It had been so long since he felt a deep connection with anyone, let alone a woman that he was attracted to. And so one kiss led to another and time and space lost all meaning. They both had sand in their hair by the time they sat up and took several deep recovering breaths.

The moon was high and to the east now and its light flitted on the tops of the waves. The wind had dropped and the air was soft and warm.

"I was here earlier this evening, wishing that you could be with me and here you are. It makes me hopeful that all my wishes might come true."

"Pray tell, Mr. Sparling, what are all of your wishes?"

Percy sat up tall, his tone becoming serious. He paused to gather his thoughts. He did not want to misrepresent himself.

"Mary, I will be leaving Niagara tomorrow. I plan to move until I find a peaceful place where I can build a home and live a purposeful life. I have been wandering alone for too long. If you would join me once I am settled or if you would come away right now, I believe I couldn't be happier."

Percy was staring out on the lake as he stated his proposal. Mary was looking up into his face. When he finished, he met her gaze. There was an awkward pause and then Mary kissed him again.

"Mr. Sparling, my employment obligations are until the end of this month. I believe that I will be asked to continue on with the Falconbridge's but should something else arise,... should there be some other proposal,....." and her voice faded.

He kissed her again. Her responsiveness was confirmation enough for him and his mind frantically began working out the logistics of communicating and sending for her, even though he had no idea where he was going. When he began to verbalize this she pressed her fingers to his lips and said,

"Let us enjoy this," as she turned to the moonlit water. He put her arm around her and they sat for a long time looking out at the lake. An owl hooted mournfully into the night and Mary shivered.

"I should be getting you back. It is late," suggested Percy half-heartedly but when she stood and began shaking the sand from her dress, he stood as well. She grasped his hand and they silently walked back to the hotel. Percy let her guide him up the service stairs to the first balcony. Outside his door, Mary kissed him again. He brushed the hair from her cheek and soaked in the gentle curves of her face. He leaned in to kiss her again but she pulled back and smiled.

"Good night Mr. Sparling. Pleasant dreams," and she quickly turned back towards the service stairs.

"Good night Mrs. Miller," and with those words he withdrew his key and pushed it into the lock and the door swung open into his room. The deadbolt was not engaged.

"What the?" Percy said loudly. He looked at the open door in disbelief. He knew he had locked it before he left. He had felt the bolt slide into place.

"Mary!" he called out loud. She had almost gotten to the staircase when she turned and tried to calm him.

"Shush darling. You'll wake the dead," she whispered.

Percy's mind was racing and so was the fury that was building inside of him. All of his plans for the future rested on him delivering the plans tomorrow. Without the plans, he had no future. He took three long strides into the room and opened the top drawer of the bureau to find it empty. How? Who? The documents were there just before Mary came to call. He had checked. He had put them in the drawer, closed it and locked the deadbolt on his door. How could this have happened? Who knew where he was and what he had?

Mary's silhouette was in the doorway.

"Mary, did you tell anyone that I was here?"

"No, darling, but you did tell Mrs. Clements and Fiona. They told me."

"But how could they know I'd be out of my room?" said Percy. He was stepping towards Mary and something in the way she stepped back into the hallway made him lunge forward and grab her arm.

"Mary, tell me you had nothing to do with this!" His voice was loud and jagged.

"Percy, I don't know what you mean. Let go. You are hurting me." She shook her arm free and lunged for the adjacent room. She swung open the door to room fifteen and nearly had it closed but for Sparlings foot. He burst through the door throwing Mary against the wall. Sparling stood in the doorway in rage focused on the trembling woman stepping toward him. Percy pushed her backward and pinned her to the wall.

"Who else knew I was here?" Percy demanded.

"No one Percy. I didn't even know until you came today."

"I knew Sparling," came a deep voice from the bed.

Percy kept his palm on Mary's shoulder and held it to the wall while turning to see the outline of Jesse Ward sitting on the bed. In the dimness of the room, he was just a silhouette, a man holding a gun, but Percy knew his voice.

"Let her go."

A cloud descended over Percy's heart. The betrayal he felt fell swiftly and the rage inside him burst open. He could feel the floor falling away and then his anger lifted him, spinning him like a hurricane. He faced Mary again, his eyes burning with rage.

"How could you?" With his powerful hand he reached up and clenched her jaw.

"I said let her go," and a blast from a revolver deafened the three of them. The projectile sent splinters of wood in every direction and as the room filled with acrid smoke Ward moved to block the door. Percy released Mary and spun to face Ward but before Jesse could fire another shot, Mary in fluid motion pulled her knife from her sleeve, pressed the button to spring it open and from behind, pulled the blade across Percy's throat.

The blade met little resistance as it sliced through his larynx. For an instant, all three of them stood assessing the situation. Jesse held the gun point blank at Percy's chest, Mary had fallen back ready to stab or slash again with her knife and Percy stood holding both of his hands to his throat. The pain of the wound had not registered. The pain he felt was betrayal and he rounded on her once more. His giant hands had clenched into fists above his head and as Mary cowered low another shot rang out. This time it hit its mark and Percy could feel the piercing fire enter his back and lodge into his lung. His fists hit the wall as Mary rolled away. He could hear his own ragged breath as he inhaled and knew that he had to escape. With one great shove he pushed himself off of the wall and as he was charging toward the door put his shoulder into Ward. Jesse crumpled to the floor in a heap as the revolver skittered across the floor. While Ward and Mary lie side by side, Sparling staggered out of the door. They could hear him stumble away along the landing.

"Did you get them?" gasped Mary.

Jesse struggled to get up. "You alright?"

"I'm fine. Did you get them?" she asked again.

"Yes. Under the pillow."

"Jesse, it's better if I cut you."

"Huh?" He was still recovering from the collision.

"You're going to have to fall for this and it's better if I cut you. It will make things easier."

"Do what you must."

And with that, Mary put her thumb on the tip of Ward's nose and forced it up to expose his throat.

"Not too deep," Jesse pleaded.

With great concentration Mary used her knife to cut a straight line from his chin to his collarbone taking great care to avoid major arteries.

"Ow, I said, not too deep."

Mary stood and tossed him a towel.

"Stay there. I'll take care of the plans. I was never here."

She walked to the bed, turned over the pillow, seized the plans for the construction of the Welland Canal and left the Park House Hotel, slipping into the darkness of the night by the service stairs.

While Percy was making his escape his breathing became increasingly laboured. He staggered along the balcony leaving small splatters of blood along the glossy floorboards. Each step was heavier than the last and he could feel gravity pulling him down the stairs and into the lobby. One lamp glowed faintly from the desk and he saw a door swing open and more light spill onto the floor as he pushed himself towards the exit. He thought he heard his name being called. When he passed through the entrance door of the hotel, he realized that he wasn't breathing anymore. Percy felt like he was underwater and his legs pumped up and down though he didn't feel the floor. He felt like he was floating. The cottages on the street before him became rocks and corals and the trees, towering kelp waving in the surf. He felt the cold of the ocean creeping into his body. The lamp at the Montreal Telegraph office swam in front of him. Its orb pulsed and shifted and he heard his name again and in that light, he could see the face of his mother, Sarah Sparling reaching out to him. He could feel her hand in his and they were both swimming to the surface. She pointed to the bottom of a skiff that Percy knew as his grandfather's. He and his mother would reach up and scare the old man again and so, with outstretched arms he reached up and kicked with all his might to the surface. They were in the bay off of Skerries and soon he would be laughing in the arms of the only people he ever loved. He was getting closer and closer to the boat rising through the dark water and into the light. When he broke the surface, there was nothing.

"Dad? Dad, how much of this is true? How could you know what Percy Sparling was thinking when he died? How could you know what happened at the Welland Canal? How could you know what went on between Percy and Mary? How much of this are you making up?" challenged John.

There was more interest in his voice than condemnation. He was accusing his father but at the same time the tone of his voice revealed that he had been seduced by the story just as I had been. We'd been sitting now for over ninety minutes. I had refilled our cups throughout Mr. Birk's dissertation and the tea leftover in the pot was cold. John had drained his coffee long ago.

"You know son, I've always told you never let the truth get in the way of a good story but I swear, most of what I tell you is fact."

"Most of what you've told us?"

Well actually, all of it. I have the outline of the story pretty much as it was related to me, wherever I wasn't directly involved. I just might have added a little colour to the black and white images. You know, like how a prism refracts when light passes through?"

"And who 'related' this story to you, Dad?" probed John.

"Well, that will all be revealed in good time my son."

"Uh-huh, well speaking of time, Dad, we really do need to be getting back. Mom will have set the table by now and will be expecting us both home for dinner soon."

Robert's son was teetering between disbelief and fascination with his father. I don't think John had begrudged spending the afternoon listening to the story but he wasn't going to give his father the satisfaction of knowing that he was entertained by it and it looked like his patience had worn out.

"That is so. Your Mother should not be kept waiting. Mr. Friesen, I do thank you for your hospitality. I have enjoyed our afternoon together. It has been wonderful to relive some of my glory days. And to see that fireplace. Ahhhh that brings back memories."

Robert Birk's face was glowing. His cheeks were flushed and his eyes were bright and if we hadn't run out of time, he looked like he could have kept on talking for many hours.

"Well, it was a pleasure to hear your story Mr. Birk. But when am I going to hear the rest of it? What happened to Jesse Ward? What happened to Mary Miller?" I asked.

"I guess I did just leave you hanging there, didn't I?" and he gave me a quick wink. "I think it should be arranged that you come up and visit us and

I will tell you the second part of the story. It ventures far beyond Grimsby Park and involves some pretty famous characters. Why don't you come up next weekend? Maybe you could bring a copy of that newspaper article?

"I'd love that. I'll get it copied this week," I said enthusiastically.

"John, can you write down my address for Mr. Friesen so he can come by? Why don't you come for lunch next Saturday? Son, you better make space in your busy calendar as well if you are going to hear the rest of this. It is a story that ran deeper than I ever could have imagined and it taught me that when it comes to human nature, there is always more than meets the eye."

A week later I was ringing the Birk's doorbell with a cardboard cylinder tucked under my arm. I had copied the newspaper article Mr. Birk had asked for. John answered the door.

"Welcome." John stepped back and let me into a spacious apartment. There was a pleasant view of a ravine. The building was new and the furnishings were tasteful. Whatever Robert Birk did before retirement, he did very well.

"My father is in his study. Come and meet my mother."

I followed him into the kitchen. A silver haired head was bent over a cutting board. John's mother was slicing sandwiches from corner to corner. She raised her eyes at the sound of our footsteps, smiled and began rubbing her hands on her apron.

"Welcome. We are happy to have you," she said as she held out her hand for me to shake. "I do hope you like tuna fish."

"I do Mrs. Birk. Thank you for having me for lunch."

"It is our pleasure. Robert is going to entertain you two in his study this afternoon. John, could you take this tray in? I'll be along in a moment with the sandwiches."

"You're not joining us Mother?" asked John. His disappointment was palatable. He clearly got along better with his mother than with his father. I suspected that John thought his mother's presence might moderate his father's imagination and keep the story more factual and to the point.

"No, dear. I've got some shopping to do. You three enjoy yourselves. Your father has been locked in his study in preparation. He has been looking forward to this all week."

So, I wasn't the only one. I gladly followed John who reluctantly carried the tray around the corner, down the hall to a large oak door. John gently kicked the bottom of the door with his toe as if to knock.

"Don't kick the door!" came a shout from inside.

John turned to me with a look that said, "Are you sure you want to do this?" I just smiled while fondling the cylinder in my hand. It felt like my admission to Mr. Birk's office and I was anxious to present it to him and hear Part Two of his story. John was decidedly less enthusiastic.

We entered the room. John set the tray on a coffee table that sat between a leather couch and a large leather armchair. Mr. Birk's office was big. It held a wide desk that was covered with stacks of papers, file folders and photos. On the wall behind the desk was a bulletin board pinned with more of the same. Mr. Birk was a busy man.

"Welcome Mr. Friesen. It is a pleasure having you here. I hope you don't mind if we eat our lunch in my office. My reference material is here so if I need to show John here," and he nodded in his son's direction, "any material proof, it will be more expedient to do it here than in the dining room. Besides, Mrs. Birk has some shopping to do so we can 'bach' it here if you don't mind?"

Just then Mrs. Birk swooped into the room, added a plate stacked with sandwiches to the table, leaned to kiss her husband on the cheek and said,

"Have a grand time boys. I'm off to shop. Nice to meet you Mr. Friesen, lovely to see you my son and don't bore these boys too much Robert." She closed the door behind her as she left.

Mr. Birk picked up a large manilla envelope from the table beside him and tossed it into the lap of his son. The corners of the package were worn and discoloured and John had to unwind a string that held it closed. This was something Mr. Birk had held onto for some time.

"What is this, Dad?"

"Reference material. Thought you might require it."

John withdrew a stack of paper an inch thick and started to read. Meanwhile, Mr. Birk lifted one of the triangular sandwiches to his mouth, took a bite and suggested he get started as there was much to cover. While John's eyes rolled across the pages in his hands, I sank down into the couch and listened to Robert Birk continue his story.

PART TWO

RING THE BELL

It was an unofficial delegation of concerned citizens that took the train into St. Catharines. They told themselves and the ones they left behind that they were going to support those who were subpoenaed in the trial of Jesse Ward. Penelope Clements, Officer Belcher and Dr. Campbell were called to the stand and their neighbours wanted to be there to see that justice was done. They told the envious who gathered on the platform that they were going to ensure that peace and tranquility would return to their beach community and that they would etch each detail into their memory to relate upon their return.

Meanwhile, Jesse Ward was confined to a cell in the Town of Grimsby. He had only spent time in jail once before. He was once rounded up in a raid on a Winnipeg Publisher that was printing pamphlets for Trade Union Organizers. His mission was to infiltrate the group, gain their trust and then inform his boss of their actions. When the raid took place he was arrested with the socialists and detained. But that was just a short stint. He was in and out in four hours. This time there would be a trial and he was likely to spend several weeks alone in a cell.

The jail in Grimsby was cool and damp and small. He had a cot and a barred window and a washstand with fresh water. There was a chamber pot and the walls, ceiling and floor were washed with the same yellow ochre. It was a dismal place.

His jailor was nice enough. Henry was an older man, round and, like Jesse, talkative. Henry genuinely enjoyed having a celebrity to guard. The efforts of H. H. Wylie, the Park owner, to keep this scandal secret were wasted. The whole region of Niagara was aflame with the murder at the Park House Hotel. For two days no one talked of anything else. Murder being a rare crime, made this the most sensational news story to hit the region for years. That it happened in the idyllic milieu of Grimsby Beach was even more of a scoop. So, while Henry relished the lurid questions from passersby, Jesse sat wondering where Henry had developed such an imagination.

"He's as calm and pleasant as a kitten, until he isn't and then watch out."

"He was covered in blood when they brought him in."

"I've heard said that he and the victim were courting the same gal."

Of all the rumours and lies that were told, it was the latter that stuck. What didn't stick, much to the chagrin of Henry the jailor, was Jesse Ward's celebrity. Only two days after Percy Sparling's murder, Kaiser Wilhelm invaded Belgium and England declared war on Germany and if that didn't eclipse the murder at the Park House Hotel, the following day's declaration of war by the Dominion of Canada on Germany did. Murder on a local scale took a back seat to murder on a global scale and the hustle and bustle that followed a declaration of war sucked the steam out of the story. Henry was quite disappointed. Jesse Ward was not.

Jesse was happy to hear through Henry that the Grimsby Old Boys had met under the direction of Colonel Hugh Rose and Captain W.W. Kidd to mobilize the 44th Regiment for duty protecting the Welland Canal. With fewer visitors to gossip with, Henry had time to describe the physical features and family backgrounds of each soldier in the local regiment. Jesse's cell was windowless so while he sat captive, he was able to visualize every young face marching down Main Street en route to the Canal. He prayed that the thirty-five young men, 'Grimsby's finest' were Henry's words, would be up to the task.

Jesse was also happy, though not surprised, to learn that Judge Falconbridge would be presiding over his case.

"That Judge Falconbridge is a right fine judge. You will get a fair trial with him Mr. Ward. He will be thorough and just and if you are guilty, then he will find you guilty and if you are innocent, he will find you innocent," professed Henry.

Jesse could not suppress a snort. It took every ounce of his will power not to respond in words. He would have loved to launch into and spin a story to break the monotony, to entertain himself and his jailor.

"Don't be downhearted, Mr. Ward. The Judge is a good man and Yours Truly has put in a good word for you," Henry puffed up his chest.

"Well, thank you Henry. That is comforting."

But Jesse was not downhearted. He was amused by Henry's naivety and innocence and by extension, the general public's ignorance of what the facts really were. They spent so much time prating about the news of the day without knowing what the truth really was.

One story that concerned Jesse was the news of a fire that consumed thirty-five of the Grimsby Beach cottages. Only eight days after its first murder and five after the country had declared war, the community was struck again by tragedy. According to Henry, a coal stove was knocked over which started a chain reaction in the closely packed cottages. One burning cottage led to another and the frantic work of the bucket brigade was no match for the flames. Henry intimated that Jesse was very much involved in this string of bad events as he started it off with a murder and as everyone knows, bad things always come in threes. It was easy to slough off Henry's interpretation of the events but the idea did stick in his mind. Was the fire started by a mishap or was there a more insidious reason? Were Clan na Gael agents taking revenge for a thwarted mission or did his own agency have a cause to create a "disturbance". From time to time those in his profession created events like this to distract the enemy, to throw them off the scent or to buy time when plans were not going to schedule. If the Grimsby Fire was indeed a disturbance, Jesse Ward was not aware of it.

In some ways, it was a blessing that Ward had the fire and the war to occupy his thoughts. He had to wait nine weeks until his sentencing. In the meantime, there had been only one court appearance. Several witnesses had been called and their testimony entered into the record. Doc Campbell was first on the scene. The Doctor's cottage was only a few yards from the Hotel and his chronic insomnia allowed him an almost immediate response to the report of pistol fire on the warm and quiet night. He was the one who examined Percy Sparling. He was the one who had found a bullet wound on Percy's back and a slash on his throat. Doc Campbell recounted how Percy was alive but non-communicative when he was found and how he died shortly thereafter.

Mrs. Clements, who was one of the last people to have spoken to Mr. Sparling before his death, was hysterical while on the stand. She was a relic from Grimsby Park's campground days and her religious fervour was in full display during her testimony. She stated that while she didn't like the man, she wouldn't have wished murder on him or any of God's creatures. She said that she was shocked that such a heinous act could have been perpetrated on such a spiritual site.

Officer Belcher, in his 'state of facts' manner, described the details of the murder scene and the capture of the accused. He was quite complementary of Ward and his respectful demeanor as he was taken into custody easily and without incident.

"He is a model prisoner and a gentleman," were the officer's words.

Mary Miller was put on the stand. Jesse noted that while her dress was still black, it was new. He wondered if she might have had difficulty removing Percy's blood from her sleeves for while there wasn't much blood found near the body, he had left a considerable amount in his hotel room, on the balcony and down the stairs into the lobby. She was calm and composed on the stand. She answered all questions matter of fact, stating that she knew the deceased but that they were not romantically involved and that she hadn't seen him in a month's time. When the prosecuting attorney wanted to delve deeper into her relationship with Percy, Judge Falconbridge cut off his line of questioning saying that it was gossip-mongering and had no place in his court. In the end, very little evidence was revealed. They had a victim. They had an accused and he had pleaded guilty. Had the public not had a war to distract them, they would have been more disappointed. The who, where, what and how were known but why was never answered.

October seventh was the last day Jesse Ward saw Henry the Jailer. "They'll be sentencing you today Mr. Ward. Best of luck. I hope they go easy on you. You are a fine man."

And that sentiment was common amongst those in the court that day. Under the direction of Judge Falconbridge, the jury was to deliberate a sentence with the facts that Percy Sparling died of a bullet to the lung and that, while his throat was slit, very little blood was found by the body. No mention was given to the fact that he left a trail of blood throughout the hotel dutifully cleaned up by Vannetter. The Judge also highlighted that the accused, Jesse Ward, sustained a wound to his throat as well and possibly had to shoot Percy Sparling in self-defence. How the bullets might have ended up in Percy's back the Judge didn't explain.

While the Jury deliberated, Judge Falconbridge left the courthouse and was seen taking a walk. Many present stood to stretch their legs. Few people left. Most did not want to miss the sentencing. One woman, dressed in black, approached the accused.

"She was the one who testified," one woman observed. "Mary Miller," she whispered to her friend. Those in attendance watched Mary lean close to Ward and whisper. The message was short and acknowledged with the nod of his head. No one was close enough to discern what was said and Ward's expression did nothing to betray their secret. Those who possess an eye for subtle detail noted that she reached out with one hand and placed it on Ward's forearm and gave it a gentle squeeze. This simple act fueled the rumour that this was a crime of passion, that Percy Sparling was the unlucky vertice of a love triangle and that his passing strengthened the bond between the two survivors.

But then the woman in black, the widow, did something unexpected. She picked up a carpet bag, her luggage, turned on her heel and exited the room. Evidently, she wasn't staying for the jury's decision. The men smoking outside on the courthouse steps overheard her directing a carriage to the train station and those who knew the schedule knew that she was headed off to Toronto or some stop in between. Her departure added another layer of mystery to the story and sent those interested in the outcome through a maze of conjecture and hypothesis. Many hours were spent arguing and counter-arguing about the 'why' of this murder and the debate lingered across the Niagara Region and beyond.

The bailiff delivered the message that the jury had reached a decision and some boys were directed to find the Judge and bring him back from his promenade. Ten minutes later, Judge Falconbridge was presiding from his desk on the dais while the crowd sat balanced on the edge of the courtroom pews. The Judge gave three smart thwacks of his gavel despite the fact that he already had everyone's attention.

"Jury, have you reached a decision?" he asked.

The court foreman stood and responded, "Yes we have your Honour."

"Mr. Ward, stand to face the court," commanded the Judge.

"And what is your decision?" said the Judge, turning to the foreman.

"We had found that Percy Sparling was shot at approximately 3:45 am the morning of Sunday August 2nd and that although he sustained other injuries, he succumbed to the bullet lodged in his lung. We have found the accused, Jesse Ward, guilty of this offense but have reduced his charge to manslaughter because he also sustained wounds and that the victim entered his room uninvited suggest that he was acting in self-defence."

A quiet murmur bubbled up from the crowd, which the Judge quickly interrupted.

"Thank you, Foreman, and thank you jury for your time and energy in reaching this verdict. Mr. Ward, you are sentenced by this court to serve 10 years less 35 days in the Portsmouth penitentiary at Kingston. Do you have any final words to say to this court?"

All eyes turned to Ward who was looking down at the defense table. Everyone waited while Jesse composed his thoughts, hoping that he would deliver the answers that they wanted to hear. Ward glanced furtively at the Judge and then down again. He was not distraught but appeared shy to speak. There was something that he wanted to say and Judge Falconbridge gave him one more opportunity.

"Mr. Ward, if there is something you wish to say to the Court, you best say it now."

Jesse looked at the Judge and then the Jury and said in a calm voice,

"I believe my sentence is fair and just."

There was a long pause when no one said anything. Most in the audience including the Judge sat with their mouths open, fully expecting more words to spill from Ward's lips, but none did. The silence was broken when the Judge gave three more raps of his gavel and declared the Court adjourned. The throng stood to add Jesse Ward's final words to the list of peculiar characteristics of the case and they took the discussion outside and to their homes and taverns to continue it there.

A detail of the case that the public never found out was that Jesse Ward served only fourteen more days of his sentence. He was transferred that day to Kingston where he was housed in solitary confinement but with warm meals and plenty of reading material. Without Henry the jailor to keep him abreast of the war in Europe, Jesse used the daily papers. To his great pleasure the news sheets were current and up to date. The war news was buoyantly optimistic and a welcome distraction, for Jesse found the oppressive emotion of regret creeping into his thoughts whenever he wasn't reading.

He felt sympathy for Percy Sparling and for all men like him impassioned by political turmoil and imbalance. As a young man, he himself had been pulled into a battle that really had nothing to do with him. He knew the seductive attraction conflict had on young men but unlike most, Percy had a real and legitimate reason to fight. The government to which Jesse Ward was employed did everything to impose English Rule on the Catholic inhabitants of Ireland and to some extent, suppress their influence here in Canada. Jesse knew the view from the other side. He understood Sparling's motivation to interrupt British supply lines, to sabotage a major artery of transportation, to disable the Welland Canal. That Sparling died for this cause was made all the more distressing because it was by Jesse's hand and in his mind, it didn't need to go that way.

On the twenty-first of October, a guard told him to gather his belongings and follow. They left solitary confinement and meandered through half a dozen barred gates and cell blocks to reach the outer walls. Ward was only a passing curiosity to the other inmates. From the cells along the main corridor, they watched him come and go. He had had no contact with any other inmate and met only a few guards. His stay was unusual and short and mysterious.

With his bundle under his arm, he took a deep breath as he stepped out into the courtyard. Today, on the east side of Lake Ontario it was raining and foggy and when he was marched out to the main gate, he could see the fuzzy outlines of two individuals standing at the entrance to the prison. Behind them, a long car parked on the street. The guard removed his hand cuffs and pointed towards the two standing in the rain. After a dozen steps he recognized the Warden standing beneath his black umbrella with Mary Miller. She was dressed in a long blue coat, a matching hat and she held a blue umbrella. They both turned to look at Jesse as he approached.

"Thank you, Warden. The Minister sends his gratitude," said Mary.

"You are most welcome Miss Black. It was my pleasure," said the smiling Warden. She had obviously charmed him as well. The Warden turned away and headed back into the gates.

Mary slid her arm through Jesse Ward's and led him back to the car.

"Nice to see you in something other than black, Miss Black," said Jesse.

"You don't know how nice it is!" replied Mary.

"I see the Judge himself is on the welcoming committee."

"He has another job for you," she said.

The driver opened the door for the two new passengers and Jesse and Mary slid into the sedan beside Judge Falconbridge.

THE PURSUIT OF HANS TAUSCHER

"Robert, you will arrive at my office at 6 am each day and every day except Sunday when you will have the morning off. On Sundays you will start at the strike of twelve."

I was being instructed by Mr. Vannetter about my hours. My brother Jacob got the same speech when he was taken on by the hotel but now that he was guarding the Welland Canal with twenty-nine of the other "Grimsby's Finest", I was to take his place. My first real job.

Some would say that I was a little young for employment but now that the war was on, the bookings for the hotel had dropped off and the responsibilities diminished in kind. Moreover, with young men champing at the bit to leave their family farms and their predictable dead-end jobs, there was a shortage of labourers and my familiarity with the Park House Hotel made me a perfect candidate for the position.

"Discretion is the first virtue of all employees. You are not to discuss the comings and goings of guests or visitors and you must never approach a guest or a visitor outside the property of our establishment. Is that clear?" asked Vannetter.

I nodded that I understood but I also knew that Mr. Vannetter was a hypocrite. He participated in great volumes of gossip regarding hotel guests with Cook. In their late evening smoking sessions, the mannerisms, relationships and financial success of the Park House guests were favourite topics as they stood on the landing behind the kitchen unaware that I was casually sitting beneath them petting my dog.

"Punctuality is the second virtue. I expect you to abide by the times I have laid out for you. You must be prompt and you must be dressed and ready. Your brother Jacob was a model employee and I expect you to follow in his footsteps."

"Yes, Mr. Vannetter. I understand. Thank you for hiring me Mr. Vannetter," I said, in an attempt to stop him talking. Jacob had repeated this speech word for word so many times that I wanted to interrupt and hopefully distract my boss before he got to the third virtue of being a Park House Hotel employee. But Vannetter would not be deterred.

"And the third virtue is honesty. If you see something amiss, it is your duty to inform me directly. I will not take any infraction of this lightly. Not disclosing information will result in your termination. Is that clear?"

"It is Mr. Vannetter. It is clear." What was really clear was that Mr. Vannetter was desperate for someone to load and unload wagons, haul water and laundry up and down the stairs, collect shoes and boots to be shined and every other manner of task the job called for.

"Good then Robert. You must go and see Cook. He has some work for you."

I left my boss at his desk and made my way to the kitchens. The cook and his two assistants were enveloped in the oppressive humidity created by the myriad of boiling pots and saucepans bubbling on the stoves. I found the cook instructing one of his underlings on the correct consistency of ham gravy. Seeing me approach from the corner of his eye, he turned my way and said,

"Hey there Toke. I hear they will be paying you a full wage here from now on."

Cook is a jovial fellow and I liked the fact that he called me by the name everyone else called me. Only my teacher at school and Mr. Vannetter call me Robert.

"That's right Cook. Mr. Vannetter said that you have something you need me to do?"

"Bins need to be emptied and the linens just came in. You can fold them. John will show you how."

I nodded to John who was busy stirring a pot and then I went to collect the trash from the bins around the kitchen. The discarded leaves and seeds and cores of the fruits and vegetables used for the day's menu went into a corral of sorts behind the hotel. It rotted away for a day or two before the driver and I forked it onto his flatbed wagon and he took it away to fertilize someone's orchard. I dumped the garbage and went back into the steamy room. John gave me a lesson on folding linens. Before Iong, I had mastered tablecloths, napkins, and the long runners that sat beneath the weekend buffets. He even taught me the subtle arts of being a sous-chef. He showed me how to stir a sauce without burning the pot and how to clean a pot when I got distracted from stirring.

As I would come to learn, John had an overdeveloped sense of responsibility. This became obvious to me when he enlisted. I realized that he was teaching me his job. He was worried that Cook would be left short-handed when he went off to kill some Huns. It was regrettable that his sense of responsibility to his King also got him killed in a trench at Pachendalle. So as weeks turned to months, I got John's job along with my own. I still had to unload wagons, and take out the trash but the occupancy of the hotel continued to decline as the war rolled on so adding sous-chef to my list of jobs never became more than I could handle.

On a spring day the previous year, my brother Jacob had delivered a large and corpulent woman to the front of the hotel. I had just finished hoisting some luggage up onto a departing wagon when Mr. Piott, who owned the fanciest carriage in the Park, was delivering the same lady to precisely the same spot in front of the hotel veranda. He was helping the woman down. She held onto his hand for dear life as she teetered on the small step and in the end Mr. Piott had to catch her as she fell off of the stool. The scene and her European accent triggered my memory. At that time, she had been accompanied by an older man with a broad moustache, but today a much younger man followed her out of the carriage. I offered my assistance.

"You will take our bags to the lobby." He demanded.

I nodded and noted that besides not having any manners, that he carried the same Germanic accent. On one arm he led his companion up the stairs, while in the other arm he carried a small dark valise. He had it tucked tightly against his body. It was clear that this was a piece of luggage that he alone would be carrying up to his room. While I set their first load of luggage down in the lobby, he went to the registry desk while the large woman collapsed on the circular settee positioned in the center of the foyer. Her legs were splade out in an indelicate manner and she was fanning herself with a lace kerchief. She looked overheated.

"Young man, could you fetch me a glass of water?" she asked.

"Right away Madam" and I reversed directions and headed toward the kitchens.

I was nearly out of the lobby when I heard the man shout at me from the reception desk,

"Where are you going? I told you to bring our bags to the lobby!"

It was an uncomfortable situation. There was no way to please both of them and with Mr. Vannetter right there to observe my actions I froze, but only for a second. In my momentary hesitation I sided with the woman's thirst over the man's boorishness. He stomped his foot when I turned and went to the kitchen. I avoided the man's gaze as I strode through the lobby with the glass of water. He was, at that moment, being rude and demanding to Mr. Vannetter who, to my pleasure, had no more success with him than I. I gave the woman her water and fled out the door for their luggage. When I returned the man was standing amongst his bags while Vannetter was helping the woman to her feet. The man motioned me to follow him up the stairs and I hurried to keep up. Of course, he was only carrying his valise under his arm and with his long legs, took the stairs two at a time. He turned to the left at the top of the stairs, walked along the balcony past two doors and stopped at room five.

"Place the brown luggage here for Madame Gadski. That black one and the ones left in the lobby you will deliver to my room, room four."

As I dropped the brown bags I noticed that embossed beneath each handle in gold was the name, Madame Johanna Gadski. As I read the name I remembered Jacob describing to my mother that she was a famous singer. I shuffled down the hall and found the door to room four ajar as the man had already opened and entered. I placed his black bag just inside the door and made my way down to the lobby for the other bags. I met an out of breath Madame Gadski who was on the arm of an out of breath Mr. Vannetter. He had expended much of his own energy supporting her as she climbed the stairs. I moved quickly down to the lobby and was back with the remaining bags before the Madame had entered her room. Mr. Vannetter, sweat on his brow, gave me a pleading look and was about to ask me to assist him assisting her but I swooshed past without giving him a chance to open his mouth. I was on my way to room four where to my great disappointment, the man was waiting for me.

"The large bag goes on the bed. The medium one goes by the washstand and the small one goes on that chair. I will leave my boots out to be polished and would like them returned by five am. I wish to have cold water in my basin at six am and a hot bath arranged for seven am. Madame Gadski and I will have our breakfast in the dining room at 8 am," and as he picked up the unused towel from the washstand and threw them at me he said, "And send fresh towels right away."

I had to bend down to pick up one of the towels that had dropped to the floor. It was a fresh towel. I had carefully folded it and placed it on the washstand the day before but I bit my tongue, picked up the towel and fled the room. I was just passing the room adjacent when Vannetter emerged. We exchanged looks of exasperation.

"Who is he?" I asked as I shrugged my shoulders.

In a rare move of tenderness Mr. Vannetter put his hand on my back and silently guided me to the top of the stairs. We had travelled several yards before he whispered in a conspiratorial tone,

"That is Franz von Papen."

He looked at me like I should know the name. I shrugged my shoulders higher. He continued as we moved down the stairs.

"Franz von Papen is a colleague of Hans Tauscher who is Madame Gadski's husband. Both Papen and Tauscher are wealthy Bavarians. They are wealthy and important patrons Robert. They are well connected and we want to make the best of impressions. Be discreet, be punctual and be honest and no matter how difficult they are, treat them like gold."

"He wants me to replace his fresh towels with fresh towels," I complained.

"Then get him fresh towels. Get him whatever he wants. They are here for four nights and they need to have the best four nights of their lives."

Vannetter was starting to wag his finger at me. Gone was the conspiratorial tone. Gone was the tenderness. I bowed my head to him and went off to the linen stores for the towels. I placed them on Franz von Papen's doorstep, knocked on the door and quickly left.

"Doesn't Bavarian mean "German"?" I asked the Cook early the next morning.

"Bavaria is a state in Germany, yes," responded Cook.

"Then why are Germans staying in our hotel when we are at war with them?"

I was helping Cook peel potatoes first thing in the morning. He had already admonished me once for cutting the pieces up too small and I found I was doing it again. There was something cathartic about the clack of the blade on the cutting board.

"Not every German is the enemy, Toke. There are German settlements all over Canada. People have been coming here from Germany for decades, just as they have been from any other country. Look at Henry Schneider. His son John signed up with all the other boys from Grimsby. Just because you're German doesn't mean you fight for the Kaiser."

"Well, I bet Franz von Papen does. He is the meanest guest we've had since I've started working here."

"I've heard that he's really taken a shine to you," Cook chuckled.

"Well, you don't have to polish his boots three times a day or bring him fresh towels every hour."

"Just remember Toke, that when you practice Discretion and Punctuality, not to be too Honest," he laughed again.

Mr. Vannetter and Cook were good friends but that didn't mean that Cook didn't poke fun at the hotel manager from time to time.

"Mr. Vannetter doesn't like him either and he likes every paying customer that comes into the lobby."

"Yes, well, we could surely use more of the paying kind. Finish up that bowl there Toke, empty the bins and then see what your Lord and Master Mr. Vannetter needs you to do. I am going for a smoke."

I did as I was told. I peeled the potatoes but when I went to empty the bins into the refuse pile I was interrupted by a well-dressed man who seemed to know who I was. He called me by my nickname.

"Toke," he said.

Assuming my working voice, I replied, "Yes, sir. How may I help you?" He looked familiar. He was thin, middle-aged and he moved gracefully. His hair well-kept and his suit tailored to fit. It was as though he had a family resemblance to someone I knew but I couldn't place it.

"I have a task I need done and you are the man to do it," he flattered.

It was something about his posture and his gait and the setting we were in. It was here behind the hotel where I had seen this man before.

"Well thank you sir. I hope I can live up to your expectations."

But his clothes were different. Was he wearing glasses the first time we met?

"You have a guest at this hotel that I know you are familiar with. I need inside his room. I need to organize his luggage."

This request gave me pause. I tilted my head and squinted at him. I imagined him without a moustache and without the glasses and put him in simpler clothes and then I remembered.

"Sir, employees of the Park House live by a set of virtues. Discretion is the first, and honesty is the third."

"And what is the second virtue?" he asked.

"Punctuality, but I hardly think that it should matter in a situation like this. It is the first and third that would keep me from honouring your request," I said haughtily.

"I respect your sense of duty. You are a model employee. Mr. Vannetter would be proud of you but this matter is of utmost importance to the war effort. You would be helping our boys in Europe to defeat Kaiser Wilhelm."

"How will 'organizing' someone's luggage help us defeat Kaiser Wilhelm? How do I know you aren't helping Kaiser Wilhelm, Mr. Ward?" I said boldly.

There was something in his manner that made me trust him. Something told me that I didn't have to fear the man accused and convicted of the only murder ever committed in Grimsby Beach. His eyes narrowed.

"That would be Mr. Wallace to you Toke. You are a very observant young man and that is a skill that should be used to help us win the war."

"I wonder what Percy Sparling would say about that?"

It was a nervy thing to say to an adult, let alone a murderer but I sensed that I was safe. My curiosity of how a man that was in the first year of a ten-year prison sentence was standing directly before me was getting the better of me. How did he escape from prison? The well-dressed man winced.

"That was a regrettable situation," he said.

And then there was silence. He was letting me absorb his words, letting them steep in an understanding. He was admitting to me that he was Jesse Ward, convicted of manslaughter, out of prison and disguised as 'Mr. Wallace'. My mind was spinning. Why would he risk coming back to the scene of his crime and why was he all but admitting who he was? I stood there with my mouth open. But then I remembered that very few people had actually come face to face with Jesse Ward in Grimsby Beach and those who attended the trial saw him from behind the prisoner's box when he was dressed in a prisoner's uniform and sitting in a prisoner's box. The man before me had disguised himself and was confident that he could pass himself off as someone new.

"Toke, you have a brother serving overseas, don't you?" He paused and let that realization weigh on me. "You can find me at the Lakeview. The sooner the better," and then he turned and disappeared around the corner of the building.

I stood there at the refuse pile for another minute with the bin in my hand before I went to see Mr. Vannetter.

WASHINGTON D. C.

“They’re abusing their accreditation!”

“While they are in this country and for as long as we stay out of this war, we will honour they’re diplomatic immunity.”

“You know he was at Veracruz.”

“I was made aware.”

“You know he's been trying to sell to Huerta.”

“Yes. He has diplomatic immunity in parts of Mexico as well.”

“And he’s been trying to buy for Germany.”

“I am aware. Is there anything new you can tell me?”

Captain Blain was sympathetic to his young lieutenant and his own flat expression hid a shared frustration. The gun lobby in his own country would sell bullets to their own execution, if it was profitable. He was trying to look calm and collected by opening one of the envelopes his secretary had placed on his desk.

“Last month Papen returned and we don’t know where he is. Smith thinks he may have crossed into Canada!”

“Well then, he does so at his own risk, doesn’t he?”

“As if? That border is like swiss cheese. You’d think they’d exert some effort protecting it.”

Blain withdrew a sheaf of photographs from the brown paper and started leafing through them.

“Do you know this woman?”

He held out the clearest image for Lieutenant Thrasher to see.

“No, but she’s a beauty, even dressed in black.”

The young Lieutenant wanted to scan the other people in the photograph for recognition but his eyes wouldn’t leave her jawline. She was looking to her left and had her fingertips pressed up against her lips as though she were stifling a giggle.

“Taken at the Irish Embassy in Sheridan Row.”

The captain was reading the notes that came with the photos.

"That's Johanna Gadski in behind and I'm sure that's Tauscher just behind her," observed Thrasher when he was able to tear his eyes away from the outline of the torso dressed in black silk.

"Take these," Blain said abruptly, handing over the rest of the photos, "and find out who she is."

"Thanks Captain. This is the nicest assignment you've ever given me."

"Just stay on task Lieutenant. We don't need any more complications than we are already dealing with. Dismissed."

Lieutenant Jeremy Thrasher knew the 'dismissed' meant that the conversation was over. That his Superior Officer was finished listening to his complaints about the rights and freedoms of the military attachés to the German diplomat to the United States of America. He was out of Blain's office and just passing his secretary's desk when she said,

"Message for you. Came while you were meeting with Captain Blain."

"Thanks Miss Redstone."

"Any chance that 'thank you' could be in the form of a nice quiet dinner?" she asked.

Captain Blain's secretary was good at her job. She had worked her way up from the typing pool to assisting progressively higher-ranking officers. Her goal was to work for a General one day but her ascent seemed to have stalled with the captain.

"Sorry Miss Redstone, I have plans tonight."

"It doesn't need to be tonight. I just need a date to put on my calendar," she drawled, batting her eyes.

"Sorry, Miss Redstone. I have plans then too."

He turned and smiled and even though it was the fourth time she had failed to make a date with the Lieutenant, she still melted as he walked away. Lieutenant Jeremy Thrasher was ruggedly handsome and it made an impact on nearly every female at the Bureau. The supervisor of the typing pool claimed that the productivity of her typists dropped ten percent every time he walked through their office. She said he alone was costing the government thousands of dollars in distracted looks and type-o's.

He opened the envelope on his way down the hall, read the four words typed on the page and stopped abruptly. He read it a second time before changing direction and heading towards the foyer and the doors that exited onto the street.

It was three blocks to the Central Police station and Lieutenant Thrasher knew that he could get there in 9 minutes at a brisk walk but today was hot and muggy. Three months and he still had not acclimatized to the humidity of this city and he was sweating profusely before he had walked half a block. The streets today were unusually busy and he couldn't help but notice that these pedestrians were well dressed and in a jovial mood. One man carried an armful of banners over his shoulder, the colours and messages carefully rolled up. He was surrounded by a harem of white blouses and dark skirts and wide hats billowing with flowers. At each intersection, this group was joined by another one of similar in size and composition until Lieutenant Thrasher found his way impeded by the foot traffic. He was caught in the flow of the crowd and he resolved to slow his pace instead of pushing his way through.

Just in front of the Criminal Investigations Precinct the entire group was stopped as a heavy wagon pulled by two heavy drays crossed the street in front of them. It was a paddy wagon manned by five constables, their boots and badges glinting in the sun, their presence sucking the frivolity of the crowd. Many in the crowd flinched at the sound of the heavy metal wheels grinding over the cobblestones as it trundled past.

By the time Thrasher broke free of the herd and entered the revolving door of Precinct Twelve, he was soaked. The desk sergeant was occupied but looked up and nodded in the direction of the captain's office. There was familiarity and respect between the men in uniform and they were able to communicate effectively without any words. Thrasher knocked on the office door and didn't wait for an invitation. He stepped inside and closed the door behind him.

"Ah, Lieutenant. Glad you could make it. I'd like you to meet Paul Koeing. They picked him up yesterday trying to light a bonfire on 13th Avenue, in Brooklyn."

The detective was speaking to the Lieutenant but looking at the short and dishevelled man sitting on a metal chair in the corner of the office. He had been handcuffed to a water pipe that was coming out of the wall.

"Good evening, Mr. Koeing. I've been following your work. You have been a busy man."

Koeing just glared at his captors. He was tired but still angry. "Maybe you can tell me why I had to ride in the back of a paddy wagon all night long?"

"Because you have been committing Federal offenses Mr. Koeing and for this reason, we had you brought to D.C."

It was a straightforward and accurate answer but it also served to intimidate him. Paul Koeing shifted and sat straight up in his chair. He knew that Federal offenses carried a heavier penalty and that his clean record in New York would carry little weight in a Washington Court.

"What do you mean 'Federal' offense?"

"I mean that you are working for a foreign office carrying out acts of terror on American soil. In a federal court of law this can be interpreted as espionage or an act of war and can be punishable by death."

"What do you mean 'Foreign' Office?"

"I mean that your instructions and no doubt your pay come from a country that is currently at war with the entire British Commonwealth and many European countries. You should be more careful who employs you, Mr. Koeing."

Koeing looked like a trapped animal. Both the Police Captain and the Army Lieutenant guessed that Koeing didn't know who he was working for, that he just collected his money and instructions and carried out the fire bombings without ever understanding the real purpose of his attacks. Still they used every tool and lever they had to turn him and it appeared to be working.

"Mr. Koeing, I can tell you, with great accuracy, where and when you planted each bomb. I can tell you specifically the explosive and the method of detonation you prefer and I can even tell you how your boss chooses his targets. I might even be able to predict future targets. Your footsteps are that easy to follow."

The Lieutenant paused and let that sink in before continuing.

"Your capture was inevitable and so is your conviction. I can promise the latter will be swift and so will the punishment. The United States Government is not at war at the moment but it still views the bombing of its citizens as terrorism."

Another pause.

Koeing was squirming in his seat. He was flushed and exhaling short bursts and it was through these puffs of air that he said, "I didn't know."

"Pardon me Mr. Koeing. Did you say something?" asked Thrasher.

"I said, I didn't know. I never knew who I was working for."

The admission was recorded by the captain in the case file. The sound of his pen scratching on the paper dominated the room.

"But you could know, couldn't you, Mr. Koeing?"

The Lieutenant was pacing around the room with slow rhythmic steps and tapping his fingertips together in front of his face. He looked like he was in deep thought. Koeing said nothing, so Thrasher continued.

"You are a private investigator when you are not an arsonist, isn't that right Mr. Koeing? You could, using your investigation skills, learn more about your employer? It could make a big difference in your sentencing if you could gather some information for us."

In the stillness and silence that followed, Koeing gave a brief and defeated nod.

"Good! Make the arrangements, Captain. I'll clear it upstream. Good day Mr. Koeing. It was a pleasure to meet you and I know we will meet again. Captain, may I speak to you outside?"

The two uniforms left Koeing chained to the plumbing, crossed the foyer and exited the building. It was not uncommon for these two to meet outside. Their conversations often involved sensitive topics and the open air provided a privacy that the Precinct could not. Today however, the street was anything but private. The crowd Thrasher had followed down fourth street had assembled at the corner of the building. Banners and flags had been unfurled and as the throng shuffled into position a beautiful woman sitting atop a white steed came front and foremost. She wore an ivory robe bordered with gold braid. Her long tresses were bejeweled with a tiara and a matching broach.

"Suffragettes." said Lieutenant Thrasher. "How did you get the honour?"

"Mayor requested that they start and end their parades here. Some of our more stalwart citizens made some threats last time and it's easier for us to keep an eye on things if they start and end here at the station."

"Who is the rider?" Thrasher noticed that while the princess sat on top of the horse, a man in army uniform stood beside holding the reins.

"That is Inez Milholland. Wrote for the Tribune as a war correspondent until her pacifist views got her sent home. Italy threw her out of the country. She's a privileged socialite who thinks her voice is more important than it is."

"Not a friend of the Suffragettes, Captain?

"They've been asking for the vote for how many years? Over a decade? And the goings on in England, what with smashing windows and burning post boxes. Where does it end? And I'm not convinced that dressing up like Joan of Arc and bunging up Pennsylvania Avenue is going to amount to anything. It's just going to anger the masses."

"There are some provinces of Canada that are about to extend the right."

"Maybe so, but what do I care what goes on up there? I've got to keep the peace here in the capital and the likes of Ms. Milholland doesn't make my job any easier."

"I sympathize with you Captain, my condolences. Now about our Mr. Koeing. Could you make sure that he has a good steak dinner before he is sent back to New York and that he is released from the 9th Precinct in Manhattan in broad daylight? For him to be of any use to us he needs to be welcomed back into the arms of Clan na Gael as soon as possible.

The Police officer nodded his head. "I will make it so," and he left Thrasher watching the demonstrators file in behind the Grand Marshall of the parade. The Lieutenant was joyful. This was a very lucky turn of events. While the Bureau knew much about the bomber's methods, they had no clues as to who he was. Just how they came to arrest him was a detail that he would seek out later. Right now, he had to process the paperwork that would turn Mr. Koeing into a free man and a double agent.

THE LIST

Mr. Vannetter had a list. I mean, Mr. Vannetter always had a list but this morning he had a list just for me and the title of this list was 'Papen'. I don't mind having many jobs to do. It makes the work less onerous and breaks up the monotony of menial labour but I did mind that every task on the list was a personal job for the rude and unpleasant man in room four. It was as though I had become his personal butler and I resented Vannetter for letting it happen.

"Can't Agnes do some of these?" I whined.

"Mr. Papen has specifically asked for you Robert. Now do your job well. Remember, discretion, punctuality and hon,......."

"Honesty!" I interrupted. "Yes, I know. Honesty. Well, I honestly would rather stuff this list,"

"Robert!" Vannetter interrupted. "Mind your manners and do your job with pleasure!" he said angrily. It didn't sound like my boss was finding much pleasure in his job either.

The list was exactly twenty-two items long, was largely repetitive and mostly had to do with Papen keeping his face and boots clean. I'd missed items one to nine that morning but was expected to fulfill the rest of the day's requirements from then on. The list looked like this;

1. 6:30 am Hot water for washstand
2. 6:35 am Cold water for washstand
3. 6:36 am Fresh Towels
4. 7:00 am Brush suit, Buckle polish
5. 7:05 am Boots - polish and dubbin
6. 7:30 am Breakfast Reservation, Clean Room
7. 8:30 am Boots - polish and dubbin, Brush suit
8. 8:35 am Hot Water for washstand
9. 840 am Fresh Towels
10. 9:00 am Post Delivery
11. 10:00 am Coffee
12. 11:00 am latest newspaper
13. 12:00 noon lunch reservation
14. 1:00 pm Cold water for washstand
15. 1:05 pm Fresh Towels

16. 1:15 pm Boots - polish and dubbin
17. 4:00 pm Cold water for washstand
18. 4:05 pm Fresh Towels
19. 5:00 pm Brush suit
20. 5:15 pm Dinner Reservations
21. 8:30 pm Warm Water for washstand
22. 8:35 pm Fresh Towels

As it was already past nine am, I avoided the task of posting his mail, deciding that he could do it himself, so I went to see Cook to make sure there was some fresh coffee for the Lordship's ten am coffee break. In the time between, I attended to my other duties which that morning included helping Mr. Swanson unload his wagon into the Hotel storeroom.

"So how is your family keeping Toke?" Mr. Swanson asked.

"Well Dad is spending much of his time at home working but Mother is here. She is working with Women's Auxiliary. They are gathering rations and writing letters."

"And how is your older brother?"

"Jacob will soon be off to Europe. He has spent the last ten months with the 44th guarding the Canal. They've been training all the while and he and several others are ready to fight."

"Well, I wish him the best. Tell your mother that for me. And how are things here at the hotel? My wagon load is a lot lighter these days."

"We're down to half on the weekends and nearly empty throughout the week and there are some strange guests. Really demanding and uppity."

"These are strange times. Makes me feel uppity from time to time."

We finished with the load and I went to the kitchen to see how I could assist Cook but the kitchen was empty. I knew Cook's habits and routines so I started to clean and straighten up the counters and that is when I noticed Cook's list. I was halfway through reading about how Papen liked his eggs when Cook came through the bifold doors.

"That's my list," Cook said with disgust. "I thought you were exaggerating when you were describing how persnickety he is. What a pompous child!"

"That pompous child is going to want his coffee in five minutes. Can I take what is in this pot?"

"You can, and add this to his tray," and Cook placed a shortbread biscuit on a porcelain plate embossed with the Park House Hotel label.

"Always go above and beyond," Cook said with a flourish.

"I would like him to go above and beyond," and I looked suggestively up to heaven. Cook smiled and gave me an encouraging pat on the shoulder, guiding me towards the service stairs.

"Good luck. Give him my regards."

I skillfully guided the tray up the narrow stairs, walked around the balcony to the front of the building and set the tray on a small table to the left of the door. I knocked briskly three times, picked up the tray again and stepped back. The door swung open immediately and Papen stood there in his crisp suit scanning me up and down. He wasted no time in berating me.

"You missed the nine o'clock post. You will have to take it now before the train leaves."

"Of course." I said obediently.

"And you are using too much dubbin," he said, staring down at his boots. "I had a devil of a time getting it off my hands last evening. How am I supposed to dine with grease all over my fingers?"

"I will be more careful today, sir." I set down the tray on the table and when I turned around, he was holding out an envelope.

"This must go out immediately," he commanded, "and be sure my eleven o'clock paper is today's paper."

I don't think he could see the steam coming out of my ears but I swear my blood was boiling. I did my best to keep my emotions in check as I left the room with the envelope. I descended the main stairs into the lobby and waved the envelope at Vannetter when he tried to get my attention and kept going out the front door without saying a word. I was still fuming when I crossed the street and climbed up the stairs to the Montreal Telegraph Company.

The Telegraph service was really only one of the services provided here. It was a general store and sold anything from medicines to souvenirs and it handled all of the post for the community. I was striding my way to the post wicket at the back of the store and recognized Jesse Ward, a.k.a. Mr. Wallace, studying the label on a bottle of hair tonic at the end of the aisle. He caught my eye briefly, placed the bottle back on the shelf and disappeared from view behind a display of canned peaches. I continued toward the post-box. It hadn't occurred to me before, but the sight of Ward made me look at and read the address on Papen's letter before I slipped it through the slot. My nine am task completed, I turned around and exited the store. I was on the first step when I heard,

"Hey there Toke." The voice came from behind an open newspaper. A glance down at the trousers beneath told me it was Ward. He lowered the paper and smiled.

"How is your day going?" he said.

"Fine Mr. Wallace."

I emphasized his surname as I said it. I wanted to reinforce that I knew who he was and that I had the power to reveal his true identity. He didn't seem to care.

"Wonderful. I was wondering if you had given our discussion any thought?"

"No," I said. "Not really," I lied.

"Well, time is of the essence. There will only be a few opportunities," he pointed out and then paused. "I noticed that you were posting a letter. Any idea where it is headed?"

He looked at me knowing that I knew the answer. He was testing me to see if I would give him the information. I was enjoying the fact that I knew something he did not.

"I might," I said and I started descending the steps in the direction of the hotel.

"Well, I'm at the Lakeview if you remember. Have a great day," he said as I walked away.

A BLACK WIDOW IN BALTIMORE

"Who is she?"

"A paper supplier."

"A paper supplier?"

"I know. She's a little out of the ordinary, isn't she? It was her husband's business which she has taken over since his death."

"Does she have what we need?"

"She does."

"Did you do a background check?"

"I haven't had a chance. She just showed up wearing her mourning dress and carrying a box of samples. We never dealt with her husband. She seems pretty desperate to make a sale."

"Well, bring her in and let's see what we can negotiate."

The two men were trying not to be too obvious as they studied the woman waiting outside of the office. They were looking out of a glassed wall out into a waiting room where a secretary's desk sat up on a loft high above the printing presses below. It was late afternoon and the day shift was winding down. Ray Brown poked his head out of the office and beckoned her in. As he held the door open for her, he introduced his partner.

"And this is my brother Stan. Stan Brown," and he waved his hand between them, "meet Mrs. Mary Miller."

Stan stood up behind his desk and extended his hand to her. She was one of the most attractive women he had ever seen, certainly the most beautiful he'd ever seen in his shop. "It is a pleasure to meet you Mrs. Miller. Please sit down," and he pointed to a chair centered opposite his. "My brother tells me you have some product that we may be able to use?"

"Yes, I do. My company doesn't make large volumes of any one type, but we do pride ourselves on the quality." She took out a sample box that held twenty or so different sheets of paper in pristine condition.

Stan Brown rubbed each sheet between his fingers as he went one by one through the samples. He was measuring the tooth and weight of each page and he was nodding his approval as he did so.

"Excellent quality Mrs. Miller. What kinds of volume can you guarantee?"

"That would depend on what you might be selecting Mr. Brown. Our supply of bond paper is quite high right now."

"What about this one? It's cotton I believe."

"Right you are Mr. Brown. It is mostly cotton. That is a specialty paper. We don't have a large supply of that and I'm afraid that we will not be making it more of it. My husband was responsible for our formulas and while he left me his recipe book, the suppliers of some materials were lost with him."

"We're sorry about your loss Mrs. Miller," interjected Ray.

"Yes, yes, we are sorry about your tragedy," added Stan and without missing a beat he asked, "How much of this specialty paper do you have?"

"Well, it's right here in the box." She began sorting through some folders and pulled a printed sheet. She used her finger to scan down the list of products and said, "Here it is. It says here we have 25 reams."

"And how much would you sell a ream of this paper for?" asked Stan. He was still fingering, bending and folding the page measuring and taking account of its qualities.

"Would $5 per ream work for you Mr. Brown?"

The brothers looked at one another. Ray, who was behind Mary Miller, nodded his head and smiled at his brother. Stan nodded his head and responded, "Yes, Mrs. Miller, I think we can make that work. Ray, can you make up an invoice for Mrs. Miller while I write her a cheque?"

"Thankyou Mr. Brown. This is my first sale since my husband passed on and it has been difficult. I greatly appreciate your business."

"The pleasure is ours. Tell us why we have never heard of your husband's business before? He didn't sell here in Baltimore. Is it based in New York?"

"New York State, Mr. Brown. We lived in Ithaca and when he died I moved to New York City to live with my sister."

"Well, welcome to Baltimore Mrs. Miller. I do hope we can do business again. Raymond will make the pickup arrangements with you. It was nice to meet you," he said, holding out the cheque.

She took the cheque, folded it carefully into her purse and left the office. Ray scheduled the pickup and delivery with Mary, ushered her to the exit and returned to his brother's office just as Stan was removing a bottle of Canadian Club and two tumblers from the bottom of his desk. He poured two generous drinks and held one up to his brother.

"Mrs. Miller doesn't know what a deal she just made us," said Ray.

"Mrs. Miller just made us richer men," said Stan. "Pretty, but not too smart."

Mary stepped out into the street and smiled to herself. She had just spun a web.

THE LAKEVIEW

"This is today's paper?"

"Yes, sir."

"This is local news then?"

"It is what we have."

"Well, what you have won't do. I need you to order me daily copies of the Times."

"The Times sir?"

"Yes, from New York."

"Sir, we don't get the Times here sir."

"Yes, and that is why you will order it for me."

I knew that even if we could order it, it would never arrive on the same day it was printed. I didn't want to point this out to him.

"Yes sir. Will there be anything else sir?"

"Have you made my lunch reservation yet?"

"Not as yet sir."

"Well then, you could busy yourself doing that and then be prompt with my cold water at 1:00 pm."

"Yes, sir."

And so, I left just as angry and humiliated as before. I had truly come to hate the man and I think it was this emotion that drove me to the Lakeview Hotel to begin collaborating with the convicted murderer, Jesse Ward, now known as James Wallace.

The Lakeview Hotel sat on the high end of the bluff above the lake. It was a five-minute walk from the Park House, across Bell Park and up towards Spooney Bridge. It was a majestic structure, bigger than the Park House even though it didn't look like it. The three-story structure was surrounded by towering white pine which dwarfed the roof ridge and made the gingerbread peaks look like a doll house. Both of the Park hotels had their advantages and disadvantages. The Lakeview was secluded and if you were in the executive suites, you had a panoramic view of the lake. It was suited to those who wanted a quieter, more tranquil vacation. The Park House on the other hand had the advantage of being close to the general store and the Midway. It had easy access to the beach and the Auditorium and while not everyone appreciated the hustle and bustle of the Park House, it was the more popular of the two.

I went through the front doors and right up to the desk. Mr. Vannetter managed this hotel as well but the reception was manned here by Harry Nelles. I'd known him all my life. He and my brother Jacob have been lifelong friends. Just why he hadn't already enlisted and wasn't fighting beside every other eligible young Canadian, I wasn't sure. But I was happy to see him because I thought I wouldn't have to explain myself when I asked him for information about a guest.

"Hey Toke, what brings you here?"

"I've got a favour to ask Harry," I said like I was out of breath. I wanted him to think that I was in a hurry and that the information was important and time sensitive.

"No problem, Toke, what is it?"

"I've got a message for a Mr. Wallace. Could you tell me what room he is in?"

"You can leave the message here with me Toke.

"No, Harry. I've got to do the delivery. What room is he in?" I asked.

"Now Toke, you know I can't tell you that. Discretion is the first virtue of,......"

"Yes Harry, punctuality is the second and honesty is the third," I interrupted. I lowered my voice as I continued, "and if you don't tell me the room number, I'm honestly going to tell my brother Jacob that I saw you on Spooney Bridge with Becky Carlson last week and I'll do it punctually."

Being seen with the opposite sex anywhere in the vicinity of Spooney Bridge implied a romantic connection. Becky and my brother had been going steady up until the day he went off to guard the Welland Canal and I knew he wouldn't appreciate his best friend honing in on his gal. Harry's eyes were shifting left and right like he was looking for an avenue of escape. When he realized that there wasn't one, he also lowered his voice and said, "Twenty-three."

"Thanks Harry." and I ran across the lobby and bounded up the stairs. Before rapping on room twenty-three I looked left and right but there was no one on the balcony. The door opened shortly after I knocked.

"Ah, Toke. Good to see you." Jesse Ward poked his head out the door and looked left and then right. "Why don't you come in?" and he stood aside to let me pass, put his hand on my shoulder and pulled me inside his room. He spoke again, once the door was closed.

"That fact that you have chosen to come and see me suggests that you may be willing to bend your vocation's virtues for the sake of our national security."

I just nodded my head.

"And so, you need to know how you can help."

Ward paused and waited for me to nod my head again. I did.

"I need to know who Papen is corresponding with, so I need you to take notes of who and where his letters are being sent. That should be easy since your nine am responsibility is to post his mail." I must have had a surprised look on my face as I wondered how he obtained that information.

"Yes, I know of your list. I will also need to know the nature of the work he is doing. This will require a search of his desk and papers but that is my job. Your job would be to get me into his room. We might arrange this while he is dining this evening?"

He stopped and looked at me for approval. I said nothing and only nodded.

"Good then. Let's try it tonight. Five-fifteen, isn't it? How about I meet you on the service stairs at five-twenty? Don't forget the key to his room."

All this transpired so quickly, I am sure I didn't truly comprehend it all. I was speechless and I nodded again when I couldn't think of anything intelligent to say. Ward opened his door, stuck his head out and again, quickly looked left and right.

"Excellent. Off you go then. See you at five-twenty."

He stood aside and I found myself once again on the balcony alone wondering what I'd just agreed to.

WASHINGTON D.C.

"Baltimore? Are you sure?"

The Lieutenant had just been handed a briefing from agent Smith.

"That's what was relayed to me. She left Baltimore and took the train to Grand Central."

"Do we have anyone in Baltimore?"

"Not that I know of."

"Well, check. It would be nice to know what business our Black Widow has there. Did you learn anything about the Embassy?"

"Only that the activity there has increased significantly since the war began. Bills and receipts have tripled. They are doing more entertaining now than ever before. We have a contact with their catering company."

"That is valuable. Could we get some of our own to work one of their parties? It would be good to have some flies on the wall."

"I think that can be arranged."

"It would be nice to get an invite as well. I'd like to see what our Irish friends are up to."

"You sir?"

"I'm getting a little tired of sitting behind this desk. It would be nice to do some field work."

"I'll see what I can do."

"And Smith, see what our contacts in New York know about her." Lieutenant Thrasher was tapping the corner of Mary Miller's photograph. "She seems to have appeared out of nowhere and now she seems to be everywhere."

"Aye, aye, Sir!" and with an overexaggerated salute, the agent disappeared down the hall.

Thrasher eyed the stack of files before him. Every investigation regarding espionage or sabotage came across his desk and since England declared war on Germany, it grew higher each day. He slipped the photo of Mary Miller into her file, closed it and slid it into his desk and took another from the top of the pile. To his amazement and shock, the same photo of Mary Miller fell out of the next folder. There she was again, laughing at whatever Hans Tauscher was saying, with the Indian conversing with the Irishman in the background. The name on the new folder was Ram Chandra Bharadwaj.

The dossier described Ram Chandra as the new president of the Ghadar Party, a political movement bent on disrupting British Rule of India. The Party was made of expatriate Indians and it was having some success on the Pacific Coast raising funds to support resistance efforts on the Asian continent. Listed under informants was Bhagwan Singh, a Sikh national who sought political asylum in exchange for information on the terrorist activities acting within the borders of British North America. Thrasher picked up his phone.

"Miss Redstone? Is Captain Blain available?"

"Hello Lieutenant Thrasher. It is nice of you to call."

"You're most welcome Miss Redstone. Can I speak to the captain?"

"I'll put you right through."

Thrasher was tapping the edge of the file on his desk when Captain Blain answered.

"What is it Thrasher? I'm busy."

"I need to see you right away Sir. It is quite urgent."

"Very Well. But come quickly. I have meetings all afternoon."

"I'll be right there Sir. The Lieutenant retrieved Mary's file from the desk drawer, slapped it on top of the file of Ram Chandra and carried both down the hall to Captain Blain's office. He left Miss Redstone batting her eyes as he walked past her desk and entered his superior's office unannounced. The captain was in conversation with someone on the phone and directed Thrasher to take a chair. Thrasher sat while drumming his fingers on the files in his hand while tapping his toe on the linoleum tile.

"Yes, General. Socialism is a symptom of disloyalty. Yes, we will do everything in our power. Yes, you too..... I look forward to it too... Goodbye.....Yes, I know.... Goodbye.....Goodbye." Captain Blain rolled his eyes, pressed down the switch and dialed a single number. "Miss Redstone. No more calls for the next hour," and he hung up the phone. "What is it, Thrasher?"

Thrasher pulled out the photo and lay it before Captain Blain.

"Sir, I found this in two files. The first file was the woman's, the one in the photograph. The second file was the East Indian in the background. The photo was taken at a Park Ave. apartment in New York City. The East Indian is responsible for funding the resistance movement in India and the woman has been observed in Baltimore and New York City."

"Yes Lieutenant? And what does this mean?"

"Sir I believe the woman is involved in espionage attempts involving German and Indian forces."

"And?"

"And, I would like your permission to investigate."

"We have agents in New York."

"Yes, we do but none have the security clearance."

"And you think that you and you alone are the one to follow and apprehend this woman? Lieutenant, I am short-handed here. The brass upstairs has got me investigating anyone hinting at sedition. If someone bad mouths the Red Cross, or War Bonds or harbours any pacifist ideals, if they are Jewish or foreign, they fall under suspicion of the Bureau of Investigation. We aren't even at war and they are wanting us to develop a strategy against draft evasion. And you want to leave this office and go chase a skirt?"

"Sir, there isn't another agent with the perspective I have. I've seen the files on each person in this photograph. The German is Hans Tauscher, the Irishman is Clan na Gael, the Sikh funds terrorism and the one person we know least about is her. I think it would be wise for someone with my scope to investigate. I believe I am the best man for the job." Thrasher finished his plea with so much determination and confidence that Captain Blain sighed, "And how much time would you need away from your desk?"

"A week, maybe two."

Blain hesitated. "A week then but be sure you are in your office in seven days. Dismissed."

MANHATTAN

It wasn't a nice neighbourhood but it was near to her work and it was affordable. Mary dropped her carpetbag on the dusty floor and placed her key on the scarred and beat up table by the door. Life in the Dominion Police force was not glamorous. She hoped that she wouldn't have to stay here any longer than needed, but there really was no way of knowing. Things in her line of work had been heating up. Fires were popping up everywhere. It was a struggle to stay focused, to keep stories straight and not get burned by the flames.

This was her second day in this dingy apartment. It was dirty and noisy down in the financial district. The docks were nearby and the whistle blasts of steamers and freighters pierced the air throughout the day. The streets below were crowded and claustrophobic and the buildings blocked out any sunlight that would have brought warmth and light into the room. She sighed and longed for home but knew her purpose here would help protect the home she loved. Already she had made useful contacts. Posing again as a widow, she moved around the lower east side trying to find a buyer for her deceased husband's revolver. It was an 1873 Colt Single Action Army Revolver in pristine condition and in her version of the story it had been his pride and joy. Many of the shops didn't deal in used weapons but she visited them anyway under the guise that she was hoping some collector might give her top dollar for a weapon that she had no use for. This was how she found herself in the shop of Hans Tauscher at 320 Broadway.

"Good morning, Madam." The words were uttered in a soft Texan drawl, musical and friendly. "It is my pleasure to welcome you to our shop. We don't get many women in our store, let alone beautiful women like yourself."

"And good morning to you. Is Mr. Tauscher here?"

"No, Mr. Tauscher is away on business, but I can assist you on his behalf. My name is Bridgeman Taylor. How can I help you?"

"Well, I wish to sell my husband's revolver. He passed away some months ago and I am told the gun is a collector's item. I would like to get a good price for it."

"Yes, of course you would. We don't usually buy or sell used guns here at Krupp's but many of our patrons do collect firearms. We could take it on consignment if you'd care to leave it here?"

"I would not like to part with it just yet Mr. Taylor. There are many dealers in the vicinity. One of them may be prepared to buy right away."

"Yes, of course. I understand."

The conversation having taken its course, Mary sought a way to prolong it, so she started to look into the glass cases at the handguns that were for sale.

"Are you interested in purchasing a new revolver Madam? We do have the finest selection of pistols in New York City. The Luger M25 is made just for a lady's hand."

"No thank you," she said, still looking into the display case. "I'm just being nostalgic. My husband had quite a collection at one time. He spent many hours cleaning and polishing them. Being here in your shop is like being in his study."

"Was he a military man Madam?"

"He was ... of sorts. He was from a long line of Fenians, Mr. Taylor. He was always plotting against English Imperialism. His grandfather tried to invade Canada and while his father was less interested in revenge and retribution, he would have liked to have followed in his grandfather's footsteps. My husband was still in a rage about the loss at the Boyne. He was forever plotting to free North America from British rule."

"And you think that was a foolish notion?"

"No, I do not. I am quite relieved to live here in the United States. I am not a Monarchist and I think the world would be a better place if we were rid of them totally. I don't know why those people in Canada continue to bow down to an English King."

"I'm afraid, Madam, that they do more than bow down to England. They will arm and feed and fight for her."

"Yes, I suppose they do but I don't know what can be done about it. My husband's grandfather met with little success and I dare say there is not much that can be done now."

Mary continued to look at the gun cases but in truth she focused not on the contents inside. Her focus was on the reflection in the glass where she could see the shop's attendant studying her. The pause in conversation did not last long.

"You might be surprised what can be done. If I may be so bold, I would like to invite you to dine with me. We could discuss this matter further and enjoy a good meal."

"And you wouldn't mind eating with a widow Mr. Taylor?" she asked coyly.

"Not at all, it would be a pleasure. I think your husband and I would have gotten along well and I would consider it an honour to entertain his wife for an evening."

"And when might this invitation be?" she said, batting her eyes in a subtle gesture.

"Well, I was thinking of this evening. The work day is nearly done and I know a very good restaurant just around the corner. I will just close up the shop and we can go, that is, if you accept."

"I accept."

"You can leave your husband's revolver here ...forgive me, I do not know your name."

"My name is Mary Miller," and she held out her hand, which he shook gently and replied,

"It is a pleasure to meet you Mrs. Miller. As I was saying, your husband's revolver is safe here. You could pick it up tomorrow and resume your hunt for a buyer then."

"Yes, of course. Thank you."

And that is how Mary Miller met Franz Wachendorf alias Horst von der Goltz alias Bridgeman W. Taylor. At dinner Mary shared her life story which was fictitious in all of the details she thought would win the trust of a German spy. And in turn, Bridgeman Taylor described every detail of his fictitious life as a native Texan. He did not tell her that his birthplace was really Koblenz, Germany, that his American accent was fake, that he once stole a draft of a confidential agreement between Mexico and Japan that led two-thirds of the

U.S. Army to converge on the southern border with Mexico. He avoided mentioning that he had served in Pancho Villa's revolutionary army in Mexico where he changed his name to Horst von der Goltz and he neglected the fact that he was currently employed by Franz von Papen, military attaché to the German diplomat in Washington, D.C. who had organized an espionage ring for the purposes of sabotage and subversion. But it didn't matter. Mary was convinced that Bridgeman Taylor was a spy simply on the fact that he was employed at Hans Tauscher's shop and Bridgeman Taylor was suspicious of any beautiful woman who walked into a gun shop on her own. Despite their mutual suspicion, they shared a wonderful dinner and enjoyed the evening lying to one another.

On the following day, when Mary went back to Hans Tauscher's shop, Bridgeman Taylor was leaning over the counter speaking earnestly to a red headed fellow with a ruddy complexion. He was 20 years senior to Taylor with thinning hair and a large paunch. Their voices dropped as soon as she entered and the older man looked put out for being interrupted. Bridgeman, on the other hand, quickly composed himself, smiled and greeted her warmly.

"Ah Mrs. Miller, you are back for your gun." He was looking for a reaction from his companion who was surprised to see a woman in the shop, let alone a woman that owned a gun. The second man stood up and looked at her with something that resembled respect.

"Mary here owns an 1873 Colt Single Action Army Revolver. Are you in the market for a collector's pistol Donovan? She's looking for a buyer and I wouldn't bid low because I hear she's a crack shot." Bridgeman winked at her as he said this. Little did he know that she could shoot the bull's eye out of a target at 30 paces.

Seamus Donovan squinted one eye like he was taking a closer look at her and said, "And where does a lady as yourself learn to shoot?" In his world, there wasn't one woman who could tell the difference between the barrel and the butt of a gun.

"Me Dad. He was Irish like you and he wanted me to be able to defend myself."

"Well, here's to your dad. Where are his people from?"

"Cork, until the English pushed them off the land." Mary said this with as much disdain as she could muster. She nearly spit on the floor but thought that might be overdoing it.

Donovan looked at Bridgeman Taylor and smiled. "And where did you find a lass like this?"

"She just walked in the door, Seamus."

"Well, she's a keeper. Bring over to O'Brien's Saturday next. There are people who would like to meet the likes of her."

"You better ask her yourself Mr. Donovan. She's an independent thinker," Bridgeman advised.

"Well?" asked Donovan.

Mary looked from one man to the other. "What's O'Brien's?"

"Just a pub where like minded people share a drink," offered Donovan.

"Saturday next? In two days?" she asked.

"Aye." nodded Donovan.

Throughout this exchange Mary was stealing glances at Taylor. She wanted to know if the story she spun last night had been convincing enough or if he suspected that she was more than a widow trying to pawn off her dead husband's gun. To her discontent, she couldn't tell. Unlike most men's faces, his was difficult to read. In the spur of the moment, she decided that the opportunity to infiltrate a ring of anti-Imperial terrorists was too good of an opportunity to give up. "Okay." she said.

GRIMSBY BEACH

When I got back to the lobby of the Park House, Mr. Vannetter was sitting at the reception desk with his head in his hands. I thought it best to console him seeing I might need to ask him for Papen's room key later that afternoon.

"Mr. Vannetter, I have 30 minutes before I have to have cold water up in Papen's washbasin. Is there something you would like me to do before? Or maybe you would like me to take over the reception desk?"

"Oh Robert, that would be a blessing,...." and without looking up, he rose from the stool and shuffled back to his office and closed the door. Vannetter suffered from severe headaches from time to time, probably due to the stress of managing two hotels. I took advantage of his bouts of pain whenever I could because it gave me some control over a job that I had little control over. Sitting at the reception desk beats emptying out garbage bins anyday and although I was really offering help so I could avoid something more menial, I found myself with access to all of the hotel keys and incoming mail. I decided to start gathering information for my new associate, Mr. Wallace.

Behind the desk is a cubbyhole for each room where correspondence and keys are stored. I was pleased to find an envelope and spare key in cubbyhole number four. Once I scanned the lobby to know I wasn't being watched, I pocketed the key. I worked out an excuse for taking it should someone notice its absence and then I found a pen and paper, copied the return address on the envelope addressed to Papen. I blew on the ink until it was dry and slipped the paper inside my pocket beside the key. I then returned the envelope back into its slot. My first job as a spy took less than thirty seconds and I spent the remainder of the time sitting with very little to do. At twelve-fifty, I knocked on Vannetter's Office door and informed him that I was off to fetch the cold water for Papen. I heard a groan from deep inside and the sounds of him moving so I went off to the kitchen to find a pitcher.

I came back out of the kitchen with the jug of water and saw Vannetter had returned to the reception desk. I was relieved to know that he wasn't likely to notice the missing key as his head was still in his hands. In another minute I was standing before Papen's door and finding myself less apprehensive about being in his presence again. There was something about invading his privacy that gave me confidence.

When he opened the door, Papen immediately consulted his pocket watch. He frowned. I was right on time which gave him nothing to berate me about. He seemed most content when he was complaining but today he seemed distracted and too preoccupied to be bossy.

"Put it there," he directed me to the washstand. "And I will have fresh towels at one-o-five?"

"They are right here sir. I will place them beside the basin and I will take your boots on my way out."

"Very well," he sighed, "Dismissed."

Papen was obviously a military man in manner and disposition and I considered myself to have gotten off pretty easy that afternoon.

Besides attending to Papen, I spent the rest of the day doing my regular chores. Cook had me fold the linens and peel some potatoes. The front veranda lobby had to be swept. Mr. Swanson arrived and I helped him unload his wagon. It was a regular afternoon at the hotel until late in the day another guest arrived.

I was just finishing sweeping the veranda when Mr. Piott's carriage rolled up. As the passenger backed out of the carriage, I could see by his suit that he was clergy and when he turned around I recognized him though I didn't know his name.

"Toke, help Father McGarrity with his bag," directed Mr. Piott.

"Sure thing." I said and did what I was told.

Father McGarrity was at the reception desk when I brought his bag into the foyer and I overheard him say to Vannetter,

"Would you let Franz Papen know that I've arrived? I should like to dine with him this evening."

"Certainly, Father. Your room is on the third floor, number twenty. Robert, take Father McGarrity's bag up to his room for him," ordered the manager.

I nodded and did what I was told. As I set his bag down on the third floor, Father McGarrity asked which room belonged to Papen and ignoring that discretion was the first virtue of a Park House employee, I told him, "Room four." The Good Father smiled at me, unlocked his door and closed it behind himself.

I didn't think much about the new guest until a few minutes later, when I heard a commotion coming from the second floor. I was carrying some sheets up to the third floor when I heard muffled shouts. Curious, I set down the sheets on a table near the service stairs and walked around to the front of the building. Through a closed door I recognized the voice of Franz Von Papen taking someone to task. I was taking pleasure in the fact that he wasn't shouting at me until I heard the second voice. It was Father McGarrity, responding to the German in a very mild and surprisingly calm voice. Whatever he said had calmed Papen and their words became indistinguishable after that. So, I moved closer. I held my breath and cocked my ear towards the door but I still could not discern their words. I crept closer. My ear was an inch away from Papen's door before I could hear every word.

"They are most discreet. The Irish Transvaal order is most secretive. They are all good men who can be trusted," pleaded the good Father.

"It is too big. There are too many involved. It must be focused and it must be organized. You Irish are too passionate. You are too willing to die for a cause."

"That may be but we have this under control. We will be ready in another month. If you could have the order filled it will all go as planned."

"Tauscher will place the order."

"Then he will need to send it to our office in Ithaca. Tell him the order is to remove tree stumps. There are a lot of tree stumps in Ithaca."

Their voices grew quiet after that so I moved down the corridor and back to my pile of sheets.

WASHINGTON D. C.

"Is he really the nephew of Napoleon?"

"Grandnephew."

"No wonder he's a real ball buster then."

"Hey, he's the reason you have a job. Without him and Uncle Teddy there wouldn't be a Bureau of Investigation."

"Yeah, I guess. Hey, have you found anything on our Widow?"

"She was located in Manhattan and is currently working as a secretary for the Clan na Gael."

"Is she an Irish National?"

"We don't think so, but really, we still don't know much about her?" The phone rang out and Thrasher picked up. "Uh-huh. Five minutes. Thank you, Miss Redstone." He stood, hung up the phone and buttoned his jacket. "Blain wants to see me."

"And what about Koeing? Does he remember who his boss is yet?" the agent asked as he followed the Lieutenant out of his office and down the hall.

"Nothing yet. We really don't believe he knew who was signing his cheques. We have him under close surveillance. It should only be a matter of time. Have you heard of a business called National Press?"

"Nope."

"How about Atlas Press?"

"Nope."

"How about Acme Machining Company?

"Nope. Nope and nope. Three strikes, I'm out. What is the connection?

"I don't know. In the last two weeks all three businesses were bought up by the World Hydraulics Company. Internal Revenue flagged it."

"Do you want me to check it out? I've got little to do until Koeing spills the beans."

"Yes, that would do. Find out what they make and where they distribute to and give the file to Ariganello. I'll be out of town for a few days."

"Yes sir. Don't do anything I wouldn't do."

"And what wouldn't you do?"

"I've never found out and that's why you need to be careful."

The agent saluted Jeremy and left him in front of Captain Blain's office.

"You may go right in." said Miss Redstone and Thrasher did just that.

Seated in the chair across from Captain Blain was a diminutive brown skinned man in a linen suit. His hair was black and matted down on his head and his large brown eyes were cast down in deference. He nodded to the Lieutenant as he entered but did not look directly at him.

"Mr. Singh, I would like to tell Lieutenant Thrasher here, what you just told me."

THE KOMAGATA MARU

The small man raised his face and his large brown eyes. He cleared his throat and in a melodic English accent calmly described his experience on the Komagata Maru.

"I am a student of law, Lieutenant. I was born in the holy city of Amritsar in the Punjab. I was raised Hindu and spent my entire life there until I went to New Delhi to pursue my education. I only tell you this because I want you to know that I had Sikh friends as a child and as a consequence, came to know their language and their thoughts. As we grew older, our political and religious views drove us apart and even though most every Hindu, and Moslem and Sikh are united in their desire for an independent nation, we hold different positions on how to achieve this goal.

I was taught in the Durgiana Temple to voice my displeasures in ways that are peaceful. My Sikh brothers have other methods and I am afraid that they are planning to use violence to rid the English from our country. I fear what actions Britain will take in retaliation. I fear for my people and that is why I am here.

When I graduated from the University, I was offered passage to British Columbia. I have an uncle who emigrated there many years ago and he said that my services could be used by Indian expatriates. And so, on April four 1914, we left Hong Kong with three hundred and forty Sikhs, twenty-four Muslims and twelve Hindus. We arrived in Vancouver one month later and the reception was not welcoming. At first the customs officials were not going to allow any of us to leave the ship. The food and water stores were running low and the officials refused to replenish them. Sometimes we had to go without food and water for two days. Our case went to court and we languished like that for two months. In the end, only twenty-four of us were allowed to land. Fortunately, I was one of them and now I am here to tell you that the Customs Officials in Vancouver were correct in denying entrance to many of the passengers on the Komagata Maru.

As you see, I do not wear a turban nor do I carry the kirpan, the knife and I do not wear the muslim kufi on my head. For this reason, the other passengers knew I was Hindu and because they only heard me speak Hindi, did not expect I knew Punjabi. Some of the men were careless. The prolonged wait, hunger and thirst, made them so and they began to talk about revenge on the British Empire. They spoke of a movement that raised money to arm the resistance back home. They talked of sending arms to the Freedom fighters. I am sure that not all of those who were turned away from the Dominion of Canada were revolutionaries but I know some were."

The Captain and the Lieutenant looked at one another. The captain gave a slight nod while Thrasher tried to suppress an 'I told you so' expression.

"Mr. Singh, can you remember any names, places and dates you overheard?" Blain asked.

"Yes. I will tell you all I know."

"Mr. Singh, how did you find your way to us? Vancouver is a long journey from here."

"Lieutenant, my uncle is a proud Indian. He wishes that the English would leave our country but he believes it must be done with peaceful resistance and he believes those that will use violent means will create havoc and ruin. There have been movements in South Africa that have been successful in this manner and he would like to replicate them in our homeland. My uncle sent me here to Washington because he believes you will listen to what I have to say."

"Did you not try to inform the officials in Vancouver?"

"They did not wish to listen." Singh said sadly.

There was a brief pause and then the captain picked up his phone, dialed one number and said, "Could you please send for Swithers?" and he hung up. "Mr. Singh, I want you to tell us everything you remember about your time on that ship, every conversation, every name, event and date that you can recall."

"I will. That is why I am here."

There was a knock on the door. Thrasher opened it and a sergeant entered.

"Sergeant Smithers, continue to take Mr. Singh's statement. We need every detail he can remember. Thank you for bringing this to my attention and Smithers, make sure Mr. Singh has something to eat and drink. He has had a long journey and be sure to record his accommodations here in Washington should we need more information. Mr. Singh, thank you for coming to see us. We will treat the matter seriously. Please enjoy your stay here in Washington."

The Indian rose and bowed his head to the captain and then to the Lieutenant and followed the Sergeant from the room. Thrasher closed the door.

"The Germans and the Irish and the Indians." stated Captain Blain.

"The sun never sets on Britain and now she is going to be putting fires out all over the world."

"Lieutenant, this makes the woman in your photograph all the more important. Find out who she is and what her connection is to all of this. Our resources are thin in the west and this matter is one that needs to be pursued."

"Yes sir." Thrasher spun around, smiled to himself and returned to his office. Alone, the Lieutenant opened a file folder and studied the photograph and address of Mary Miller once more. The address was in the banking district of lower Manhattan and the photo showed the beautiful woman dressed in black clinking champagne glasses with Hans Tauscher. Evidently, she hobnobbed with the upper crust of society. It was no surprise that her attractive looks would gain her access into New York's elite. That she worked as a secretary in a dingy little office during the day and toasted with wealthy people in the evening made her all the more interesting.

He studied the photo more closely. While Mary Miller was the main subject, Tauscher, the arm's dealer, was easily identifiable in his profile. He was smiling. He was enjoying Mary's company. In the background was the man of dark complexion wearing a robe and a turban. He was in a serious discussion a freckled man. Although the photo was black and white, Thrasher thought his hair was likely red. He looked Irish.

Jeremy leaned back in his chair. 'What a party this is,' he said to himself. A wealthy German, an Irishman, an East Indian and the Widow of unknown origin were engaging in a social gathering in Midtown, Manhattan. He committed the photograph to memory, placed it back into the file folder and slid it into his top desk drawer and locked it. He opened the bottom drawer and withdrew his revolver, checked that the chambers were loaded and slid it into the holster under his left arm. He stood, grabbed the bag he had packed that morning and headed to the train station.

MIDTOWN TO THE LOWER EAST SIDE

Lieutenant Thrasher's first glimpse of New York City was Grand Central Station and it gleamed. The glossy stone was not yet two years old and it ricocheted sunlight throughout the main concourse. Sculptures and friezes adorned the great hall. It was more like a palace than a train station and his early morning arrival found him lonely in the giant expanse. His footsteps echoed through Graybar Hall and down to Lexington Avenue. Outside, the city sounds were muffled and far away for the area around the world's largest train station was still barren, an empty expanse where building materials were left abandoned. Broken stone and rubble lay before the pride of the New York Central Railroad. Grand Central was a phoenix rising out of a derelict construction site.

He turned up 42nd street to find a line of hacks and taxis waiting along the curb and under a row of giant umbrellas shoe shiners waited for oxfords and treadwells to make their way to their stands. It was not D.C. sticky. The day was fine and he was enjoying the comparative dryness in the air, so he walked. At Fifth Avenue he stopped to take in another new building. The New York Public Library sat like a fortress, a wide expansive bastion guarding the knowledge within. It was built as a research library but looked more like a bank. Thrasher thought it looked imposing and less inviting than a public building should be and he smirked at the thought that it held all the secrets of the world.

He headed south down Fifth avenue. In Midtown, the scents of the city were mild. The sewers in the center of the island moved their effluent quickly away and the residents were wealthy enough to pay sweepers to remove the horse manure in a timely fashion. The windows of the three story walk ups were so clean that they reflected the images of the opposite street. The fenders of the automobiles were waxed and polished. There were trees shading the sidewalks and the pedestrians strolled at a leisurely pace like they had no better place to be. The women carried parasols while the men carried cigarettes. Even the horses clopped along the cobblestone 'in lento'.

At thirtieth Avenue he felt like he was walking into a cathedral, the boulevard like the center aisle in the sanctuary of America's architectural achievements. Direct sunlight was absent and he could feel the stone and steel closing in around him. He saw the Flatiron building, twenty-two stories high, its knife edge separating Madison and Fifth. The Everett Building towering sixteen stories and the Germanic Life Insurance Building Street twenty-one stories; looming over the tenement housing at Union Square. Thrasher suspected that the tallest buildings were the newest and his casual glances at corner stones proved him right. His theory clinched as he passed the brand-new Consolidated Edison Building three blocks south. It was twenty-six stories tall.

He continued south and was now deep in the canyon and as the street's numbers diminished the building heights and human activity augmented. Cars, carriages, wagons, bicycles, and automobiles weaved their way up and down the road as pedestrians crisscrossed in every direction. Constables waved their arms and blew their whistles at every intersection, keeping the chaos moving. Alleyways became narrower and darker and the smell of human civilization rose from the sewers. Leisure was a stranger here. Streetcar chimes, car horns, shouts of street hawkers, the put-put of combustion engines and the clop of horse hooves blended into the cacophony.

A street vendor stood behind his cart of oysters, his patrons slurping the contents off of the shell. A well-dressed father was buying flavoured ice for his daughter while poorer children put their lips on the block of ice being chipped and sold by the pound. As the streets narrowed, the pedestrian traffic moved onto the street and Thrasher followed suit. The sidewalks had become clogged with wagons and stalls selling fruit and vegetables and breads. As he moved southward, he noticed that the resident's words were strange to him, languages that he couldn't place or had never heard before. He noticed that their skin was darker and that their eyes followed him. As much as he was watching them, their dark eyes were watching him and for the first time in his life, Jeremy Thrasher felt like he was in the minority. He had left his military uniform in

Washington but still he felt conspicuous, his clothes, his skin and his upright posture marking him as an outsider.

As the numbered streets ran out, Thrasher left the Bowery neighbourhood and entered Chinatown. He had experienced this culture in Toronto and marvelled at the strength of a people who could successfully transplant themselves into most every major city of the world. A Chinese city within a city, complete with its own food, entertainment, celebrations and industry. Chinatown gave way to City Hall Park where Thrasher saw one of the oldest city halls in the United States. He had been walking nearly an hour and in that brief period he felt that he had passed nearly every nationality and social strata present in the United States of America. He was now in the Financial District and knew that his destination was a short distance away.

THE MALLORY STEAMSHIP COMPANY

Situated between the docks and the Stock Exchange, the four-story building was looking run down. Soot had discoloured the red brick and the wooden frames around each window suffered from neglect. Paint peeled around each grimy pane of glass and weeds grew between the paving stones that lined the path.

If you climbed up to the second floor and turned left you would find a door with gold stencil lettering that read, 'Mallory Steamship Company' and if you looked inside the door you would see Mary Miller working diligently from eight am to five pm. You might see Mary filing, answering correspondence or balancing the accounts but presently she was making a copy of a list. This list had three columns, the first entitled, Name, the second, Address and the third, Donation.

The names listed in the first column were all Celtic in origin. The addresses were from across the United States but the majority came from the Chicago area with some being as far away as San Francisco. The amounts in the donation column ranged from hundreds to thousands and when she summed this up, the total was just over ten thousand dollars. The amount was shocking the first time she tallied one of these lists but once she learned that over four million Irish immigrants had settled in America, she knew she was looking at the end result of a well-organized and aggressive National fundraising campaign. She suspected that much of the money would be ferried back to Ireland to fight for home rule but she also had evidence that some would be siphoned off for sabotage and espionage here in North America. She was careful and meticulous in her work. Mary was left alone here for most of every day, her clerical work only interrupted when Seamus Donovan dropped off an envelope of cash for her to count or letters for her to file or answer. Every once in a while, he asked her to take a walk while he had an impromptu meeting with some other mysterious gentleman. On these occasions she was careful to take all of her notes with her.

Mary had been the secretary at the Mallory Steamship Company for three weeks and was becoming familiar with its diverse operations as receipts and requisitions filtered across her desk. Besides the steady stream of donations that needed to be recorded, the company did import and export merchandise from Europe and beyond. Exports to Europe were increasing by the day as the war raged on. The shipyards were clogged with frigates and freighters carrying flour, wheat, oats, corn, lard, hams and bacon destined for England but Mary's desk was littered with orders for brass plates and mineral oils as munition factories in Britain tried to keep up with the demand from the front lines. The prices for everything were going through the roof and as long as there was a supply of goods to buy and sell, there was a steady and profitable income for the shipping business. Her days were filled with counting and accounting. Her evenings were spent fulfilling a rich social calendar.

Each workday was followed by an obligatory hour at the pub. Donovan insisted that she attend, that this was part of the job but Mary knew that he just wanted a pretty woman on his arm when he went through the door. That she always left him there to drink to excess didn't seem to bother him, like her daily refusal to his advances. He was relentless. She was friendly but firm and used her 'widowness' as an excuse. When she invented the character she would portray, she was expecting her black dress to provide a stronger barrier, but she had come to learn that social norms were no match for lust.

Weekends were more highbrow affairs. Her presence was sought on the Upper East Side and at Lenox Hill where the apartments were lofty and ornate. She would take a carriage up to Central Park and enjoy the fresh air as she escaped the dankness of Water Street and the stench of the Seaport district. Adorned in the same black dress, Mary fended off just as many suitors and admirers as she did in the bars. The men here were just more sophisticated in their approach. Many were German, attachés to the Consulate in Washington, or entrepreneurs who had business with the American Government. Even Count Johann von Bernstorff, the German Ambassador, attended one party held at Hans Tauscher's apartment. There was usually a delegation of Irish and on one occasion Sikhs from the Punjab in India.

These get-togethers had the pretense of being light and fun but there was always an aura of tension amongst the guests. The opposing forces usually divided down Nationalities and it appeared to Mary that the Irish didn't really trust the Germans and the Germans didn't really trust the Irish and the Sikhs didn't trust anyone. While in her presence, the men kept their conversations to witty anecdotes but it was common for small verbal skirmishes to erupt when they thought she was out of earshot. Mary was convinced that she was excluded in these discussions because she was a woman rather than a suspected enemy spy. Overall, the social gatherings didn't yield a great deal of useful information but they were a pleasant distraction from the more mundane spying she was doing at the office. And so, for another week, Mary Miller, copied lists of donors and suspicious orders onto paper, stuffed them in envelopes and mailed them to a post box in Toronto. The work was routine and monotonous until a new stranger knocked on her office door.

"Come in?" she said, not getting up from her desk.

The door opened and a grey fedora entered, quickly removed by a hand to reveal charming smile and piercing blue eyes.

"Good day. I don't mean to intrude. I was looking for the office of Gibson's Manufacturing and I appear to have gotten lost." By the end of his sentence, Jeremy Thrasher, dressed in a gabardine suit was one step into the office, his square shoulders filling the frame of the door.

"You are in the right building." she smiled, "Wrong floor. They are up one more level."

She put down her pen and placed her chin in her hands. She wanted to steady her gaze so that she could better study his face.

"Thank you. I am sorry to disturb you," he said, still rooted to the spot.

"If you go up one flight, turn left, you will find them just above where we are now," she directed but he didn't move. He looked down at his feet.

"Just one floor up," she repeated.

He slowly looked up and locked eyes with her. Mary felt a faint flutter in her abdomen.

"I'm sorry. I'm just surprised to find a woman like yourself in a place like this."

"A woman like myself?"

"A beautiful woman like yourself," he said, his eyes never leaving hers.

It was a line spoken to her before by so many other men but until now, it never had any effect on her. She lowered her hands to the sides of the desk to steady herself and where she usually kept a witty retort for occasions like this, she found none.

"Well, thank you Mr....?"

"Thrasher. Jeremy Thrasher. And what name do you go by?"

"Mary Miller." She stood, came round the desk and held out her hand. He took her hand in his and they shook. Jeremy was thinking that the photographs he had stuffed in his desk did not do her justice. Each line on her face gracefully met another until the whole effect was balanced organic symmetry.

"Well, it is a pleasure to meet you. I'm sorry about your husband. Was he lost in the war?"

"Before the war, Mr. Thrasher. Over a year now." Just why she added this last detail surprised her. Did she want him to know that her black dress wouldn't stay on forever?

"Well, I'm sorry just the same. Say, do you know a good and inexpensive restaurant nearby. I really should have lunch before my appointment."

"I do. Kresge's is just around the block."

"Kresge's? Thanks......Would you care to join me?" he asked shyly. "My treat."

Without any hesitation Mary heard herself say, "Just let me clear my desk."

She busied herself to the task. Before she knew it, he was holding open the door to the deli and then she was giving him recommendations on what to order and he was laughing at the mustard dribbling down the corner of her mouth. Before he knew it, he was paying the bill. Conversation had flowed so easily between them that the time seemed to have evaporated and they both felt that they were back at Mallory's far too soon.

"Can I take you to dinner?" asked Jeremy.

"Tonight?"

"Yes, tonight.

"Two meals in one day, Mr. Thrasher? Are you trying to sweep me off my feet?"

"I guess so," he shrugged. "I mean, I hope so."

"In that case, the answer is yes. I am done at five pm," and she put the key in the office door but found it already open. Mary knew that Donovan must have returned while she was out. She lowered her voice and said, "See you at five," and then quickly slipped into the office.

Lieutenant Thrasher walked out of the Shipyards without learning anything new about Mary Miller. He would have admonished any of his agents for squandering the opportunity he had just had. The experience made him aware of the power of female operatives. He made a mental note to recruit more females in his department. Had she been 'playing' him? He didn't think so. He didn't want to think so and, in any case, none of their conversation went near political or personal information. For the entire hour it took them to consume two Rueben sandwiches, they only discussed their escapades at trying to adapt to life in New York City. They revealed to on another that they were from a small town but neither asked for specifics. Both were purposely vague lest the questions came back to them. It was as though they didn't want to lie to one another, so they both avoided topics they might have to fib about. It was the most honest conversation Jeremy had had with a woman in years and he wondered how he was going to sustain it this coming evening.

"And who was that?" growled Donovan.

"Who was who?"

"The stiff you were with in the booth at Kresge's," he sneered.

"That was Jeremy Thrasher." Mary steadied her voice. She hadn't seen Donovan or any of his compatriots keeping watch over her, but obviously they had. She thought it best to be forthcoming and truthful as much as she could possibly be.

"And who is Jeremy Thrasher?"

"Jeremy Thrasher is a businessman visiting New York. I just met him. He took me to lunch and he is taking me to dinner."

Donovan raised his eyebrows. “Dinner too? This guy must be a regular Don Juan. What did you discuss?”

Mary knew Donovan was jealous but she also recognized that he would be concerned about the security of the transactions that went on in this office, so she tried to console him.

“Donovan, we only talked about what it is like to live in New York City. He didn’t ask me anything about Mallory Shipping and I didn’t tell him anything about Mallory Shipping.” There was a long pause and then he said,

“Well, be sure that you don’t. We’ve spent a lot of time and effort setting up this operation.”

He took an envelope from the breast pocket of his blazer and threw it on the desk. The thud it made told Mary that there was a thick wad of bills stuffed inside, hundreds, maybe thousands of dollars.

“This goes to Bridgeman Taylor. He will be by tomorrow. Maybe he will have time to take you to dinner too?”

With that, Donovan got out of the chair and huffed out of the room. Mary sighed, greatly relieved that he was gone. She closed and locked the door and sat at her desk. She completed the minor accounting she had left to do and then opened the safe to deposit the envelope for Bridgeman Taylor but when she picked up the package, the shape and weight told her there was more than just cash in there. The envelope was common. She had lots just like it so she tore it open knowing that she could replace it without anyone knowing. Bills of various denominations fell out along with a passport. The passport was new. The photograph was recent and no stamps smudged the pages inside but it was the paper itself that held Mary’s attention. The tooth, weight and composition were quite familiar to her. She had sold it to Brown and Brown in Baltimore only weeks before. Mary took the bills and passport, sealed them in a new envelope and locked it in the safe.

GRIMSBY BEACH

The few guests that were staying at the hotel were already in the dining hall. I checked to see that Papen and McGarrity were seated with menus in their laps before I made my way to the second floor and the service stair landing. The key to Papen's room was weighing heavily in my pocket. It had been there since I had taken over the desk for Vannetter earlier in the day. Luckily for me, Vannetter's malady had distracted him from noticing. This was the kind of detail he seldom missed and it was fortunate that Papen himself had not misplaced his key and needed the replacement.

Mr. Wallace was there waiting for me. Without a word, he nodded and followed me to Papen's room. I stopped in front of his door and while Wallace looked both ways, I took out the key and opened the door. Wallace slid inside and when I tried to follow he put his hand up and told me to leave the key in the door and depart. I was happy to oblige.

The next morning when I arrived at work, Mr. Vannetter asked if I knew why Papen's spare key might be on the reception desk. He had found it there first thing in the morning. I shrugged my shoulders and went to fetch the hot water for Papen's six-thirty washstand. By seven am I had also gathered the towels, brushed his suit, polished his boots, and made his breakfast reservation. At seven-thirty I entered his room to clean it. I didn't notice anything out of the ordinary. I really didn't know what to expect but there was no evidence that I had let James Wallace into the apartment the night before and evidently, Papen hadn't noticed either. When he returned from breakfast and his walk, I brushed his suit and polished his boots a second time, fetched more hot water and fresh towels and then waited for his daily post. This morning, Papen handed me three envelopes which I promptly took to the kitchen where I copied the names and addresses of each on a scrap of paper. The first envelope was addressed to Consul Carl A. Leuderitz in Baltimore, the second to Bridgeman W. Taylor in Washington and the third to Hans Tauscher in New York. I gathered up the envelopes and tucked the paper in my pocket.

The sun was beaming that morning as I descended the veranda stairs and crossed the grounds to the post office. The poplar leaves were flashing brightly in the wind and this matched my disposition for it looked like I had gotten away with admitting Wallace into Papen's room and I had successfully gathered some more of his personal information. All I had to do was find the time throughout the day to give it to Wallace and even that problem was solved when I entered the store.

I caught a glimpse of him standing by the coffee grinder reading a newspaper as I made my way to Post wicket. He let me post the letters before motioning for me to come to him. I stood breathing in the rich aroma of freshly ground coffee while he spoke through his newspaper.

"I have to get in tonight as well."

"Again? I don't have the key and I won't be able to get the key. Mr. Vannetter is healthy today." My sunny day was clouding over.

"You'll find a way," he said confidently. "Same time, same place," and he folded up his newspaper and started walking out.

"You don't want this?" I asked, holding up the paper I had scribbled on.

"Thank you." He snatched it out of my hand, turned and left.

I was racking my brain as I went back up the stairs of the hotel. I crossed the veranda and when I entered the lobby, I locked my eyes on the spare key for room four hanging just above Mr. Vannetter's head. Unfortunately, he caught me looking and was able to follow my gaze to the pegboard behind him. He looked over his shoulder and then back to me with suspicion all over his face. The mystery of Papen's key showing up on the reception desk still plagued his mind and I just gave him a big piece of the puzzle.

As the day's chores rolled on, I looked for ways to snatch the key but I was faced with the fact that Vannetter was wary and watchful. It was Cook who gave me the inspiration.

"Hey Toke. I need a bag of flour when you have a chance," he said.

"Sure thing," I replied. It wasn't until I was in the storeroom and noticed that we had only one bag left that the idea hit me. I lugged the bag to the back corner of the storeroom and hid it beneath a few bags of potatoes just in case Cook came down to look for himself. Then I told him we were out of flour. I won't repeat the epithets he uttered before he told me to go and borrow a bag from the Lakeview. Now Cook is my superior, but it was here I deviated from the chain of command. Instead, I went directly to Mr. Vannetter and told him that Cook was in a rage because he needed flour right away but we were out of flour and suggested that I go and borrow one from the Lakeview Hotel. I told Vannetter that as much as I wanted to oblige Cook, I needed to deliver cold water to Papen in a few moments, so I could not.

For his part, Vannetter, gave out a great sigh, and knew right away that there was only one man for the job, and that was him. I told him that I would watch the desk between my tasks and off he went. It was then that I took Papen's spare key and replaced it with another from a drawer full of orphan keys kept low behind the registry desk. I was confident that Vannetter would not discern the cut of one key for another and would never be able to discover my ruse unless he possessed both keys at the same time and I planned to have the real spare key back on its peg well before that might happen. I was coming down the service stairs for a jug of Papen's cold water when I saw Mr. Vannetter, sweat on his brow, heaving a 30 lb bag of flour onto Cook's counter. It was then I knew that my plan was in motion. At least I thought my plan was in motion. The wheel of my plan had many spokes and some were a little loose. My scheme became wobblier as the evening wore on.

I fulfilled my list of duties to Papen and waited for 5 pm. Unfortunately, unbeknownst to me, Father McGarrity and Papen did not make good dining partners the previous evening. As I was to learn, there was an altercation late in their meal. As their dessert arrived, the attending waiter overheard Papen call Father McGarrity a "Celtic Charlatan" and he left the dining lounge and stomped up the stairs to his room. Mr. Wallace must have completed his search and vacated the room before Papen returned but it appeared now that the Irish Priest and the hot-headed German would not dine together a second time. Had I known this, I would have worked out some other plan as this left James Wallace waiting on the second-floor service stairs while Papen was still in his room. Having gone to significant personal effort to obtain the spare key, I needed a way to draw Papen out of his lair.

My method was crude and perhaps short-sighted but time was short and I was under a great deal of pressure. I knocked on Papen's door and insisted that I brush his jacket. Papen, who had no need of his jacket that evening, jumped at the opportunity to have someone work for him. He opened up the door, took it off and gave it to me. I, in turn, wasted no time in taking it to the laundry, fetching a hot iron off of the stove and burnt a hole right through the back of the expensive garment. The smell was horrific and I was saved from asphyxiation when the laundress grabbed the iron from me as she rushed to open up a window. I ignored her curses as I hung the smouldering coat on a hanger and carried it back to Papen's room. It was still smoking when I handed it to him.

While he was still speechless and immobile, I took leave and sought out Mr. Wallace. My hypothesis was that once Papen got his voice back, that he would race down to find Vannetter, show him his jacket and insist on me being fired. I was right. Both Wallace and I could hear him shouting in the foyer while I unlocked the door and let the spy in. Like the previous night, I left the key in the door and left Wallace to his own devices. I escaped down the service stairs, meandered my way through the cottages and went to sit on the beach. It gave me time to contemplate what my mother was going to say and what other jobs might be available to me.

MANHATTAN

By four-thirty pm Mary Miller was contemplating her future. She was entertaining thoughts she had never considered before. Did she want to end her career in espionage? Did she want to settle down? The thought of children had never entered her mind before and she could pinpoint the exact time when these ideas entered her head. It angered her that her chosen path in life could be derailed so easily. But her nerve melted when she recalled the moment Jeremy Thrasher removed his fedora at her office door and smiled. How long had it lasted? Four, five seconds and yet the brief exchange of energy would cause her to question the road she'd been on for years. She had been dedicated enough to risk her life and when necessary, to take the lives of others during her service for the Dominion Police. For an individual who never questioned her motives, this lack of faith was jarring.

Moreover, she was questioning her own professional judgement. She had met many clever agents in her day. Agents that could make you believe anything they wanted you to believe. She herself had fooled so many. She knew the tactics and methods and here she was willing to believe the words and gestures of a man she knew next to nothing about. Mary Miller, agent of the Dominion Police, the Black Widow, was listening to her heart rather than her analytically trained mind. There was something in his voice and his mannerisms that made her want to trust him and had her intuition not served her well before? Suffice it to say, Mary Miller was on edge while she waited outside the restaurant. She screwed up all the resolve she had to slow her pulse and her thoughts. She was a professional, she told herself and she vowed to behave like one.

Lieutenant Thrasher was watching from the alley across the street. Along with vowing to hire more female agents, Jeremy also vowed not to let his heart obscure his objectivity. He knew very little about this woman. She worked in the New York headquarters of Clan na Gael, had travelled to Baltimore and has been photographed socializing with German, Irish and Sikh Nationals. As he watched her now, he noted her pacing. She was calming herself, gathering her thoughts, controlling herself. This was a woman who had much on her mind.

Thrasher was just about to step out from behind the fire escape ladder and head off across the street when he noticed a large red headed man watching Mary as well. He was standing behind a mailbox just down from the restaurant pretending to be reading a paper but obviously stealing long glances at his dinner partner. Jeremy left the alley, turned left away from the restaurant, crossed the street on the next block and circled back. He was able to get a good look at the red head as he passed him swiftly. He kept this pace even when Mary looked up to see him. Her smile was short-lived as he grabbed her arm and led her around the corner and away from the restaurant.

"You have an admirer," he said, picking up the pace. Mary looked back over her shoulder, simultaneously alarmed that she hadn't noticed and that her date had.

"You were watching me?" she asked. He nodded. "You're Police?"

"Of sorts," he responded.

They made another left and crossed the street. Jeremy led them through the doors of a dry cleaners and to the surprise of the proprietor they moved around the front counter and into the back room. They passed unnoticed by another worker who was pressing shirt collars and exited the back door into an alley. Both Jeremy and Mary looked up instinctively. Both of them had used this method of evading followers and knew the angle of the sun and its shadows would help reorient themselves when they got back onto the street.

They were catching their breath in the alley when he said, "Mary, I do not intend to ruin your cover. You are working for the English aren't you?

She narrowed her eyes. "I work for the Mallory Shipping Company Mr. Thrasher."

"And?"

"And what?"

"And the English or the Dominion Police?"

There was no point in lying. He seemed to know who she was.

"Dominion Police," she admitted.

"That's the same as the English in the eyes of Clan na Gael. If they find out, that will be the end of you."

"Then I won't let them find out, will I?" Mary had turned to face him using her deep dark eyes to hold his gaze.

Lieutenant Jeremy Thrasher stepped closer to her and held her elbows in his hands.

"I wish I were that confident." He was looking at her with concern in his eyes. "It's bigger than just the Irish. Germany has agents too. Do you know who you are rubbing shoulders with?"

"Do you know who I am rubbing shoulders with?"

"I do, at least, some of them I do. You are toasting champagne with some heavy hitters. I hope you have an exit plan."

Mary narrowed her eyes and wondered how he knew so much. "And just who are you Mr. Jeremy Thrasher?"

"Well, for now, let's just say I'm a friend and if you are going to go back to working in that dingy little office of theirs, we are going to have to find a way of shaking their suspicions away from you."

"We could walk into their pub and show them they have nothing to worry about. The Clan meets at O'Brien's on South St. every night."

"That's a ballsy thing to do." He paused to consider this. "Are you sure?"

"Never underestimate the power of a pretty face," and she smiled and batted her eyes. Jeremy admired her bravery and confidence.

"It might just work. Are you sure?" he asked a second time.

"I'll lead the way Mr. Thrasher and you should let me do the talking."

Jeremy held out his arm, Mary took it and they made their way down to the wharf.

GRIMSBY BEACH

I didn't quite know how I was going to explain to my parents how I lost my job at the Hotel so I didn't mention it when I got up that morning. Dad was still in Hamilton on that day but Mom was busy making me breakfast. I was the beneficiary of my Dad's and Jacob's absence. She was focusing her attention on me and it was only making me feel all the more guilty.

My mother had started daydreaming when Jacob had gone away. For a woman whose virtues included alertness and presence of mind, this was a drastic change. She would stare off into space contemplating where he was, what he was doing and whether or not he was going to make it back home. It was a look many of the women living in the Park carried and it weighed on them. I didn't want my newfound unemployment to add to my mother's load so I dressed for work like I did every other morning and headed off to the Park House so she wouldn't ask any questions.

It was a strange feeling walking up the steps and into the foyer of the hotel. I had prepared myself for a brutal public firing, one where Vannetter could really scream his head off and be justified for doing so but with each step toward the reception desk my feet got lighter and my fear smaller. I had imagined the worst so I guess I felt I had nothing to lose by facing the music. To my surprise the orchestra of doom never showed up. Vannetter was there at the desk checking over the register and when I greeted him with a, "Good morning Mr. Vannetter" he looked up and smiled.

"And good morning to you Robert. Isn't it a glorious day?"

It wasn't what I expected. He was beaming at me while I waited for the axe to fall. It didn't.

"Mr. Swanson will be making a delivery at ten am. Could you please make yourself available to help him unload his wagon?"

I was speechless. I nodded and shuffled off to ask Cook what illness had infected our boss.

"You can thank Officer Belcher for that," Cook told me when I inquired. "He wandered into the lobby just as von Papen was letting Vannetter have it. Nice work on his jacket by the way and just so you know, Margaret, our

Laundress, never wants to see you near her Laundry again. Anyway, Papen's eyes were popping out of his head as he was screaming at Vannetter. That's when Belcher came up from behind and tapped him on the shoulder. Papen wheeled around on Belcher but when he saw Belcher's uniform, he clammed up right away, turned and gave Vannetter one more stink eye and then stomped across the foyer and up to his room. That man must have a sharp respect for the Police because just thirty minutes later, he carried his own luggage down the stairs, settled up his bill and sought out some transport to the train station. He even left Madame Gadski behind. Our esteemed leader has been floating on a cloud ever since. I've never seen him happier to see a guest vacate our hotel. And to think he has you and your ironing skills to thank for it, which brings me to asking, why were you ironing his jacket?"

"It's a long story," was my only response. I was contemplating Papen's quick departure and if James Wallace was aware of it.

"Well, when we both have more time, I would like to hear that long story. In the meantime, I need some things from the Lakeview. Here's my list. I need them straight away," instructed Cook.

For the second time that morning fate fell in my favour. I needed an excuse to find Wallace and Cook sent me to the place I'd most likely find him. I wasted no time and ran across the Park and up Temple Lane to the Lakeview. Harry Nelles was working the reception again. He was still smarting from my threat to tell Jacob about him putting the moves on Becky Carlson.

"Hey Harry, could you tell me if Mr. Wallace is in his room?" I asked, a little out of breath."

"Well Toke, no I couldn't. Discretion is the,.........," he started but I interrupted him by reaching across the desk and spinning the register so that I could read it. I was running my finger down the page when he added, "Oh and I heard about your new job in the laundry. I hear they're giving you your own personal iron."

"Yeah, send your uniform over anytime and I'll flatten it out for you," I said just when I read in the registry that Mr. James Wallace had checked out at nine thirty-five that morning. Harry pulled the registry book back, spun it around to face him and closed it with a thwap. I turned, fumbled for Cook's list in my pocket and went to the kitchen.

O'BRIENS PUB, MANHATTAN

"You're sure about this?" Jeremy asked as they approached the pub.

"Just let me do the talking." Mary responded.

She entered O'Brien's on his arm. There was a bell that rang when the door opened but it was barely audible for the din of voices inside. The place was packed. Nearly every chair was occupied and the bar was lined shoulder to shoulder with men that had one elbow on the bar and one foot on the rail, each nursing a pint. Thrasher noticed one of them elbow his companion in the ribs when he saw Mary come through the door and this reaction repeated itself until everyone standing were looking their way. This spread to the tables seconds after that. The conversations had halted and the din diminished to a murmur until one large freckled faced man stepped forward and said,

"Aw, if it isn't Maud Gonne herself comin' to have a drink with her kin. Nice of you to join us."

The unfriendly greeting came from Seamus Donovan. Jeremy heard the threat behind it. Mary acted like she hadn't heard it at all. She found a gap between the men at the bar and squeezed her way through. She ordered a pint for herself and one for Thrasher.

"Who's your friend Mary?" someone asked.

"Yes, who are you?" said a menacing voice into Thrasher's ear. The giant of a man came from behind and stepped between him and the bar.

"I'm just here for a drink," Jeremy said. He was trying to sound friendly but he'd wished he had his revolver with him.

The giant moved forward forcing Thrasher to back up until he was against the wall, a dartboard just to the left of his head.

"I said, who are you?" the giant repeated as he patted down Thrasher's body.

The Lieutenant was suddenly happy not to be carrying his revolver. His search complete, the giant placed a large hand up on the wall to the side of Thrasher's head. Jeremy could smell his breath and sweat and was planning evasive maneuvers when a sharp thud caused the giant to shout and turn away.

Jeremy looked up to see a knife embedded in the wall above his head. It had a small bead of blood on it.

"This one will go in your eye if you don't sit yourself down and be polite."

Mary was holding a second knife, a sister to the one stuck in the wall above Jeremy's head, by its tip. The men at the bar had moved a respectful distance away from her. The giant, holding his bleeding finger in his other hand, took a step away from Thrasher and sat in the closest chair. Mary folded up her knife, slipped it up her sleeve, and carried the two pints of ale over to where Jeremy was standing. Jeremy, meanwhile, reached up behind his head, worked Mary's other knife out of the wall, folded the blade into its handle and put it in his pocket. She then looked down at the men sitting at the nearest table, lifted her chin in the direction of the bar. They and the giant got up and left the chairs vacant. When Thrasher and Mary sat down, the man who first welcomed them into the pub sauntered over.

"You're a true daughter of Erin Cumann na uBan, Mary. Maud Gonne would be proud."

"I don't know if she'd be proud of her countrymen fighting amongst themselves, Donovan."

"We're in desperate times Mary, desperate times. I don't think you can blame the boys for being nervous when you bring a Yank in here."

"Yank or no, I'd only bring a friend and you know it."

Donovan squinted his eyes and scanned Thrasher. "Do I now?" He paused for effect, turned and let them alone.

"You alright?" Mary asked as she sipped her beer.

"Not a warm reception, and nice throw," he said, winking at her. "Glad you had the second knife."

"Always carry a spare."

"That's good to know."

Thrasher was doing his best to look relaxed as he drank his beer. His hands were tingling, his heart was racing and despite the beer, there was a metallic taste in his mouth. He felt like he'd narrowly escaped death. The excitement over, most of the men went back to their conversation. It seemed as though knife throwing and the frisking of patrons were not uncommon occurrences in this establishment.

It wasn't easy to get a good look at anyone. The room was dimly lit and the men inside stood or sat close together with their heads bowed conspiratorially. Jeremy was surreptitiously scanning the faces in the crowd when he recognized the man who was watching Mary from outside the restaurant. "Your admirer is the second to last guy at the bar."

"That's Donovan's brother and so is the behemoth with the scratch on his finger."

"Lovely family." Dropping his voice to a whisper he added, "So do you think this will bring you back into the fold?"

"Can't say. This is a squirrely bunch. Finish your beer and let's go back to my place."

"That's an interesting invitation," he said, wanting to verify that he had heard it correctly.

"It is and I'm sure we can make it interesting. In our line of work, there isn't time for romance," Mary said as she squeezed his arm.

Lieutenant Jeremy Thrasher was quite taken aback by the forward proposition. He had had propositions from women before but none of them have ever been so direct but no other woman had ever defended his life by throwing a knife across the room either. They both finished the ale quickly. About half of the patrons in the bar took notice when Mary and Jeremy got up to leave but only one caught Jeremy's attention. Cowering in the back at a table beyond the bar was the nervous and pale face of Paul Koeing.

GRIMSBY BEACH

I carried the bag of vegetables from the kitchen at the Lakeview to the kitchen at the Park House and then I helped Mr. Swanson unload his wagon. As usual he was a wealth of information. His job delivering goods across the Niagara Peninsula and his penchant for gossip made him a library of world affairs and he was always on the lookout for new news to share.

"Good day Toke! Any news from your brother Jacob?"

"We had a letter last week. He made it to France. He said they were giving the Huns hell."

"That's good news. Hopefully this will be over soon and Jacob will be back here to help us carry all of this," he said, shouldering another sack of flour. "I hear you will be hosting the new recruits next month."

"Yah. Mr. Fair has secured enough wood and ice for twelve nights. We get one battalion a night as they march their way from Niagara to Hamilton. They are camping on the field."

"Well marching will be good practice for them. There are a lot of footsteps in being a soldier. Poor souls might have to walk across all the countries in Europe before this is over."

"Mr. Swanson, how is it that so many countries are involved in one war? Why does Russia care what happens on the French border? Why do we care what goes on in Serbia?" I asked.

"Good question Toke. I've been asking questions like that since I got back from South Africa a decade ago. The more interesting question is what made a young man like me board a boat to South Africa a decade ago and why young men willingly join up today to fight in battles that are not theirs?" Mr. Swanson paused to think. "I believe it all comes down to one human condition that affects us all. Something that has been woven into our souls from the dawn of time, all the way from Adam and Eve in that lovely Garden of Eden to where we stand today in this lovely jewel of a place. It has been passed down from generation to generation, starts as a seed inside infants and grows to be a mighty oak when we are at our tallest, our strongest, our fittest and at the prime of our lives." Silence followed. Mr. Swanson had said a lot but didn't answer the question.

"What human condition is that Mr. Swanson?" I had to ask.

"Stupidity," he answered. "Just plain dumbness. You are better off staying home Toke. If you want to help the war effort go off and get a job at Radiant Electric Company. They just got a contract for one hundred thousand fuses. Or go to Metalcraft Manufacturing. They're making shells and you'll make me and every other taxpayer in Grimsby get a return on our investment. That was a fine decision by the Grimsby Council to invest. That company is employing every man in Beamsville and Grimsby who wasn't fool enough to go off to war. In short, and no disrespect to your brother Jacob, my advice, which comes from direct experience, is don't go over the ocean to get yourself blown to pieces."

I nodded my head, considered his words and got the feeling that my brother Jacob was in more danger than I previously thought. When we were finished with the load I went to the kitchen where I folded the linens and napkins. Afterwards I swept the veranda and delivered fresh towels to the rooms. Without waiting on Von Papen's every whim, I seemed to be racing through the list of morning tasks left for me by Vannetter. It was when I went to ask my boss for more to do when he presented me with an envelope.

"This was left for you this morning."

The envelope had no return address and only the name "Toke" written on the front. I took the envelope to the back of the hotel and set myself under the kitchen steps. I opened the envelope and read;

Dear Toke,

Can't thank you enough for your assistance. Your efforts have helped us gather information that will help us defend our country and the Commonwealth. It is incumbent on us all to do what needs to be done in these difficult times. It is best if you do not mention my name(s), past and present. There are some mysteries that should not be solved. Burn this. J. W.

I held a match beneath the letter and envelope and made sure it was aflame before I dropped it on the gravel to turn to ash. Once extinguished, I stomped on it to scatter the pieces and that was that. My association with J. Wallace and my life as a spy was over.

Grimsby Beach seemed to slow down after that. As the war went on, there were fewer and fewer visitors. There were rations on food and fuel. Ferry service diminished to one boat a week and while the train stopped twice a day, few people got on and even fewer got off. The live acts on the Midway disappeared and the Merry-Go-Round only operated on the weekends. Grimsby Park was a shadow of its former self and although moving pictures did come to the Auditorium, attendance was spotty. A malaise settled in our community as an early end to the war seemed further and further away with each passing month.

Jacob's letters became less positive. He always tried to end the letter on a cheery note but there were more and more references to how difficult living conditions had become. Jacob had never been one to complain but bad food and his soggy feet became recurring themes. He recounted Ypres and the lingering smell of chlorine that had disabled hundreds of soldiers. He wrote of the screeching blasts that turned spring fields into a moonscape of mud. A year later he told us of how hundreds were snagged in barbed wire while machine guns took whole platoons out in minutes. At Beaumont Hamel, over half of the Newfoundland Regiment were killed or wounded in less than 30 minutes. But now Jacob was writing from a cave just West of Vimy. They were resting before their big push up the Ridge and Jacob was describing some of the art that his mates were carving into the soft chalky walls.

"Some fellows are regular Rembrandts. Our Sergeant carved our insignia. It has the crown and even the scallop shell. Other boys are making images of their girlfriends. A herring choker carved the Bluenose and there is even a mailbox sculpted right into the rock. It is cool and quiet down here in the Souterrain, but I know what awaits us."

I could see that as time went on, Mom would worry more deeply. Her smile, which had been a constant feature on her face before the war, appeared less often and for shorter stints. She would stop her knitting in the middle of a stitch and I would catch her looking off into space or she would wipe a dish over and over again with the towel until it could not get any drier. She seemed trapped by her thoughts and she never ventured very far from the cottage.

Two families who lost their sons at Ypres left in June and when they learned the news they didn't return to Grimsby Beach for the remainder of the summer or the summer after that. The optimism of the first year was shrinking and when the British Prime Minister Lloyd George called together our Prime Minister Robert Borden, W.M. Hughes of Australia, General Louis Botha of South Africa and Sir Edward Morris of Newfoundland every one suspected things were not going well. The main issue in the next Federal election became conscription and while most of the Niagara boys that were of age were already serving overseas, there were parts of the country who opposed mandatory service vehemently. At times it felt like the country would be torn apart and there were many disparaging remarks about the French in Quebec and the Irish Catholics who did not wish to sacrifice their sons for the Union Jack.

It was an awfully depressing time and I felt sidelined. Too young to enlist and with barely enough to do in my vocation, I had collapsed into the general depression of the times. And then a guest arrived at the hotel that brought me back up on my feet.

MANHATTAN

"We're going to my place," commanded Thrasher.

"That wasn't in my invitation," said Mary.

"I regret to say that we will have to delay that invitation. There was a guy in there who knows who I am and if he knows who I am then you aren't safe either. I'll clear out my apartment and then we'll do yours." Jeremy was walking faster and faster as they moved from the pub. Mary was struggling to keep up without breaking into a run.

"How does he know you?"

"We caught him setting fires here in the city so we pulled him into Washington for questioning. I thought we had him turned but seeing who he is drinking with I think he is still working with the Clan."

"Washington?" she asked.

"Washington."

"So you are Bureau of Investigation?" she asked.

"And you are Dominion Police. Isn't it nice when neighbours work together?" Jeremy stopped outside a brownstone. "I'm on the second level. I'll only be a minute. I suggest you wait in the alley," and he disappeared inside the door.

Mary slid into the darkness and kept a watchful eye on the street. Before she knew it, he was back carrying an umbrella and a suitcase.

"Okay. Let's go get your stuff," he said and they made off down the street and around the corner.

In five blocks they made a right and stopped at the first door while Mary found her key.

"Let's not be long," commanded Thrasher.

"I'll take less time than you," replied Mary and together they climbed two flights of stairs to the third floor.

The hall was dark and quiet as they moved swiftly to the door. Mary had her key ready and she entered the dark room first. She detected it right away. Her nostrils flared at the smell of sweat and ale hanging in the air but before she could slide her knife out of her sleeve, Mary was body checked across the room. Her feet left the ground and her body flew to the wall and bounced to the floor. Jeremy watched Donovan's hulk of a brother steady himself and then stomp toward her motionless body. He felt for Mary's knife, still in his pocket, drew it out and snapped the blade. The click stopped the giant in his tracks where he slowly turned toward the sound and on recognizing Thrasher, his mouth twisted into a menacing grin.

"We meet again," said Thrasher and he crouched down to ready himself for the giant's attack but the behemoth stopped his approach and just kept smiling. It was then that Jeremy felt an arm come up and under his and a hand press down on the back of his head. A leg had appeared between his own and along with a second arm around his midriff, he was thrown off balance and at the mercy of a second assailant. He did however, have Mary's knife in his free arm which he swung down between his own legs and into the thigh of his attacker. The man howled until Thrasher withdrew the knife from his leg, turned to face the screaming man and thrust in and up under his rib cage, slicing through the diaphragm and into his pleural cavity. The screaming stopped immediately and the man fell as his lungs collapsed.

Jeremy could feel the presence behind him. He knew the giant would be upon him before he could turn around so he ducked down into a ball hoping that his smaller shape would be harder to kick or punch. But neither came. In their place fell the full force of nearly 300 pounds of sweaty flesh. Jeremy could feel the air whoosh out of his lungs and he fully expected that a giant hand would reach out and crush his throat or punch his kidneys or bash his skull, but that never came either. Just the crushing sensation of being pinned to the floor by hundreds of pounds of human. The heft of the man wasn't allowing him to draw in much air but he had breath enough to lift a massive arm off his shoulder and kick the tree trunk leg away from his own. He slid and rolled and wriggled out from under his attacker and only when he kneeled to catch his breath did he see one of Mary's knives buried in the back of the giant's neck. It had separated vertebrae and sliced through his spinal cord. He looked dead and even if he wasn't, the giant couldn't move anymore.

"Good throw," he managed to say.

"Thanks." Mary was already emptying a drawer of clothes and a desk of papers into a carpet bag. "Are you good to go?" she asked.

Jeremy struggled to his feet still holding the bloody knife in his hand. "I think so."

"I'll take that," and she took her knife from Thrasher, wiped it on the back of the giant's shirt, folded it and slipped it back up her sleeve. Then she reached over, withdrew her second knife from the giant's neck, wiped it on his shirt again, closed it and slid it up her other sleeve.

"Do you do this every time you invite a gentleman back to your apartment?" he asked.

"Not every time." she smiled at him. "Let's get to the train station."

BUFFALO, NEW YORK

Jesse Ward, aka James Wallace, was staying in a large Victorian house on the east side of Delaware Park. It was an upscale neighbourhood. The homes were large and ornate and most employed at least one butler, one maid and one gardener. The grounds were well kept. This is where the elite of Buffalo lived and James found this assignment a pleasant distraction from the derelict inns and pubs he was normally put up in. This home was the property of an acquaintance of Judge Falconbridge. The owner was away at the time so the home, the grounds and the staff were at Jesse's discretion.

He had just returned from a walk about the neighbourhood when he passed the unusual home of Darwin D. Martin, a wealthy executive of a soap manufacturing company. "Prairie style?" he said to himself. The contrast of this modern home and the Victorian estates surrounding it was extraordinary. Jesse did not know what to think. Change had always been a present in his line of work. Shifting from one assignment to the next set him in constant motion. He wasn't unlike an actor shuffling from one city to another, assuming one identity on Monday to play a different role on Tuesday.

But there had always been something solid he could hold onto. Something steadfast and secure that he used as an anchor to balance himself and get his bearings when he wasn't quite sure who he was and who he was working for, his aunt's farm for instance. It didn't seem to matter how many years had passed; the family homestead always seemed the same. The rubble foundation under the house and barn was as strong as ever and his aunt never considered painting the house any other colour than white. As a youth, this place was a touchstone that told him where he had come from, who he was and who he wanted to be. In his adult life Jesse had fewer opportunities to visit the farm so he had to seek other anchors.

Even before his stint as a mason, he was drawn to stone edifices. The permanence of the material and the skill required to shape it was something he always admired. From the ornate details of the Victorian buildings to the more reserved and recent Edwardian structures, Jesse found solace in their facades. While they weren't as warm and inviting as the whitewashed farmhouse in the Ottawa Valley, they made him feel that the society and culture he was a member of, was stable and secure. This neighbourhood on Buffalo's north side made him feel the same way. And then he passed the Martin House. This house, designed by Frank Lloyd Wright was like nothing he had seen before, another sign that the world was changing.

Still his walk was pleasant. He had to remind himself that even though the country he was in wasn't at war, much of the rest of the world was. It would have been easy to forget his purpose here if it weren't for the butler delivering coded messages and telegrams every time he came through the door.

"Breakfast is ready for you sir," said the butler as he held out the latest coded message.

"Thank you Charles."

Jesse unfolded the note. It read;

M. at O. 8pm

'M' he knew, stood for McGarrity and 'O' represented O'Hallarin's, an Irish pub near the Buffalo dockyards. It was written in a good hand on a slip of quality paper. He hoped the information was as good as the handwriting.

"Charles, I am unoccupied until this evening. What should I see of Buffalo while I am visiting?"

"The zoo is nearby and the Albright Gallery is a pleasant walk across the park, Sir," offered the butler.

"Then that is what I will do. Thank you for the suggestion. I will take my breakfast now, I will dine out for lunch and I will have my dinner at six pm."

"Very good, Sir."

Giving orders to others felt foreign to Jesse but he had a role to play and he was impressing himself at how well he could pretend to be the well-to-do gentlemen. After breakfast, he changed his shirt and collar. He was glad that the fashion of a high collar was still in vogue as it nearly covered the scar on his throat. As he left the house, he felt buoyant about the prospects of the day. The zoo held many exotic animals, many of which Jesse had never seen before and he enjoyed the walk across the park to the Art Gallery. Also new and novel to him were the Impressionist paintings that hung on its walls. He left the gallery questioning the value of these works and wondered who would want to hang a blurry landscape image in their home? It was another sign of change.

He crossed the park once again to return home where he bathed and napped until dinner. He sat alone at the table and was served a delicious plate of roast pork. Jesse bestowed compliments to the cook and thanks for the service and then he made his way to his room to change into his work clothes. He hung the suit he had worn throughout the day carefully in the wardrobe and put on a pair of wool trousers and a checked shirt. He added a well-used hat and exchanged his pair of dress boots for the work boots he usually wore. By the time he had finished the costume change, he was transformed from a gentleman to a workman. He could pass for any one of the gardeners he had seen on his way to the zoo and art gallery. Charles was there in the foyer to see him off.

"You are best to use the kitchen door, Sir," he suggested.

"Good idea Charles. I assume it will be left open should I arrive back late?"

"Yes, it will, Sir."

"And you said the Omnibus is the fastest transport into the city?"

"It is Sir and it is most inconspicuous. Although it does not return this way after 9 pm."

"Then I may have to find some other means. Thank you, Charles. Have a pleasant evening."

"I will do my best Sir. Do be cautious."

"I will."

And so Jesse Ward joined the crowd of passengers on the bus travelling down Main St. to the heart of the city. He enjoyed his day and was appreciating his lodging and the help within. Obviously, the butler had some working knowledge of who the guests were or at least, who they worked for. His help and assistance gave Jesse a boost of confidence and positive outlook to the task he had tonight.

O'Hallarin's was near the wharf. He had no trouble finding it. The pungent fragrance of stale beer drifted to his nose as he entered the large pub. It was very popular with the local stevedores and sailors who worked the Great Lakes but presently it was quiet. The afterwork crowd had gone home to dinner and there were only a smattering of patrons at the tables and at the bar. McGarrity was not among them but it was still thirty minutes until eight pm. Jesse went to the bar and ordered a pint and found a table with a clear view of the room. He scanned the small crowd wondering if McGarrity was meeting with any of the men already here. Most were in groups of two or three playing cards or telling stories, passing time. One group of three were playing darts by the far wall. None of them looked dangerous enough to be holding a meeting with a high-level member of Clan na Gael. There was one lone individual with his hat pulled down and his head on the table. He looked too drunk to hold a conversation with anyone. Jesse sat and waited. Eight pm went by. Eight-o-five pm went by.

A barmaid came and asked Jesse if he needed his ale topped up and it was during his response to her that he saw McGarrity slip in and sit at the table adjacent to the dart board. Jesse declined more beer and seized the opportunity to cross the room with his mug in hand. He asked to join the threesome in the game. He took a circuitous route so his approach would not face McGarrity directly and by the time he stood between the dartboard and McGarrity's table his quarry was still alert but unalarmed. To his good fortune the dart players welcomed him and they proceeded to play a game called 'cricket'. In situations like this, Jesse usually found himself the center of attention as he told one of his tall tales but he knew he was there to observe and eavesdrop. It took great personal restraint to remain quiet and his efforts were rewarded. Before Jesse threw a dart a tall and lanky man entered and went directly to McGarrity's table. His features were severe. High cheekbones and a pronounced brow were accentuated by his short-cropped hair. Over the banter of the dart game, Jesse could make out a Texan accent.

Jesse and his partner were losing the match and their opponents were taunting them at each throw making it challenging to eavesdrop but he did catch some words and phrases. He distinctly heard the words "Maine", "Dupont", "Canal" and he thought McGarrity called the other man 'Taylor'. Of greater interest was an exchange made from the Texan to McGarrity. It was an envelope whose contents caused it to bulge. Both McGarrity and his guest departed before the dart game was over. To the consternation of his opponents, Jesse made an excuse as to why he had to leave before the game was over and he headed off after McGarrity.

McGarrity was only halfway down the next block before he went into another pub. Jesse approached cautiously, pulling down his hat before he walked past. He noted that it was another Irish pub and thought he might be recognized if he were to double back and enter the establishment. He took note of the location and called it an evening. Caution is the parent of safety he told himself. He had put himself in harm's way many times in his vocation, but in this instance, he needed to be inconspicuous. He had been sent over the border to observe and document the movements of Father McGarrity and it would not serve his purpose if he were discovered. He boarded the omnibus back to Delaware Park and this gave him time to consider what he had heard and seen.

He surmised that 'Taylor' was not from Texas. His demeanor was too formal and manner of speech was exaggerated and unnatural. His mention of a "canal" might refer to Erie or the Welland canal. Jesse's experience posing as a stonecutter on the locks of the Welland Canal and the current military efforts to guard it suggested that this was a likely target. He knew that "Dupont" was a century old company that until recently, had a monopoly on the production of gunpowder. "Maine" was the northernmost state on the eastern seaboard and did not fit nicely into the puzzle he was assembling in his mind but not all clues, he told himself, always fitted nicely into every picture. He was distracted many times throughout the dart game and it may have no consequence at all. And then there was the envelope. It could have contained money or plans or anything really. He did conclude that 'Father' McGarrity and the stern looking man were plotting something and the directions were being given by the guest to McGarrity. There could be no question as to who was in charge. The tip he received earlier that day regarding this meeting was a good one. He wasn't privy to the source of the information but would make sure that his report would acknowledge the accuracy of the intelligence he had received.

He was still mulling over what he had learned that evening as he approached the service entrance. He opened the kitchen door to find Charles's head enveloped in a cloud of steam. He was ladling soup into a taurine.

"A little late for dinner, isn't it Charles?"

"We have two more guests sir," he said as he continued to transfer the soup from the pot.

"Guests?"

"Yes sir, and they would very much like to speak with you."

The door between the kitchen and dining room swung on a hinge through which Jesse could just hear the murmur of two voices. Curious to see who had arrived he pushed his way through the door to find a chiselled good-looking man sitting adjacent to the beautiful features of Mary Miller. Their heads were bent together and their conversation was hushed and intimate.

"Well, look who is here!"

Mary stood and embraced Jesse.

"Good to see you Mr. Ward," she said as she held him in a tight embrace. Lieutenant Thrasher noted the discrepancy between the cool formality of her verbal greeting and the close warmth of her physical embrace. She hung onto Jesse Ward longer than he thought appropriate for a regular working relationship. He guessed that these two had had a more intimate connection in the past. "And this is Lieutenant Jeremy Thrasher of the Central Intelligence Agency."

Jeremy stood as he was introduced and reached out his hand to Jesse Ward who shook it. Just then, Charles brought in the soup.

"Don't let me interrupt your dinner. Please sit down and tell me where you have been," prompted Jesse. "You've been down here for some months now, haven't you?" Jesse asked Mary.

"Baltimore and New York City," nodded Mary as she took a spoonful of soup.

"And what was in Baltimore?" asked Jesse.

"The Brown Printing Company. I was asked to verify that they were printing forged documents for German citizens. We had news that Consul Carl

A. Luederitz was providing fake passports to agents here in the U.S. I took some time isolating printing companies that might be involved and then I sold them the paper they needed and Brown and Brown used it. The paper had a distinctive marker in it so we could identify and track it. One of the forged passports passed over my desk just weeks after I sold them the paper."

"And what was in New York City?"

"I got hired as an accountant by the office of Clan na Gael in Manhattan. I ,....."

"Wow," interrupted Jesse. Both Jeremy Thrasher and Jesse Ward were staring at the beautiful Mary Miller with admiration and respect. They didn't know any women and very few men who had the nerve to infiltrate organizations as ruthless as the Clan.

"And as their accountant, I oversaw contributions coming in from all the major cities across the country. Thousands of dollars flowed in to fund their cause. There are over four million Irish here in the U.S. and many have it in for the Dominion of Canada and her ties to England."

"And what is the Bureau of Investigation doing about the Clan?" Jesse had turned his attention onto Lieutenant Thrasher who did not shrink from the accusation.

"We are aware of the Irish organization but most are American citizens and in this country, they are free to donate their money to whatever organization they wish. Besides, most of our resources have focused on the German Consulate in Washington. We are not at war with Germany but we have observed suspicious activities amongst their military attachés and we suspect that they are behind a series of arsons in New York City, colluding with the resistance in Mexico and India and the purchase of hydraulic presses across the country."

"Why would they want to buy hydraulic presses?" asked Jesse.

"They are needed to make ammunition and if they have control of them, they can control the production of shells," explained Thrasher.

"Speaking of shells, I overheard Father McGarrity in conversation tonight and the mention of Dupont came up."

"Who is Father McGarrity?" asked the Lieutenant.

"Clan na Gael," said Mary. "He has been drifting over the border for months posing as a Catholic Priest. We suspect that he orchestrated a train derailment a year ago and an attempt to steal plans for the fourth canal at Welland."

"Dupont is manufacturing most of the gunpowder in this country," added Thrasher.

"What else did the good Father say?" asked Mary.

"I didn't hear very much. I really only heard four words. 'Dupont', 'canal', 'Maine' as in the State of Maine and 'Taylor'."

"Taylor?" asked Mary.

"Yeah, I think it may have been the name of the guy McGarrity was meeting with."

"What did he look like?" asked Mary.

"Tall, thin, short hair, bony face," described Jesse

"Did he have an accent?" added Mary.

"Yeah, but it didn't sound authentic. He was trying to sound like he was from Texas but he was from somewhere else."

"That's Bridgeman W. Taylor. I met him in Hans Tauscher's shop in Manhattan," she said looking at Thrasher. "He helped me get the office job at Clan na Gael. He's in Buffalo right now?" asked Mary.

"Well he was as of two hours ago. Who's Hans Tauscher?" asked Jesse.

Jeremy spoke. He knew the file on Tauscher backwards and forwards.

"Tauscher is an arms dealer. He has been peddling the German luger to every police force in the country. He's even approached our General High Command. He rubs shoulders with some very influential people in business and in government. He is quite at home here in the States but we feel like he may be more loyal to his home country."

"So how is it Mr. Thrasher, that your government is host to foreign diplomats who are nothing more than spies and saboteurs to your allies and neighbours?" accused Ward.

“My government believes in holding its friends close and its enemies closer. And do you think there are no spies in your country Mr. Ward?” replied Thrasher.

He paused for a response but didn’t get one. Both Mary and Jesse were aware that espionage was alive and well in Canada and that their country had meagre resources to deal with the problem. Diplomats within the Dominion were vetted by Britain and the United States. Canada had to rely on foreign governments to guard the security of its own parliament. The Lieutenant then turned to Mary.

“Mary, if Taylor is in Buffalo, you should not be seen. It is no longer safe for you here or anywhere in the United States. Clan na Gael is in every American city.”

Mary nodded. “I will go back to Canada as soon as possible.”

“And I,” said the Lieutenant, “must return to Washington.”

He was looking at Mary and when she looked up, there was regret in both of their eyes. Jesse Ward immediately felt invisible. It was as though there had been three people sitting around the dining table and then one vanished. He spoke up as if reintroducing himself to the room.

“And I will track McGarrity here in Buffalo. I am sure that he is taking directions from Bridgeman Taylor and if they are going to make an attempt on the canal, I best stay close to him.”

Jesse looked from Mary to Jeremy. Neither responded. They were deaf to him. Jesse shrugged, sighed and said, “Well, I’m turning in for the night. Good night to you both.” Neither responded. They just sat staring into each other’s eyes.

GRIMSBY BEACH

Since the departure of James Wallace, aka Jesse Ward, life for me was pretty static. It was as though the community was suspended in time during the war. Many of the cottages remained closed up, shuttered and empty throughout the summer season. Fiona Falconbridge had not visited since the beginning of the war. I was beginning to wonder if I remembered what she looked like. Still, my infatuation was steadfast.

The only significant change in the Park was that Harry Wylie died. He had owned Grimsby Park for six years and in that short time, gave much of the Park a carnival like atmosphere. His descendants had no interest in running it so they sold the Park to the Canada Steamship Lines. I imagine the transportation company thought they could profit from hosting and entertaining visitors as well as delivering them to the resort. In essence, very little changed. The staff and the procedures used to keep the hotels and amenities running were the same and other than the Steamship Line logo showing up on more advertisements, brochures and pamphlets, most people were unaware that there was a change in ownership at all.

A less significant and more personal change was that my boss, Mr. Vannetter was kinder and more respectful to me. He even called me Toke once. I often wondered about the source of this transformation. He seemed to have forgiven me for my adventures with the iron and my complaining of difficult and demanding guests. He did not bristle when I was late for work or when I could not be found. Even when he had good reason to admonish me, his strictness had faded. My boss had become a kinder, gentler man. I pondered this out loud once in the presence of Cook. He was smoking a cigarette on the landing while I was leaning on my broom when he informed me that Mr. Vannetter's kid brother had been killed in action at Beaumont Hamel.

And so I knew. I knew that Mr. Vannetter was suffering a loss shared by so many families. A loss that caused some to withdraw into themselves and deny them the simple pleasures and joys of daily life, like my mother, who hadn't lost her eldest son, but was plagued by the possibility of losing him. And then there were others, like Mr. Vannetter, whose loss made them appreciate the fragility of what is before us. That our lives and the people we share our lives are delicate and needed to be honoured and cherished. I stopped leaning on my broom and got back to work.

BUFFALO, N. Y.

Jesse Ward gave it three nights. He had not received any other coded messages so he repeated the actions taken before. Each night he dressed in his gardening garb. Each night he took the bus into the city. Each night he entered O'Hallarin's bar and each night he ordered a draft ale and drank it alone. He sat with his back to the wall with a view of the whole room and each night Father McGarrity failed to show his face. It was this part of the job that he loathed. The waiting was so tedious. On the third night, the threesome he played darts with showed up. He was hopeful that they would see him sitting and ask him to join in but his untimely departure in their first match gave them cause not to invite him, so they didn't. He sat for three nights with nothing to show for it.

"It's time we got you back to Canada," Jesse said to Mary the following morning. He had just come into the dining room to find Mary having her breakfast.

"You won't get any argument from me," said Mary. "I'm going stir crazy cooped up here."

At that moment the doorbell rang and they could hear Charles footsteps as he made his way to answer the front door. He came back with an envelope and handed it to Jesse. Inside was a note that read;

M. in G.B.

"Looks like McGarrity has crossed the border. He's back in Grimsby Beach. No doubt he's carrying out the instructions of Bridgeman Taylor."

"Does it say how long he has been in Canada? You haven't seen him in three days. He could be ready to carry out their plans at any time," pointed out Mary.

"It doesn't say but you're right. Time is of the essence and we don't want to use the bridges. I can arrange for a boat to take us back over the border for tonight but that gives McGarrity another day. I know someone who may be able to help. Pack your bag, Mary. I've got to send a telegram."

GRIMSBY BEACH

I just happened to be in the Montreal Telegraph office picking up the daily news for our guests when Henry Mullens called me over to his wicket.

"Here Toke, this is for you. Some kind of coded message. Hope you can read it," he said, holding out the slip of paper towards me.

This was the first telegraph I'd ever received. At first, I thought there must have been some kind of mistake and then I thought it might be from my brother but when I saw J. W. at the bottom of the slip I knew who it was from. I read it right there and then. I didn't understand it until I had crossed the road and was climbing the steps of the Park House Hotel.

`Organize M's baggage. List contents. J.W.`

"Organize" was the term Wallace used when he went through Papen's room. While I hadn't stayed to watch him do it, I imagine he searched amongst Papen's papers and clothing and suitcases for anything that might be of interest. Evidently, Mr. Wallace wanted me to carry out the same search for someone known as "M" and keep track of what I found. The request was both terrifying and exhilarating at the same time. My life had become predictable and boring in those months so I decided to check the Park House's registry first for whom the "M" might represent before I committed myself to the crime of break and enter.

Luckily, Vannetter wasn't at the front desk. I crossed the foyer and spun the registry around. There were only nine rooms booked for the night and not one of the registered guests' names started with 'M'. I looked back throughout the prior week and while a Mildred Mason stayed four nights before, she had stayed only one night and had long since gone.

I dug in my pocket for the telegram and reread it. There were only five words and I didn't think I misinterpreted them. Mr. Wallace sent it to me thinking someone known as 'M' would be staying at the Parkhouse but what if they had chosen to stay at the Lakeview? That would make the task more challenging. To make off with the spare key in my own hotel wasn't easy. To do so under the nose of Harry Nelles at the Lakeview would be nearly impossible.

Nevertheless, I made up my mind to check the Lakeview registry for any 'M's' and decide later if I needed to steal a key before breaking into one of the rooms.

While Vannetter was out of sight, I took the opportunity to make the short trip to the other hotel. All the way I was imagining ways of distracting Harry while I searched the register and stole a key. By the time I was climbing the outside steps and crossing the lobby, I still had no idea what I was going to do or say. To my great delight the receptionist was absent. I repeated my earlier actions, spun the register and ran my finger down the page. There was only one 'M' on the page and the name jumped out at me like fire, 'McGarrity'. He had checked in two days prior and I was sure this was the 'M' Wallace was referring to. I was just eyeing the spare key to McGarrity's room when I heard Mr. Vannetter's voice behind me.

"Robert? What are you doing here?"

"Oh, Mr. Vannetter." I turned around to see Vannetter with Harry in tow. "Cook sent me over for some supplies," I lied.

"Well get him what he needs and then get back over here. We have a little crisis. Mr. Nelles here is going off to war."

Vannetter said this as he turned to Harry and put a hand on his shoulder. I looked at Harry sympathetically and with some measure of envy.

"As he's terminating his employment today, he will have to train you to take his place."

"Here, at the Lakeview?" I asked.

"Yes, here at the Lakeview. Now get those supplies to Cook and get back here right away," instructed Vannetter.

I made the motion of leaving the premises, walking the five minutes to the Parkhouse and then turned around and walked back. I couldn't believe my luck. The Lakeview was just completing renovations and promised to be the grander of the two hotels. It cost $1.50 to stay at the Parkhouse and $2.00 to stay at the Lakehouse. Amongst hotel staff, it was considered more prestigious to work at the Lakehouse. The guests were richer and the tips were greater. By the time I got back to the Lakeview's front desk, Harry was waiting for me. He looked a little lost.

"When do you ship out?" I asked him.

"I've got basic training for eight weeks before they ship me out. I will be in Thorold for most of that time and then we will take the train to Montreal.

The timbre and tone of Harry's speech was odd. Gone was the bravado that punctuated every other verbal discourse he and I had ever had. He was speaking automatically, like a machine, devoid of emotion. I decided that he was regretting signing up, that he was sorry for succumbing to the social pressure to fall into the ranks, to do his part. Every young man, myself included, felt its pull. The difference for Harry was that he knew, unlike those who signed up at the beginning of the war, just what he was getting into. Enough letters had made it home and were shared amongst neighbours and they showed a stark contrast to the glorious fighting and victories described in the daily papers.

"Are you scared?" I didn't ask in a mocking way. I was asking for future reference. If the war lasted another two years, I would be in his shoes.

He nodded. "They're going to conscript us anyway. It's better to sign up."

"Sure, it is," I said, trying to sound supportive and that was the last word he or I said about the war. He took me on a tour of the hotel describing his duties as we went. He had worked here for four years and I could see that he was going to miss it. Besides some modern features that are absent at the Parkhouse, the Lakeview ran in pretty much the same way and I was confident that I could do the job. I tried to convey that confidence by suggesting that he leave early and spend time with his family before heading off to Thorold. He was receptive to the idea and after he took one last mournful glance around the lobby, Harry Nelles left the Lakeview in my hands.

My Dad always said that I was lucky. If we were playing cribbage, I would always draw a five when I needed one or when we were fishing, I'd always snag the biggest catch and I thought my luck had showed up again in a big way that day. I had just landed into the best possible job in the Park. At least the best possible job that I was qualified for. I would have more responsibility and more money and I was pretty sure that it would impress Fiona. I felt a surge of pride and renewed confidence in myself. Things were looking very good for me. And then I put my hand in my pocket, felt the telegram there and was reminded of the reason I'd come to the Lakeview in the first place.

It felt like destiny. When I needed access to McGarrity's room, I was put in charge of every room key in the entire hotel. It felt like I had been chosen for the task by some higher being. Little did I know that the day my new job at the Lakeview hotel started, that that was the day my luck would run out.

PART THREE

THE ANNIE LARSON AFFAIR

LAKEVIEW HOTEL, ROOM 14

When I awoke I had the overwhelming sensation of pain. I'd never felt so engulfed before. It was as though every nerve of my body was on fire. I tried to see why. As my left eye struggled to flutter open and focus, I became aware that my right eye wasn't opening at all. The message my brain sent to my hands to reach up and clear the sleep from my eyes wasn't being obeyed. The message my brain sent to my legs only moved the right one. The left was immobile. It was when my knee raised off of the bed that I heard voices.

"He's waking up," said a female voice.

"Thank God." said a male with relief.

I felt their weight on either side of me. The movement of the mattress made me winch and the man took a step back which allowed my left eye to bring him into focus. It was James Wallace. He was dressed in a tailored suit. He wore an expression of pity and concern.

"Can you give him something for the pain?" he asked.

"I'm doing that right now," the woman said and I felt a tug on my right arm.

"Where am I?" I asked.

"You're in the Lakeview Toke."

I looked around. It was a room I'd never seen before but I could hear the waves on the shoreline and behind Wallace I could make out the thick trunks of the towering pine trees that surrounded the hotel.

"I'm just going to check this bandage Toke," said the woman and she lifted a covering over my right eye. I winced again. The light was blinding.

"Try not to blink," she added. "That's healing well," and she laid the bandage back over the eye.

I could feel a warmth start to creep over me. The pain was lifting and I began to feel like I was floating off of the bed.

"Toke, do you remember anything?" Wallace asked.

"Mr. Wallace, he's not going to be able to answer you for some time. You'll need to let him rest."

I saw his face become blurry and then my one good eye closed and I floated away.

A TRAIN RIDE TO NEW YORK

Forty-eight hours after James Wallace had left Buffalo for Grimsby Beach, he was on his way back over the border. He was, once again, on the trail of Joseph McGarrity with increased fervour. He had seen what the imposter priest had done to young Toke and he felt responsible for the young man's injuries. Moreover, the latest intelligence suggested that while McGarrity's plans for the Welland Canal had been foiled, he was still very much involved in sabotage activities. So, he bought a ticket to New York City and followed.

The train from Buffalo was full. Two of the passenger cars were commandeered by the U.S 27th Infantry Division. The troops were on their way to Grand Central where they would transfer on their way to Camp Wadsworth in Spartanburg, South Carolina. This left one car for the rest of the passengers who had to shuffle and squeeze their way into every seat. Wallace found himself sandwiched between an elderly woman and a middle-aged gentleman and across the aisle was a mother and her three children. The gentleman to his right hid behind a newspaper, its headline describing the failed allied attack on the Dardanelles. The elderly woman busied herself with her needlepoint while the young mother gazed out the window at the passing farmland, her kids poking and prodding each other but generally behaving themselves.

"That's detailed work you're doing." stated Wallace.

"It passes the time and it's good for my arthritis. Keeps my fingers nimble."

"Must be a challenge. My mom was a knitter. She didn't have the eyes for the fine work you're doing. Her projects were big ones. She once knitted my dad a scarf that was ten feet long. Big loopy thing. Had to wrap it around his neck four times to keep it off the ground."

The gentleman beside me snapped his paper. It didn't deter Wallace.

"One time my mum knit a sweater for my brother. It could have fit him and me and me Dad. She had no sense of proportion, that woman. God, I miss her. Another time,..."

The gentleman snapped his paper twice this time but it only spurred Wallace on.

"As I was saying another time my mom was baking a cake ..." but before he could go any further the man folded the newsprint onto his lap and glared at James.

"Am I disturbing your reading Sir? I can't say there's much good news these days. I see the allies had a time in the Dardanelles. That's in Turkey, isn't it?"

"Allies? You call them allies? They are going to drag us into a war that isn't any of our business," The man was surly and curt and still glaring.

James Wallace wanted to tell him about the German spies that wined and dined with the rich and powerful of his country. He wanted to describe the intricate network of fundraising and campaigning that sent thousands of American dollars to Ireland to attack England from behind. He wanted to let the ignorant ass know that American soldiers were already fighting a German backed militia on the borders of Mexico. But he didn't. Instead, he turned his attention to the children sitting opposite, eyes wide with the confrontation going on before them.

"Hello children. Do you like riding on trains?" The eldest continued to stare, the middle child clutched her mother's arm more tightly and the youngest nodded.

"You like trains too. I could tell. One time I took the train all the way from Toronto to Vancouver. It was supposed to take three days but it ..."

The man with the paper got up, tucked his paper under his arm, pulled his valise from the overhead rack and left. James slid over to occupy the new found space and continued his story.

"...it snowed mounds and mounds of it. In one spot the drift was higher than the train and it stopped us right there in the middle of a mountain pass. Imagine that? The snow was so high that the big powerful locomotive couldn't move forward. The snow was so high that the conductor and crew broke out shovels and asked for volunteers. It seemed like great fun to me so I joined up and we all shovelled ourselves silly. We dug for 10 hours and the porter brought us hot chocolate and biscuits. And I think I have some biscuits here."

Wallace reached into his bag and withdrew a package of Peek Freans. "That is, if it is okay with your mother?" The children looked up to their mother with pleading eyes. She smiled and nodded and Wallace shared the biscuits.

"Anyway, we shovelled snow all through the night, scraping and scooping out snow as high as we could reach until there was a tunnel just big enough for the locomotive to get through. The train moved ahead slowly behind us as we dug deeper and deeper into the snowbank. We dug until the sun came over the horizon, its light flitted through the roof of our tunnel and made it a beautiful pale blue." Wallace got a far off look in his eye as he gazed up at the ceiling. When he looked down at his audience, he could see that the children had already eaten his gift. "It was one of the most beautiful sights I have ever seen. We stopped the work to eat more biscuits,.... would you care for another?" and Wallace handed out the package to everyone. "We had more biscuits and the engineer told us to get on the train. He thought that it was possible for the train to smash its way through the rest of the drift so we stopped our work and prepared to board. But when I walked by the coal car, the engineer singled me out and said, 'Not you! You're a good shoveler. We'll need your help to shovel coal. We'll need a good head of steam to blast through that snowbank' and he took my snow shovel away from me and handed me a coal shovel. I climbed up into the engine, opened the furnace door and felt the warmth of the fire within. 'Well, get on with it" the engineer says to me and I threw shovel after shovel of black dusty anthracite deep into the belly of the train. At each shovelful, flames leapt out of the furnace door and I could hear the water bubbling and gurgling away in the tank. I was like a machine; stooping and scooping and throwing coal until the furnace wouldn't hold any more. The water in the tank was rolling around and steam was escaping from every seam. The metal before me started to glow and that's when the engineer told me to stand back. He reached up with his left hand and engaged the drive wheels. We could hear them slipping and screeching as they spun on the rails. Meanwhile his right hand was on the brake keeping us from barreling towards the snow. 'READY?' the engineer yelled above the noise. 'READY?' he shouted again and when he gave up on my reply he shouted, "HERE SHE GOES!' and he released the brake. We could hear the cars lock together as the engine lurched forward and swooped into the tunnel of snow. The heat from the engine melted the beautiful blue ceiling as we passed and the water rained down on the cars. When we were nearing the end of our tunnel, the engineer gave the throttle another crank and shouted, 'HANG ON!' and we burst through the snow bank in a cloud of steam that followed us all the way to Vancouver and that children, is why I like riding on trains. They always lead to adventure. And do you know the morale of this story?" Wallace looked into the wide eyes of the speechless children. "There isn't anything we can't do, when we work together and that includes, fighting the Turks in the Dardanelles," and he winked at the elderly woman.

The children smiled. One of them clapped and the mother mouthed the word, 'Thank you'.

"You are most welcome. I enjoyed telling it. What good is an adventure if you can't share it with someone?"

"Well, I hope this trip is completely absent from that kind of adventure," said the old woman. "But I did enjoy your tale and thank you for making more room in the car. Such a dreadful man."

The rest of the trip was quiet. The kids went to sleep. The mother resumed gazing out the window and the old lady worked away on her needle point. James Wallace used his time to eat the last biscuit in the package and contemplate what he would do when he reached New York. He had been briefed on Mary Miller's time there. He knew where she worked, where she lived and the pub she frequented. He also had the address on Park Ave where she attended parties. He let the information float as he drifted off to sleep and hoped it would organize itself and settle into a plan by the time he woke. He hoped finding Joseph McGarrity would be as easy as shoveling a train out of a snowdrift.

BARRED

There was a crowd of boys around the veteran. His long beard shook as he told his story, the hardee on his head cocked to one side. They were all sitting at the base of a Civil War monument.

"And there was me, just a tyke not much older than you, picking up the Stars and Stripes and yelling at the Confederates, 'You come and take this!' and didn't they all turn their guns on me. Shot was buzzing around my ears until our artillery gave them a blastin'. When the dust settled, the battle was over and I counted five bullet holes in the flag I was holdin."

The boys were wrapped up in the story and only noticed Wallace's presence when he cast a shadow over them.

"That sounded like a good story. Wish I'd heard it from the beginning."

"Well, Sir, I am here every day. Can't say I know where all these fine young men will be but I'll be right here come rain or shine. I could tell it to you then."

"Thanks for the invitation. Could you tell me where O'Brien's Pub is?

"We can take you there mister." Two of the boys, both chewing on cigar butts looked up. "But I don't think you'll be welcome."

"And how would you know where I'd be welcome?"

"You're not Irish and O'Brien's is just for them."

"Just the same, I'd appreciate it if you could point it out to me. There might even be a fresh cigar for each of you if you could help me out."

Simultaneously both boys spat out the tobacco in their mouths and nodded. "Let's go then," and they headed off towards the docks. As Wallace followed, he noticed that one of the boys was shoeless. Although it didn't appear to bother him, he had a painful looking rash up the back of his leg. The other boy looked like he would be shoeless soon. He had no laces and the souls were worn unevenly. There was no school for them and Wallace wondered what circumstances kept them out of the warehouses and factories that took advantage of child labour. These were kids whose survival depended on knowing what doors and windows were open to them, who would let them in and who would keep them out and he suspected that they might be correct about him being barred from the Irish Pub. He had followed the boys two blocks when they abruptly stopped. James nearly walked into them.

"Is it here?" he asked as he looked up and down the street.

The boys said nothing. The shorter of the two pointed to the sign in the window beside them. The status of an entire and fresh cigar instead of a butt plucked from the gutter was irresistible to these boys.

"Ah, you'd like payment now?" said Wallace as he read, 'Cuban 5 cent cigars'.

Wallace went into the store, made the purchase and came out with two cheroots. He handed one to the taller boy and put the other in his pocket which he tapped with his open palm and said, "When we get to our destination." The tall boy smiled as he put the tobacco into his mouth. The shorter boy scowled and began walking, beckoning Wallace to follow.

They made their way to Five Points. It was a slum like no other, its inhabitants a desperate lot. It was a short boat ride from Ellis Island and most of these immigrants saw no other part of America. They had survived the transatlantic crossing and navigated the immigration screening and came to Lower Manhattan to search out the family and friends who came before them. Wanting for money and shelter, many became stuck in the mire of the tenement buildings and low wage labouring jobs. James Wallace had seen nothing like it before. The cobblestones were broken and uneven here. Puddles and pools of water sat tepid and stinking. A horse lay in the gutter. Emancipated and bony in life, it looked even sorrier in death. Children, shoeless and dressed in rags, sat in the same gutter fascinated by the stillness of death that lay beside them.

Ship bells and shouts rang up Broad Street. They were descending into the lowlands towards the docks and there was great motion where the street ended and the water began. Wagons rolled along the waterfront delivering and picking up cargo while stevedores and longshoremen busied themselves along the pier. Not far along South street they came to squat red brick with the sign, 'O'Brien's'. Wallace took the cigar out of his breast pocket and handed it to the boy.

"Thank you, boys. I'll take it from here." and the boys sauntered back the way they had come, two long sticks of tobacco protruding from their mouths.

The window of the pub was grimy and dark. James could make out the outline of a face peering out, a sentry? It did not look welcoming. There was an older man in a ratty coat and a bowler hat standing on the opposite curb selling bagels stacked on a stick. His white beard quivered as he advertised his goods.

"I'll take one," Wallace said as he took a position with a clear view of the pub. He fumbled in his pocket for some coins.

"That will be one penny." The old man enunciated each syllable carefully and his voice climbed in pitch with each word. He had a heavy Hebrew accent.

"These look good. Did you bake these?"

"That would be the Mrs.'s. She's the baker in the family. I'm just the salesman," said the Jew as he tried to look over Wallace to catch the attention of his next customer.

"I used to be a salesman. I sold dry goods, musical instruments, and hardware." Wallace took a bite of a bagel and glanced at the entrance to the pub across the street. He was measuring and noting the setting; the distance from Broad St., the neighbouring buildings, its proximity to the water. When the bagel seller started chanting his sales pitch again, Wallace continued.

"I used to travel from city to city with a suitcase of samples. Sometimes I'd open up my case and sell on the street just like you and other times I would go door to door. It was an interesting job. I liked it. I met all sorts of fascinating people." Wallace noticed a giant of a man exit the pub and slap a flat cap onto his ginger-coloured head.

"Is that so?" asked the bagel seller, who continued to scan the street for other customers.

"It is so. One time I knocked on a door only to find the lady of the house engaged in the rehearsal for a play, the rest of the cast was practicing a recital for their upcoming performance. As luck would have it, this play was a musical and just before I rapped on the door the entire chorus was struggling to find the harmony between the soprano and the altos. As I introduced myself to her, she winced at the discordant sounds emanating from her salon. The melodies were so disjointed that I immediately offered my services, demonstrated the Czechoslovakian pitch pipes I had with me and sold her one. Within minutes the troop was singing together like a choir." During his dissertation Wallace saw two young toughs knock on the Pub door and wait to be invited in. A rough looking face peered through the door and the frame, asked the men a question and then let them in.

"Bagels, Fresh Bagels here!" The Jew was back at it, apparently not that interested in Wallace's stint as a travelling salesman.

"And then there was the time when I was selling hats,...."

The Jew rolled his eyes and for the first time in several minutes looked directly at Wallace and interrupted. "If you are not going to buy my bagels, I would appreciate it if you departed."

"Then I will have another. They're most delicious. Compliments to your wife. She is a master baker." Just at that moment, James Wallace recognized Joseph McGarrity. He had come around the corner and was making his way to O'Brien's door.

"That will be two pennies." The old man was noticeably perturbed.

"Two pennies. My first bagel was only one." stated Wallace, his eyes still on McGarrity.

"Yes, and the price will keep rising the longer you stand before me. I thank you for your business, now please move on."

McGarrity had been questioned and let into the pub while Wallace had worn out his welcome with the Jew. He paid the two pennies, pulled another bagel off of the stick and ambled a short distance away. There was a collection of kegs piled nearby that had a view. He sat down, chewed on his purchase and waited. As the moments passed three more men entered, each underwent the same interview process at the door. Only one man left and it wasn't McGarrity.

"And who might you be?"

Wallace looked over his shoulder to see a rough looking character with shaggy black hair and stubble on an impressively square chin. His voice was deep and threatening. Wallace stood, turned and thrust out his hand. "Mr. Jesse Ward at your service. Pleased to meet your acquaintance, Mr.,......?"

"Shove off." The man stared down at him and did not take the hand that Wallace offered.

"My apologies. I didn't know these were your kegs. I was only resting my feet."

The menacing glare was punctuated with an almost imperceptible nod. Wallace was silently and not so subtly being told to 'shove off' a second time. He was about to take another go at apologizing when he noticed the man's dark eyes focus across the street in the direction of the pub door. The motion lasted only a fraction of a second but Wallace could see his eyelids narrow and his dark irises shrink. They were both watching the same door. Wallace instinctively turned his head to see another bloke come through the pub door and stagger up the street. It wasn't McGarrity. When turned again the eyes looked less threatening and the voice less aggressive.

"Leave." the dark man advised and Wallace reluctantly capitulated. He resolved that, as the two young boys predicted, he would not be allowed into the pub and that sticking around here would only aggravate this dark stranger more. He headed back up Broad St. to the first alley and turned right. Again, his senses and sensibilities were assaulted. He had to make his way past garbage and rats and the unfortunates who had no roof over their heads. Toothless, grimy and covered in rags three individuals were sharing what was left of a loaf of bread. He dug in his pocket and placed coins onto the ground before them. They expressed wide eyed gratitude as Wallace walked on. He resumed his count and paced out another thirty steps. It took him only ten strides to confirm the back entrance to the pub. Empty kegs sat beside a heavy door and one window was emitting light, steam, smoke and the meaty fragrance of stew. The second window was also lit and he could just hear the singsong lilt of the Irishmen inside. His ears pricked at the mention of McGarrity's name.

"McGarrity needs two more."

"Well, I won't risk mine. I've done my part."

"And you think your part is done? You think any of our parts are done?"

"This isn't our fight, Seamus. Those guns should be going to Ireland."

"Yes, guns should be going to Ireland and we've got the likes of Roger Casement and McGarrity working on that now. Don't you see that we can stab England in the back in East India as well? The enemy of our enemy is our friend."

There was silence in the room. Wallace sat on his haunches beneath the window sill leaning on the kegs and barrels beside him. McGarrity's name was mentioned but his voice was not part of the conversation. Wallace began to worry that he might have left out the front door. He started to stand but sank quickly back down when the door beside him swung open. Unnoticed amongst the barrels, he heard a match strike and the quick whistling puffs of someone lighting a pipe.

"I don't like it, Donovan."

"No, I don't like it either but what I like less is the English ruling our country. It's time we put a stop to it. I'll go and I'll take my brother. McGarrity set this up with Mallory's and I trust him."

Wallace sat until the men went back inside. He stretched his stiff legs as he stood and told them to walk back to Broad St. and to the place of Mary Miller's employ. Her report was detailed and accurate so it took no time at all for him to locate the four-story red brick building that held the office of Mallory Shipping Company. The problem was that there was little cover around the rundown building and it had started to rain. Wallace pulled his collar up around his ears and stood as close to the wall as possible but there were no eaves on the roof and there really was no protection from the elements. It was water seeping down his neck that turned his investigation in another direction. Mary had also described the location of Hans Tauscher's store on Broadway. He left the warehouse district and headed on up the hill.

WASHINGTON D C

"He said his name was Jesse Ward?"

"That's what the report said, Sir. He was nosing around one of Clan na Gael's meeting places and he nearly compromised our surveillance. Henderson scared him off before he could get any closer to the building."

"Did Henderson give a description?"

"No Sir."

"Well, wire him and tell him to be more thorough next time. We can't have any interference with our work."

"Yes Sir."

"And tell Ariganello to report to me asap."

Lieutenant Thrasher came back from Buffalo to a desk high in files. He had spent the morning separating them into stacks categorized by theme. There was the forgery pile, the bombing pile. the arson pile and the pile for hydraulic presses. A fifth held any propaganda and subversive activities. He cross referenced these with nationalities; German, Irish, Mexican and East Indian; the four corners of his desk representing four corners of the world and he separated each file accordingly. A problem arose when more than one nation had a connection to a file. If collusion amongst these diverse nations was to be believed, the English had a great deal to worry about. Every place the sun set on the British Empire, there were fires were burning. How this might affect the United States of America was his department's concern. Thrasher's filing was interrupted by a rap on the door.

"Ariganello, come in."

"Welcome back Lieutenant."

"Thank you, Sergeant. Tell me what you know about hydraulic presses."

"Well, as you are aware, over the last few months several small manufacturing companies have been bought up by the World Hydraulics Company. These companies make hydraulic presses for many applications, stamping, shearing, pulverizing, etcetera. But all of them make hydraulic presses that are used to pack rifle ammunition and artillery shells, anything from 37mm to 280 mm. And every one of them has or has had military contracts. Internal revenue flagged this as suspicious and, in my opinion, they were right to do so."

"And did you find out who is behind World Hydraulics?"

"Not yet, we're still tracing down the ownership. We have a list of names on their board of directors but we haven't isolated it to any one person. We suspect that they may be aliases or not real at all."

"Well keep on it. We do not want to lose control of our arms production, particularly if we end up fighting in this war."

"Yes, sir." and the sergeant left the Lieutenant alone.

'Jesse Ward' Thrasher said to himself.

CARGO

Three twenty Broadway was just around the corner from City Hall. It was a popular location for imported products given the proximity to the wharf and the Customs House. Gun shops were no exception. Tauscher's store was well kept with lettering on the window advertising 'High Powered Rifles and Automatic Pistols'. A bell marked his entrance and over this he heard, "Be with you momentarily. "There was one customer when Wallace walked in. A gaunt and gangly man was leaning on a glass counter having an intimate conversation with a red head. They were leaning towards one another in close proximity. Wallace could hear a murmur but couldn't make out any words. He feigned interest in the rifles lining the wall and followed a palisade of firearms to the back of the store. There was a glass display case of revolvers beside a doorway with no door. It had a curtain.

"Good day. My name is Henry Muck. Do you see anything of interest?" The gaunt man had come around the counter approaching Wallace while the other man was leaving. The red head moved quickly and with purpose, the force with which he opened the door caused the bell to clang wildly. Both men watched him go.

"I wish to purchase something for my uncle. He is a hunter but I am not. I'm sorry to say that I know very little about guns."

"Well, you've come to the right place. What kind of hunting does your uncle do?"

"Ducks. Ducks and geese I think?"

"Well, he would be using a shotgun and they are just over here on our back wall."

The clerk swept his arm in that direction and they moved to a display of several heavy looking rifles standing vertically on a rack mounted to the wall.

"We have only two models on display. There is a third in the back but it is small and made for women and we don't get many of those in here." The clerk let out a soft chuckle and Wallace followed suit, not fully understanding what they were laughing at. The clerk brought down one of the guns and popped open the chamber. "Single barrel, twelve gauge, all high carbide and very reliable in the field. The sight on this rifle is unparalleled. He would bring back a lot of game with this," and he snapped it closed and handed it to Wallace.

"It is quite heavy." Wallace was holding it awkwardly. He was fumbling with the trigger. "Are they all this heavy? My Uncle is smaller than me," and he handed the gun back.

"Well, the twenty gauge might suit him better. It doesn't fire as much or as far. He'll have to be a better hunter with it. They are in the back. Give me just a minute."

Wallace watched the clerk disappear behind the curtain. He used the opportunity to approach the counter on the opposite side of the store. There was no cash register but there was a desk behind the counter. He slipped behind it and scanned the papers filed in two neat piles. One pile held orders and the other receipts. Heavy sounds emanated from the back room. The clerk was moving crates and boxes. Wallace relaxed his pace. There were three orders, two revolvers and one rifle made to the Krupp's factory in Essen, Germany and there were two receipts for two more handguns. He found all the desk drawers locked. The noises in the backroom halted and he swept around the other side of the counter just in time to see the barrel of a twenty-gauge barrel push out through the curtain. The clerk followed with a smile on his face.

"Here we are. I think you will find this weight more suitable."

Wallace was studying the contents of the glass case before him. The revolvers were laid in plush velvet lined boxes, the steel within them polished and oiled. He lifted his head as the clerk approached and raised his arms to receive the gun.

"Walnut stock, single barrel of the finest carbide steel. You won't find a better weapon in its class."

Wallace shook it in his arms measuring its heft. He looked down the barrel and ran his finger along the relief of the oak leaves carved in the wooden fore-arm and stock. "It is beautiful and I think the right size. How much does this cost?"

"This one is forty-five dollars. It is a reasonable price for a firearm of this quality."

"Yes, that may be, but do you have a firearm of lesser quality? One that doesn't cost as much."

"Well, yes, I do. I'll just have to go into the back again. You'll have to excuse me."

Wallace waited for the curtains to fall together and then he followed. "Can you use buckshot and birdshot in the same gun?" He poked his head into the backroom. The clerk was reaching deep into a box in a long line of boxes. A small space, this storeroom was stuffed with wooden crates.

"Yes, same gun." said the clerk breathlessly.

"Lots of boxes." Wallace observed.

"Yes, and I'll be grateful when they are all gone. Ah, here we are. This one is essentially the same as the twenty gauge I already showed you, just not as fancy," as he pulled a rifle out of the straw it was packed in. Wallace noticed that each crate was stout and solid. On the ones he could see, each lid had a label stencilled in the bottom right corner. He glanced down at the closest one and read, 'Mallory Shipping Galveston Texas'. He stepped back through the curtain and waited in the store.

"It is the same gun without the carving detail." They were both back in the store amongst the shiny cabinets and rich wooden paneling. He held it out for Wallace to hold but Wallace only leaned in to take a closer look, his arms at his sides.

"This one is forty-one dollars," said the clerk offering the rifle a second time.

"I'll have to think about it some more. Thank you for your help today."

"It is a quality firearm. For the price, you will not find a better gun.

"Yes, thank you, I understand. I'll just have to think about it some more," and Wallace backed his way out of the door and headed back down towards the dockyards.

THE ARREST

Wallace followed Fulton St. down to Pier 16. It was the most direct path back down to the Mallory Shipping office. This time he didn't hesitate to enter the building. He climbed to the second story and passed by the door where Mary Miller had worked only the week before. He could hear voices inside but did not stop to listen. He walked to the end of the row of workrooms and offices and sat on the first step of the stairwell. In this position, he had only to lean forward to catch a glimpse down the hall. It was a short wait. The click of a door latch echoing down the hall brought him to his feet. He risked a quick look and saw a large man leaving the Mallory office and heard a voice call out, "Make it quick Sean." The closing of a door was followed by approaching footsteps, so he silently scrambled to the landing above and moved out of sight. When the pedestrian moved onto the flight below him, he descended the stairs to see the outside door closing. He followed.

He peered through the door window to see the large man cross the street and disappear around the corner. Once again, he gave chase. His quarry walked with determination. Wallace jogged across the street and trailed at a distance. As they came to the waterfront Wallace closed the gap. The wharf was a hive of activity. Gulls cried as they swooped through the salty air and there were so many men and carts moving along the pier that Wallace felt inconspicuous while just four paces from the man.

The progress of this chase only slowed when the man stopped in front of a warehouse to watch a boxing match between two sailors, each a representative of their ship. A bookie was holding wads of bills wagered on the match and comrades were shouting their encouragement. Wallace and the other man stood side by side while the contestants sized each other up, their bare torsos rippling with muscle and anticipation. But before a punch was thrown, the man was on the move again. He skirted the crowd and walked up to the warehouse. Beside the door at which he stood was a knotted rope protruding from the wall and a sign that read '12 D'. He pulled the rope and stepped through a wooden door.

Wallace stood watching this from the safety of the crowd. They were shouting taunts at the opposition and boosting encouragement. 'Bid your time Johnny!' 'Watch his chest Franz!' 'Keep your hands up!' But the fighters were a slow blur to him, circling and bobbing at one another. Wallace was examining the building for other doors and windows. There were none visible. He didn't like following anyone into an unfamiliar building without an alternate means of escape. Perhaps it was the adrenaline and testosterone pulsing through the crowd around him. He backed out of the crowd and went directly to the door, pulled the rope and climbed inside.

The clamour outside faded as the door swung closed. Light penetrated only a small window on a distant wall. It took time for his irises to dilate so he stood stock still in the dim light trying to make sense of the shadows. When the shapes and images began to form he took tentative steps along an aisle of barrels lying on their sides. There was the heavy sweetness of rum or molasses emanating from them and from the wooden planks on which he stood. As he moved deeper into the warehouse, he heard the heavy sound of scraping coming from an adjacent room. Again, he looked for other exits and saw none. Wallace swallowed, wet his lips with his tongue and then he started to whistle 'A-Roving'.

He did not sneak. He exaggerated the weight of his steps and forced the melody from his lips. He did not want his presence to be a surprise and yet the door frame was instantly filled with the silhouette of the man with a surprised and very annoyed look on his face.

"Sean?" inquired Wallace.

"And who might you be?" growled the large man.

"I was told to come and help you. I was told that urgency was in order and by the sounds of it, you might need some help."

The large man squinted one eye and cocked his head to one side. "And who sent ya?"

"This is the Mallory warehouse, isn't it? I was told by the office to come to warehouse 12 D and give you any assistance you might need. My name is Ward. Pleased to meet you." Wallace extended his hand.

The menace on the other man's face disappeared as he whipped his hands on his pants and shook Wallace's hand. Never before had anyone sent someone to assist him and he was grateful.

"Well let's get to work shall we. What is it that you want me to do? You are the boss," stated Wallace and the other man clearly enjoyed the title.

"We need to be making space in here," and they moved into an alcove that was higher and drier than the rest of the warehouse. Wood shavings were strewn about to absorb moisture and the smell of cedar rose from the floor. "This is special storage. We need to clear out this lot and make space."

For the next twenty minutes the two men lifted and rolled and hauled a melange of crates and barrels out into the main warehouse. When the room was empty, the man handed Wallace a broom and told him to sweep the wood shavings into the corner. "We'll sweep 'em back into the center when the new crates get here."

"And what are we moving in here?' probed Wallace.

The large man cocked his head and squinted again. "Donovan never told ya'?"

"Must have slipped his mind. I forget things too. Just the other day I left my hat on the bar of O'Brien's. I didn't notice until the rain was bouncing off the top of my head. So, I turned back and me friend Malcolm had it in his hand as he was leaving the bar. He's a lifesaver."

"I don't know any Malcolm."

"Skinny like me, only a foot taller with red hair?"

The other man was shaking his head and looking at Wallace suspiciously again. Wallace stepped behind a large crate and motioned for the man to pick up the other end. He hesitated but did as Wallace asked.

"Anyway, I got my hat back which reminds me of the time I lost my coat on the ferry to Stanton Island.,.... and Wallace distracted the other man with a long-winded story that saw him lose one coat and find three new ones in his search and it fulfilled the purpose. By the end of the story the big man's suspicions were calmed. Wallace considered his ability to talk and distract an asset, maybe his best skill for this line of work. There were many occasions when he talked himself out of an uncomfortable situation and it worked again just now. They had just set down the last box and Wallace secured the man's confidence by withdrawing a flask from his inner pocket.

"Fancy a swig?" Wallace asked, holding out the container.

"Thank you. I could use a drop."

"It does help to fortify the soul, gives one stamina for work like this. Is there more that we have to do?"

The big man lowered the flask from his mouth. "The cargo meant for this space should arrive any moment. It's good you showed up. I'd never had this place cleared out in time and I could use your help with what's comin' in. Those crates are heavier than these," raising the whiskey to his lips another time.

"What is it? The cargo I mean."

"Rifles mostly. They're meant for East India. Rebels there are going to push the English out of that country." The Big man shared this secret in a conspiratorial tone. He put the back of his hand up to his mouth as if to block the view of his lips should someone be trying to read his message, but there was no one else there. He obviously enjoyed letting Wallace in on this classified information but quickly stood, screwed the cap on the flask and handed it back when they heard voices coming from the larger warehouse. "They're here. Get your back ready to do some more liftin'," and he stood to greet the newcomers. From his seated position, Wallace looked for a means of escape. There was none.

"Seany, the wagon's being drawn around back. Go open the bay doors and let him,...........who's this?" A small and stocky man approached Wallace, alarmed at his presence. Two other men fell in behind him.

"Wallace is my name. I was just lending a hand to Seany here. We've cleared out this space together."

"I can see that. But who told you to do it?" The stocky man was giving this full attention to Wallace who could feel the weight of his scrutiny.

"He told me his name was Ward!" The Big man stood, anger flushing his face. He didn't like being lied to. "He told me the Office sent him over to help me."

Wallace sat seemingly calm, cursing his error while his mind was racing for a way to talk himself out of this one. The two other men came out of the shadows and Wallace was stunned to recognize one of them as Joseph McGarrity.

"'Ward' you say?" McGarrity stepped forward and took a good look at Wallace. No doubt Father Joseph McGarrity would have recognized the name as the murderer of Percy Sparling but he had only brushed by Wallace in a pub in Buffalo and had never set his eyes directly on the accused.

"Who sent you here is my question?" the short stocky one continued.

Wallace continued to sit on the crate, he tried to remain calm. No stories came to mind and he began to feel a trickle of panic flow through him. There were too many inquisitors in front of him, too much scrutiny to baffle them with words and no more whisky to share. He stood, speechless.

"Take him in the alley." It was McGarrity's voice, a flat and unemotional command. Wallace could only think of Toke Birk and what this man did to the young boy. Now it was his turn. It made Wallace hate McGarrity all the more. The Big man and his partner grabbed his arms and pushed him out into the warehouse and out a back door. In only a matter of seconds, his back was against the wall and his arms held firmly. The stocky short man before him pulled back and then put all his force into a blow to the stomach. Wallace folded over. An uppercut straightened him again as the small man's fist contacted his jaw. It was while the short man was unfolding his knife that they all heard a whistle from the end of the alley way. Wallace's assailants looked up to see three men racing toward them, the silhouettes of two wore the tall constabulary hat of the New York Police department. The men dropped the limp body of Wallace and scattered.

In his last minute of consciousness, Wallace's eyes closed to the flashlight held in the policeman's hand. "Not in his eyes" commanded a voice. "Pick him up and take him to the station."

"Sir, the other's?" questioned the officer redirecting the light in his commander's face.

"Not in my eyes! Jesus Constable!" shouted the commander and in that brief flash of light Wallace recognized the unkept shaggy hair and square chin from the day before.

"Sir, the other men. They've escaped."

"Yes, Constable, they've escaped. Let them go. Put cuffs on this one. Drag him back onto the wharf and make a show of putting him in the paddy wagon. Mind his head though."

WASHINGTON D.C

Name:	*James Wallace*
Alias:	*Jesse Ward*
Where born:	*Essex, England*
Age:	*34*
Height:	*5' 7"*
Weight:	*135 lbs*
Complexion:	*Fair*
Hair:	*Brown*
Eyes:	*Grey*
Occupation:	*Merchant / Mason*
Sentence:	*10 years*
Where sentenced:	*St Catharines, Ontario*
Date of:	*October 3rd - 1914*
Crime:	*Manslaughter*
Remarks:	*Left middle finger stiff; talkative.*

"He's walking up, Sir."

"Thank you, Ariganello. I'll be right down." Lieutenant Thrasher looked over the rap sheet again. 'He gets around for someone convicted of manslaughter' he thought as he slid the page back into the file. He took the file with him down the hall and into the observation room. Wallace was sitting on a cot holding his head in his hands.

"Last time I saw you was in Buffalo"

Wallace looked up and returned his head to his hands. "Last time I saw you I wasn't seeing double. There was only one of you. I liked that better."

"If you had stayed in Buffalo, I would have liked that better."

"Thrasher, where am I?"

"You are in Washington D.C."

"That would explain the journey."

"I hope you were comfortable."

"That's not how I would describe it." Wallace looked down to his wrists and began rubbing them. "Your officers cuffed me. I feel like I was hit by a train rather than riding in one."

"You got hit by the train before we picked you up and we cuffed you to keep you safe from Clan na Gael. It's better if they think we arrested you."

"Yes, thanks for that. I don't mean to be ungrateful. It would have been worse if your men hadn't appeared. How did you find me?"

"Always carry more than two aliases with you. Our agent observed you watching O'Brien's Pub and you used your alias. I recognized it immediately. We had you tailed thereafter."

"Well, thanks again."

"You can thank us by recording your whereabouts and your contacts while you've been in the United States of America. I have procured a stenographer for you."

"And what if I don't wish to share my whereabouts and contacts?"

"Jesse, you very nearly compromised our surveillance. This isn't really a request. Your release will be contingent on what you provide us. We can detain you based on your rap sheet. You have served less than two years of a ten-year sentence for manslaughter. I am sure the Dominion Police would prefer that you earned your freedom than served it in an American prison."

"Thrasher, there is something you need to know right away."

"Write it down Ward. Write it down."

"I'll tell you now. Mallory Shipping is sending crates of rifles to Galveston Texas. Joseph McGarrity arranged it through Hans Tauscher's shop."

"Galveston?"

"Galveston. Tauscher's storeroom was stacked to the ceiling with crates stamped with Mallory's seal. They are going to be moved to their warehouse, or maybe by now they have been moved. I was helping to clear space for them just before your men found me in the alley." Ward was rubbing his forehead. Accessing his memory was making his head hurt. Thrasher looked skeptical.

"Galveston? Why would they send guns to Texas?"

"I overheard two Irish complain that they were bound for East India."

Thrasher's mouth dropped. The image of Mary Miller laughing at something Hans Tauscher said. The photograph where an Irishman and a Sikh were in a serious discussion. And that Hindu's story of the Komagata Maru and the terrorists aboard. It all fell together.

"Did you gather any documentation on this?"

"No."

"I will send in the stenographer. Be as detailed as you can. Ariganello here will get you anything you might need." Lieutenant Thrasher made to leave but hesitated. Ward noticed him standing there, one more question swirling between them. The Lieutenant's face had softened and in a subtle way his eyes were pleading. Jesse had seen that expression when he first met Thrasher, an unexpected warmth in an otherwise hard exterior. He had seen it in Buffalo when Thrasher was gazing in the eyes of Mary Miller.

"She's in Europe," was all Ward needed to say.

LAKEVIEW HOTEL, ROOM 14

The next time I awoke, it was my mother's face staring down at me. She had her hand on my forehead and while it was a struggle to put her face in focus it was good to see her. She also had an expression of concern and relief and it was a great consolation to have her there. Nothing compares to a mother's soft words of encouragement and gentle touch. I don't know how long I drifted in and out of sleep. My mother's face was drawn and gaunt so it could have been days. The only time I remembered staying conscious for any length of time was when a knock came at the door and Judge Falconbridge entered.

I had known of the Judge all of my life. He was one of the most respected members of the Grimsby Beach community. He was the master of ceremonies for nearly every event held in the Park and he introduced many of the speakers and performers who headlined at the auditorium. More importantly he presided over nearly all of the court cases throughout the Niagara Peninsula and he did all this while maintaining a thriving law practice in Toronto. To me, he was a celebrity. But it was the fact that I lusted after his daughter that made me nervous and for a few fleeting seconds my foggy brain thought this might be the subject of his visit.

My mother took her hand off mine and stood as though he was entering a courtroom. He was a big man in height and girth and he dressed in a fine suit. He wore the air of dignity around him like a cloak and I swear the atmosphere changed as he came into the room. His deep baritone voice gently persuaded her to sit back down.

"Don't get up Grace. Your son deserves your attention. He has done a great service for us all. A service greater than he could know and I'd say he's paid a price for it. Both of you deserve to know the cause of your injuries Robert and I intend to tell you all that I know."

It was an introduction like I had never heard before and although my left arm was in a cast from my wrist to my shoulder, I was able to sit up to hear his story.

"Grace, your son Robert here has been observant, diligent, intelligent and daring and judging by the expression on your face, discreet."

Indeed, my mother was surprised at the list of superlatives describing her youngest son. I, of course, did not recount every moment of my days working at the Park House Hotel to my mother. Oh, I complained about von Papen's list of things to do, of the endless sweeping of floors, of polishing boots, of Mr. Vannetter's demands etc., but I left out the misdemeanors; break and enter, the burning of dinner jackets and the theft of room keys. She was unaware that I had been aiding and abetting a spy or that I had put myself in danger on more than one occasion, the most recent of which left me in the broken state I was presently in. The Judge, intending to bestow praise on me, was raising the ire of my mother who looked like she wanted to break my other arm. Fortunately, he recognized that maternal protectiveness can, at times, endanger the offspring it is designed to protect and he continued.

"Grace, your son was drawn into this by circumstance. I am told that his employment at the hotel put him in a unique position to help us prevent serious sabotage attempts on our canal at Welland. As you know, our 44th Regiment, has diligently guarded it since war was declared but we have been privy to groups within Canada and the United States who have planned to disrupt supply lines across the continent. Only last week a rail bridge in Maine was destroyed by explosives and we believe the plans were executed by the same radical group. You will recall the murder of Percy Sparling two years ago? He was in league with that group as was von Papin, who, Robert, you served so well. And there have been others. Now that America is close to entering the war, the German diplomats and their military attachés in Washington D.C. have been detained or deported. Hans Tauscher, who also stayed at the Park House was among them. They were all involved in ways to hinder our war effort. There was even a consulate in Baltimore involved in forging passport documents."

"And Father McGarrity,....?" These were the first words I spoke since the Judge had entered the room.

"And Father McGarrity too. We believe he took instruction and money from the German government and hired men to do the work. Percy Sparling was among them."

"When he came back into the room...." I started but stopped. My memory was still foggy and the retrieval of images fuzzy.

"When he came back into his room and found you there, he must have known his plans were nixed. Anger is the sister of fear and Robert, he must have been very afraid of failure. According to Mr. Vannetter, McGarrity was in such a rage that he continued to thrash you even though you were unconscious. Vannetter himself sustained a gash on the head when he tried to intervene. The important thing is that McGarrity will no longer be able to organize any more sabotage attempts and that you, yourself, are okay."

"And are you sure Father McGarrity will not return?" said my mother. She was still concerned for my safety.

"Our sources say that he is on his way back to Ireland. He will fight England from there from now on. Robert, I must go. You need to rest and heal and get back on your feet. Mr. Vannetter needs you."

Judge Falconbridge gently patted the cast on my left arm, stood, bowed to my mother and left the room. My mother returned to my bedside and sat down and didn't know what to say, so she said nothing.

My memories slowly returned. They came whenever I started to fall asleep which only served to jolt me awake with their violence. At first, I saw only McGarrity's fists and knuckles but eventually I saw myself in the room before the attack. I was standing at his desk with one of his letters in my hands when I heard the latch in the door click. I heard the hinge creak as I quickly read the last sentence and salutation on the page. I heard him bellow and stomp his way to my side where he snatched the letter with his left hand and brought his right down on my head almost simultaneously. I could recall nothing after that except that the letter was from someone named Bridgeman Taylor and that the last sentence stated that *"all is ready".* Whatever their plans were, they were never realized. According to Judge Falconbridge, I played a role in thwarting whatever plot they had been scheming. My presence in McGarrity's room reading his mail was enough to disrupt their mission and while it caused me bodily harm, I was assured by all around me that I had accomplished something important.

My mobility returned with my memory and it wasn't long before I was able to leave the hotel with the aid of crutches and move back to my parents' cottage on Victoria Terrace. My recovery included long walks under the canopy of white oak and white pine, leisurely strolls amongst the cottages, and reading by the shoreline of Lake Ontario. I was serenaded by the swoosh of water pulling and pushing its way through rock and sand as I napped in the shade of the great canopy of Grimsby Beach Park.

While I was unable to return to work for some time, my convalescence had allowed me to live out a long-held dream. When summer returned, so did Fiona Falconbridge. We spent many a day fishing in her father's boat and while I felt better with each day, I played up my injuries to extend my holiday. In the end, I never did get to work at the Lakeview Hotel. Just months after renovations were complete a fire destroyed the entire structure. It was another devastation for our beautiful community, a list that began with espionage, a sabotage attempt and a murder at the Park House Hotel.

BURLINGTON, ONTARIO

When Mr. Birk had finished talking, we all sat in silence for a moment. By the look on his face, he was still recalling the past. He was locked in some long-gone emotion, reliving a smile he received from Fiona, or an admonishment from Franz von Papen, or he might have been experiencing the terror of being attacked by an imposter priest. Wherever Mr. Birk was, he was completely in that time and space. He sat absentmindedly running his finger up and down his temple along his scar. He traced and then retraced a path from his ear to along his cheek bone and up to the corner of his eyebrow.

John in the meantime had finished reading the papers that had landed in his lap an hour before and was staring in disbelief at its cover page. He was the one to break the silence. "United States Bureau of Investigation? Is this what Jesse Ward wrote to get out of Washington?

"It is." Mr. Birk had a very satisfied look on his face.

"How did you get a hold of this?"

"That, I never found out. I assume Lieutenant Thrasher sent it or gave it to Jesse Ward and he in turn, sent it or a copy of it to me. I would have never been able to relate this story without it."

"And your scar Dad. You always told me it was a fishing accident."

"Well son, it was, kind of. I was fishing in a way."

"The Dominion Police?" John continued. He was sitting up now.

"Well, I was never officially working for them. Like I said, circumstances just drew me into it."

"But Vannetter, Cousins, Mary Miller and Jesse Ward or Wallace....."

"Yes, in some capacity or other, they were all Dominion Police although I never knew it at the time and I never would have found out if Jesse Ward hadn't sent that report. I guess most of them had died or retired and Mr. Ward thought that the statements he made for the U.S. Bureau of Investigation wouldn't do any of them any harm. I guess he thought I deserved to know. You know, at the time, the Annie Larson Affair became the largest court case in the history of the U.S Judicial System and I think he

wanted me to know that I had a small part to play in it. I think it might have alleviated any guilt he had for my being injured."

"What happened to the shipment of rifles?"

"It came out in the trial that once they got to Galveston they were put on a train to San Diego and then loaded onto the Annie Larson. But through a long series of misadventures, they never did make it to India. It is a story unto itself. The relevance to my story is that it critically wounded the foreign espionage ring in North America."

"And my grandfather?"

"Well John, I never found evidence that your grandfather was involved. He was never mentioned in that report and other than the day he came to see me when I was convalescing, I never discussed anything about these events with him. I never had the nerve to ask. Still, he must have been. He was there when Jesse Ward was released from prison, a prisoner he sentenced not two weeks before. He worked for the Ministry of Justice and he knew all of the agents you've mentioned. Mary Miller, in particular, worked for him directly."

"Judge Falconbridge was your father-in-law?" I asked.

"Yes, he was and he was imposing one at that," replied Robert.

"So, you married Fiona Falconbridge." I said triumphantly.

"It was Fiona who made our lunch Mr. Friesen. She and I have been together all this time."

"That's amazing!" I said. It was intriguing, exciting and romantic and I felt privileged to have heard it. I was still putting all the pieces of Robert's story together when his son spoke.

"That is an amazing story Dad and I am sorry I doubted you. This is incredible. Why did you never tell me this before? Why did Mom never tell me about this?

Mr. Birk sat back in his chair and looked up at the ceiling. He started to speak and stopped himself. On his second attempt he said,

"I'm not sure. It was a tumultuous time in our history. There were some wonderful things about it but there were tragedies too. For many years I

never wanted to talk about it and you have to remember, for many decades, until I got that envelope, I didn't know the full story. But our visit to Grimsby Beach last week stirred it up again. It made me dig up Jesse Ward's report and refresh my memory and I am happy I got to share it with you. You know we spend so much of our lives looking at the world through a pinhole. It's like we can't stand far enough away from the scene to get perspective, to see the whole picture. At least, it's been that way for me. I guess the answer to your question, son, is that I wasn't ready to tell this story. Even when I knew all the facts, I couldn't untangle it all and I had trouble forgiving those that acted against me. I didn't recognize that there is always a story within a story, always a layer beneath the one you are standing on, a backstory that gives us perspective on the motivation of those around us. History helps us comprehend why young men joyfully signed up to fight in South Africa and France. Helps us understand why a skillful tradesman would risk his freedom or even his life to sabotage a canal. Why someone might impersonate a priest or why a beautiful woman would learn to throw knives with deadly accuracy. Sifting through the layers helps us realize that there are many ways people rationalize their choices and that there are many forces lurking beneath what we think is simple and benign. The difference between what we think is right and wrong depends on the baggage we carry around with us and the size of the peep hole we look through. Boys, there is always more than the ear can hear and more than the eye can see, and until we accept that, we will be at a loss to explain much of what goes on in this world."

Then, there was a hush in the room. The tension that existed between the father and son had vanished and a peaceful calm and contemplation enveloped us all.

GLOSSARY OF PEOPLE, PLACES AND EVENTS (IN ORDER OF APPEARANCE)

Percy Sparling – Other than the fact that he was found barely alive with two bullets in his back and his throat slashed in front of the Park House Hotel early in the morning of August 3rd,1914, I know little else. He was rumoured to be in a love triangle with Jesse Ward and Mary Miller.

Jesse Ward- He was sentenced to 10 years for manslaughter for the murder of Percy Sparling, He was found in the victim's room after Percy's body was discovered and he was observed to have a brief conversation with Mary Miller just before his sentencing. He told the court reporter that he thought his sentence was fair. His arrest record shows his age at 67. I choose to make him much younger for this story.

Welland Canal – There have been four different canals used to raise and lower boats between Lake Erie to Lake Ontario. The fourth and final canal was under construction during this story. It began in 1913 and was completed in 1932. Remnants of the third canal, the target in this story, are still visible. A moderate hike along the Bruce Trail will bring you to the swing bridge mentioned in this story. If you park at Woodend Conservation area just east of St. Catharines and walk west for 3 km you will come to the old canal. If you walk another 300 m south you will come to the swing bridge. Although it doesn't swing anymore, the gears used to turn are still intact and the structure still carries trains over 12 Mile Creek.

Merriton- This community immediately east of St. Catharines was named after

William Hamilton Merritt, a prominent local entrepreneur and founder of the Company. It was first known as Slabtown and was an important crossroads for industry and transportation.

Booth's Railway- J.R. Booth was a lumber baron. In 1892, his lumber complex was the largest operation of its kind in the world. To transport logs out of the Algonquin highlands he built the Canada Atlantic Railway which stretched from Georgian Bay to Ottawa and then down to Vermont.

Mohawk Ironworkers- Mohawk men have a long and storied history of working on iron structures. I have no idea if they worked on the swing bridge at 12-mile creek but I thought their inclusion in this story would help honour their contribution to the infrastructure and defense of our nation.

Morningstar Mill- There has been a grist mill at the site of Decew Falls since 1812. Wilson Morningstar rebuilt the mill in 1885 and worked there until his death in 1933. Morningstar received 1/12 of the flour produced by the gristmill as payment. The mill is presently owned by the City of St. Catharines and is open for viewing.

Battle of Slabtown- A local and violent skirmish, this battle between the Orangemen of Meriton and Irish canal workers typifies the enduring tension between British aristocracy and Irish laborers. That seven of the Irish were shot leaving two dead while the Orangemen perpetrators were exonerated and honoured with medals of valour shows where the balance of power rested. They didn't call it British North America for nothing. You can read more about this at;

https://brocku.ca/social-sciences/geography/wp-content/uploads/sites/152/The-Early-History-of-Merritton.pd

Sann Road Aerodrome

Although not in existence until 1918, (4 years after my characters witnessed it), this historical site was too good not to write into the story.

https://lincoln.library.on.ca/looking-back-the-beamsville-aerodrome/

Grimsby Park– Religious retreats began on the property of J.B. Bowlaugh in 1846 who eventually deeded 12.5 acres to the Ontario Methodist Campground in 1875. Initially visitors camped in tents but by 1880 more permanent cottages were constructed. Several remain today. Two hotels opened within the park and according to the 1885 program, over 50,000 people visited the previous year. The Grimsby Park Company went bankrupt in 1909 when it was sold to H.R Wiley. He added a midway and a dance hall. He transformed it significantly until his death in 1916 when property was purchased by the Canadian Steamship Lines who sold it off in 1949. It has been a residential neighbourhood ever since.

Bell- Between 1801 and 1951, four different foundries in Troy, New York made over 100,000 bells. One of them rang in Grimsby Beach from 1885 until 1957. It was commissioned to hang in the temple but was thought too heavy once it had arrived. A platform was constructed in what became known as Bell Park. One of the many photos of the bell there is one with a sign that threatens a fine of $25 to anyone ringing it without good reason. Wouldn't it be interesting to hear the bell ring again?
Bell Park- Bell Park had a bog hole causing the ground to be very damp. To eliminate the wet ground, the spring was damned up and drained into a heart-shaped moat. The drained centre became a beautiful flower garden and grassy area and was accessed by two wooden bridges built over the moat. It was large enough to hold many of the classes offered each summer as part of the programme of activities. Water grew scarce in later years and was drained into the lake. When H.H. Wylie bought the Park in 1910 the moat was filled.
Park House Hotel- In June 1875, the Directors of the Ontario Methodist Church Campground Company voted to construct a restaurant 70' long and 24' wide with sixteen bedrooms and storerooms. Later in 1875, a 100' addition was approved for the restaurant. This restaurant became the Park House Hotel. It was torn down ~ 1930.
Lakeview Hotel- At the August 28, 1882 meeting, the Board voted unanimously to take immediate steps to erect a good hotel containing about 50 rooms fronting the lake on the west end of the Grounds. At the October 13, 1882 meeting, plans were approved for a hotel 32' x 100' and three storeys tall. The first storey was to be 12' high, the second storey 10' high and the third storey 9' high. The total cost of the project was not to exceed $4000. Lakeview House Hotel was more ornate than the Park House Hotel as it was decorated with ornate fretwork. It burned to the ground on August 13th, 1914.
The Temple- Built in 1888 to shelter congregations and audiences, this round structure dominated Grimsby Park for 34 years. It was 100' high and was reported to have seated ~3000 spectators. The roof was notoriously leaky and the structure was raised in 1922. Today a cairn commemorated by Queen Elizabeth in 1939 sits in a small parkette on the site.

Turbinia- The first steam turbine ship on the Great Lakes, the Turbinia started delivering passengers to Grimsby Beach in 1913. It was requisitioned for service during WW1 and left the Great Lakes. It returned in 1923 and left the Great Lakes for good in 1926.
https://www.greatlakesvesselhistory.com/histories-by-name/t/turbinia
Mary Miller- Mary Miller testified at the trial of Jesse Ward that she had known Percy but hadn't seen him the 3 weeks leading up to his death. She was seen having a brief conversation with Jesse Ward but left on the train just before he was sentenced. Everything else about her is my invention.
Hans Tauscher- Hans Tauscher was an officer of the Imperial German Army during WW1, the husband of Johanna Gadski and a military attaché to Johann Heinrich von Bernstorff. He was an arms dealer who sold weapons for the Krupp corporation in Manhattan, N.Y. He was accused of plotting sabotage against the Welland Canal and implicated in the Annie Larson Affair but was acquitted by a federal jury. He died in Manhattan in 1941. There is no evidence that he ever visited Grimsby Beach.
Madame Johanna Gadski- Madame Gadski was the wife of Hans Tauscher and a renowned opera star who sang at all the important houses in Europe and North America. She was employed with the Metropolitan Opera House in New York from 1890 to 1904 and again from 1907 to 1917. When the United States entered WW1 in 1917 all performances from the German repertory were suspended. Gadski was given the choice to resign or be dismissed. During the remainder of the war, she lived in the U.S. but returned to Germany in 1922 where she died in 1932.
Franz von Papen- Over the course of the First World War there were 15 sabotage attempts made in North America. These were funded by Imperial Germany through agents like Franz Von Papen. Papen was deported in 1915 after organizing an attempt on the Welland Canal and financing Rebellion Forces during the Mexican revolution. Once back in Germany he served as a battalion commander on the Western Front, a Lieutenant Colonel in the Middle East before being appointed the Chancellor of Germany in 1932. There is no evidence that he ever visited Grimsby Beach.

Horst von der Goltz- His real name was Franz Wachendorf but he also went by Bridgeman Taylor. Goltz published a book about his life as a spy and even starred as himself in the movie, The Prussian Cur. He, along with Hans Tauscher and Franz von Papen were accused of plotting to sabotage the Welland Canal. He was caught and testified against the other German agents.
Joseph McGarrity- McGarrity became the leader of Clan na Gael in 1926. Prior to that he was part of the Irish delegation that visited the German Ambassador in Washington D.C. to see how they might join forces to fight Britain. 'Father' McGarrity's actions in this story are purely fictitious as is his impersonation as a priest. In real life the Clan na Gael under his leadership consistently supported more violent means of resistance to British control. Clan na Gael is just one of many groups that have morphed in time to become Sinn Fiene.
Consul Carl A. Luederitz- worked in the German consulate in Baltimore and was involved in forging passports for German-Americans who wished to return to Germany.
Johann Heinrich von Bernstorff- German Ambassador in the US during the early years of the war. He was deported back to Germany when the US entered WW1. He was involved in forging passports to assist German-Americans who wished to return to their homeland, he managed a fund used to finance many of the sabotage efforts in British North America, and he supported the Pan-Indian Rebellion. Ironically, he became the President of the German Association for the League of Nations, (which promoted world peace), in 1920.
Sikh Forces– Clan na Gael and German agents worked with and funded Sikh leaders to plan a Pan-Indian rebellion in British held territories. Clan na Gael and Germany supported the Ghadar Party in India which wanted independence from Britain. Taucher, Papen, McGarrity, and Bernstorff were all implicated in the Annie Larson Affair which was a plot to send arms to revolutionaries in India. The plot was thwarted by British Intelligence and resulted in the Hindu German Conspiracy Trial, the longest trial ever held on US soil at the time. This story is a novel unto itself.

Mallory Steamship Company- An Irish-American shipping company implicated in the Hindu German Conspiracy. They owned and operated the schooner, the Annie Larson.

The Dominion Police- Created in 1868 after the assassination of Thomas Darcy McGee, this small force arose out of fear of Fenian aggressions at the time. Responsibilities included protecting Federal buildings, naval yards, and railways, providing body guards for government leaders, secret service work, and enforcing counterfeiting and human trafficking laws. In 1920 it became a part of the R.C.M.P.

The BOI (FBI)- After the assassination of President McKinley in 1901, there was a perceived threat of anarchy in the United States. To combat this, President Roosevelt directed Attorney General Charles Bonaparte (Napoleon's grandnephew), to organize the Bureau of Investigation (BOI). This department was responsible for enforcing Federal Crimes and investigating crimes against the state, went through many name changes before it became what is now known as the FBI.

Fenians- The Fenian Brotherhood were a political organization in the 19th and 20th centuries dedicated to an independent Irish Republic. From the United States, they started conducting raids into Canada in 1867 and have been implicated in sabotage attempts on the Welland Canal. The ultimate goal of the Fenian raids was to hold Canada hostage and therefore be in a position to blackmail the United Kingdom to give Ireland its independence.

Clan na Gael- Successor to the Fenian Brotherhood and a sister organization to the Irish Republican Brotherhood, Clan na Gael raised funds in America for the Pursuit of Irish Independence. They were the largest contributor of funds to the Easter Rising of 1916 and the Irish War of Independence (1919-1921). Leaders of the organization met with the German Ambassador in the US and Franz von Papen. This was followed by a mission to Berlin to discuss how Irish Nationalism and the German War Effort might help one another. They thought it best to fight England from both sides.

Maud Gonne- An actress who fought for Irish nationalism despite having been born in England. Inspired by the plight of evicted Irish farmers, she advocated for Home Rule. She was also the love interest of W.B. Yeats, inspiring much of his poetry.

Paul Koeing- Koeing was a private investigator based in New York City. He was hired by Franz von Papen to conduct a sabotage and bombing campaign against businesses in New York owned by citizens from the Allied nations.

South Africa- mentioned when Mr. Singh comes to Washington to relate information he learned on the Komagata Maru. He describes the success of Peaceful Protests there. They were organized by a young law student who later brought the idea back to his home country. This individual was Mahatma Gandhi.

Komagata Maru- In 1914, the Komagata Maru, a steamship carrying 376 immigrants from the Punjabi region of India, was turned away at the Port of Vancouver. When the steamship returned to India, the British Army imprisoned and murdered many of the passengers. The incident is a dark stain on Canadian Immigration Policies at the time. There was evidence of some radicalized revolutionaries aboard the ship, (which was procured using a German agent), however, the long ordeal and frustration the passengers must have experienced would radicalize the most peaceful of humanity. The heavy-handed manner in which the Government of Canada dealt with the passengers has been commemorated with a park in Brampton, ON.

Inez Milholland- American Women's Rights lawyer, journalist and pacifist. She campaigned for the Suffrage Movement throughout her life.

Erin Cumann na uBan- An Irish Republic Women's paramilitary group formed in Dublin in 1914.

Martin House– The Martin House was designed by Frank Lloyd Wright and built between 1903 and 1905. It is considered one of his most important works and is well worth a visit. It is located at 125 Jewett Parkway in Buffalo, N.Y.

Albright Gallery– Now known as the Albright Knox gallery, the Albright Gallery was completed in 1905 and has a long history of collecting and exhibiting impressionist and post-impressionist art. The Group of Seven formed in Canada are said to have been inspired when some of its members visited the Gallery. It has a small but diverse collection of impressionists and is well worth a visit.

Souterrain Caves- These limestone caves are just north of Vimy Ridge and were used by both the British and French as shelter during their failed assaults. When Canada took over the mission, the Canadian soldiers used their leisure time to carve reliefs into the soft rock walls. They wrote their names and carved messages to their loved ones before assaulting the Ridge. More creative soldiers created images of their home in Canada. Fearing that these carvings would be lost, an organization called CANADIGM mapped the caves and captured many sculptures as 3D images. Some of these can be seen at the War Museum in Ottawa.

Radiant Electric Company & Metalcraft Manufacturing-Both companies were in business during the First World War. They were major employers in the Grimsby area providing fuses and shell casings for the war effort. The Council of Grimsby invested in the Metalcraft Manufacturing Company.

Henry Muck- An American citizen who worked for Hans Tauscher and provided much of the evidence against him.

Excerpt from Anodyne, the sequel to More than the Ear Can Hear, More than the Eye Can See

"I think the frame outshines the subject, like they're trying to make a purse out of a sow's ear."

"You haven't looked at the painting long enough, mon chère. Joseph Turner is talking to you. He is telling you a story. He is telling you the future."

She took a step to the right and leaned over and read the label.

"The Fighting Temeraire. Looks ghastly."

"Looks more ghostly I think. What you don't know is that that ship came to Admiral Nelson's rescue at Trafalgar. It captured and lashed two French ships to its gunnels and continued firing its cannons until the French turned their tails back across the Channel. The Temeraire was a 'Victory' ship."

"Then why is it being towed?"

"It is going to its grave, to the breakers who will salvage the timbers and nails. The steamer pulling it up the Thames would have been a new generation of boat and I believe Turner was being nostalgic. He was an oficiando of ships, couldn't *not* paint one once he saw it, and here I believe he is lamenting the past glory of the English Admiralty. See how the Temeraire is emerging out of the gloom all silvery, ghostlike and majestic while the tug is a sooty smudge before it? It tells us where his passions lie, doesn't it?

"Tells me that his passion doesn't create beauty."

"*'Love of beauty is taste, the creation of beauty is art.'* Ralph Waldo Emerson. Wonderful poet but he, like you and most every man on the street, had limited scope when it comes to art."

"Well I think art should be beautiful."

"But it is a representation of life and life isn't always beautiful is it? I would think someone in your profession would know this. Art is the great communicator. It lectures and teaches to the illiterate and it captures the imagination in ways that no prose is able."

"A picture is worth a thousand words?" offered Mary.

"Well, this one certainly is, maybe ten thousand. What time of day do you think it is in the painting?"

"Dawn? Sunset? I don't know. It could be either really."

"Exactly!"

"Exactly? How could it be both?"

"Well, if you are looking at the modern paddlewheeler belching out a sulphury coal cloud it is dawn, but if you are looking at the majestic vessel it tows, it's sunset."

"Dawn is the future, sunset is the past."

"Precisely."

"And it doesn't look like Turner liked the future as much as the past."

"Very good! Manfred did say that you were a clever one. How is it that you came to work for the Judge?"

"In which capacity?"

"Surveillance and espionage, of course! I have no need of a nanny. I assume that being a governess for Fiona Falconbridge was a ruse. The girl must be a woman by now. Surely your employment in their home wasn't really necessary?"

"It was a contrivance, mostly, though I did come to grow fond of her. She is a lively girl, although naive. The Judge wanted me to protect her as much as he did our government's interests. But to answer your question, the Judge and I met at a party and I impressed him in the manner in which I fended off the advances of the men that approached me. He said that he had never seen so many young gentlemen thrilled to be turned down by a woman. He asked if I might teach the skill to his daughter and he recognized that it might also be useful in the field. He had just taken up as chair for the Dominion Police and he was looking to expand the force. He saw the opportunity to enhance his department and help to prepare his daughter for the challenges of adulthood."

"Manfred always was a double dipper. That man could accomplish more in an hour than most people did in a day. At school we called an hour a 'manfred minute' and a day a 'manfred month'.

"You went to school together?"

"We attended King's College, until I dropped out. At that age I didn't share the same drive. I got almost one year of law before I flew the coup, but Freddie stuck it out. Of course he could have gone to the bar after his first year. I, on the other hand, wouldn't have had the patience to make it after a decade. But I found greener pastures."

They passed beneath an ornate marble header into another gallery, the souls of their shoes echoing in the empty rooms.

"The Judge does hold you in high esteem," complemented Mary.

"The Judge is too kind."

"He says that you have elbowed your way into the Government here and made yourself indispensable to them."

"Influential, maybe, but indispensable?"

"You are a Lord. How many Canadians can say that? Some of them must resent a subject from the colonies taking a seat in *their* House of Commons?"

"There is a degree of animosity but politics is all about animosity and fortunately for me, Lloyd George appreciates my input, but here now Miss Miller, you and I are here in the National Gallery to appreciate art, even when it isn't the art that is beautiful." The middle-aged and balding man scanned the young woman before him. He thought he was being coy and debonair. She thought he was leering.

"Is that why we are here Lord Beaverbrook?"

"Oh, please, call me Max. It is why we are here, amongst other things. Look here, here is an entirely different genre of '*art*'. It is from another world isn't it?"

"It's vulgar."

"That it is and I'm showing it to you now because that is where you are going."

The eerie scene of dead tree trunks in a wasteland of shell craters and war debris showed a few tiny figures of soldiers making their way along a makeshift walkway of planks. Above them, diagonal searchlight beams slashed the sky. Mary read the tag.

"A copse of trees? Not exactly war propaganda. I thought you were trying to get a seat on the war cabinet?"

"I was but I have been left to come up with a project of my own. I discovered this artist digging a latrine at Etaples. Like you and I, he is Canadian. He is amongst a new school of painters that are applying Impressionism to the Canadian landscape and here, in this case, to the Belgium landscape. Effective isn't it?"

"Maybe, but it's not pretty."

"No, but neither is war and the image helps me sell newspapers."

"Ahh. I see."

"Ahh, but it's not just for profit my dear. I propose to have a record of our contribution to this war. There is a persistent attitude here in London that we are a colony of canon fodder. We have only just now won the command of our own troops and it is already showing promise. Our lads are gaining respect amongst the allies."

"Well that is worth something."

"That is worth everything, Miss Miller. It is time for our country to stand on its own feet and our efforts here have the power to do just that."

"That sounds treasonous *Lord* Beaverbrook."

"I will never forget my roots. They are inextricably nested around my heart. I can serve on both sides of the Atlantic, just as you are about to do, which brings us to the other reason we are here."

"Which is?"

"Your contact."

"Who is?"

"Evelyn."

"Evelyn?"

"That's all you will need to know. They will instruct you on the when and where and how. You simply need to wait at your hotel for their contact."

"And Judge Falconbridge couldn't have told me that?"

"Oh, he could have, but I wanted to meet you. Your reputation intrigued me."

"Is that so?"

"Our day doesn't need to end here Miss Miller. There are many fine restaurants in the vicinity and I have an apartment just a block away."

"I am honoured by your invitation Lord Beaverbrook, but our day does need to end here." Mary flashed her eyes. The expression on her face was inviting. Her words were not.

"Ahh, turned down by a master. I can see why Freddie wanted you to educate his daughter. I feel simultaneously disappointed and thrilled. To a man who usually gets his way, you are an enigma."

"I'll take that as a compliment and I thank you for the tour of the Gallery. It was most illuminating."

"The pleasure was all mine and of course, if you should change your mind, my invitation is always open."

Mary extended her hand, which Max Aitken lifted to his lips and kissed.

"I bid you farewell. Best of luck on the continent. Evelyn knows how to contact me should you ever require assistance."

Mary said nothing but bowed her head before turning to leave Lord Beaverbrook alone in the cavernous hall of marble.

ACKNOWLEDGMENTS

First and foremost, I have to thank Kate Sharrow for directing me to the archives of our local paper, The Grimsby Independent. It was a story within those pages that inspired this tale. Kate is also responsible for the design of the cover.

Secondly, Adrian Brassington cajoled, prodded, and pushed me to complete a version of this story that is much more readable than the first draft I gave him. His advice and encouragement has improved the story beyond measure.

Thirdly, much appreciation to Jim Sakic, George Brasovan, Lynn Anstey, and Doug Friesen for their honest feedback and advice and to Hiio Delaronde for his Mohawk translations.

Finally, a thank you to all in the Grimsby Beach Community that help to make this unusual and quirky place, a pleasant place to live.